PRAISE FOR

What a Woman Needs

"A romantic story . . . The engaging, descriptive writing will draw the reader in, and Fennell's knack for believable dialogue will keep them hooked. Smooth pacing and an amusing plot make this modern-day maid-to-order romance worth the read."

—*RT Book Reviews*

"Fennell has such a heartwarming and colorful way of creating, that there isn't a reader alive who won't love her stories. She packs [them] full of sexual tension, imagination, humor, and just plain romance."

—*Fresh Fiction*

What a Woman Wants

"Fans of Fennell's quirky style will enjoy the entertaining misadventures."

—*Publishers Weekly*

"The dialogue was fun and witty."

—*Night Owl Reviews* (Top Pick)

"Fennell's modern storytelling and witty dialogue are the highlights of her latest novel . . . With quick pacing and an entertaining plot, Fennell's latest will have readers laughing as they turn the pages."

—*RT Book Reviews*

"A lighthearted, feel-good romance . . . This book has a little something for everyone. Fennell shines with her newest book and will have readers in tears with giggles!"

—*Debbie's Book Bag*

"A pure joy to read . . . [A] clever and colorful author!"

—*Fresh Fiction*

continued . . .

FURTHER PRAISE FOR JUDI FENNELL AND HER NOVELS

"One of the best books I've read. I don't know who could set it down after the first few pages . . . An excellent choice."
—Joey W. Hill, national bestselling author of *Naughty Bits*

"Rip-roaring fun from the very first page . . . This book is one for the keeper shelf."
—Kate Douglas, bestselling author of *Dark Refuge*

"Judi Fennell is a bright star on the horizon of romance."
—Judi McCoy, author of the Dog Walker Mysteries

"Will keep the reader enraptured."
—*Publishers Weekly* (starred review)

"Sizzling sexual tension, plenty of humor, and a soupçon of suspense." —*Booklist*

"One of the most exciting and fun reads I have ever encountered." —*Fresh Fiction*

"[Fennell] is proving herself to be a solid storyteller."
—*RT Book Reviews*

"Phenomenally written . . . One of the best stories I have read this year, and I highly recommend it to anyone who loves a happy ending!" —*Sizzling Hot Books*

"I had a smile on my face and a sigh of contentment . . . Lighthearted but full of emotion. The story stirred in me feelings of falling in love all over again. It was just downright enjoyable to read!" —*That's What I'm Talking About*

Berkley Sensation titles by Judi Fennell

WHAT A WOMAN WANTS
WHAT A WOMAN NEEDS
WHAT A WOMAN GETS
WHAT A WOMAN

What a *Woman*

JUDI FENNELL

BERKLEY SENSATION, NEW YORK

THE BERKLEY PUBLISHING GROUP
Published by the Penguin Group
Penguin Group (USA) LLC
375 Hudson Street, New York, New York 10014

USA • Canada • UK • Ireland • Australia • New Zealand • India • South Africa • China

penguin.com

A Penguin Random House Company

WHAT A WOMAN

A Berkley Sensation Book / published by arrangement with the author

For information, address: The Berkley Publishing Group,
a division of Penguin Group (USA) LLC,
375 Hudson Street, New York, New York 10014.

ISBN: 978-0-425-26832-2

PUBLISHING HISTORY
Berkley Sensation mass-market edition / March 2015

PRINTED IN THE UNITED STATES OF AMERICA

10 9 8 7 6 5 4 3 2 1

Cover illustration by Daniel O'Leary.
Cover design by Judith Lagerman.
Interior text design by Kristin del Rosario.

To my family and the friends I consider family.
You know who you are and you know why.
Thank you.

Acknowledgments

Thanks to Dan Levi for your fifth-year reunion revelation that was the spark for this story. It would have been so much easier, Dan, if you'd asked me out instead of pulling out one hair from my head every day of ninth grade.

Guys' Night Out . . . Plus One

THREE hunks in aprons were the best advertising in the world for a maid service. Make one of them a Hollywood movie star, and there was no way Mary-Alice Catherine Manley could fail to get the publicity her fledgling business needed.

Make all three of them her brothers, and the picture only got better.

"You really won?" Gran gripped the doily-covered arm rests and leaned forward when Mac returned from the watershed poker game with her brothers. "Oh Mary-Alice Catherine! I wish I'd been there."

"Me, too, Gran." But it'd been enough of a coup to get a "you can play" from the three of them; there'd been no reason to push for an invitation for Gran, too. That would have raised too many red flags and maybe given their plan away. "You should've seen the looks on their faces when I told them they'd all have to be fitted for Manley Maids uniforms. I wish I'd had a camera."

She'd make sure there were plenty of cameras around when her brothers started work on Monday.

"So who are you going to pair them up with?" asked Gran, who was onboard with the plan in hopes of getting the brothers married off. Whatever worked. Mac just wanted the publicity. "We have to plan carefully. You know the kind of crazy that follows Bryan around."

Bryan was the Hollywood movie star, and Mac didn't think he minded crazy. He'd taken to that lifestyle like a duck to water. 'Course, you had to teach a duck to swim, as odd as that sounded, so maybe she and Gran could teach Bry a thing or two about women, since his recent choices were about as feather-brained as ducks.

Mac plopped onto the sofa that'd been in the same spot for the twenty-six years she'd lived with Gran after their parents had died in the car accident, the worn depression cradling her butt as usual. "I was thinking I'd tell them when they pick up their uniforms. That'll give you some more time to figure out where you want them. Though Sean's already called dibs on the Martinson estate. I didn't see any reason to object."

Gran tapped her bow-shaped lips. "The Martinson estate? But it's empty. He won't meet anyone that way, Mary-Alice Catherine."

Mac let her full name go by. Gran was the only one who used it since she'd dubbed herself Mac, back when she'd done anything to be like her brothers—male name, included. Given that tonight's poker game was her attempt to catapult her company into the same kind of success her brothers had earned for themselves, she hadn't gotten over that competitiveness yet, had she?

But tonight was her win, fair and square. Well, maybe not quite so fair. She *had* spent a lot of hours learning to play poker online and to count cards to improve her chances, but her brothers played together every month. She had to even the odds.

Tonight she'd beaten them at their own game and she was going to enjoy every minute of her victory and the possibilities it meant.

And Bry had said she had nothing comparable to what

he, Sean, and Liam had to bet on the game? Clearly, he had no idea. Yep, she was definitely going to enjoy the win.

"Actually, Gran, the Martinson house won't be empty. Merriweather's granddaughter is moving in. Besides, Sean specifically requested that place. It would have looked odd if I'd said he couldn't have it. Maybe he'll fall in love with the granddaughter." And maybe pigs would fly, but if it kept Gran's spirits up and created enough word-of-mouth, this was worth every bit of her hard work.

"The granddaughter, huh?" Gran tapped her forefingers together. "It just might work. But what about Bryan? We can't assign him to just anyone. It'll have to be someone who won't mind having Mr. Movie Star around."

Gran said it with more love than the rest of them did when ragging on Bryan about his stardom. Ever since he'd gotten a role with one of the biggest female leads in the industry, they hadn't been able to resist teasing him, and Bryan hadn't been able to stop smiling. Until tonight.

"I really think he should help that widow you just had a call about. The one with all those children."

"You want me to send Bryan into a house with five kids? Gran, that'll drive him nuts."

"Or teach him tolerance. We don't want him getting too big for his britches, do we?"

Gran had a point. And Mac *would* like to see Bryan try to clean a house overrun with five kids. None of her brothers were the quitting type, but this would test Bryan's mettle. She owed him a lot more than that for the pranks he'd pulled on her over the years.

"Okay, so what about Lee then, Gran?"

"Oh I know the perfect place for Liam. That nice Cassidy girl. She's going to be lonely when Sharon leaves to have her baby. Liam can keep her company."

"What do you have against Liam?" Cassidy Davenport was as spoiled and high maintenance as they came. More Bry's type, but if Bryan went there, the only thing he'd end up cleaning would be Cassidy's sheets. And the shower stall. And the table top . . .

"Now Mary-Alice Catherine Manley."

Mac winced. The first time Gran had said all four of her names in that tone, she hadn't felt the layer of skin it sliced off for about an hour. The effect hadn't lessened over the years.

"That Cassidy girl simply needs someone to pay attention to her. And our Liam needs to get his head out of his—well, off himself and into the rest of society. Have you noticed how preoccupied he's been since he broke things off with Rachel? It's not good, and if anyone can take Liam out of himself, it's that Cassidy."

The problem was, Cassidy was just like Rachel, though on a far bigger scale: all designer-this and celebrity-event-that. Rachel had put Liam through the wringer and Mac wasn't so sure shoving a replica-on-steroids in his face was all that kind. Still, he definitely wouldn't fall in love with Cassidy, so she'd actually be doing Liam a favor by thwarting Gran's matchmaking attempts.

She felt sorry for the guy. He was the only one of her brothers to have come close to the altar, and the fallout had been tough to witness.

"Okay, but if he wants to bite my head off, you need to talk him out of it."

"Never fear, honey. Your brother will love it."

Mac wasn't so sure about that, but she wasn't about to argue with Gran. Her grandmother had raised four grandchildren on meager savings, love, and not much else. The woman had grit.

"Oh. I forgot to mention something."

"What, Gran?" Mac hid her worry. Gran had been forgetting a lot of things lately. That was one reason she'd agreed to Gran's wacky plan of trying to marry off her brothers while having them work for Manley Maids, even if the chances were as slim as . . . well, as Mac being able to pull off a win tonight. And lightning rarely struck in the same place twice. Still, it'd give Gran something to keep her mind occupied.

"Mildred's grandson moved back home this week." Mildred

was her grandmother's childhood friend whose recent move into an assisted living facility had spurred Gran to do the same. "You remember Jared? The one who was injured in that car accident?"

"Yes, Gran. I remember Jared." As if she could forget him. Besides being a professional baseball player who'd sustained season-ending injuries in a bad car accident, and being her oldest brother's best friend since forever, Jared had been her first crush. And her longest. And her most embarrassing. She'd followed him around like a star-struck teenager. And that'd been *before* she'd been a teenager. God, she'd fallen out of the tree fort once when she'd been spying on him, only to land *on* him and his date and, well, it hadn't been her best moment.

It also, sadly, hadn't been her worst.

"Well Mildred and I were chatting and it came up that now that Jared has moved back, he could use help, what with the house being so old and his injuries. It's been tough for her to keep ahead of it, and, well, one thing led to another, and she wants to hire you to clean it. Isn't that wonderful? I rounded up some business for you and you can help Jared out, too."

That was her grandmother: kindest heart this side of the Make-A-Wish Foundation. Too bad it was with *her* biggest nightmare.

Mac gritted her teeth. Refusing would be childish and petty—and it'd make Gran ask too many questions. Besides, it wasn't as if *she* had to do the cleaning. She wouldn't even have to see Jared. "Yes, Gran, it sure is. When does she want someone?"

"Not *someone*, dear. You. I told her you'd come. Mildred doesn't want just anyone in her home."

Great. So much for that idea.

She couldn't do this. She couldn't. To see Jared . . . All that humiliation hitting her right in the face again . . .

But arguing with Gran was fruitless; she'd win in the end anyway. Mac had learned that early in her teenage years, which had saved them both a lot of angst.

She just hoped she was lucky enough that Jared wouldn't remember that night she'd never forget.

Then again, she might have used up all her luck in the poker game.

She sighed. "When am I supposed to be there, Gran?"

"Tuesday, dear. This Tuesday."

Which gave her three days to gird herself to see him again.

It wasn't going to be enough.

But she was a big girl; she could do this. After all, she wasn't that same girl who thought Jared was the only man alive. And considering his relationships kept par with his homeruns, she wasn't the only one to think so. And if there was one thing Mac Manley could never abide, it was being one of a pack. Jared no longer held any thrill for her.

"Okay, Gran. Tuesday it is. I'll be there with bells on."

Chapter One

THE woman had bells on.

Jared blinked, then rubbed his eyes and looked out the front window again.

She wore bells.

Then she rang his bell.

And, yeah, she was a pretty little thing, so she did kind of ring his bell.

She rang it again—the doorbell, not *his* bell.

Jared shook his head and willed his legs to move. Well, the working one. The other just hung there and let his crutches do the work. Funny how he still thought about the mechanics even though his muscles now made the actions on their own, but then, habits you taught yourself when relearning to walk tended to stick.

He opened the door just as she went to knock on it with the pot in her hands, and Jared had to jump back to avoid hot soup—which sent pain shooting through him and almost took the crutches out from under him.

Damn. His body might have been repaired by the best surgeons in the country, but idiotic moves like that reminded him real quick of what he'd gone through—both during *and* after the accident.

Other things he'd learned when relearning to walk also stuck.

The woman's bells jangled. "Hello. I'm—"

"Wearing bells."

"Not exactly." She hefted a pot of delicious-smelling something with a, "Here. Hold this," at him and he had to shove his crutches into his armpits to balance on them and his good leg. "Actually, I'm carrying them. My grandmother thought you might want them back." She hefted a leather slab of sleigh bells off her shoulder, knocking her baseball cap askew. "Where do you want 'em?"

The woman was about five-two, yet entered the house like a tornado. Jangling bells included.

"I don't know. I wasn't planning on bells in my future." Jared waved the pot toward the left. "Just drop them on the chair over there."

She did. Dropped them right onto the chair. Then they slid off and hit the hardwood floor with a nerve-destroying reverberation. He hoped to hell they hadn't destroyed the floor.

And then he saw her outfit. Matching green pants and shirt with MANLEY MAIDS embroidered over the left breast pocket.

Oh shit. He knew exactly why this woman had entered the house like a tornado—she *was* a tornado. Mac Manley could stir things up like only acts of God and Nature could.

Liam's little sister had been the shadow they couldn't shake their entire childhood, and her crush on him . . . Talk about embarrassing. And annoying. Every time he turned around she'd needed to be rescued because she'd tripped or fallen or hurt herself thanks to the stars in her eyes whenever she'd looked his way. And the nightmare she'd put his dates through . . . Jared shook his head. She'd caused him no end of trouble.

And if that uniform and her presence meant what he thought they did, he could guarantee she'd end up causing him even more.

Jared took two crutch-swinging hop steps with the pot, and—yeah. That wasn't going to work. Some sloshed out from under the lid and damn if it wasn't hot. Not even five minutes and his prediction had come true. "Hey, a hand here?"

She looked at him as if he had two heads.

He picked his crutches up by clenching his arms against his torso and lifting them with his armpits. "Injury?"

"Oh. Crud." She grabbed the pot and carried it into the kitchen, steam rising from the pot when she set it on the counter. "Sorry. I wasn't thinking. You okay?"

Okay? With busted ribs, a couple titanium rods, a bum knee, and the prospect of arthritis at an early age, not to mention a career on a downward slide thanks to the so-called accident his former girlfriend Camille's boyfriend had caused, and now Mac, here, in his grandmother's home where he was recuperating, looking hotter than his best friend's terror of a sister had a right to?

No, he sure as hell wasn't okay.

JARED *Nolan had certainly filled out nicely.*

It was Mac's first thought at her first up-close and personal glimpse of the baseball hero who'd filled her dreams long before that going-away party his parents had thrown to kick off his major league baseball career.

But he could work those crutches something fierce, and his flexing chest and biceps were a nice result. Abs and thighs, too. Physical therapy had done good things besides getting him upright again because he certainly didn't look as if he'd come close to death. Matter of fact, he looked to be the picture of health, the perfect cover model for the men's health magazine he'd been on before the accident.

She was very sorry to admit to herself that she had looked at that cover. A few times.

But she wasn't here to ogle the client. She never ogled clients. She never ogled *anyone*. Especially Jared. She'd worked so hard to make Manley Maids successful that by the time she *could* look at anything other than work, her eyes were crossed with exhaustion.

He, however, definitely straightened them out.

Get over it, Mac. Remember your embarrassment? Remember his derision?

The night she'd turned seventeen came back in humiliating clarity. She'd followed him out of the house, certain the reason he'd been at her birthday dinner had more to do with her—finally—than hanging with Liam. She'd just *known* he was going to give her her first kiss.

But then he'd headed down the walk and she'd run after him, grabbing his arm before he could leave.

She still cringed at the memory.

"What do you want, Mac?" he'd asked, shrugging into the black hoodie that had made his blond hair blonder and his green eyes greener. Not to mention the way it'd hugged his broad, sculpted shoulders and arms that she'd imagined wrapped around her more times than she could count.

"I want you to kiss me, Jared." She'd nibbled her lip nervously, unable to believe she'd finally said the words out loud. She hadn't wanted to be the only girl in school who hadn't been kissed, but she'd wanted her first kiss to be special.

To be from Jared.

He'd stopped putting the hoodie on with his other arm halfway in, and had looked at her with his eyebrows almost in his hairline. "Kiss you? *Get real, Mac. I could've had my chance anytime I'd wanted. And I didn't. Doesn't that tell you something?"*

It'd told her he was cruel. He was uncaring. Had no compassion.

And didn't have even one iota of interest in her.

She'd wanted to curl into her skin and disappear. Or have the ground open up and swallow her whole. She'd never felt so stupid in her entire seventeen years.

And with Nan Marone, gossip extraordinaire, grinning at her over the hedge, the entire school would know exactly what the hottest guy in town thought of her before she made it back inside to lick her wounds and pretend that everything was all right.

Thankfully, now, it was. Jared might have been her first crush, but she was a long way from that self-conscious, lovesick seventeen-year-old. "Are you sure you're okay? The soup didn't burn you?"

"I'm fine."

That he was.

Mac rolled her eyes when he turned around and shoved his fists onto his hips—a really good look for him, and one she didn't need to notice. Because if she did, Gran's hopes would skyrocket.

Hey, wait a minute . . . Did Gran actually think she could hook Mac and Jared up like she was trying to do for Liam, Sean, and Bryan?

Jared leaned against the counter and crossed his arms, his crutches falling against the butcher block. "Are you really here to clean?"

That was the idea. But was it Gran's?

"I'm certainly not here to cook." Mac nodded at the pot. "That's from my grandmother."

A ridiculous idea because chicken soup was a cold remedy, not a cure-all for broken bones. And even if it was, Jared had been out of the hospital for a while; he was certainly capable of getting around if he'd moved in here to get the place ready to sell for his grandmother.

"That was kind of her. Please thank her for me."

"Or you can give her a call while I get started. I know she'd love to hear from you." Ever since Mildred's request for her to personally handle this assignment, Gran had done nothing but regale Mac with Jared's wonderfulness, seen fully through the eyes of his grandmother. Gran and Mildred loved talking about their grandkids.

Now Mac was wondering how much of that regaling was because Gran was thrilled Jared was doing okay or because she wanted Mac to be thrilled about Jared. Too bad Gran wasn't aware of their history. Of the embarrassingly obvious wishes that she'd wished she could take back and pretend had never been. Especially since the object of those wishes had been aware of them all along.

Mac picked up a misshapen blue ceramic mug. Mr. Davison's fourth grade art project. She had the same one, though hers was a little more even than Jared's. "How about if I start upstairs and work my way down? Will that interfere with your schedule?"

Jared looked at her as if he didn't understand a word she was saying.

She set the mug down next to a picture of thirteen-year-old Jared with Mildred at one of Jared's Little League games. Mac knew exactly how old Jared was in that picture—actually knew it to the *day*; that's how infatuated she'd been with him. Her poor deluded, prepubescent self . . .

"Princess, what are you doing here?" He laid the dishtowel on the side of the sink, folded up all nice and neat.

Any gratitude she felt for his neatness was instantly gone with the use of that annoying nickname she'd hated since the first time he'd called her that. "I'm here to clean your grandmother's house."

"No. I mean, why are you *really* here?"

"*Really* here? I don't understand the question."

Jared stared at her as if he were trying to figure her out, but finally shook his head and turned away.

And winced.

He stumbled a little and Mac was at his side, under his arm with hers wrapped around his waist before he could protest.

"I've got this, Mac. I have the crutches. You don't have to try to carry me."

"I'm not trying; I'm doing. I don't need you breaking something on my watch." She grunted with the effort it took to keep him upright. He might not be aware of it, but he was no lightweight. All that muscle put some major poundage on him.

Not that she was paying attention or anything.

"So you're saying it's okay if I break something later?"

Wow. His tone put Gran's skin-slicing ability to shame

because Mac figured out right away that he wasn't her biggest fan. Still harboring resentment that she'd practically been his shadow all those years ago? She'd love to tell him to get over himself—that she had—but Gran and Mildred wouldn't be happy if they were fighting, so it was time to cut her losses.

Hands up, Mac backed away. "Okay. Fine. I'll just get started and you go do what you do and I'll stay out of your way." Far, far out of his way.

He gripped the countertop and worked the one crutch under his arm. "Fine. You do that."

"Fine. I will." She should probably hand him the other crutch that was by the sink, but screw it. If he was so "I got this," let him get his own damn crutch.

She spun around and strode toward the back steps. She'd find the farthest corner of the house from here, and take out her emotions on the dust—

Except she needed her cleaning supplies that, between the soup and the bells, she hadn't had enough hands to carry in. Which meant she had to go back downstairs. Past Jared.

Great. Fabulous.

Executing a ninety-degree turn that would stop an army drill sergeant in his tracks, Mac strode toward the front door.

"Leaving so soon?" He didn't have to sound so happy about it.

She turned around and was steamed to find him smiling. "Look, Jared, I'm here as a favor to your grandmother and mine. If you have issues with that, take it up with them."

She so would have loved to slam the door behind her, but it was Mildred's front door, not Jared's, and she wasn't about to let him see her sweat.

Because, damn it all, with that smile, he actually *could* still make her sweat.

Chapter Two

SHE left just as she'd entered: a tight little package of tornado, stirring things up in a way no one else he'd ever met could.

Jared pinched the bridge of his nose. The grandmothers were nothing if not obvious, and while he hated to hurt their feelings, he wasn't going to suffer through Mac's brand of torture long enough to get anyone's hopes up. Camille's "little game" of playing up to him to get as much as she could out of him had put him off women even before her supposed ex-boyfriend had tried to mow him down in a jealous rage. So *if* he ever decided to settle down, the decision would be his, not his grandmother's. And it definitely wouldn't be with a pain-in-the-ass who'd made his life miserable.

The same one who blew back through his front door, swirling grass clippings and leaves in behind her. Some cleaning lady she was.

"You weren't raised in a barn, Princess."

The old nickname rolled off his tongue as easy as if he'd seen her last week, so he didn't even think about it.

But she obviously did because she stumbled on the first step.

"I beg your pardon?"

He'd rather have her beg for something else.

Oh, hell. What was wrong with him? This was *Mac*. Terror of the tree fort. Tagalong extraordinaire.

Who'd grown up to be one hell of a gorgeous woman.

When had she grown up? She'd been a cute kid—well, when she hadn't been covered in dirt and grime and grass stains—but now . . . Gone were the chubby cheeks and freckles, skinned knees, and her brothers' T-shirts. Now she had legs and curves and cheekbones and lips . . .

Jesus. Mac had had a mouth on her back in the day, but it'd been verbal. Now . . .

"I said that I know for a fact that you weren't raised in a barn, so would you mind telling me why you left the front door open? Seems to be counterproductive to the cleaning thing you profess to be here about."

She stormed back into the kitchen, temper in full view.

Damn, she was too pretty for his own good when she was angry. Green eyes flashed like emeralds beneath bangs so black they could be blue, the rest of her hair tied back in a ponytail that stretched halfway down her back. It was the same style that she'd worn when she was ten, though she sure as hell didn't look ten now.

"Have I ever told you how to play baseball?" She rammed a finger into his chest.

Jared looked at it, then into her eyes, trying to remember why staying away from her was a good idea. "There was that pickup game when I came home from college senior year—"

Her hand fluttered. "You were going to run over Nicky. He was a third your size. You were too stuck on winning to see what you were going to do. I had to say something."

"So your point is?"

"I don't tell you how to do your job; don't tell me how to do mine. I know how to get this place into shape."

Jared laughed. "Only you, Princess, could follow an anecdote of how you told me how to do my job with the declaration that you *don't* tell me how to do it. Are you getting the irony?"

She glared at him. "My name is not Princess; it's Mac. Use it. And for our grandmothers' sakes, we have to make this work until this house goes up for sale, so you stay out of my way and I'll stay out of yours."

"Is that like the not telling me how to do my job thing?" He probably shouldn't tease her, but that'd never stopped him before. She just made it so easy.

"Fine. Whatever." She tossed up her hands and spun around, storming off toward the staircase.

What a view it was.

Jared uncrossed his arms and gripped the counter. These next few weeks ought to be anything but boring.

MAC counted to a hundred—twice—and she still hadn't calmed down. That man . . . How could she have ever even *thought* she'd had a crush on him? Arrogant, self-centered . . . Life was one big party to Mr. Prostrate-Yourselves-At-The-Feet-Of-My-Greatness Jared Nolan. Her teenage self had been such a sucker for a pretty face. She ought to be thankful he'd laughed at her—

She swatted a cobweb off the floor lamp by the reading chair in one of Mildred's spare bedrooms. The face was still pretty, but Jared Nolan could take a flying leap for all she cared. No one mocked her and got the chance to do it again. No one. Certainly not Mr. Caveman, alpha, He-Man Jared, all testosterone and muscle, ordering everyone around and expecting them to like it. Perfect for a professional athlete, but as a general rule? Notsomuch.

Mac swiped at another cobweb in the corner behind the lamp, but it was beyond the reach of her rag. Poor Mildred; the woman should have moved out a long time ago. These old Victorian houses were just too hard to keep up, especially for people her grandmother and Mildred's ages.

Too hard for her, too, with these ten-foot ceilings. At

five-two, even eight-foot ceilings were a challenge. Which meant she had to go *back* to her old pickup truck to get her ladder. Past Jared and his sneering condescension.

How could someone as sweet as Mildred be related to him?

Tucking the dust rag into her utility belt, Mac ran down the stairs, hoping to avoid Mr. Sarcasm this go-round.

She didn't make it.

"Had enough?"

She momentarily thought about flipping him the bird, but that would A) be childish, B) give him further cause to ridicule her, and C) not be worth her energy when she had too many other things to do.

So she ignored him and headed out to the truck. She grabbed the ladder and hefted it onto her shoulder, then went back into the house.

Jared met her at the door. "Here, let me help you."

"Back off, Nolan. I've got it." She hefted it once more just to make a point. How he thought he'd carry a ladder with crutches was beyond her. She hadn't expected him to have them when she'd handed him the soup and she'd been too busy trying to keep the bells from falling to the floor to notice until he'd pointed it out. She didn't need to be told twice.

Jared stepped back, hands up. "Hey, I was only trying to be helpful."

"Not interested." She stomped past him toward the stairs.

"With that attitude, don't be surprised if it's not available when you are."

"Seriously, Jared? Nothing you do would surprise me. I know exactly what kind of guy you are." One who reveled in destroying a young girl's dreams. Callously.

It was a good thing she was holding on to the railing because halfway up the stairs, the ladder jerked her to a stop.

She looked over her shoulder.

Jared held the end. "What the hell does that mean?"

She glared at him. "Let go of the ladder."

"Not until you tell me what you meant by that crack. I haven't seen you since what? Your senior year? And if you recall, I was exactly *not* that kind of guy back then."

He didn't say anything for a second. He didn't have to. He remembered. She really wished he didn't. *She'd* like to forget that night.

"And since we haven't seen each other since then, how could you possibly know a thing about me?"

"How could anyone not? You're always plastered all over the media. Which actress are you dating this week? What endorsement deal did you just sign? Who tweeted what about you now? How can I *not* know what you're up to?"

"You seem mighty interested in a guy you claim to not be interested in."

She hadn't said she wasn't interested in *him*. She specifically hadn't said it because she didn't want him challenging her. She knew Jared; had grown up with the guy. He was all about taking dares and bets, one of the reasons he was the perfect friend for her brother. She'd been glad Liam hadn't invited him to that poker game because he would've been one more person she'd have had to beat, and after losing her adolescent heart to the guy, she wasn't sure she would've been able to.

"Mac?" He gave her that cockeyed smile that she'd thought had been so cute years ago.

Unfortunately, now it was just plain sexy. So she was *not* about to give him any satisfaction by arguing with him. She was over him. Had been when he'd laughed at her.

"Or maybe you *are* interested?"

He took a step closer and if Mac hadn't been so shocked that he'd even *think* she was still interested, she would have high-tailed it up the stairs.

"That would explain the attitude."

Mac stared at him. There were no words to describe this guy's hubris. And she'd thought she'd come up with so many of them while she'd put her broken heart and dreams back together.

"Okay, okay." Jared turned on that killer smile that put him on the entertainment magazine covers as well as the sports ones. But she was immune.

Even from that dimple in his left cheek.

Really.

"I'm a good sport, Princess. Come back down here and I'll sign whatever you've got. Or I'll even give you a peck on the cheek if that's what you want."

Of all the arrogant, egotistical—

Mac stormed backward down the stairs, the damn ladder preventing her from turning around.

So she dropped it, all clings and clangs as it hit the hardwood. Crap. She hoped she didn't have to refinish the treads.

But it'd be worth it, since she could now stare Jared in the face at eye level and point a finger at him. "Are you out of your—"

She never got the last word out.

Because he kissed her.

His hands clasped the back of her head, his thumbs tilting her jaw, his touch searing her nerve endings as she tried to process the jolt of electricity that shot through her, sending her on a roller coaster ride of need and want, and had her legs threatening to give out. God, she would have killed for this when she'd been seventeen. Of course, she wouldn't have been able to handle it when she'd been seventeen.

She wasn't so sure she could handle it now.

But then the kiss was over. And if her lips weren't still tingling—and he weren't grinning like a Cheshire cat—she might have thought she'd imagined it, some holdover from her teenaged dreams.

But then reality rushed back in and it took all her self-restraint not to whack him across the face even if he did deserve it. She was *not* going to let Jared get under her skin. "What the *hell* was that?"

Jared chucked her under her chin. "Kiddo, if you don't know, you have a lot more problems than ugly uniforms to worry about."

She could only gape as he gimped back into the living room on one crutch—and she didn't know if it was because of the uniform comment, his arrogance, that damn kiss, or . . .

The fact that she'd enjoyed it.

Chapter Three

"YOU sure you don't need any help up there?" Jared's voice echoed—for the third time in the last half hour—up the hardwood steps, bounced off the bare walls, and slithered under Mac's skin to grate on her nerves.

Help? She didn't need his help. She didn't *want* his help. She wanted nothing to do with him. He'd loved tormenting her when they'd been younger; time obviously hadn't changed anything. *Kissing* her, of all things—

"Mac? I wouldn't want you to fall and hurt yourself."

Sure he wouldn't. And he'd kissed her because he wanted her. Not.

She exhaled. "Sure thing, Gimpy. Just hobble your way up here and climb this ladder to do the crown molding." There. He wanted to help? He probably thought she wouldn't take him up on it. Then he could go around saying he'd offered but she'd turned him down. Fine. The man wanted to prove he was all that? Let him.

Mac snorted. Yeah, right. Jared work? Jared had had everything handed to him on a silver platter his entire life. She never remembered him mowing the lawn or raking leaves. Jared had been all about baseball his entire life while she'd had chore after chore after chore.

She winced. That wasn't fair to Gran. Gran had done her best, but the four of them had been a handful. Chores had been necessary, not something to keep the kids occupied while Gran went off and ate bon-bons.

Thunk.

That was *not* a crutch on the staircase.

Thunk.

Oh hell, it was.

Mac scrambled down the ladder, careful to keep all the soapy water in the bucket, but almost took out the swing-arm porcelain lamp that'd been in Mildred's living room years ago until the boys had toppled it.

She rubbed her hairline. Four stitches had prevented it from crashing to the floor.

She almost wasn't as lucky this time, though at least she didn't need stitches. Still, she did take a healthy *thwack* to the shin. "Son of a—"

"I can hear you."

"Good. Then listen up, Jared." She set the bucket down and wiped up the water that'd dribbled over the edge. "Stay down there. I'm perfectly fine without you and I really don't feel like explaining to the cops how you broke your neck when you fell down the stairs."

It was one thing to challenge him; it was another entirely to spend time in the same room with him. *Especially* since that kiss.

"I can manage stairs when I need to, Princess."

She ignored the nickname. He'd enjoyed pissing her off with it when they were younger; she wasn't going to give him the satisfaction now. "Well right now you don't need to. I've got everything covered. Why don't you make yourself comfy in the den and turn on a game or something?"

Silence. She didn't even hear the slide of a crutch.

"Jared?"

"Yeah. Whatever."

She heard the *thunks* again, but this time they were headed toward the foyer.

She leaned against the doorframe and put a hand over her thudding heart. She was going to have to set the record straight with him. She wasn't that same girl who still thought his blond hair and green eyes were *to die for.* To go and kiss her like that . . . It was just like him to toss the crush in her face.

Well she definitely wasn't crushing on him now and he could take his stupid kiss and . . . and . . . well, go kiss someone else.

She grabbed the bucket and headed into the bathroom to change out the water. Poor Mildred hadn't cleaned the molding in years. It was going to take Mac a long time to get through this place if every room was as neglected as this one, and she didn't want to have to be here one minute longer than necessary. Not with *him* in the house.

She filled the bucket with clean hot water, then headed back in, glancing over the banister to the foyer below.

He'd taken her advice. She'd be surprised except that Jared was a sports nut. And not just *any* sports nut; he'd been so into the game that his parents had moved a personal trainer into his house. It'd been a big topic of conversation at her house because her brothers loved sports. And if they did, she did. Those stitches on her forehead were nothing compared to the broken bones and sprained ankles she'd had over the years. Gran had put up with a lot. The poor woman had probably thought she'd been getting a cute little girly-girl in ruffles and lace, but Mac had been all about knee pads and baseball bats.

She laughed at herself now. So young and trying so hard to keep up.

She caught a glimpse of herself in a mirror with her Manley Maids shirt on. Her company. Her business. Like Sean and Liam's ventures and Bryan's movie career, this was her success or her failure.

She shrugged. Failure was not an option. She *was* going to be as good as her brothers.

Even if it meant putting up with Jared Nolan.

JARED hobbled into the den, Mac's little directive ringing in his ears: "Go relax and watch a game." Really? A game? Did she not get that he ought to be *playing in* the damn game? Or was that little dig to get back at him for kissing her?

Why *had* he kissed her? That should be the *last* thing he'd wanted to do to Mac Manley. God knew, he'd had the chance when they were younger. Hell, she'd even asked him straight out to do it.

He shook his head, remembering that night. He wasn't surprised that she'd wanted him to, but her request had shocked the hell out of him.

She was Liam's little sister. There was a guy code, and baby sisters being off limits was, like, rule number one. She'd never gotten it, always following him around with puppy dog eyes, and butting in on his fun whether it was with her brothers or his dates. He'd finally had to nip it in the bud. So to speak.

He grimaced, remembering the look on her face when he'd said the first thing that'd popped into his head. But he'd been worrying about draft picks and signing bonuses; dating a high school senior had never been on his radar—even if she hadn't been Liam's sister.

He probably could've been nicer about turning her down, but it'd put an end to the crush, which was better for everyone.

Yet now he'd gone and kissed her. Must be the pain meds.

Except he hadn't taken any today.

Or maybe he'd just wanted to shut her up. Which it had.

Or maybe, now that you're both adults you want to see if there could be anything between you—

He shut *that* up real quick. She was still Lee's baby sister and that put her on the Do Not Touch List. For life.

Then explain the kiss.

He couldn't. And now that he knew what kissing her was like, he knew enough to know that that little peck had been a mistake.

Mac tasted good. Felt even better, and the kiss . . .

He was Out. Of. His. Mind. If it wasn't the meds, it had to be the pain itself making him think this shit. He'd had no business kissing Mac. No business even thinking about her like that. About any woman for that matter. Not now. Not for a long time.

He banged his shin on the damn footstool. Grandma had these dainty things all over the house, and on a good day, he wasn't dainty. Give him crutches and he was a walking disaster. Or rather, a *not* walking disaster. He couldn't wait for the doctor to take him off these damn things.

Jared dropped onto the sofa, grabbing the stupid crutches before they clattered onto the delicate little side tables filled with glass and porcelain figurines, the quintessential little-old-lady's parlor. A den it was not. A den would have padded leather chairs, a big comfy sofa, a flat screen, and an ottoman the size of a Fiat for a coffee table, like the one he had at his place.

Where Camille still lived.

That pissed him off to no end. Camille had strung him along while still playing house with her previous boyfriend Burke on the sly, using *his* bank account to rack up stuff for the two of them. Then Jared had been stupid enough to think he'd loved her and had her move in.

That's when the fun began.

The boyfriend got jealous and staged an "accidental bump" in a parking lot, landing Jared in the hospital and Burke in *his* bed. Sadly, with eviction laws being worse than divorce laws, Jared was the one who'd gotten screwed; the criminal investigation had gone belly up when Burke's alcohol count had come in within the legal range and he'd claimed it was an accident.

Accident, Jared's ass. The guy hadn't put the truck in drive instead of reverse *by accident*. Jared had seen his eyes and the determination on Burke's face. But the media circus of a civil trial—even if he won—wouldn't get him back into shape any faster.

So here he was, stuck with knick-knacks, doilies, and Mac Manley until the eviction went through.

He looked at the ceiling. She was up there, in his grandmother's house, going through things . . . The grandmothers had probably planned this. Too bad they didn't know Mac was over her crush.

He'd hoped she would've been after that time he'd told her to wait for him in the tree fort years ago, and she had. For six hours.

He'd been home by then for batting practice in the cage his father had had built in the backyard, but he'd had a clear view across the field to see her grandmother standing at the bottom of the ladder while Mac had climbed down.

Not his best day. He'd known that even then. She'd been a kid, after all. But so had he and he'd been desperate to hang with the guys, and just as desperate that she wouldn't. So he'd put her where he'd known she'd stay and he wouldn't have to worry about her showing up to wreck their afternoon.

She hadn't looked at him for two weeks afterward, and the look she'd given him when he'd ended their kiss now reminded him of the one she'd given him back then.

And damn if he didn't get the same hollow feeling of guilt as before.

Not to mention a few others . . .

Sighing, he grabbed the remote as he remembered sliding his fingers behind her neck and feeling the heat there. Of bypassing her cheek when her mouth was right there. And the soft crush of her lips, the scent that said she wasn't wearing perfume because she didn't need any. The warmth of her breath as he stole it, and the sweet movements of her lips against his until he'd come to his senses.

He changed the channel. The kiss had been a boneheaded move and one better served from the teenager he used to be. But now he was thirty-five years old, for chrissake. He ought to be able to handle suddenly being attracted to her.

He flipped to the History channel. Okay, so maybe it wasn't so sudden. She *had* driven him nuts since the first time he'd seen her, riding the motocross trail he, Liam, Bryan, and Sean had built in the field separating their neighborhoods that first summer after he'd moved in. For a few seconds he'd been stunned to see a girl—a little girl at that—with her attention so fiercely focused on each dirt mound as she rode over it, until he realized that she was shearing off parts of them, undoing all their hard work.

He'd called out to her, and she'd missed the turn, taking a header over the highest mound, the one that had the sweetest air. He'd been pissed off that she'd ruined it, but he'd had enough compassion to make sure she was okay before he'd started yelling at her.

Only . . . she'd yelled back. Something about breaking her concentration, which he wouldn't have done if he knew *anything* about riding the course, and he better leave her alone or she was going to tell her brothers and that would not end well for him.

He'd been surprised at her attitude, and, thinking back on it now twenty-some years later, he'd had to admire her spirit, too. Her grit and determination to both ride the motocross *and* tell him off.

But he'd seen that same grit and determination in getting her way one too many times with her brothers. Like the time Liam had had to bring her along on the Halloween parade because she'd insisted on showing off her costume, which had put an end to their house-egging plans.

Probably had kept him from getting into trouble, but still. She'd ruined their fun.

Then there were the too-numerous-to-mention times she'd tagged along to the swimming hole and the pickup ice hockey matches and T-ball games, and hell, everywhere he'd turned, Mac had been there. Put a real crimp in his idea of fun, and he hadn't believed that Liam and the guys had put up with it.

Liam had just shrugged and said she was his sister, she was family.

Jared stretched his arms across the back of Grandma's scalloped-edged sofa with its floral fabric and ruffle-edged pillows, feeling like a behemoth in a froufrou dollhouse. Family as Liam described it was a foreign concept to him. His parents' sole reason for having a son, it seemed, had been to get him into the major leagues. Well, at least his father's had been. He'd even gone to the extreme of building a batting cage in the backyard and moving Bill, one of the biggest trainers in the industry, into their home to work with him. That was when his life had become a series of training sessions with miniscule breaks for school and friends tossed in.

He'd cherished those times with his friends.

Something crashed overhead. Jared sighed and pushed himself to the edge of the well-indented sofa. And just like those times, Mac would somehow manage to get involved, usually when they'd had to rescue her from one disaster or another.

Seemed that damsel-in-distress issue hadn't gone away.

Chapter Four

JARED was about to head toward the stairs when someone rang the doorbell.

He glanced up the stairs. "Mac?"

"I'm fine."

She'd say that even if she weren't, but she was a grown woman now; he was no longer responsible for her safety.

He opened the door.

"Hey, Mr. Nolan." A tow-headed kid of about seven stood on the front porch.

With a baseball and glove.

"Uh, hi."

"My dad said you're staying here and I was wondering if you could help me work on my throw. I want to play in the majors like you when I grow up, so I gotta practice. My dad said you had a batting cage and trainer when you were my age. I bet that was cool."

"Yeah, it was." Sort of. There were times when Jared had felt less of a prodigy and more of an indentured servant. As if his parents had spent all the money as an investment and he'd better give them a good return. Which was why it was so ironic that they rarely came to see him play. Dad had his bragging rights and Mom had the cachet of being a celebrity's mother; apparently that was enough for them.

"So will ya? Help me, I mean? I got a good arm, but Dad says it needs work. He was helping me 'til he had to go back for his last tour."

Oh hell. Autographs were one thing, throwing a couple of pitches something else entirely. He wasn't ready for this. "His last tour?"

The kid nodded solemnly. "Afghanistan. It's where he lost his legs in a roadside bomb. That's why he can't throw with me a lot. It's hard for him to catch from the chair."

The wheelchair. Jared had seen way too many people in those during his stint in rehab, where he'd been angry that he might never play again, something that was now put in perspective by what this boy's father had lost.

No way could he turn this kid down. "So what's your name?"

"It's Chase. Chase Williams. I'm the starting pitcher for my rec team. I beat out Dylan, but if I don't practice, he might get it next year, you know?"

"Yeah, I know." Mitch Weymouth was on *his* mound now and it sucked big time to see someone else where he was supposed to be. "Let me grab my glove and I'll meet you out there."

He pointed to the clearing between the front porch and the street trees, trying to calculate how long it was going to take him to get up to his room, dig through the duffel bags Camille had thrown together while he'd been in the hospital, and hopefully find the glove she'd said she packed. He wouldn't put it past her to have hocked the thing online.

The kid jerked his head toward the step where Jared saw another glove. "My dad sent his over. He wasn't sure you'd have yours."

Because no one was expecting him to play again. There'd been so much speculation in the media that he kept the TV off for just that reason.

"I do have it, but I'll use his if you want." It'd save him a trip up the stairs, and Chase's dad would talk it up that *the* Jared Nolan had worn *his* glove. Besides being the least he could do for the guy who'd given so much for their country, let the media get a hold of that info. Show *them* he wasn't out for the count. "Okay, Chase, let's go."

"Cool!"

It actually *was* kind of cool for Jared. He still had his pitching form, though he wasn't about to throw a ninety-miler at a kid, but the motion felt right—even if he had to prop himself up with a crutch. He'd always planted with his left leg and wound with the right, so the injury hadn't affected that. The actual follow-through, however, was going to take some work. The physical therapist at the hospital had considered walking more important than keeping his pitching form . . . Jared hadn't agreed.

"Take a couple of steps back now, Chase," Jared said after they'd warmed up. He threw the ball into his webbing while the kid hopped into place a few feet back and windmilled his arms.

"My dad says I arc high when I go longer because I'm thinking about the distance."

"So we have to get you not to think about it and the only way to do that is by practice." Easier said than done as Jared knew from personal experience. Learning to walk again had taught him the brutal lesson of focusing more than his old trainer ever had.

"But what if I can't throw the ball all the way to you? Won't it be hard for you to get it?" Chase pointed to the crutch. "My dad has trouble sometimes."

"You let me worry about getting the ball. Your job is to pitch it."

"Okay, but Dad said to make sure I don't tire you out or injure you any more than you already are."

What was he, an invalid? He could catch a damn ball for chrissake.

Wisely, Jared kept his mouth shut. The way the kid said "Dad" told Jared all he needed to know. The guy was Chase's hero. With good reason. Giving up two legs for your country was much more heroic than hitting a ball into the grandstand. He was Jared's hero, too. Even more so because he was his son's hero.

Jared choked on the lump in his throat. He'd always wanted his father to be his hero . . . but he hadn't been. Not when he let Mom control everything, practically worshipping the ground she walked on. His father's existence seemed to be merely to give his mother whatever she wanted and taking her wherever she wanted to go. To Jared that wasn't a marriage, it was a high school crush on the head cheerleader gone bad. That was never going to be him.

"So how far do you think this is?" Chase asked. "Fifteen feet?"

"Nah, more like twenty-five. Let's see what you got from there."

"Okay, here I go!" Chase did his wind up and let the ball fly.

It landed right in the webbing. The kid had a decent arm, though he could use some coaching. "Nice. That had some speed to it. Probably could go another ten feet."

Chase bounced on the balls of his feet. "You think? Can I try it now? What if my arm's tired? What if I won't be able to because I used up all my power with these last throws? My dad says I don't want to burn out."

"You can keep second-guessing yourself or you can try it and see."

Those were the very words Dave, the physical therapist from the team, had said when he'd visited him in the hospital right after Jared had gotten word from the doctors that he'd probably never play again.

Dave's comment had hit home. Jared wasn't a quitter. Never had been, never would be. No one told *him* he couldn't do something, not his doctor, the team's GM, or his therapist.

Or even Mary-Alice Manley.

MAC looked out the window pane she'd just finished cleaning. Jared was still at it.

Dammit.

Why'd he have to be so nice to that little boy?

She carefully pried the last piece of glass wedged in the wood casing around another pane that a tree branch must have broken. No wonder there were leaves and other debris strewn across the floor. Mildred should have called sooner; these windows were in bad shape—which was why Mac had a front row seat to something so sweet she wanted to cry.

Seriously, why did he have to do this? It was easier to hold on to her anger when he was a pompous jerk, but being propped up out there on one crutch to play catch with a neighbor kid was undermining Jared's pomposity.

Especially when he almost fell over reaching for a pitch.

She gasped and grabbed on to the ladder as if that would keep him upright.

Why do you care?

She didn't. Jared had broken her heart so many times it was amazing it'd ever healed. It shouldn't matter that he was playing catch with that boy; he was still the same Jared, right down to that stupid *Princess*. Condescending jerk.

Who played ball with a kid he didn't know.

She gently raised the sash to clean the outside of the window. It'd take a lot more elbow grease than she could give it from the inside, but that would be a project for another day. Right now, she just wanted to clean it so the duct tape would have something to adhere to when she covered the broken pane.

"Work on your follow-through, Chase. You want to keep your eye on the target the entire time. You look away, the ball's gonna go the way you look. Stay with it."

Okay, so maybe a quick cleaning job to the outside of the window was an excuse to listen to what Jared was saying so she'd hear something to remind her of the condescending jerk he could be. And with the maple in front of the window, it wasn't as if he could see her watching anyway.

Unfortunately, the only thing she heard from him was encouragement, which didn't help her cause. Nor did the fact that he still looked good out there, crutch and all.

Then again, when *hadn't* he looked good?

She groaned and swatted a cobweb. She'd wasted enough

time on Jared; she needed to get back to work and stop spying on him for no apparent reason.

Unless teenage crushes that had grown into full-on adult fantasies counted as a reason.

Mac shook her head and swiped the paper towel over the glass, then pulled her arm back in and shut the window. She didn't need a reason. Didn't want one.

What she wanted was to finish and go home. Get out of here with her heart intact.

Then she reached up to get that one last cobweb and . . . the ladder buckled.

JARED double-hopped to stay upright, but his left leg was taking a beating. Too much standing and now too much fancy footwork; it was all he could do not to take a header as if he were sliding into home base.

He managed to keep his foot under him with minimal assistance from the one crutch. He should have shelved his pride and brought the second one out because he was beat. But at least Dave would be glad to know his left quad was working well enough to do its job.

"Hey, buddy, let's call it for the day. Don't want to overdo it, you know?" Jared underhanded the ball to Chase, and made it to the stairs before collapsing onto them in a semblance of taking a seat.

Luckily, the kid was too excited to notice. "Thank you so much, Mr. Nolan. My dad's gonna be so impressed. He said you know all about the game. Can I come over again?"

Jared looked at the hopeful face. "Sure, but let's give it a few days, okay? We don't want to wear out your arm." Or *his* legs, though he was happy with the way his left one had held out. "You're going to want to ice it when you get home because it'll be sore tomorrow."

"Oh, yeah, like you guys in the majors do, right? You have trainers and stuff."

Jared smiled and tapped the kid's baseball cap visor. "Yup, we have stuff."

"Um . . ." Chase scrunched his face. "Can I ask you a favor?"

"Playing ball wasn't one?" He flicked the visor up.

"I mean another one." The kid looked nervous.

"What is it?"

"I was wondering . . ." Chase hopped off the second-to-last step and ran onto the porch, coming back with a permanent marker.

"You want me to sign your glove?"

"And my dad's, too. I think he'd like that."

Jared took the pen, not bothering to answer. Autographs were no big deal, but giving one to Chase's dad, who wasn't able to do what Jared had just done with his son . . .

Man, that almost did him in.

He scrawled a quick *Thanks for playing ball with me, Jared* on Chase's and *Thanks for allowing me to play ball with your son. All the best to a true hero, Jared Nolan* on his dad's. The ironic thing was, the guy would think *this* was a treat, but all he'd have to do was look in the eyes of his son to see a real one.

Jared held up the marker. "Anything else? The cap?"

"Really?" Chase's eyes lit up as he swiped the cap off his head.

"Really." He scrawled his name nice and big and handed it back. "Now don't forget to ice that arm. We want you to be able to use it for a lot more years."

"Yeah, so I can grow up and be just like you someday."

A lump clogged Jared's throat. He'd heard that for years from kids, but now, when he might be facing the end of his career, the words hit home a lot more.

He cleared his throat. "You take care, Chase. I'll see you again."

"Okay, Mr. Nolan. And thanks."

"Call me Jared."

Jared didn't know it was possible for a smile to be as big as Chase's was.

"Thanks, Mr.—I mean, Jared!" The kid took off so quickly the cap went flying off his head. Chase stopped, ran back and picked it up, then headed for home, hollering, "Daaaaad!!!" the entire way down the block.

He'd made the kid's day, would make the dad's, and felt a lot better about his prospects at making it back for next year's spring training. Okay, so it hadn't been a double header, but, damn, playing that little bit of ball had felt good. Life was looking up.

But then he opened the front door.

Chapter Five

MAC shrieked from upstairs as something crashed.

Jared hobbled to the stairs as fast as he could. "Mac? Are you okay?" Or was she going to need rescuing again?

She groaned. "Don't come up here."

Rescuing it was. Jared sighed. Some things never changed. "I'm coming up."

"I mean it, Jared. I don't need your help."

"It's my house and I can come up the stairs if I want."

"It's not your house, it's Mildred's, and she's paying me to clean it, so butt out."

Bossing him around again. Um . . . no.

Besides, he knew for a fact that Mac wasn't charging his grandmother. That'd been unexpected. And a very nice gesture. She'd surprised him.

He hopped up the first step because he owed it to Liam to make sure his sister was okay. *And* because he was actually a good guy.

Yeah and look where that got you with Camille.

He winced when he landed on the next step awkwardly,

his ribs—and his ego—protesting. Damn Camille and her boyfriend.

"I mean it, Jared. I can hear you trying to sneak up here. Crutches aren't designed for sneaking."

"I don't have to sneak, Mac, in case you've forgotten. I live here." And he wasn't using his crutches.

"As if I could forget."

She muttered it, but he heard it.

It was stupid, really, that her tone could get to him.

Oh get the hell over it, Nolan. Your ego's bruised because she doesn't worship you anymore? Seriously? So she's hot; big deal. She's still the same ol' Princess in need of rescuing.

Yet here he was going to her rescue once again. Old habits definitely died hard.

He gripped the banister and hauled himself up the last step to the landing, giving him the perfect view into the front bedroom, Grandma's sewing room, the room Mac had chosen to start with. Crap. There were way too many pointed things in that room. She could get hurt and, with her track record around him, probably had.

"Are you all right?"

"Do I look all right to you?"

She was sitting cross-legged with her hands planted on her thighs in a pile of mannequins his grandmother had used to make dresses, looking both guilty and annoyed.

The ladder by the window explained the guilt. She'd been eavesdropping and he, obviously, was the reason for the annoyance.

"Hear something you didn't like?" He leaned against the door frame and crossed his arms. It took the weight off his leg. "You look like you could use a hand." He tried not to crack a smile.

He failed miserably.

"Do not start clapping." Mac half rolled over one of the dress forms and got to her knees, brushing her hands on her backside as she did so.

His smile disappeared.

Somewhere along the line, amid the ass-hugging green pants and curves that ought to be well hidden by the golf shirt but weren't, Mac had grown out of the freckles, scraggly ponytail, frayed shorts, and secondhand T-shirts that'd made her look like one of the guys.

What a woman Mac had become.

"Oh my God."

He yanked his gaze off her curves and tried to focus on what she was saying. "What?"

"Do you know what's under here?" She tapped the dresser and brushed a strand of hair off her face.

Another one remained on the bridge of her nose and either she didn't feel it or she didn't care, but Jared wasn't going to tell her and risk getting his butt chewed for telling her how to do something. "I'm guessing a colony of dust bunnies and a lost shoe or two?"

"Not quite."

She leaned over, reached under the dresser, dragged out an old hat box, and pulled out a . . .

. . . kitten.

It was about the size of his fist, a bluish gray with a spot of white on its nose, and had a tail that curled all the way up to that nose and then some.

A tail that twitched.

"That's not a stuffed animal, is it?"

The little thing mewed. It wasn't even old enough to meow.

"And there are three more where this came from." She tilted the box forward a little. "That explains the trail of debris from the broken window."

Another one with a spot on its nose, though the rest of it was black, an all-white one, and a calico with lopsided markings on its face.

"Where's the mom?" *he asks hopefully.* Jared shook his head. He had a bad feeling about this.

Mac set the blue gray one down and picked up the calico. "I think she might be by the side of the road. I saw her when I drove in this morning."

"So she's . . . dead?" He lowered his voice, which was ridiculous. It wasn't as if the kittens understood him.

"If that's her. And if it is, these little things are in danger." She set the calico back in the box with its siblings. "They need to eat regularly and their lethargy has me worried."

"So you're telling me we have to take care of a bunch of newborn kittens?"

She stood up and straightened her shirt.

"Not *we*, Jared. You. *You* live here, remember?"

"I don't know the first thing about taking care of kittens, Mac."

"You feed them, show them the litter box, and pray they don't like to scratch furniture."

"And then what?" Those things were *tiny*. "Seriously, Mac. I can't take care of kittens."

She picked up the hat box. "Seriously, *Jared*, it's not that hard."

"We should take them to the animal shelter."

"Again, not *we*. You." She held out the box. The one with the live, defenseless baby animals inside. "You live here after all. Wasn't that what you were saying earlier?"

Only Mac could make the correlation of living in the house with having to take care of stray pets. And they shouldn't even be *called* pets, since they could barely open their eyes. He wasn't someone's parent for God's sake, and with the lack of pointers from his own, he shouldn't be.

He leaned away from the hat box. "We need to get them out of here."

She lifted the box a little closer. "At the risk of repeating myself, Jared, there is no *we*. There's you. So be my guest. Go drop them off at the shelter where they may or may not be adopted. A two-foot-square wire cage and getting separated from their siblings does beat hanging out together and having free reign of a nice old house, don't you think?"

He wasn't going to cave to her reverse psychology. "If you want them so much, why don't you take them?'

"I have to work for a living. Here, as a matter of fact. I don't have time. You, on the other hand, *live* here. You *sit* here. Aside from the occasional game of catch, you have nothing to do but rest and recuperate. Surely you can handle taking care of four tiny kittens."

Yup, she *had* watched him and Chase.

He shook his head. Not what he needed to be focused on right now.

Kittens.

Here.

His.

He'd love to tell her he couldn't do it, but, number one, he never admitted defeat, not even when it was staring at him through the windshield of a Ford F-150 pickup with his girlfriend's lover sitting inside it, and number two was . . . He forgot what number two was because Mac was looking up at him with such hope in her eyes that it could make him say yes, and he had a feeling it just might.

"What am I supposed to feed them? It's not like I have cat food sitting around." He wasn't saying yes.

"You need kitten food, and if I'm not mistaken, kitten formula. These little guys need to be bottle-fed. Probably need help going to the bathroom, too."

"Hold on there, Princess. Bottle-fed? Are you out of your mind? I've never held a bottle in my life. And as for the bathroom thing, you can forget that." It'd been humiliating when *he'd* had to have help in the hospital; no way was he dealing with anything having to do with *that*.

She grabbed his hand and placed a kitten into it, then curled his fingers gently around the soft fur.

"First time for everything, Jared. You weren't born knowing how to throw a ball, right? So you had to learn. Might as well learn this." She stuck the hatbox on her hip and rested her left wrist on the rim, three kittens poking their noses up over it. "I'll look for something we can use as a litter box. You pick the location."

He was *not* saying yes to this. "What about the basement?"

"These little guys can barely see. Do you really want

them to have to navigate old worn stairs that lead to a stone floor? One wrong step and it's bye-bye kitty."

He hated that she was right.

He hated it even more that he was actually going to do this.

He'd always wanted a pet. But with his mother horrified at the prospect and Dad wanting him to focus on his training, pets had been scratched from his Christmas list every year. The betta fish he'd won at a Fourth of July carnival one year hadn't made up for it, and with the time he had on his hands now, it'd be the perfect opportunity to get one. Or four, as the case may be.

"Fine. I can always put it in the laundry room."

"Exactly." She handed him another kitten. "Now you have to take them to the vet."

"The *vet*? I have to fork out money for these things?"

"I'm sure a vet bill or two won't break you. I hear pro ball players earn a decent living these days."

That was *if* one was playing the game. Luckily though, his agent had earned his commission with the injury clause he'd negotiated for Jared, so money wasn't added to the list of Jared's worries.

Mac plopped another kitten onto his shoulder.

"What are you doing?"

The imp actually looked like she was trying not to laugh. "I'm letting them get used to your scent. Animals, cats especially, are very scent-oriented. They have glands in their cheeks and forehead that they rub against humans to mark them. Might as well start now and get the bonding process going."

"Bonding?"

"Yes, imprinting. So they know you're their mother."

"I am *not* their mother."

"But you are, since you're going to be feeding them."

Uh, maybe this wasn't the best idea . . . "Can't you do it, Mac? You seem to have a greater affinity for these things than I do."

She lifted the last one from the box and rubbed her cheek against its face. "Awww, what's the matter, Jared? Little kittens can knock you off your game? I've seen you pull out a grand slam in the ninth inning with two outs and an oh-and-two count. Keeping four kittens alive isn't nearly as much pressure."

"You saw that game?" It'd been one of the best moments of his life. When the ball had come at him, he'd known it'd go long even before he'd connected. And then, the feeling of running the bases with the win on his shoulders . . .

God, he missed the game.

"Of course I saw it. Gran always puts your games on. She and Mildred are glued to the TV when you play. They could be sports commentators."

"Your *grandmother* follows baseball?"

"Why is that surprising? Why wouldn't she? She's friends with *your* grandmother, after all."

True. Grandma was his biggest fan. Surprising that his parents weren't, but then, he'd stopped trying to figure out his parents' attitude toward him years ago. He didn't get why they were so apathetic about his career when they'd put so much into it, but he'd given up expecting them to watch him play before the end of his first season.

But Mac watching him play? He had to wonder *why* if she was over him.

Oh for fuck's sake, Nolan. Get over it already. Half the nation saw that play.

"Okay. Fine. I'll do it."

"I knew you wouldn't let them down." She took the kittens from him and put them back in the box, then looked around the room. "So I'm guessing you can't drive."

He swung his braced leg. "Good observation."

She tapped the black one's nose and picked up the lid she found beneath the rocking chair. "To finish my thought . . . Since you can't drive, I guess I'll have to."

"Hey, don't do me any favors."

"Really?" She arched her eyebrow. "And you're planning to, what? Ride your broomstick to the vet? Crutch your way there with a hat box balanced on your head? Send out a tweet asking some local fans to drive you?"

He shuddered. That last one was a nightmare waiting to happen. "Fine. You can take me."

"No, you can go *with* me, since I'm the one doing *you* a favor."

Jared had to wrap his brain around that logic. That was like her not telling him how to do his job.

She hiked the hat box higher on her hip and stepped over the mannequin that had started this. "We should go now. I don't know how long they've been without their mom, and with animals this young, every minute counts."

Being around Mac, Jared had the same feeling.

Chapter Six

WHAT had she done?

Mac was sitting in the close confines of the beat-up old truck that'd been her first major purchase after she'd gotten the business license. It was the perfect size for her, one of those scaled-down pickups, but with Jared in it . . . The thing was too small. Too confined.

Good thing she hadn't driven Bryan's Maserati. It'd been his bet in the poker game, and while it might be a cool ride, it was even smaller inside than this.

A tour bus would be too small with Jared in it.

"Wow, Mac. Where'd you find this thing—in a kid's meal at a fast-food joint? Carmel corn box?" Jared's leg was at an awkward angle and when he pulled the seat belt across his chest, it was an inch shy of making it to the lock mechanism. "This isn't going to work." He yanked it. "I don't get in a car without a seat belt."

"Move the seat back. Then it should reach."

"If I were a pretzel I could move the seat back."

She exhaled and bent down to do the honors. Thank God

the latch was on this side of his seat so she didn't have to crawl across his lap—

She yanked the latch.

The seat flew back with a screech.

Jared braced himself with a hand on the ceiling and the other on the back of her seat. "First time?"

She shrugged, not willing to admit she'd been rattled. By his nearness or the screech, it was anyone's guess and she wasn't so sure she wanted to. "I don't get many passengers, and having that seat up close works for me when I put stuff there."

He pulled the seat belt back across him and this time it buckled. "Here's hoping the airbags still work."

"I'm driving to the vet, Mr. Crankypants, not on the autobahn. You'll be fine."

"Uh huh." He adjusted his leg once more, then pulled the hat box from the dashboard onto his lap. "How far is it?"

"A few miles." She put the truck in gear and backed out of Mildred's driveway, being careful to check both ways before pulling onto the street because she understood his trepidation. He'd been injured in a car accident; he had every right to be leery about riding in one. She herself was always extra careful on the road, having firsthand knowledge of how much an accident could impact lives. Looked like she and Jared had something in common.

She glanced at him out of the corner of her eye. She didn't want to have anything in common with him. She was still so embarrassed about following him around all those years. He'd known and so had her brothers. Her friends had teased her, everyone thinking her "little crush" was "cute."

"So how'd you come to start a maid service, Mac?" Jared asked, nudging the lid of the hat box back in place when the kittens poked their noses out.

"I needed money for college, and it was something I could do on my schedule. Plus it was a lot more lucrative than working at a fast-food restaurant."

"What'd you go to college for?"

"A good education?" Not an MRS degree like he'd probably assumed, since he always seemed to think the worst about her.

"I meant, what did you study?"

"Oh." Damn. She thought she was beyond feeling like an idiot around him. It'd been a perpetual state for her whenever he'd deigned to smile at her all those years. Which had been rare. "Business administration. I'd gone for English, but realized I'd be closer to making a living wage in fast food. And once I had a few regular cleaning clients, I saw that I could actually make a business out of this. I have four women working for me at the moment, and business is good. With my brothers helping out—even though they're temporary—I'm hoping word of mouth will grow the client base even more."

"So you're using your brothers for publicity?"

Why he sounded surprised, she didn't know. He had endorsement deals; he knew the value of celebrity. "I'm certainly not using them as long-term employees. I'm surprised Bryan could commit to a full month as it is. And Liam and Sean have their own things going on, but, yeah, I'll take what I can get. Guys in maid outfits are a good draw."

"So what about me? Are you planning to use me to get your name out?"

"Why would I use you?"

He raised his eyebrows. "In case it's escaped your notice, I do tend to make the news every now and then."

She'd noticed. Way too many times. "But you're not one of my employees. I'm building my business on my *business*, not capitalizing on my clients' names. And you're not even my client. I'm not going to violate Mildred's privacy by running your name through the media."

Jared opened his mouth, then shut it.

"What?"

He shook his head. "Nothing."

Oh it was something. She could see it in the way he was staring at her, and it made her uncomfortable.

In two different ways.

Dammit. She hated that she was still attracted to him.

She really didn't want to be. Didn't want to notice him.

And she certainly didn't want him looking at her that way. In *any* way. She was not going to make a fool out of herself over him again. She'd grown up, knew what she wanted out of life. And it wasn't to play second fiddle to the man she ended up with. And that's what she'd be with Jared.

Oh, not the celebrity thing. It was a given that any woman with him would have to take a backseat to the PR machine. No, it was the fact that, by virtue of the feelings she'd worn on her sleeve all those years, he'd had all the power in their relationship. She'd been head-over-heels for him while he . . . He'd probably wanted to *toss* her head-over-heels. The way he'd looked at her that night she'd begged him to kiss her was a perfect example.

Mac shook the memory away before the tears stinging the back of her eyes decided to put in an appearance. At least Jared hadn't led her on; that was a point in his favor. But she took two off for the callous way he'd turned her down.

She pulled into Dr. Bingham's parking lot, glad to see only a few cars. Good, there wouldn't be a long wait. She had to get busy on Mildred's house. It needed more work than she or Mildred had thought, and since she was doing this for free, she didn't want her bottom line to suffer. She was working this in around other clients, so that'd be less time to think about Jared. All bonuses.

"I'll drop you at the front door, Jared, and bring the kittens with me after I park."

"Just park the truck, Mac. I don't need to get dropped off like an invalid."

The anger in his voice surprised her—enough to the point that she did what he said without arguing.

She grabbed the hat box quickly, and got out of the truck without making a big production out of it.

Unfortunately, Jared Nolan in the vet's office with a box of kittens turned out to be a very big production.

The minute he walked in, everyone knew who he was. And, seriously . . . put a hot, injured baseball player—who was single—with a box of kittens in a small office in his hometown, and it became an event. Every kid in the place wanted his autograph—which he gave out sincerely—and every woman wanted him, period. Thankfully, he didn't act on *that* while she was standing next to him, but she saw the pieces of paper that presumably had phone numbers make their way into the back pocket of his shorts.

"Mr. Nolan?" The receptionist's cocked head and soft smile were pure come-on. "Dr. Bingham will see you now."

Mac saw the stars shining in the woman's eyes and rolled her own. "All righty then, Jared." She put the box of kittens on the reception desk. "I'll be back to get you in a bit."

"Mac." Jared's voice was low.

"Yes?"

"Could you . . . That is, would you mind coming back with me? In case I don't catch everything the doc says. I've never done this before."

She might have enjoyed this bit of unexpected insecurity from him if half the waiting room weren't watching them.

And he knew it, too, and was using it. She'd look like a real piece of work if she left him here. Poor Jared Nolan, injured with a hat box full of kittens, left to his own defenses by the maid.

That wouldn't play well in the press, and press was what she needed right now. There might not be such a thing as bad press for someone of Jared's celebrity, but for someone trying to build a business on word of mouth, one bad phrase could sink her reputation.

Plus, much as she hated to admit it, she felt sorry for him. It had to suck being at other people's mercy when he'd been used to doing everything himself, and doing it well.

"Fine." She picked up the box. "Let's go."

The receptionist stepped out from behind the desk and led them down the hallway. "Let me know if there's anything you need," the woman said to Jared as if Mac weren't walking between the two of them.

Jared flashed his megawatt smile at the woman when they reached the exam room. "Thank you, Mimi."

Charmer.

The woman giggled as she pulled the door shut behind her.

Giggled.

"Go ahead and take a seat, Mac," Jared said, pointing with his crutch to the lone chair beside the exam table.

She set the box on the table and shook her head. "I'm good." She turned the chair slightly. "You take it."

"We aren't doing this."

"Doing what?"

"This. This pissing contest."

"I am not having a pissing contest with you, Jared. I don't do pissing contests."

"So then have a seat."

"What's the big deal? Why won't you?"

"Because you're the woman."

"You so did not just say that."

"What's wrong with it? You are. And I'm a gentleman."

She begged to differ, but she got tripped up by the fact that he'd noticed she was female.

Too bad he hadn't had that revelation twenty years ago.

The kittens started mewing again. "Might want to take off the top," she said, making no attempt to do it herself. Which was hard not to. She liked kittens as much as the next person. Wanted to get two for her place, actually, so it wouldn't be as lonely now that Gran had moved out.

Jared lifted the lid. "Geez, Mac. They're so tiny. Helpless."

"Haven't you ever seen a kitten before? They're not exactly rare." If she didn't know any better, she'd think he was scared. Nervous. Unsure.

That would be the day. This was Jared Nolan, MVP two years running, she was talking about. The guy had the world at his feet; he didn't have a thing to be nervous or unsure about. Never had, which was probably why he'd been able to dismiss her feelings so callously—er, easily; if someone had done that to him, it would've rolled off his back as easily as it'd rolled off his tongue.

But her? Notsomuch. His rejection had hurt.

Thankfully, the exam room door opened before Mac went down that road again, and Dr. Bingham entered.

The woman was gorgeous and everything Mac was not: five-nine, blonde, with a body to make swimsuit cover models green with envy even if she did cover it with a lab coat. Exactly the type of woman Jared went for.

Surprisingly, though, he didn't seem to notice.

Even more surprising, Dr. Bingham didn't seem to notice.

How could she not?

Mac didn't have a clue. She might be over Jared, but she was honest enough to admit the guy was still hot.

"Hello. I'm Jennifer Bingham. Nice to meet you." She shook Mac's hand first and didn't linger over Jared's.

Seriously, was the woman blind?

"So what do we have here?" Dr. Bingham picked up one of the kittens, and held it close to her face, a quintessential chick move that would have Mac questioning Dr. Bingham's motives except the woman didn't break her veneer of professionalism.

She went over what and how to feed the kittens, how to get them to use the litter box, speaking to Jared as if he was anyone and not one of the hottest pro athletes of the day. He could have been a troll with three eyes for all the personal attention the vet gave him.

He'd never be a troll, with three eyes or otherwise.

The woman had to be blind.

"I'd like to see them back in a few weeks, but if you have any questions in the meantime, feel free to give me a call." Dr. Bingham handed them her card. "This is my service; they'll be able to get in touch with me anytime."

Again, no innuendo, no come-on . . . Jennifer Bingham was unlike other women in this town, and it made her someone Mac could want to be friends with.

"Thanks." Jared smiled at her as he pocketed the card, but the smile didn't reach his eyes. Wow. It must be true: Even with a beautiful woman in the room, Jared Know-It-All Nolan was out of his league. Because of kittens.

Mac was going to enjoy watching him try to take care of these things.

JARED was so screwed.

He maneuvered himself back into Mac's sardine-can work truck and looked at the kittens in the hat box. They were too small. Too needy. Too dependent on him. If Mac hadn't been in the exam room, he would've just turned them over to the doctor and left. He didn't know how to take care of these things and he didn't need this kind of responsibility in his life. Not when his entire focus had to be on rehabbing himself back to MVP status. Nothing less would do; he'd gone out on top and that's the way he'd return.

But Mac *had* been there, looking as if she knew everything about raising kittens and had merely been humoring him by taking him along for the ride. No way was he going to admit defeat.

He looked over at her. At her cute nose, perfect lips, high cheekbones, long lashes that shielded eyes so green they ought to be called shamrock, and the ponytail he could never remember seeing her without. She was the same Mac Manley he remembered . . . but different.

"Take a picture; it lasts longer."

Well *that* was different. Back then, she would have looked at him shyly out of the corner of her eye and given him that smile that lit up her face, thankful for the iota of interest he'd shown.

He winced inwardly. He could've been nicer. Should have been. "I don't need a picture, Mac."

She glanced at him, her teeth gnawing on her bottom lip. She'd always done that when she was nervous. Like when—

"Hey, do you remember when we put the zip line across the creek?"

She'd insisted on coming with them—or she'd threatened to tell their grandmother, which would have killed that afternoon right then.

"And you guys got stuck halfway across and had to pull each other with Sean's belt to get to the other side?"

He settled the hat box onto his lap when she drove over a pothole and the kittens shifted inside. "But you made it across."

"I didn't weigh as much as you muscle-heads, so I didn't drag the line down."

She'd been nervous as hell to get on the contraption they'd made—they all should have been. That thing had been dangerous. But her brothers had brought her along, so Jared had had to go with it.

In hindsight, he appreciated that they'd cared about her enough to bring her. At the time . . . Not really. "That was a fun afternoon."

"Until Johnny Heavers found that snake and chased me with it."

"Your brothers took care of him for you."

"Yeah. They did." She smiled that same smile that she'd worn that day when Johnny had run home in tears with her brothers chasing him, leaving Jared alone with her.

He'd rather have gone after Johnny, but the guys had had the right since they were her brothers and someone had to stay with her. He'd been annoyed and probably not as nice to her as he should've been, but he'd always been careful not to complain around her brothers. Hadn't wanted to test the friendship over their sister.

"Bryan shoved the snake down the back of Johnny's shorts. Good thing it was a garter snake, because if it bit him, at least it wasn't poisonous."

Jared smiled. He'd wanted to get Johnny a time or two when they'd been kids. "*Did* it bite him?"

Mac shrugged. "I don't know. "

"If I were Johnny, I'm not sure I'd admit it if it did, you know?"

She laughed. "I wonder what he's doing these days. He was always causing trouble."

"I heard he joined the circus as the snake handler."

She rolled her eyes. "You are so not funny."

"Oh I don't know. I thought that was hilarious."

"And you thought Mariellen Meselnick was hot, so that just shows what your opinion is worth."

"Mariellen *was* hot."

"Yeah, but not for what you were selling."

Jared shook his head. "This conversation is so wrong on so many levels. I'm sure Mariellen married a nice guy and settled down to raise her two-point-five kids."

"Actually, Mariellen married a woman and they each had a baby via surrogate. So your radar was totally off on that one."

"Ouch. Way to wound a guy. Still, Mariellen and another chick? Now that's hot."

Mac rolled her eyes again. "Next topic."

He smiled, enjoying one of the first non-confrontational conversations he'd ever had with Mac. "Okay, how about jumping off the boulders into the swimming hole?"

"I was never so scared in all my life. That was like a hundred-foot drop."

"Actually, it was fifteen. I went back and measured a few years ago."

"Seemed a lot higher then."

One of the kittens nudged the lid of the hatbox, and his arm brushed hers when he went to close it. "A lot of things looked different when we were kids."

"Yeah, they did." She turned into the strip mall parking lot. "You hang here and I'll run in to get the rest of what we need. It'll be quicker and I can just park at the curb."

And just like that, reality smacked him in the face. The trip down memory lane had taken his mind off the stupid injuries, but now, here he sat, kitten-sitting in the truck, having people do things for him that he ought to be doing himself.

He shifted his leg. Stupid ache wouldn't go away. How the hell did he even hope to be able to play again if he couldn't handle twenty minutes in a truck?

He set the box o' kittens on the dash and opened the door. It took him longer than it should have to get out of the damn cab, but once he was out . . . thank God. He'd needed the air and once he stretched the kinks out, he started to feel better about not only his leg, his life, and his professional prospects, but even the kittens.

Then Mac walked out of the store with a bag of something on her shoulder and another bag of something under her other arm, a few other bags in one hand, and a big flat box in the other, looking like a beast of burden—and there went that good feeling. He ought to be carrying that for her.

He crutched over. "Here, give me some of those." He reached out to take the bags and for the briefest of seconds he saw her smile.

But then she frowned. "Did you leave the door open?"

"Huh?" He took the first bag off her arm.

"Did you leave the truck door open?"

He worked the bag onto his wrist then turned around.

Hell. Kittens.

He actually made it back to the truck with his crutches before Mac could with all the other stuff, catching the calico fuzz ball before it fell off the seat onto the pavement.

"Seriously, Jared? Are you just humoring me that you'll take care of them while trying to find a way to get rid of them? If you really want me to take them off your hands, just say so. There's no sense killing them."

The woman could make him madder than an ump with blinders on. "Knock it off, Princess. I saved this one, didn't I? Of course I can take care of kittens."

She smiled then. A big, beautiful . . . know-it-all smile. "Told you so."

She dropped the bags and box at his feet, flipped her ponytail over her shoulder, and practically skipped around the truck to the driver's side.

For a guy on crutches, he'd walked into that one easily enough.

He set the little adventurer back in the hat box with the gray one—the only smart one of the bunch—and scooped Moe and Curly off the seat to rejoin their siblings before hefting the bags into the flatbed.

There would be no getting out of kitten duty now. Not with Mac grinning the entire drive back.

Chapter Seven

THREE hours gone. Mac checked the cuckoo clock in Mildred's dining room as she lugged the bag of litter through to the laundry room. Three more hours that she was going to have to spend in Jared's company. For so long she'd tried to forget about the guy and now here he was, staring her in the face.

Testing her resolve.

Why'd there have to be kittens? Why'd she have to *care* that there were kittens? Why couldn't Jared have broken the other leg instead so he could drive himself and the kittens to the vet without her?

Why'd he have to be so endearingly inept when it came to kittens?

Karma. The universe was paying her back for outplaying her brothers at poker.

She slid the heavy bag the last five feet, praying there wasn't a loose floorboard or rogue splinter on the hardwood, but she just couldn't carry this thing any farther.

She made it into the laundry room and propped the bag in the corner, then wiped her forehead and headed back out to get the litter box. *Three* litter boxes, actually. Dr. Bingham had suggested they get two full-sized ones for when the kittens got bigger, since they could be finicky about their toileting habits, and one low-rise one for them to use until they were big enough to climb into the others.

She put the litter-catch mat down, then set the boxes on it like a row of kitty townhouses. Sadly, there was very little room to do the laundry now. But since Jared was the only one staying here, how much laundry could he have?

Unless he has someone stay over.

She wasn't going there. Jared's love life was not something she wanted to think about.

"You need help in there?"

Why did he persist in asking if she needed help? Did he still see her as Liam's kid sister who needed rescuing every time he was around?

If he only knew that *he* was the reason she'd been such a mess back then. She hadn't been able to think straight when he showed up.

If she could tell Mac-Then what Mac-Now knew, this situation would be a lot different.

But hindsight didn't do her one iota of good. Speaking of . . . "No, I'm good." And she would be if she didn't keep picturing the concentration on his face when Dr. Bingham had been teaching him what to do. Or if his gaze hadn't darted to the kittens every couple of seconds. Or if he hadn't snuck in some quick petting when he'd thought she wasn't looking.

She'd been so used to Jared tormenting her that she'd rarely seen this tender side of him.

He was standing beside the sink when she walked back into the kitchen, exactly the spot she needed to go.

She was starting to get the warm-and-fuzzies for him. All on account of those darn kittens. Oldest trick in the book.

But Jared never played by the book. And he certainly wasn't playing now. He'd made his disdain for her very clear on more than one occasion. Those warm-and-fuzzies were solely figments of her imagination.

Mac strode over, turned on the faucet, and squirted some

soap onto her hands to wash the litter off. "What'd you do with them?"

Keep the conversation on the kittens. That was a safe subject.

Then again, she'd thought heading upstairs earlier would be safe, given that Jared was injured, so that showed what she knew. Kittens, kisses . . .

Great. Now she was thinking about that kiss again.

She caught herself looking at his lips.

Then she caught him *catching* her looking at his lips.

Those lips twisted into a smile. "What do you *want* me to do with them?"

He wasn't talking about kittens.

And she didn't like that he was laughing at her. Oh, not outright, but it was there. She knew because she'd been the recipient of his mocking laughter too many times not to know it when she saw it.

Well she was a big girl now and no longer love-struck. She could give as well as she got.

She leaned closer. Licked her lips. Let him think what he wanted about *that*. "What should you *do* with them?" She flicked her tongue over her lips again and lowered her voice almost to a purr. "Feed them." She tilted her head up. "*Cuddle* them." She nodded him closer. "*Pet* them."

He sucked in a deep breath.

She was trying so hard not to smile as she leaned even closer and whispered, "Then put their butts in the litter box."

She shook the water from her hands and refrained from tossing her ponytail over her shoulder, but she glanced at him as she walked out of the room. Let him see what it felt like to want. She knew all about it.

IT took Jared a couple of seconds to get his breathing back in gear. Teasing him like that . . .

He'd thought she was over her crush, but then he'd caught her looking at his lips and, well, he'd looked at hers.

And remembered what they'd tasted like.

He shouldn't have kissed her. He should have kept his damn curiosity to himself and used the childhood memories of her as a shield.

"Uh, Jared?" Mac called down from upstairs. "The kittens need you."

He exhaled. The kittens were mewing.

"I hear them." He shoved himself off the counter, stuck a crutch under each arm, and headed into the front room.

The kittens hadn't waited for the litter box.

Man, what was in that formula?

He decided against picking up the hat box, worried that the now-wet bottom would fall out, and instead picked up each kitten, gathered the hem of his shirt, and stuck it in his mouth, using it as a basket. Unfortunately, it gave him a way-too-up-close-and-personal experience with the kittens' messy paws as he headed back into the kitchen with a shirt that was now toast.

Back at the sink—a big farmhouse style one with sides as high as skyscrapers to these little guys—Jared set each one on paper towels he layered over the porcelain. It wasn't the most hygienic place to put them, but then hygiene had pretty much flown out the window since Mac had found them.

He was going to have to wash these little things. He sure hoped kittens were bathe-able.

Then the gray one slugged his white brother over the head, leaving behind a very distinctive—and stinky—paw print on his brother's pristine fur, so they were going to be bathe-able whether they liked it or not.

He hiked his own ruined shirt over his head and used it to line the sink.

The little curiosity-seekers were inspecting the walls of their temporary home, leaving tiny, not-so-nice paw prints all over the place. They weren't very steady on their legs; the vet had said that'd come with age and she'd guessed these were about three to four weeks old. They'd been well fed, so the mother had probably had her accident last night at the latest. There was a plus in there somewhere for Jared; at least the kittens weren't hovering on the edge of starvation for him to bring back to life, but the downside was that he still had to keep them alive.

The black one, however, *was* hovering on the edge of the sink.

Jared plucked him—her, actually—off the rim and set her back into the middle of the sink, then turned on the water to let the bathing commence—

Holy hell! Four kittens moved faster than he'd ever thought they could, each one scrambling to get out of the sink. The black one actually made it this time and was heading over the edge, right to the floor.

Jared scooped her up, then rounded up the others, hugging them to his chest as they clawed their way up under his chin, leaving little bloody claw marks the entire way.

"That's a good look on you."

Of *course* Mac would be standing in the doorway, witnessing him at his worst. He didn't have a leg to stand on in that department—oops. Not a good cliché to use.

"What'd you do? Try to bathe them?"

"Considering I'm as wet as they are, I think that's self-explanatory." He jostled them in his arms to keep the calico from making its way over his shoulder.

"Don't you know cats don't like water?"

"No. I don't. I never had any as pets before."

The white one made it onto his other shoulder and the gray one had chosen *now* to decide to keep up with its brothers' and sister's bravery as it tried to jump back *into* the sink. Damn, their claws might be tiny, but those suckers could draw blood.

His crutches went clattering to the floor as he tried to keep all the kittens in one place.

That didn't work and, of course, he lost his balance.

If Mac hadn't caught him, he would have broken his tailbone in addition to his other injuries when he landed.

As it was, he slid down Mac's body—something he was *not* going to think about—and those injuries got a reprieve before he hit the floor.

Who knew five-foot-two could be such a long way down?

"You want to get off me, please?" Mac sounded out of breath.

Hmmm, he liked having her under him. Preferably under other circumstances, but right now, just for a second, he allowed himself to feel Mac against him.

Liam's little sister had *definitely* grown up.

Okay, time to get off her. For both their sakes.

He sucked in a big breath, set the kittens onto the floor, and managed to roll off of her and not onto them.

He sucked in another big breath to mitigate sore-rib pain. "Sorry about that. And thanks for the catch."

Mac stood and brushed off her thighs. Thighs that were now eye level for him. "You're welcome." She held out a hand. "Need some help getting up?"

No. He didn't. Not one bit.

Jesus.

Jared plunked a cat onto his lap to hide the evidence. Nothing like kitten claws to get the guy to go into hibernation. Which is where "he" needed to stay around Mac, for God's sake.

"Not that I don't appreciate the offer, but it's probably a better idea if I get up on my own."

He slid the kitten to the floor as he turned onto his side, the little thing's claws pretty much finishing the job of sending his dick back into hiding, and struggled to schlep himself onto a chair.

Mac scooped the kittens off the floor, catching the calico before it crawled through the gap in the kickboard. "So, I guess you need some help with the bathing process."

It took him a second to realize she was referring to the *kittens'* bathing process, but that one second was enough to get the full-on image of Mac in the shower. With him. And soap. And water. And steam—the water variety and other kinds.

Hell. "Uh, yeah. Not sure how I can corral four kittens with two hands." Though at least it'd keep his hands busy so they wouldn't be tempted to stray toward her.

Except . . . they already *were* tempted.

Jesus. He'd never been this hyper-aware around Camille. Why was he around Mac of all people?

"Okay, so you get the water lukewarm while I keep them busy over here. Probably best to put only a little water in the sink and let them get used to it." She held the kittens as if they were a pack of stuffed toy animals—all sitting in her arms as if they hadn't just knocked him off his feet. The little heathens.

They did flinch when he turned the water on, but he quickly turned the stream down to almost a trickle. "This is going to take a while to fill."

Mac shrugged. "So we wait. I'm already three hours behind; what's another?"

"Got a hot date you have to get to?"

She raised her eyebrow. "It's Tuesday. Middle of the day. How many hot dates have you been on at that time? Wait." She held up her hand. "I don't want to know. You and Bryan don't have normal lives like the rest of us, and I've heard his stories too many times to want to hear them from you, too. Let's just go with, *if* I have a hot date, it's usually on a Saturday night after I've recovered from the week."

"So *do* you have a hot date this Saturday?"

"Why do you care?"

Yeah, why did he? "I don't. I mean, it was just conversation."

"So is 'what did you have for breakfast today,' but that wasn't what you picked to go with."

"Geez, Mac, give it a rest, will ya? Don't you ever get tired of carrying all that armor around all the time?" He plucked a kitten from her arms—the one in the crook because he wasn't going for either of the two in the middle that were right over her breasts.

"I don't know what you're talking about, Jared." She handed him the gray kitten when the white one started to mew. "Here. They don't like to be separated."

He jostled the little thing that was practically hopping out of his hand to get to his brother. *Her* brother. Sister. Whatever. At some point he should probably come up with names for these things so he'd know which one was what gender. There was one female in the bunch—and that was just fine with him. One female was all he could handle these days. And given that Mac was bristling at his question, one was more than enough.

"Your armor. Or maybe you prefer the chip on your shoulder?

Don't you ever get tired of carrying it around? Why not let it go? Even for a little while?"

She almost dropped the last kitten. Luckily, her sense of kitty-preservation kicked in and she was able to catch the little thing before it splattered on the floor. "Chip? I do not have a chip on my shoulder."

"Oh, right. It's normal for everyone to go around snarling at an old family friend."

"An old family friend, huh?" She set the last kitten in the sink. Their mewling stopped the minute they were all together. "Funny you call yourself that, Jared, when you weren't friends with the *whole* family."

He leaned a hip against the sink and braced a hand on the edge. "Mac, we were kids. At some point you have to move on."

"Move on—" She tossed the dishtowel she'd just taken from the drawer in his face. "Don't flatter yourself, Jared. I've moved on from that stupid crush I had on you. A long time ago."

Which she proved by storming through the doorway and leaving him with a cache of now-crying kittens.

Now crying *wet* kittens.

Who were trying to claw their way out of the sink via his forearm.

He took a deep breath and redirected his anger. It wasn't the kittens' fault that she'd left them at his mercy. And it wasn't their fault he didn't know what to do with them. It was whoever'd been driving the car that'd killed their mother, that's whose fault it was.

And, like with Camille and Burke, assigning blame didn't make him feel any better or make the situation any different. So he sucked it up and put the discussion with Mac on the back burner for after the kittens were washed.

And dried.

And fed.

And litter-boxed.

God, he hoped they'd sleep through the night.

Because with Mac's anger still lingering in the air—and the sight of her backside in those figure-hugging pants as she walked out—he wasn't sure he was going to.

Chapter Eight

MAC ran the dust mop over the molding one more time for good measure, sneezing half a dozen times more. Now she knew why Mildred hadn't done this for years; the delicate filigree molding held on to dust like powdered sugar on cake frosting. This was the fifth duster she'd gone through since she'd left the kitchen.

And Jared.

Damn him. *At some point you have to move on.* Really? Was he *really* that conceited to think that she'd been holding a torch for him all these years? Idiot. If she *had* been, wouldn't she have been all into that stupid kiss and begged him for more?

But she'd *stopped* it. She'd walked away.

Um . . . haven't really walked away, sweetie. You're still here.

Oh no. She wasn't going to have this argument with herself. She was here because she had a job to do. Nothing else. So what if he kissed her? He was still the same old arrogant Jared who thought all he had to do was crook his little finger and she'd do his bidding.

Yeah, but you did *drive him to the vet and chauffeur him around.*

That's because he couldn't drive himself. Seriously, if she had to have this dialogue with herself after every Jared encounter, someone was going to have to sign her up for the Funny Farm when this job was all said and done.

"Ah, dammit! No! Come here!" Jared's voice bellowed up the stairs, followed by a crash and a thud that sounded like him taking a header to the floor.

Great. That's all she needed; spending the next ten hours in the ER and explaining it to both their grandmothers.

Mac tossed the dust-laden duster into the big green trash bag on the floor and hightailed it off the ladder and down the front stairs in record time to find three out of four kittens huddled together between Jared's sprawled legs, while the other one—

Oh no. The other one was at the top of the basement stairs, looking back over its shoulder at its siblings, teetering over an abyss.

Those stairs were open, no risers between them. One wrong bounce and Whitey there would be a goner.

She took a step toward it and the little guy looked up at her, with his big soulful blue eyes, and let out a high-pitched "Mew."

It teetered some more.

"Don't go after it, Mac. You'll just scare it."

"It's already scared. Are you okay, by the way?" She glanced back and—uh, yeah, he was okay. More than okay, actually, since he was still shirtless. Which wasn't helping her argument about not being into him anymore.

"Yeah. I'm fine. Ribs are sore, but then, they were to begin with. No harm no foul, but we have to save that kitten."

"No kidding." Mac looked around for something to scoop the little thing up with before it realized what she was up to, but of course Mildred didn't have fishing nets hanging from her pot holder rack. She thought about tossing a dishtowel over it, but that might send it over the edge. As would lunging toward it.

She grabbed the calico kitten and set it down within arm's reach. She didn't want to have to chase two of them down the basement steps, but hopefully the white one would come toward its sibling.

"Mew." The calico played its part perfectly.

"Mew." Thankfully, the white one was on the same team. It took its first step toward them.

"Thank God." Jared rested his forehead on the floor and sighed.

"I prefer *goddess* actually if you're going to go with divinity." Mac took a step toward the calico.

"Goddess beats out princess?"

"Hands down." She wasn't going to rise to the bait, choosing instead to keep her eyes on the white kitten, ready to pounce should it change its mind.

A couple more "*mews*" and Whitey was close enough to scoop.

"Grab Larry!" Jared did some strange scramble across the hardwood, catching the calico's—Larry's?—tail between his fingers before it took off.

"MMMwwwrrrroooowww!"

"Stow it, you." Jared dragged the kitten backward toward him.

Mac winced as she plunked her butt on the floor and took the kitten from Jared. She could see the little guy's point, but a pinched tail was better than a crushed skull. "Larry?"

"Three Stooges."

"There are four kittens."

Jared got up onto his elbows. "And there was Shemp and Joe, so we're actually a kitten short."

She snorted and tucked the two mewling kittens under her chin. "You want *another* one?" She pulled the rubber band from her ponytail, letting her hair fall around them like a curtain to give them a place to curl up and feel safe.

The mewling quieted down and the kneading into her neck stopped. Thank God. The claws might not be big, but they were there and they were sharp.

"Wow."

"What?" She looked at Jared.

"Your hair."

She puffed some off her face. "Yeah, so? I get that it'll never earn me a spot on a shampoo commercial, but I'm a little more worried about calming the kittens down than what my hair looks like."

"That's just it, Mac." Jared swung his legs around, sat up, and tucked the two well-behaved kittens onto his lap. "I've never seen your hair down."

For a second—just one—she thought he was impressed. Maybe even flirting with her. But then that moment passed. This was Jared. A leopard didn't change his spots. Not even with kittens involved. And it wasn't as if he'd ever looked long enough to notice in the first place.

She climbed to her feet and held out her hands for the kittens he was holding, trying desperately to ignore that sculpted chest with just a dusting of hair that would feel so good against her cheek. Or other parts. "At the risk of repeating myself, do you need some help to get up?"

"No, I'm good."

She really wished he'd stop saying that.

She plucked the other kittens off his thighs, trying to focus on something other than where they were. "So where's the crate thingie?"

"The what?"

"The crate thing. The play yard. The thing I bought so they don't run all over the place?"

"I didn't see a crate."

"So what did you do with them? I see the hatbox lid is missing."

He struggled to his knees and she had to remember he didn't want any help from her.

"Did you *look* in the hatbox, Mac? It's a mess. I wasn't about to put them there."

"So where *did* you put them?"

He glanced at a group of pillows on the floor. "I, uh—"

"You tried to pen them in with pillows? Jared, they can climb."

"I gathered that." He yanked his crutches off the floor and used them to get upright. "I just wanted to drop them some place quick so I could sit down, then put them on my lap."

"And you thought they were going to, what? Hang out and watch the game with you? They're not dogs."

"Look, Mac, I'm soaked, my ribs and leg hurt like a sonofabitch, and I'm learning on the fly here, so if you have some infinite wisdom you'd like to impart, could you do it quickly so I can get off my feet? I am still recuperating, you know."

As if she couldn't tell, he rattled the crutches. It was on the tip of her tongue to make some sarcastic remark, but then she saw the pastiness beneath his tan. The grim lines at the corners of his mouth. The tired look in his green eyes. The slump in his shoulders. The guy was in pain. And she was human enough not to want to cause him more.

"That." She pointed to the box she'd bought earlier, then gathered the four kittens into the crook of one arm, cuddling them close to her neck. "It unfolds into a play yard so they can't run all over the place and get into trouble."

"How am I supposed to know that?"

She maneuvered the box from the wall she'd leaned it against to the wingback chair by the sofa, reminding herself that he was in pain. That she should have compassion for a fellow human being.

Who'd kissed her . . .

"It says so right here on the front cover. See this sticker? Complete instructions *and* a picture. They couldn't make it any easier."

"Except someone would have to *see* it to know that that's what it's for." He hobbled over to the sofa and sat down.

She had to work to hold her temper. Remind herself that he was mad at his circumstances, not at her.

Right?

The old self-doubt came back for just a moment, but that moment was enough. Jared had always been able to reduce her to a babbling shell of her former self—her former *confident* self. Only around him had she ever been unsure of herself.

Well, not anymore. She was a grown woman running a successful business she'd started herself. Whether Jared liked her or not no longer defined her.

"Hey, it's not my job to know what you see and don't see. Don't you have a personal assistant for that?"

"No." He spat the word at her enough that she had a feeling athletes didn't need personal assistants after they went on the disabled list.

Well, hey, no one had to tell her twice to back off from a touchy subject where Jared was concerned. So she set the kittens on the chair, then hiked the box up in front of them, penning them in, before opening one end to let the play yard slide out. A couple of screws pinged onto the floor beneath the sofa.

This time it was the black kitten who decided to go exploring and tumbled off the chair after them.

"Hey, kitten! Come back here!"

"I got this, Mac." Jared braced himself on the seat cushion and got down on his good knee to scoop up the kitten. He plopped her onto the sofa, then reached back under for the screws. "You can go back to what you were doing."

"Don't be ridiculous. We can put this up together and then I'll get back to work. It'll take you twice as long—"

"I said I have this. Go do what you need to do."

"Are you telling me what to do?"

He looked up at her, one eyebrow cocked in that devil-may-care attitude that she dreamed about as a teenager. "Has *anyone* ever been able to tell you what to do?"

It took a lot of fortitude, but she didn't fire back a nasty response since he was in pain, but that was the only reason he was getting a pass.

She corralled her anger and channeled it to jerking the play yard off the table, opening it into the hexagonal shape shown on the sticker. "So where do you want me to put this?"

He was quiet just a heartbeat too long.

"Don't answer that." She hiked it over her head—thing was more awkward in its current shape—and plunked it in the middle of the room, then held out her hand for the screws and put the sizzle she felt when his fingertips brushed her skin down to that anger she was trying to keep a tight rein on.

Yeah, keep telling yourself that's why your arm feels like something jolted you. Face it, Mary-Alice Catherine, Jared still does it for you.

She yanked her hand back, almost losing the screws in the process.

"I'll get a screwdriver," Jared clambered to his feet, seemingly unaware of what was happening with her nerve endings.

How was that possible? How could he not see her reaction? How could he not feel it, too?

She closed her fingers over the screws. He never had felt it, so she was better off forgetting him. She'd wasted enough time on Jared Nolan over the years.

Thankfully, someone chose that moment to knock on the door.

It was a woman. A very trim, very toned woman. In a short skirt. And heels. And a figure-hugging scoop-necked T-shirt. Holding a basket of something.

Come on, honey, don't be so obvious.

She now rang the doorbell.

"Mac, can you see who that is, please?" Jared called from the mudroom beyond the kitchen.

Oh, she'd see who it was all right. "No problem."

She ran her fingers through her hair—though, why? The woman on the other side of the door had perfectly cascading waves off her five-ten perfect figure, so it wasn't as if Mac could even hope to compete.

She opened the door. "Hello. Can I help you?"

The woman was gorgeous. Maybe a bit too heavy on the makeup, though, and the shirt was a tad snug. There was a fine line between sexy and tacky, and this chick was teetering on it.

"Is Jared here?" she asked with a beauty-pageant smile.

Mac refrained from rolling her eyes. Barely. "He's, um, occupied at the moment. Can I tell him who stopped by?"

"Oh, but I wanted to give him these in person." Miss Beauty Pageant held up a basket of muffins. Chocolate chip muffins right out of her favorite bakery if Mac wasn't mistaken. She recognized the Cups & Cakes foil muffin holders.

"Sorry. Like I said, he's occupied at the moment." Mac took the basket, surprising the woman into letting go. Like taking candy from a baby. "But I'll be sure to share these with him. Did you leave your name"—and number?—"in the basket?"

"Well, yes, I did, so if he could call—"

"I'll be sure to let him know. Thanks so much for coming. I'll just run these back and I'm sure he'll be in touch."

That he probably would, Mac didn't doubt. If she were Jared, she would, too. The woman was hot and if she didn't bake, at least she knew which bakery to go to.

"Oh. Well, um, okay. Thanks."

"Sure. No problem. Have a nice day." Kill 'em with kindness, all while taking their cookies. Muffins. Whatever.

"Who wa' 'at?" Jared met her in the kitchen as he crutched out of the back room with a screwdriver between his teeth.

Mac took the tool, careful to avoid touching his lips. "Might want to come up with some other way to transport this, Jared. We don't need to spend the night in the ER."

"It was the easiest way I could think of. So who was at the door and what do you have in that basket?"

Mac set the screwdriver down and dug around in the basket for the woman's card—complete with a handy-dandy cell phone number. Didn't little Miss Beauty Queen just think of everything?

"Name's Juliette Lerner. About five-ten, long brown hair. Pretty." Mac was the master of understatement. "Not sure about her baking skills, though, since she bought these. You'd think someone trying to hit on a guy would go for homemade."

Jared just arched an eyebrow and helped himself to a muffin. "Hey, the woman's got taste. She came to see me *and* she knows where to buy the best muffins."

This time Mac let the eye roll happen. "Then eat up, Casanova. But you might want to save some room. I have a feeling these aren't going to be the last sugar explosions you get."

"Jealous?"

Of the women who might actually have a chance with him? Yes. Was she going to admit that? No.

"No. I don't need sweets. I'm sweet enough as it is."

She actually got a laugh out of him.

"Touché, Mac." He raised the muffin to salute her and for the first time, Jared was looking at her with something other than derision, sarcasm, or anger.

And it shot her argument about being over him straight to hell.

Chapter Nine

THE kittens woke him up.

Again.

One was on his foot, meowing.

Another one was on his arm, also meowing.

The black one had a paw across his left eye, though it wasn't making a noise, but the gray . . .

Damn that one; it was curled up in his crotch. Where it'd slept since two AM. Jared was very sure of that time; it wasn't often that he woke up with claws to the nuts. One tended not to forget *that,* as well as the sound four hungry kittens made in the dead of night.

Thank God Mac had brought the bottle warmers up. He'd filled the bottles with water last night and had pre-measured the powdered formula, so all he'd had to do was mix them together to feed the kittens. She'd put the litter box with the higher sides on the chair beside the bed, so that hadn't been the challenge he'd thought it would be. It was rolling onto them when they'd climbed out of the laundry basket beside him on the bed for the fifth time that had really worried him, but when they'd settled down on his various body parts every time he'd put them back, he'd finally given up and let them stay put.

But now he was out of water and formula, so he'd have to get up to feed them.

With ball-boy purring contentedly in his crotch, Jared wasn't sure how he was going to manage it.

The other two ratcheted up their crying enough to wake Shemp. That's what Jared had decided to name ball-boy in the middle of the night, which made the black one Moe. Not the most feminine of names for the only female in the bunch, but he'd been too tired to be more inventive. And besides, she was a cat; she'd never know.

His leg twinged when it hit the floor. Oh, right. Leg brace. He'd taken to sleeping without it. There was just something about being a damn invalid twenty-four hours a day. Sixteen were bad enough.

He grabbed the monstrosity and lashed himself into it. He'd shower later, but these guys—and girl—needed food more than he needed a shower.

He plopped them into the laundry basket, balanced a pillow on top, grabbed his crutches, and nudged the contraption toward the stairs as the mewling escalated.

There was only one way to get them all down quickly.

Tossing his dignity out the window, Jared sat on the top step, dragged the basket onto his lap, and butt-hitched himself down the stairs, sliding his crutches beside him.

Of course it stood to reason that Mac would show up when he was halfway down.

"That's um, inventive."

That perfectly bow-shaped mouth twitched at the corners as she struggled against smiling.

"Necessity and all that." He slid down another step, bravado-ing his way out of this embarrassment. Karma was really paying him back in spades for how he'd treated her.

"Want some help?"

"No." Yes.

The doorbell rang.

Of course it did. He was in his boxers—thanks to

ball-boy—because the minute the claws had hit his nuts last night, he'd put them on. Not that they were all that effective in blocking cat claws, but they gave him a modicum of protection. And now a modicum of self-respect, though there was no way he was answering the door in them.

"Want me to get that?" Mac lost her battle with the smile.

The doorbell rang again.

Shit. "Yeah. Sure. Why not."

"Gee, you're welcome."

She spun around, a too-perky bounce to her step—which did really nice things to her ass. She needed baggy work pants. Those figure-hugging ones were going to cause her trouble around male clients.

"Hi," said a sultry voice from the other side of the door. "I'm Maeve Finnegan. I live down the street."

"Let me guess." Mac rested her hip against the door. She really needed to get different uniforms. "You brought Jared cookies."

Was it Jared's imagination or did Mac move a little to the left to block the woman?

Why do you care?

Because . . . it was nice if she was protecting his privacy and dignity. And if she wasn't doing it for him but because she was jealous, well, hey, even better. Right?

The deafening silence of his subconscious spoke volumes.

"Actually, no. I brought coffee cake."

Jared loved coffee cake. Ms. Finnegan was a woman after his own heart. Not that he would be giving it to her.

"Jared's, um, indisposed, so I'll be more than happy to give it to him and let him know you dropped it off. I'm assuming your card's in the basket?"

"Um . . . well . . . yes—"

"Good. Here, have one of mine. If you're ever in need of someone to give your home a quick cleanup, I handle all sized jobs. You know, if you're expecting special company or anything."

Jared almost blew Mac's story by laughing. The woman was a piece of work; peddling her services to someone who'd come here with one thing in mind. This entrepreneurial side was a part of Mac he hadn't anticipated.

He liked it.

"Trying to sabotage my love life, Mac?" he asked once she shut the door.

"Get over it, Jared. I'm sure there are a zillion more where she came from." She peered through the sidelight. "Luckily, the hordes aren't descending yet, so you can go put some pants on."

"Don't tell me what to do."

"You so did not just say that. How old are you—six?"

She shoved a hand onto her hip and cocked her head, the epitome of pissed off, but instead, somehow managed to kick start his salivary glands. Yeah, he definitely wasn't six.

What the hell was wrong with him? This was *Mac* of all people.

Maybe it was the coffee cake. Yeah, that was it. He was salivating for that.

"Are you planning to share what's in the basket?"

Mac rolled her eyes and set the basket on the steps. *Just* out of reach. "You better not eat all of this or you're going to get out of shape real quick."

He leaned forward. Coffee cake was worth rib pain. "Ah, so you're noticing my shape, Princess?"

"Dream on, Nolan."

The doorbell rang again, saving him from actually doing what she said.

"Oh my God. Are you *kidding* me?" Mac stomped over to the door. She was about to fling it open, but caught it and glanced back at him before stationing herself in the same position she'd been in with Ms. Finnegan.

"Let me guess," she said to whoever was on the other side. "Brownies."

"Chocolate chip cookies," said a sexy voice. It'd be nice if the door opened toward the stairs so he could see who was there, but given what he wasn't wearing, it was probably better this way.

"I'm sure Jared will appreciate them. You put a card in there, yes?"

"Well, yes, but I was hoping I could speak to him."

"He's not entertaining at the moment. Trying to recover from the accident and all. I'm sure you understand. But I know he'll enjoy these." Mac raised the basket for emphasis, then went about giving this woman her business card, too. "For any *special* entertaining you're planning to do."

"I gotta hand it to you, Mac," he said when she shut the door again. "Smooth move pushing your business like that. I could hear the innuendo from here."

"I don't know what you're talking about."

"Oh right. As if you weren't playing on those women's hopes that I'd show up."

"Feeling a little full of ourself, are we?" Mac set the cookies on the step. "Start eating those and you'll be full all right. Then no one will want to see you."

"You included?"

Mac rolled her eyes. "Sadly, I wasn't given a choice."

That stopped his chuckle. He might enjoy teasing her, but she probably didn't. She never had.

God, he felt like such a jerk. Okay, he'd been a kid, but would it have killed him to be nice to her? Or had he just taken her crush so for granted that he hadn't realized what it'd meant to her?

"I'm sorry, Mac." The words slipped out, but they were the right ones to say. He should have apologized years ago.

Mac waved her hand. "No need to apologize. I knew what I was getting into when I took this on. No one's fault."

"No, I meant that I apologize for—"

"Jared, really. It's no big deal. I'm here to do a job and I don't mind answering the door occasionally." She picked up the laundry basket of kittens. "So do you plan to get dressed at all today or are you going to be mooning the neighbors? I don't think your grandmother would appreciate that."

And apparently, neither would she. She really was over her crush.

And how wrong was it that he didn't want her to be?

Jesus, he shouldn't have kissed her. He should have stayed away. Mac had grown up and he was the one stuck in the past.

"Jared? Hello?" She waved her hand in front of his face. "Sugar fumes get to you?"

He shook his head to clear it. "Uh, yeah. I mean, no. I mean, you're right. I ought to go put something on."

He turned to leave and the doorbell rang *again*.

"Okay, I said I don't mind answering it *occasionally*. You might want to think about putting in a revolving door or I'm never going to make any progress on this place. Fending off your female admirers is *not* in my job description."

"Want it to be?"

She didn't bother rolling her eyes this time; she just stared a hole through him as she handed him the laundry basket while Ms. Persistent on the other side of the door rang again.

Dammit. He didn't need any more desserts and he didn't need any more women showing up to try to wiggle their way into his heart through his stomach. He ought to tell them all that that road was closed thanks to Hurricane Camille.

Yet it was Tornado Manley who put her hand on the doorknob. "Should I get this?"

The visitor knocked. "Jared? It's Dave."

Of *course* it was Dave. Why shouldn't it be? Who was going to be next—the entire crew of the local sports network? He'd rather have another Mrs. Nolan Wannabe.

"*Dave*?" Mac raised her eyebrows. "Should I open it?"

"My physical therapist, and not really."

"I see you, Jare. I'm not going away." Dave was peering in the sidelight, his hands cupped around his eyes.

Jared exhaled. "Fine. Let him in."

Mac opened the door.

"Hi. I'm Dave. Jared's physical therapist."

"I'm Mac." Mac gave Dave a smile Jared hadn't seen in a long time. "I'm cleaning the place for Jared's grandmother."

Dave held out his hand. "It's nice to meet y—"

"You're early, Dave."

Dave glanced at him. "I can see it's going to be a good day."

"Can it." He hadn't noticed that Dave was a good-looking guy until this moment. Five-tenish, a body that saw a gym regularly, decent face, single. It'd never been an issue before, but with Mac standing there with the smile she'd given *him* now directed at Dave, it was.

"Didn't you get my voicemail?"

"No. Been a bit busy." He held up one kitten—but that wasn't the reason he hadn't checked his messages. No, the reason was because there weren't any that he wanted. Like from his agent, the team manager, the owner . . . People who had a stake in his future. Instead, all he got were doctors' offices and media calls about what he was going to do with his life post-game.

He didn't *have* a life post-game.

Which was why he had to work with Dave. After he got dressed. And fed the kittens.

Right on cue, they started meowing again.

"Here, hand them to me so you can get to work." Mac, all sweetness and smiles, climbed the three stairs and held out her hands, looking at him as if they were the best of friends.

He wanted to tell her no, that he'd take care of the kittens, but that would be foolish. He did need to get to work.

"Come on, Jare," said Dave. "We only have an hour, and sitting on the steps in your boxers isn't going to get you anywhere."

Dave was right. Sitting here annoyed because Mac had smiled at Dave wasn't going to get him back on the mound, and telling Mac *no* just to spite her was only going to add to his workload.

He handed the kittens over, then headed upstairs to put some clothes on.

IT was a shame the man had to wear clothes.

Mac tried not to sigh as she watched him hop up those stairs, boxers not hiding the view of his glutes hard at work.

Jared had always been very well blessed in the gluteus maximus area.

"So." She smiled at Dave and hiked the laundry basket more comfortably in her arms. "You been working with Jared long?"

"I can't really discuss a patient's personal information, but I've known him for years as a friend." Dave stepped closer and shut the front door. "Here. Let me carry that for you." He took the laundry basket from her, and, sadly, she didn't feel the sizzle when his fingers brushed hers like she had with Jared.

She hated that she was still attracted to Jared. Especially when there was a perfectly nice, good-looking—she glanced at his left hand—single guy smiling at her with a certain level of interest.

"Where do you want them?"

"The laundry room. I'm sure they need the litter box. Then I have to get their bottles ready."

"Bottles?" He followed her through the narrow shotgun hallway.

"I found their mom by the side of the road. They're not old enough for regular cat food, so Jared and I are bottle-feeding them." It felt so natural to link their names. Hell, it should; she'd dreamed about it for years. But this was reality, and the reality was Jared still didn't like her and she was still stupid enough to find him attractive, but was hopefully smart enough to know those childhood daydreams had been fairy tales and Jared was no Prince Charming.

"I can give you a hand until Jared comes down if you want."

Dave, however, might be.

"Thanks." She took the kittens from the basket and set them in the litter box. "Can you watch them while I get the bottles ready?" she asked as she stood.

"Sure. I guess I should add litter box training to Jared's therapy repertoire." He smiled and there was a dimple in his cheek.

She'd always been a sucker for dimples. Just like Jared—

She put the brakes on that. She was never going to find

anyone if she kept comparing every guy to Jared. "I'm sure your patient will *love* that."

Dave winked. "I won't tell him if you don't."

"Oh, trust me. Where Jared's concerned, my lips are sealed."

As they would be the next time he tried to kiss her.

If he tried to kiss her.

Stop hoping he'll try to kiss you.

"Be right back."

She hurried to the kitchen and prepped the bottles she'd kept in reserve, then grabbed a towel from the stack beside the sink.

"Mac," Dave said, "they seem to have finished up in here. Should I bring them out?"

"Sure," she called, spreading the towel over the kitchen table. Kittens were not the neatest of eaters. "Can you manage them?"

"If I can handle Jared, four kittens ought to be a piece of cake." He walked in from the laundry room, pieces of litter clinging to his shirt.

Curly almost leapt from his arms.

Luckily, Mac caught the little white fur ball. "Um, yeah, I can see that."

Dave winked at her again. "Hey, who wouldn't want a pretty woman coming to his rescue? That little guy did it on purpose."

The compliment made her smile. Hmmm . . . he was a nice guy. Liked animals. Could put up with Jared. Dave had a lot going for him.

"So, I see you and Jared are close. Are you guys . . . cousins?" Dave set the rest of the kittens down, then stuck the bottle in Larry's mouth as if he'd done it before.

She had to coax Curly to latch on, then tapped the black one on its nose while the gray tried to grab Larry's tail and nurse on that. "Cousins?" She choked. That would be wrong on so many levels. "No. I—we—my brothers and he are friends and so are our grandmothers. I'm cleaning the place for Mildred. She wants to sell. See?" Mac twisted slightly to the left and nodded toward the logo on her shirt. "Manley Maids. I'm Mac Manley."

"Catchy name. I bet it's good for business. You have a couple of hunky guys cleaning for you?"

"Actually, I do."

"Planning to add Jared to the ranks?"

"Oh yeah, sure. Big professional baseball player gives up his dream job to clean toilets. While I think the media might love the story, you don't know Jared very well if you'd think he'd ever consider it."

"But you would?"

Mac shrugged. "I'm trying to drum up publicity for the business. If he wanted to, sure, I'd strap an apron to him." Oh, not an image she should be having. "I mean, you know, for promo only. Though my brothers don't want the promo but they are doing the work."

"You could always ask him to be a spokesperson."

And give him the chance to shoot her down once more? "Jared has other things to focus on. Isn't that why you're here?"

"True." He wedged the two bottles he was using between the fingers of one hand and the kittens lined up as if he were their mother, even kneading his palm. "But the guy can multitask, you know. He's a hell of a ball player and a hell of a guy. I bet he'd do it if you asked him."

"I'll think about it." Okay, Dave was firmly on Team Jared, so she wasn't about to enlighten him as to Jared's willingness to help her. "So how'd you get involved with professional sports?"

He gave her a rundown of his resumé and the conversation segued to the teams he'd worked with. "I met Jared the day we both started with the team. Been friends ever since."

"Ah, sharing the newbie jitters."

"Something like that."

"He's going to get better, right?"

Dave changed the angle of the bottle to get the rest of the formula in place for the kittens. "Professionally, I can't answer that. It falls under the heading of patient information. Plus, I'm not his doctor."

"But personally . . ."

"Personally, I've known Jared for a long time. I've seen how he works. How determined he is. If anyone can come back from what happened, it's Jared. He's completely focused on what needs to be done. Always has been. That's what was so surprising about the whole thing with Camille. He let his focus drift from the game."

"He must have loved her very much. "

Dave shrugged. "I didn't get it. She came out of nowhere, poured on the charm, and he was smitten. I didn't trust her from day one. But you can't talk a guy out of a girl if he wants her."

And you can't talk a guy *into* one if he doesn't want her.

Mac had tried.

So why did he kiss her?

"But I'm sure you know all this if you're friends. So tell me about you. How you started this business. I've heard a lot about your brothers from Jared, but I don't remember him mentioning a beautiful sister."

That's because he'd never considered her beautiful.

But Dave apparently did and she was woman enough to enjoy it.

She gave him a brief version of how she'd come to start Manley Maids.

"So where does kitten-sitting come in? Side business?"

Mac smiled. "By-product. I found them under a dresser. I think the mom crawled in through a broken window pane to have them, but now, with her dead, this was what Jared chose to do about them."

"Don't let her fool you, Dave. I didn't choose it. She made me take them on." Jared crutched into the kitchen.

Mac's heart skipped a beat.

Why? It was one thing to find him attractive; that was as plain as the gorgeous nose on his gorgeous face. But it was a whole other thing for her heart to be involved.

Damn it. She didn't *want* her heart to skip a beat. She didn't want to think he was sexy in a plain black T-shirt that set off his golden hair and tan so much that if someone didn't know about his accident—and he wasn't on crutches—they'd never think he'd spent time in a hospital. No one should look that good after getting out of a rehab facility from such a horrendous accident.

It was only one of about a thousand things that got to her about Jared, and no amount of arguing with herself could stop it.

"I did not make you take them on. I gave you a choice."

He arched an eyebrow at her. "Really? Take them or leave them. Pretty harsh, Mac, even for you."

"Hey, Jare." Dave hopped to his feet, popping the bottle out of Larry's gnawing mouth. "We should get to work. Can you handle these two as well, Mac?" He gave her the bottles and the kittens followed them, mewling as they snuggled in next to their siblings in front of her.

"Yes. Go ahead and rehab this guy so he gets"—*out of my hair* was what she'd been going to say, but it was a little too revealing—"better quickly." There. That was grown-up of her. Empathetic. Supportive. And totally not head-over-heels-for-Jared-Nolan she'd once been and wasn't anymore.

Methinks the lady doth protest blah blah blah.

She herded the kittens toward the center of the towel and stood. "I'll just take Larry and Curly and Mary-Sue—"

"Moe." Jared shrugged the crutches out from under his arms and gripped them together in his right hand.

Mac looked at him. "What?"

"Moe. The black one's name is Moe."

"But she's a girl."

"So?"

Mac picked *Moe* up and stroked her cheek with hers. "Moe isn't a very feminine name."

"Neither is Mac but that hasn't stopped you from answering to it."

That stopped the cheek-stroking.

Did he see her as unfeminine? Was that why he'd never been interested in her?

But . . . he'd kissed her. He knew she was female. He'd been interested enough to do that.

Or had it just been a "wonder what it's like" kiss? A punishment kiss? A condescending, sarcastic, you-are-not-worthy kiss?

Dear God, she had to stop dwelling on it. It was done. Over.

She picked up the gray. "So this one is Joe?"

Jared shook his head. "Shemp. Joe's too close to Moe."

"You named the cats after the Three Stooges?" Dave snorted.

"You got a problem with that?"

"Me? Nope. Not my pets, so it's copacetic." He took the crutches from Jared. "So, you ready to do this or what?"

"Yeah, let's fix me up."

Mac would like to fix him up all right, starting with giving him a clue that he ought to have noticed her years ago.

SO what's the deal with the maid?" Dave leaned the crutches against the doorframe once he'd motioned for Jared to sit on the doily-covered ottoman in the middle of the room.

"Excuse me?"

"Oh. Is that not the correct term? Housekeeper? Cleaning lady? Domestic goddess?" He hunkered down in front of Jared and started undoing the Velcro closures on the brace.

Yeah, Mac was a goddess—got the word straight from the goddess herself—but it was none of Dave's damn business.

He brushed Dave's hands away and undid the bindings himself. "She's Liam's sister. Owns the cleaning service. She's doing my grandmother a favor."

She was doing *no* favors for him whatsoever.

"She single?"

"Really, Dave? You're hitting on my maid during work?"

Dave stood up and held up his hands. "Whoa, Jare. I'm asking you a question, not hitting on her. Didn't know it was such a big deal to talk about a woman. If memory serves, you had a lot to say about Camille."

He had, but that'd been the pain talking, and the fact that he'd known Dave for years. Dave had interned with the team's PTs and they'd become friends. So when Dave had gone into home care, it'd been a no-brainer that he was the one Jared would call when he'd been discharged from the rehab facility.

Now he wished he hadn't. The therapist who'd worked with him at the facility had been ugly as sin. Nice guy, but not on Dave's level looks-wise. Jared would feel a lot better if *that's* who'd helped Mac with the kittens.

Oh for God's sake. He wasn't going to fire Dave because the guy was good-looking enough to catch Mac's attention. Hell, he ought to be happy about it because it'd put this ridiculous growing attraction to her to rest and she'd end up with a nice guy.

But it didn't make him feel better.

"I just don't think you want to start anything, Dave. If it doesn't work out, I'd have to fire one of you, and my grandmother would be upset if it was Mac."

So would he, but he wasn't going there.

Dave took out the angle measuring device with the weird name. Goony-ometer or something like that. He motioned for Jared to bend his knee. "You're sure it's not because *you're* interested in her?"

Jared dropped his foot to the floor, not even having to think about bending his knee, since he was about to stand up and get in the guy's face. "Interested? Oh, God, please. You don't know Mac. She's the last woman I'd be interested in. Well, next to Camille."

"She doesn't strike me as being anything like Camille."

"Yeah, well you've known her all of about five minutes. I've known her since she was five. Trust me when I say that she might not have caused the same amount of damage as Camille but that's only because I didn't let her. If I'd listened to the same instincts I had with Mac in regards to Camille, I wouldn't be in this predicament. No, women like Mac and Camille, they're best left alone if you want to keep your sanity."

AND that put the lid on that.

Mac leaned against the wall outside the parlor, hugging the kittens to her heart. Jared couldn't have been any clearer.

That was good.

Right?

Yes, it was. It was closure. Hell, it slammed the door in the face of her *what-ifs* so she could now go about her life without wondering. Sure, he might have kissed her, but the disdain in his voice spoke louder than the way his lips had molded over hers, the way his tongue had swept the seam, the way he'd slanted his head and kissed her—

She exhaled. Nope. Over. That whole attraction thing she was feeling? Done.

His loss.

Though she ought to go in and confront him. What if she was interested in Dave who'd now want nothing to do with her because of Jared's comment?

Do *you want something to do with Dave?*

Well . . . no. There was no spark. It wouldn't be fair to him to lead him on.

Okay, then. By all means, head back in there and have a discussion with Jared about happily ever after. Go on, prove yourself to him, Cinderella.

Okay, so no, she wasn't going to do that. She'd always been a little unsure about the whole Cinderella thing anyway. Chick marries the guy who'd only marry the woman who fit a shoe? Didn't seem to have much substance. She wanted a guy who'd not only pick up the shoe and put it on her foot, but would also not complain that's she'd bought the shoe in the first place.

There had to be more to the guy of her dreams than a pretty outside, and if Jared was blind enough to lump her in the same category as his ex, chances are he wasn't.

Chapter Ten

THE silence was the worst.

Jared patted the kittens Dave had plopped onto his lap before leaving, and stared up at the ceiling. She was up there and he couldn't stop thinking about it.

It was Dave's fault. "Unless you're interested in her?" Damn him for that. And damn him for putting him on the defensive. But Dave just *had* to show interest in her, didn't he?

The guy was a sadist, putting him through round after round after round of motion, movement, and pain. His knee wasn't healing as quickly as either of them would like—Dave because he was hoping it didn't signal any worse damage, and Jared because every day that his body wasn't working right was a day longer to get back to the game. And now a day longer he had to be in Mac's presence.

Both of which frustrated the hell out of him. Mac because, well, that was self-explanatory, but the game . . . He *had* to get back to baseball. There was nothing else for him if he didn't. He didn't want to have to go the open-a-restaurant route or go into commentating. He enjoyed his fans and the celebrity part of his career, but what he really loved was the game. The sense of teamwork. Of family. Of having each other's backs. Striving for a common goal. Now? Now he was floating among the wreckage the accident had made of his life, while he struggled through it, trying to find land.

But it had to be the land he wanted, not just any land. He had to play again. Had to reclaim what Camille and Burke had taken from him.

"Meow." Larry shifted, rolling off Jared's lap onto the sofa beside him. Poor little guy just blinked his blue eyes up at Jared as if to say, "What happened?"

Jared knew exactly how the kitten felt.

He picked him up, this small, fragile little thing Mac had thrust into his life.

"I guess *she* didn't do it, exactly." He held Larry up so they were nose-to-nose. "It's a good thing she found you when she did, though. You guys would have been SOL if you'd had to wait until *I* found you."

He tucked Larry under his neck, smiling when the kitten licked him. It *did* feel like sandpaper, just as he'd heard.

For all his complaining, he was glad he hadn't dumped these four at the vet's office. There was something to be said for having to reach out beyond himself. If he could get over the fact that he didn't know how to take care of them, he could actually appreciate that the five of them were their own team.

"Jared? Can I borrow you for a second?" Mac's voice reverberated through his grandmother's foyer.

She was asking for his help? Mac of the I-can-handle-it-by-myself attitude? This was the woman who'd outplayed—so she claimed—her three older brothers at a game they were all too familiar with. Jared had to see what it was that she couldn't manage on her own because the bundle of energy that fit in her little body could fill a six-five frame. Twice.

"Be right there." He hitched himself forward on the sofa, then lifted the still-sleeping kittens into the play yard thing. "Now you behave and don't wake the others," he said to Larry, plopping a quick kiss on the calico's nose.

He looked up to see Mac in the doorway.

"Looks like we better get those kittens their shots and soon."

"Smart-ass." He pulled the crutches under his arms. "What do you need?"

"If you can open the kitchen door so I can take this out to the trash, that'd be great."

"What is it?" He followed her through the kitchen toward the back porch.

"A bunch of moth-eaten linens I found in the hall closet."

He held open the back door. "Closet cleaning is part of your service?"

"Not usually, no. But I was looking for a light bulb and found that moths had gotten to these, so I figured I'd throw them out. One less thing your grandmother has to do."

Mac swept past him, far enough below his chin that he could see the top of her head. He knew she was small; he'd never realized just how much smaller than him she actually was because when he was around Mac, things always seemed amplified.

She stumbled on the last step as some of the sheets got stuck on the door handle and she fell back against him, her head *thonking* his chest right above his heart.

Case in point.

He wrapped his arms around her. "You okay?" Her skin was silky. He hadn't thought it would be. Someone who worked with cleaning products and ladders, battling spider webs and dust bunnies . . . He hadn't expected her skin to feel as smooth and silky as if she spent hours at a spa.

"I'm . . ." She glanced up at him and cleared her throat. "I'm good. Thanks."

She got her feet under her and stood, her shoulders no longer brushing his abs, and Jared surprised himself by admitting he wanted her back in his arms—which rattled him enough that he almost let go of the door.

Mac in his arms? What was he thinking? This was Mac. *Mac.* Liam's little sister. Terror of the tree fort. Date-destroyer extraordinaire. Tornado Manley.

Maybe if he kept repeating it enough, it'd stick.

She rounded the corner of the house, brushing her hands, her ponytail bouncing saucily behind her. It fit her personality. He couldn't imagine Mac without a ponytail—well, he hadn't been able to before yesterday when she'd let it down.

What a shock that'd been. Her hair was just one more gorgeous surprise, a black curtain that shimmered against her pale skin, much longer than he would've thought, since he'd only ever seen it tied back.

It'd been all he could do not to imagine it falling across his chest. Of having to sweep it off her face to pull her down for a kiss. Of flipping her over and seeing it fanned out on the pillow beneath her . . .

Okay, so maybe he *had* imagined it. He was human, after all. But seriously, those thoughts had to go. This was Mac. His friend's sister. The girl he'd wanted nothing to do with for years.

Except . . . now he was finding himself thinking about the *woman* and the things he *could* do with her.

He was going stir crazy. That was it. He'd been cooped up too damn long in the hospital, then the rehab place, and now he was stuck at his grandmother's with only a woman he didn't want to like and kittens he didn't know what to do with to keep him company.

"So how'd your therapy go?"

She even smelled good. Not sweaty and dusty or like furniture polish, but fresh and clean, with a tiny hint of flowers or something—

God, now he sounded like some bad infomercial.

"It was therapy. It's not supposed to be good. It hurt and I'm frustrated, and that's Dave's lot in life: to deal with frustrated, angry people who want nothing to do with him."

"Wow. To hear him talk, I thought he was your friend, but after that . . ."

Jared raked a hand through his hair and stuck the crutches under his arm that'd fallen behind him against the door when he'd caught her. "He is. It's just that his profession isn't one people generally find enjoyable."

"Well he seems nice."

Oh really? "He is." Jared sucked on the inside of his cheek, waiting for the questions to start: Was he single? Did he have a girlfriend? What's his number?

"Do you mind if I eat lunch in here?"

"Huh?"

"Lunch? You know, the midday meal? Since it rained last night, the porch furniture is a little wet. I'd rather sit in the kitchen if you don't mind."

It took him a few seconds to process that she wasn't asking about Dave. "Uh, yeah, sure. That's fine. I'll join you."

It took him a lot longer than a few seconds to admit why he'd volunteered to do that.

Damn it. He didn't want to find Mac attractive. He didn't want to notice these small things about her, like how she smelled or how she fit in his arms or what she looked like across from him.

Or over him.

Or under him.

This lunch was probably not a good idea.

Chapter Eleven

LUNCH was a very bad idea.

Mac hadn't expected him to ask to join her—she'd only asked so he'd know she'd be there so he could avoid her. She hadn't seen the joining-her thing coming at all.

And that made her nervous.

Jared was up to something. He'd played all sorts of tricks on her as a kid and, since he played a game for a *living*, she wasn't expecting him to have moved much beyond that, especially given his obvious disdain for her.

Then why'd he kiss you?

Probably an experiment. Or to teach her a lesson. A bet he'd lost.

Yeah, that was probably it. He'd probably bet someone that he'd kiss her someday and now he could collect. She hoped it wasn't one of her brothers. But then, those guys liked to bet on everything. They were pros. One of the reasons she'd had to have a plan before she'd taken them all on.

Not that she could see them betting on Jared kissing her. After all, they were her brothers before they were Jared's friends. Still . . . Bryan might think it was worth a shot. He liked to live life on the edge—and if she ever found out he *had* bet Jared, she'd toss him off it. Betting Jared would kiss her . . . Nice brother.

It'd been a nice *kiss*.

She refrained from touching her lips. She wasn't going to let Jared know she was even thinking about it. Mr. Big Celebrity Sports Star had enough women hanging on his every word; she wasn't going to be one of a crowd.

She opened the brown bag she'd brought her food in. It was the lunch she'd wanted back when she'd been in school: a sandwich, some chips, a soda, and a couple of her favorite store-bought cookies for dessert, things Gran hadn't been able to afford, opting instead to use the school's special fund so they could have a hot cooked meal every day, along with a baggie of homemade cookies that had embarrassed Mac to no end.

She'd never realized that Gran's homemade cookies had been worth ten times what the store-bought mass-produced brands were, seeing only the poverty in homemade things, not the love.

Now she knew better, which was why, once a month, she helped out with the community center's Kareers for Kids event by teaching kids how to bake. Her chocolate chip cookie classes were always well attended.

"So how long do you think you're going to be here?" Jared asked, pulling a giant container of some powdery thing off the top of the fridge and mixing a couple of scoops into a bottle of water. He shook it up, then gunned the contents before pulling a plate of chicken, a tomato, and an avocado from the fridge.

No PB&J for Jared. His parents were loaded, so the few times she'd been at his house—which were very few—there'd been a full spread. The Nolans lived in a large house that backed up to the same field her development did, but that was the only common ground—literally or figuratively—they'd shared. Their situations in life could not have been more different.

It'd worried Gran that her brothers, who'd always hung

with Jared, would be discontent with their life, but it'd only made them more determined to be able to provide for their families when they eventually had them. And to provide for Gran. Mac had a feeling that Bryan was paying more than his share for the large apartment Gran had moved into at the assisted living facility, but hey, Bry's star was rising. He could afford it and who was she to tell him he couldn't give back to the grandmother who'd done so much for all of them? Sort of the reason she'd incorporated Gran's matchmaking into the maid gig. She couldn't exactly tell the woman no when it was for a good cause.

"I'll be here until I finish." She munched on her sandwich. Roast beef and Swiss, with mayo and lettuce on a pita. Her favorite. "Since I'm not charging Mildred, I didn't work up an estimate. I pretty much hit the ground running on this one, so whenever I finish, I finish. There's a lot to do."

"What about your other clients? Aren't you putting someone out by giving your time to my grandmother?" He ran the knife around the circumference of the avocado, twisted the halves to separate them, then stuck the knife into the pit to remove it.

She wouldn't have thought he'd know how to open an avocado without mangling it. Actually, she wouldn't have thought he'd know how to open an avocado, period. The Nolans had had chefs and housekeepers and a grounds crew. Jared had led a charmed life. "I'm working my regulars in and I have a few people working for me at the moment to cover the slack."

"Your brothers."

She wasn't surprised he knew; while her brothers probably weren't announcing the news, the grandmothers did live at the same place. "Yes."

He set the plate on the table. "I heard you conned them into doing it."

That did not come from the grandmothers. "Conned? I did *not* con them. I beat them at poker. Won it fair and square." She crossed her fingers as she scratched a nonexistent itch on the back of her head.

He pulled out his chair and leaned his crutches against the wall. "Really. You beat three guys who've been playing poker almost as long as I've known them on your first outing *just* when you needed them to work for you?"

Her sandwich stopped halfway to her mouth. "I don't like what you're insinuating, Jared."

He sat down. "And I don't like my friends being taken advantage of. Not even by their sister."

Mac dropped her sandwich. She hadn't taken advantage of her brothers. She'd just done what she'd needed to do to win and if counting cards was a sin, it would've been carved in stone with the others. It wasn't even illegal in most casinos, so he couldn't get on her about that, either. "I did *not* take advantage of them. My brothers could've folded and not taken the bet. No one was forcing them to ante up."

Jared slid an avocado slice into his mouth and took his sweet time chewing. "Is that right?"

Her brothers played together all the time. They knew each other's strengths and weaknesses. Knew their bluffs and poker faces. She'd come in blind; she'd had to even the odds, but it wasn't as if she'd had a few cards up her sleeve that she'd slipped into the game. Sure, she'd counted, but counting was mostly for blackjack, not poker. Still, she'd been able to apply the theory to poker, but if the cards hadn't been dealt right, knowing where the flushes and straights were wouldn't have helped her if she hadn't had a hand to beat them. There'd been no guarantees going in and it was only because things had fallen where she'd needed them to that it'd worked. Otherwise, she'd be cleaning their places and Bryan's Maserati wouldn't be sitting in her driveway.

So, yeah, she'd stacked the odds in her favor, but that was because they'd been stacked against her to begin with. And it wasn't as if she was hurting anyone. The guys did some work, helped out people who needed it, and she got publicity. It was a win/win for everyone and if it happened because she'd worked a little harder to make sure things *could* go her way, well, hey . . . Gran had endorsed the plan. Actually, it'd *been* Gran's plan. Well, the idea for it.

But no one needed to know that. Least of all Jared.

She rolled the napkin around the rest of her sandwich, her appetite gone. "I should get back to work. The quicker I finish, the sooner I'll be out of your hair."

She walked past him—and was just as surprised as he was if that look on his face was anything to go by—when he stopped her with a hand to her arm.

Her bare arm. With his bare hand.

The guy ought to wear his baseball glove while she was here because heat shot up her arm so fast she almost jumped out of her skin.

This was way beyond an adolescent crush. She might have had a thing for him back then, but this . . . This was pure feminine reaction and it annoyed her no end.

"What?" She might have snapped that out a little sharper than she intended.

Jared dropped her arm like a hot poker. "I . . . Wait."

He raked that hand through his hair and exhaled. "Can you please sit down? I'm sorry I was such a shit. I shouldn't be taking my frustrations out on you."

Depended on why he was frustrated . . .

Mac sat.

And waited. Jared wasn't saying anything.

"I have things to do, Jared. And don't you have kittens to take care of?"

"The kittens are fine. Sleeping like babies." He exhaled and the words seemed to force their way past his lips. "Could you . . . you know, hang out and eat with me? I'm sorry I was nasty. I feel nasty these days. Not that that's an excuse, but it's not you I'm mad at."

"You know a lot of other people who *conned* their brothers in a poker game, 'cause that sounded pretty personal to me?"

He winced. "Like I said, Mac, I shouldn't take my frustrations out on you. Can we just pretend I never said that? I'm so damn tired of eating alone. In the hospital, they drop off your food, then leave. In rehab, they only wanted to make sure I knew how to use a fork and not to poke myself in the eye with it. Then I was on my own for meals. It got—gets—kinda lonely."

Good thing she was sitting down. Jared Nolan admit to a weakness? She'd never thought she'd see the day.

"Well I'm sure you must have had visitors." Of the female persuasion most assuredly. Nothing lured women in like a man in need. A good-looking, rich, professional athlete sort of need.

She'd thought about visiting, but why? He wouldn't have been happy to see her, so there'd been no reason to put herself through it. She'd sent cookies with Liam—which made her look like the rest of the women who'd brought him food. Ugh. So much for not being one of the pack.

"You get visitors the first week or two, when you're too groggy to know who's there. When you only really want to be alone and sleep. It's once the healing process begins, when you're on the mend, that people think you're okay and they go on with their lives. That's when the loneliness sets in. I would have been bored stiff if it weren't for your brothers. I can always count on them."

She knew the feeling. "Yeah, but weren't you sitting right there when the doorbell rang this morning? You can't tell me that that hasn't happened before."

Jared sighed. "That's not what I mean." He kneaded the back of his neck. "Friends. Family. That's what I'm talking about. I'm not into meeting new people now, especially women with only one thing on their mind."

"Wow. I can't believe you just said that. I think they take your man card for turning down guaranteed sex."

Jared shrugged. "It's not new. Groupies. Women who want to say they've made it with a pro athlete. Not my scene."

"Could have fooled me. I've seen your photo plastered all over the tabloids with one actress or another hanging off your arm."

The corner of his mouth kicked up. "Spying on me?"

Great. Just what she didn't want him thinking. "My brothers comment on it. Especially Liam and Sean. They want to know if you're outdoing Bryan in the Babe Department."

"The Babe Department? Your brothers need a hobby if they're watching my supposed love life play out across the media. The truth is, I saw those women for what they were. What they wanted. Just like I see the Juliettes and Maeves of the neighborhood. When you're in the position I'm in, it's nice to have someone around who knows you. People I can let my guard down and be myself with. That doesn't happen with brownie deliveries."

She was almost sorry for him because he was right. When you were at your lowest, you wanted people around who cared about you. "Well, there's always your parents."

His mouth twisted sideways and he glanced away. "You'd think that, wouldn't you? But they're on vacation."

He'd been in the hospital for months. "That's an awfully long vacation."

"Yup."

One word, so much not said, but oh what it conveyed.

She'd always thought his mom was a bit of a cold fish, but to not visit her child in the hospital after he'd been in an accident? Mac didn't get it. Gran would've pitched a tent in a hospital room before she'd leave any of her grandchildren alone for longer than an hour.

"But what about Mildred? Surely she visited you."

"She did. And it's always nice to see her, but you know what grandmothers are like. Always fussing. Adjusting the pillows, putting too many blankets on . . . I love my grandmother and she means well, but no one wants to feel like more of an invalid than they already are."

"And I'm sure gin rummy got old after a while."

Jared laughed, and oh what it did to his face.

Not that his face needed any help, gorgeous as it was, but the light came back into his eyes. That certain . . . glow, for lack of a better word. There'd always been this glow about Jared. A light. Like the sun, warming everyone, pulling them into his orbit. Charisma. She knew what it was called now that she was an adult, but back then, it'd seemed to her as if the sun had actually risen and set on him.

And if Mac thought she'd been in trouble *before,* she was

way beyond trouble and head-on into disaster now because a surly Jared was easy enough to keep her distance from, but this . . . This contrite, apologetic, smiling-at-her-joke Jared . . . She didn't have much defense against this Jared.

"Yes, Grandma did want to play gin rummy. Reminded me of that summer when we had the tournament. You remember?"

As if she could forget. She'd actually made it through the ranks and had had a match against him.

She'd been a decent player, but when she'd sat across from him at that table, she hadn't been able to concentrate on the cards. Her poor tongue had been tripping over itself not to say anything stupid, so much that she'd lost so ridiculously badly that the score alone could make her want to shrivel up in a corner, never mind the fact that she'd probably had stars in her eyes and a goofy expression on her face the entire match—which had lasted less than any other she'd played.

"Want a chance to get even?" Jared asked.

"Me? Now? Here?"

"Yes, why not, and of course." That darn smile of his was just so appealing. So were his charm and charisma. "Please."

And saying *please* . . .

She stood. "I'm guessing the cards are still in the same drawer?"

She didn't wait for Jared's response. Even a few-second reprieve would be welcome to put her hormones back in sync with the rational part of her brain that said this was probably not a good idea.

She headed to the sewing kit Mildred used as a wall decoration in the front parlor and opened the third drawer down on the left. The cards had been well used when Gran had brought her and her brothers to visit Mildred.

"You deal first." Jared slid the lazy Susan to the opposite side of the table after taking a pen and his grandmother's grocery notepad from it. "I'll keep score."

She shook her head. "Oh no you don't. I'm not that eight-year-old anymore. I remember how well you added—in your favor. You deal and *I'll* keep score."

"Are you accusing me of cheating?"

She shuffled the deck, then placed it facedown in front of him. "If the shoe fits."

Or was that: Pot, meet kettle?

"I'm not wearing shoes."

And earlier he hadn't been wearing pants. Or a shirt. She'd seen more of Jared's half-naked body than she wanted to. Well, no, that wasn't quite right; she'd seen more of Jared's half-naked body than was a good idea. She was still a woman who appreciated a good-looking male form, and Jared's was off the charts.

"Well, just to keep it honest, Jared, I'll keep score. Right here in the open so you can check my math. You deal."

He picked up the cards and shuffled them. "I don't like what you're insinuating, Princess."

"Now where have I heard that before?" She picked up her cards. Hey, a three-of-a-kind already. She'd love to beat him just to show him that she didn't need to con anyone to win.

Though her card counting skills might come in handy.

She beat him with the first hand.

"Beginner's luck," he said, sweeping the cards together.

"I'm not a beginner. I've played before."

He tapped the deck on its long edge, then handed it to her. "Not like that, you haven't. I distinctly remember annihilating you with every game."

"Feel good about that, do you?" She shuffled the deck, then dealt, relying on bravado to keep from revealing that the real reason he'd been able to beat her back then was she hadn't been concentrating on the cards. Not when his hair had been lightened by the sun, his skin tanned, and those incredible green eyes that she used to dream about and that smile had been right there for her enjoyment.

But she was concentrating now. She wanted to beat him.

Jared picked up the top card from the draw pile and discarded a two of clubs. "What other jobs have you had, Mac? I don't really know much about what you've been doing with your life."

Obviously Mildred hadn't been singing *her* praises as

much as Gran had sung his. She picked up the two and stuck it with the other two in her hand, discarding a six of diamonds. "I waited tables. That was pretty lucrative as well, but start-up costs for a restaurant are a lot steeper than for a cleaning business."

He picked up the six. "I guess a couple of dust mops and brooms don't cost all that much."

She passed on the eight of spades he discarded and took one from the draw pile. "And vacuum cleaners and carpet cleaners, and hardwood floor steamers. Let's not forget that. Those things add up. Especially when you multiply the cost by four or five employees. Then there's the van. I pick it up this week." She tapped the tip of the jack of hearts with the jack of diamonds. He was collecting diamonds but getting all four jacks would be tough.

"Van?"

She kept the jack and discarded the nine. "Yes, a work van. Right now I reimburse mileage and some of my employee's car insurance, but eventually, I'd like a fleet of Manley Maids trucks on the roads for branding. We're using car magnets for now to get the name out, but to look professional, you have to be professional."

Jared picked up a card from the deck and tapped its edge on the table. "I'm impressed. I hadn't really given a lot of thought to what it took to start up a business like this. I thought you just needed clients."

"You do, but there are a lot of companies competing for the business. That's why I needed something to make my business stand out above the competition."

"Hence your brothers in maids' outfits."

"Exactly." She looked at him. He was staring at her, and she wasn't quite sure how she should feel about that.

Well, self-conscious for one. She was always self-conscious when Jared looked at her. If she'd kept her big, hopeful trap shut that night on Gran's walkway, she might not feel awkward around him.

But she hadn't, so she'd had to deal with the consequences. "You going to play that card?"

"Huh?" He looked at the card in his right hand, then switched it out for one in his left. "Sounds like you have a plan, Mac."

"I'd better because you don't get ahead by wishing. You have to make things happen." She picked up another card and laid down her hand. "Gin."

JARED was looking at this woman across from him, someone he thought he knew, but hearing the words and plans come out of her mouth, he was having a hard time reconciling this entrepreneurial businesswoman with the pig-tailed kid who'd ruined a make-out session with Jamie Sheridan.

He liked what he was seeing. And that was a problem.

He threw down his hand, not even close to beating her. If she'd played him, he didn't know how. "Same time tomorrow? Give me a chance to kick your butt?" He pulled his crutches to the table and stood up.

"I'll give you the chance, just don't expect to do it. Score's not even close." She tapped the eraser end of the pencil on the paper. "Read 'em and weep, Jared."

"Big boys don't cry. And there's still time to beat you."

She shrugged and stacked the cards and the score sheet on the lazy Susan. "Big words. Let's see if you can pull it off next time."

"You're on." The kittens started making their presence known. "Man, they're hungry."

"What can I do to help?"

Kiss me. The thought popped into his head along with an image of that stupid, what-was-he-thinking kiss. He should never have done it. Should have kept his distance. Because now he knew exactly what Mac tasted like. How she felt. How she fit in his arms.

"Grab the bottles and I'll get the paper towels."

By the time they made it to the pen, there was a *lovely* mess that needed to be cleaned and four kittens to bathe. Again.

"Are you kidding me? Where does that come from? They're not that big." Jared held his breath as he grabbed a damp paper towel and picked up Larry.

Mac waved the bottle. "What goes in, must come out."

"You failed to mention that when you told me I had to take care of these things."

"It's not my job to know what you don't know." She quickly made up the four bottles, then took Larry from him once he'd cleaned the little messy fur ball up.

Larry sucked on the bottle, his slurps only escalating the mews from his siblings. Jared worked fast to get the rest of them clean, and, like an assembly line, he'd finish one, then pass it to Mac, who popped a bottle in its mouth. She had a good system, propping the bottle on the back of the previous one, so by the time he'd finished with Curly, Larry was almost done eating, and the other two were contentedly sucking away.

"I'll feed this one."

She tapped Shemp's back. "Put him here. You have to clean the pen."

"I thought they were supposed to use the litter box." He looked at the pan he'd filled for that purpose. Pristine as that desktop Zen garden sand thing his catcher had given their coach after the diatribe when they'd lost the opening game last season.

"They're babies, Jared. They have to learn. You have to teach them."

"I thought I had," he muttered, wiping down one particularly ominous spot on the carpet where someone had gone burrowing beneath the towels he'd laid down for this specific reason. "This is going to leave a stain."

"I have something in my arsenal for that. Don't worry; I'll take care of it."

"You're on." He gathered up the towels with one hand, balancing himself on his other hand and his good leg, praying to God he wouldn't topple onto the play yard, taking that out with him.

"I think there's a yoga pose like that," she said. "Balancing table, I believe it's called."

"I don't do yoga."

"Um, yeah, you kinda are." She made no attempt to hide the chuckle in her voice.

He turned to glare at her and—damn—fell over. Onto the play yard. Thankfully it was only plastic, but it still didn't do his ribs any favors.

"Jared!" Mac was beside him by the time he could take a breath. "Are you all right? What can I do?"

"Get away from me." He didn't want her help. He was so damn sick of needing help.

He felt her recoil, and saw the hurt look on her face.

Dammit. Could he ever, just once, not bark at her?

"I'm sorry, Mac." The words crawled out through his gritted teeth, the second breath coming just a tad easier than the first. The pain hurt like hell and so did apologizing. Christ, he'd done more apologizing in the last twenty-four hours than he'd done in the last twenty-four years. And all of it was to Mac.

And all with reason, which was the part he hated the most. He wasn't usually a dick, and Mac certainly didn't deserve it.

Having her here was taking a toll. Suddenly finding her attractive—and not just physically—was wreaking havoc with his preconceived ideas of her and the whole thing about wanting to stay away from emotional entanglements. That wasn't going to be as easy as he thought with Mac.

"I'm sorry, Mac. It's a gut reaction. I've had it with being poked and prodded. First the doctors, then rehab . . ." He struggled to get up onto his butt, no easy feat with his ribs protesting.

"I get that." She sat back, her fingers far enough from his skin that he couldn't feel them.

But the memory lingered.

"You must have felt so out of control. At the whim of Fate, unable to do anything for yourself, always having to rely on others. That must suck."

He looked at her. Really looked at her. "Yeah. That's exactly it. I'm so tired of asking for help, of having to relearn things or figure out new ways of doing things." Especially when he hadn't caused it. That was what rankled the most; if not for Camille's greed and duplicity, he wouldn't be in this situation and he could be living the life *he'd* worked so damn hard for. "I didn't expect you to understand."

Of course he didn't. Because he always thought the worst of her.

Mac didn't know why she'd bothered. She should have just left him there.

Except he was Jared and old habits die hard.

She rolled back onto her heels and pivoted toward the wingback where she'd dumped the kittens behind a couple of pillows. She picked them up before Curly took a header onto the floor. "These guys are all fed, and have obviously done their business. All you have to do is play with them to tire them out, then they should sleep for a few hours."

She picked up a knitting basket off the floor, dumped out the contents and put the kittens in it. "Where should I put them?"

"Anywhere." Pain flashed across his face. Real pain, not the frustration she'd seen before.

She'd never seen Jared at a disadvantage like she had these past couple of days. Never in all the years she'd known and puppy-loved him had she ever known him to be anything less than one hundred percent confident. He always had a plan, always knew what came next and how to achieve his goals. It'd made him the ball player he was—and the pain in the ass, too. So to see him suffering, sprawled on the floor . . .

"Jared, you were right. You can't do this. The kittens are too much."

"Can it, Princess. Don't go telling me what I can and can't do. I can take care of a couple of kittens, for God's sake."

"You need help."

"That's exactly what I was thinking, Mary-Alice," came a new voice from the foyer.

Another brownie delivery? Mac was sure she'd locked the front door.

She looked over her shoulder as Jared's eyes narrowed.

"Grandma."

"Hello, sweetheart. Mary-Alice is right, you know. You really shouldn't be doing this by yourself." Mildred—Jared's grandmother—took a few more steps into the parlor. "That's why I'm moving back in."

"No." Jared hauled himself onto his elbows.

"I beg your pardon?" Mildred crossed her arms and tapped her foot.

Uh oh. Mac knew what that meant. Mildred and Gran were friends and shared many of the same mannerisms. This was one Mac never wanted to be on the receiving end of.

"I'm sorry, Grandma. I just meant that you don't have to. You have your new place, why would you want to come back here?"

Mildred's eyes narrowed. "I might be in an old folks' home, Jared, but I don't have one foot in the grave. You can't force me out of my own home. I do still own this place."

"I know. I just meant—"

"I'm sure what Jared's trying to say, Mrs. Nolan, is that you shouldn't disrupt your life to take care of a bunch of kittens." Mac had to jump in and save the emotions here because she didn't want Mildred to end up getting hurt and Jared was hurting too much to think straight—as she had first-hand knowledge of. "We'll manage."

"We?" Mildred got the biggest smile on her face. "Then you'll help my grandson, Mary-Alice?"

"Um, yeah. Sure." Mac smiled as sweetly as she could through gritted teeth. She should have kept her big mouth shut. The *last* thing she wanted to do was feed Gran's and Mildred's hopes. She wasn't stupid; she knew exactly where Mildred was going with this. The problem was she couldn't stop it without hurting two people she loved.

Never mind that if she didn't stop it, *she* could end up getting hurt.

"Oh, good." Mildred clasped her hands in front of her heart like a kid in a candy store. "Now that I know you'll be staying here, I can rest easy."

"Stay here? Oh, but I wasn't going—"

"Nonsense, dear. Of course you must. Why, you see how hard this is for him." Mildred nodded at Jared.

A glowering Jared.

Great. One step forward, six steps back.

"Grandma . . ."

Mildred waved him off. "It's settled, then. Mary-Alice will stay until you're better, Jared. That way, I won't have to worry about you injuring yourself even more. Otherwise, I'll have to move back in myself." She patted Mac on her shoulder. "Thank you, Mary-Alice. I can't tell you how relieved I am."

That made one of them.

Chapter Twelve

NO way. Not happening. Mac was not going to spend a single minute of darkness beneath this roof. He didn't need another moment of "curiosity." Bad enough he'd been tempted—and had acted on it—in broad daylight; darkness put a whole different spin on things.

"Don't you think that's a wonderful idea, Jared?" Grandma had a smile on her face as big as the scar on his thigh, and telling her *no* would hurt more.

Shit.

"Uh, yeah, sure. Thanks."

"Gee, sound a little grateful, would you?" said Mac. "Make a girl feel wanted."

That was the problem—he *did* want her, as surprising as that was. And not to take care of kittens or bring him pain meds in the middle of the night.

Now if, on the other hand, she wanted to fluff his pillows, well, he might be open to that idea.

"Pain meds. Bathroom cabinet. Top shelf. Please." It wasn't rib pain that was making him speak in broken sentences.

"Mary-Alice, dear, would you mind?"

"Sure. No problem." Mac hopped to her feet and ran out the door in a way that made him decide the uniform wasn't so bad after all.

Get your eyes off her ass.

"What are you doing here, Grandma? I didn't know you were planning to show up."

"I own the place, Jared. I wasn't aware that I had to announce my visit."

"I'm sorry. I'm—"

"In pain. Yes, I know."

That wasn't what he'd been going to say, but arguing with her about Mac staying here would do no good. He'd have to do that directly with Mac.

Grandma sat on the sofa. "I wish I could help you get up, but I'm afraid I'm not strong enough and I wouldn't want to injure you more. That's why it's much better for Mary-Alice to stay. She's in better shape than me. Perhaps she can help you—"

"No." He didn't need to think about Mac's shape and he definitely didn't need it anywhere near him. "Don't bother. I can do it. I just need the pain meds." Or a couple shots of whisky just to take the edge off.

He still wasn't talking about rib pain.

Though the suckers did hurt. He repositioned himself to take some of the pressure off. "So what brings you here, Grandma?" She was way too obvious. But she would use his fall to get her way, so he and Mac would do better to humor her. What she didn't know about Mac *not* staying wouldn't hurt her.

"Two things. First, I wanted to thank Mary-Alice for doing this for me. She's such a sweet girl to not charge me. Though I am going to pay her. I don't take charity."

"It's not charity, Grandma. She wants to do it for you."

"Yes, well that's all fine and good, but this business is her bread and butter. I can't in good conscience take from her when she had to get her brothers to help out. How much do you think I should pay her, Jared?"

"She's not going to let you. You know that. I'll handle it.

I'll pay her for you. I guarantee she'll take money from me." He just hoped that'd be all she'd take from him because Mac Manley wasn't turning out to be anything like he'd thought.

"All right. And then I'll pay you back." Grandma repositioned herself on the sofa, crossing her legs at the ankles as he always remembered her doing. *Like a lady*, she'd said.

Mom had added "little old" to it.

But then, his mother was a pretentious fool. She looked down on Grandma because she'd made her own clothes and baked for the church and lived a simple life. To hear Mom tell it, Grandma had "hoarded" the life insurance money Grandfather had left, but Jared thought she'd been pretty smart. She owned this house outright and had had enough to buy her way into the facility where she was now.

She'd also been the one to insist he recuperate here. Mom hadn't opened the house to him—not that he would've gone—because they were out of town and there was no sense in paying staff for just him. "Your grandmother will take you in," Mom had said so dismissively in the hospital when he'd first woken up.

She hadn't even bothered to come to the rehab facility once he'd been on the mend; she'd jetted off to Europe instead. Sometimes he doubted he'd even come from her and if there weren't a picture or two to prove it, he'd doubt it even more.

Thank God for Grandma. She was really the only family he could call *actual* family. The rest were just biological relatives, an idealized *Martha Stewart Living* version of what a family should be, and if there was one thing he'd learned from playing team sports, biology didn't make a family. Hell, even Liam and Bry and Sean had visited him more often.

"So what's the second thing?" Jared wanted to drag himself out of that morass. His parents' failings were something he'd learned to handle over the years.

Grandma's smile disappeared. "I was hoping you could help Mary-Alice."

He loved his grandmother, but she had no idea what she was asking. Or maybe she did . . . "Grandma, as you can see, I'm not exactly in shape to do any cleaning."

"Not with the cleaning, Jared. I need help with something else. From both of you."

Her tone worried him and all sorts of things flew through his mind. "What is it?"

She clasped her hands in her lap and took another deep breath. "Well, I don't know if you've been in the attic yet, but it's rather, um, messy."

"Not yet."

"I was sort of frantic when I was last up there."

Grandma never got frantic. He was surprised she even knew the word. She'd always been calm and comforting. Over the years, whenever the fame and the pace and media coverage had gotten too much, he'd always known that he could come back here. Grandma was the slice of his childhood that he loved above everything else. Above the championships, above the MVP awards, above the nice contract, Grandma was his haven in the storm of his life. Even now, she'd been the one to offer him solitude and solace when the bottom had dropped out of his personal life and turned his professional one upside down. He'd do anything for her.

"Why, Grandma? What are you worried about?"

Her lips tightened and she stood up, now clasping her hands behind her back as she started to pace.

The kittens sat in their pen, lined up next to each other, their gazes following her as if they were at a tennis match. It'd be adorable if she weren't worrying him so much.

"Grandma?"

She looked at him. "Oh, Jared, I'm not sick or dying. Well, not physically."

"Now you really have me worried."

She patted her hair, then held out her hand. Her left hand.

"I lost my wedding ring. In the attic." She looked at him and he could see the sheen of tears in her eyes. "Your grandfather gave me that ring when we were just seventeen years old. He worked so hard to buy it, and while it wasn't as bright and flashy and big as some people thought I should have"—he loved Grandma for not throwing his superficial mother under the bus—"it's more valuable to me than anything because he gave it to me. Because of how hard he worked to make me his wife and give me a wonderful life."

She walked up to him and cupped his chin and suddenly he was right back to being a young boy whose parents dropped him off for weeks at a time so they could go on vacation and do what they wanted without having him tag along. "Your father, you, this house . . . Your grandfather didn't make a lot of money, but he gave me everything I needed, and I've been sick since I realized it was gone."

"When what was gone?" Mac asked from the doorway. "Or am I interrupting something?"

Grandma waved her in. "No, Mary-Alice, of course not. You're practically family since your grandmother is the sister I never had." She took Mac's arm and patted it. "I've lost Robert's ring." She held out her empty hand. "I was in the attic going through boxes—there are a lot of them—and it wasn't until I was getting ready for bed that night that I realized it was missing."

Grandma settled into the Queen Anne chair in front of the bay window and crossed her ankles, her hands wringing in her lap. Jared could still see the indent from her wedding ring on her finger and he did the math. That ring had been on there for almost sixty-five years, though his grandfather had been gone for thirty-five of them.

"You can imagine that I didn't sleep well that night, and the next morning, well, I was pretty frantic. I went through every box I'd been through the day before, hoping to find it." She held up her hand. "As you can see, I didn't. And I can't sell this house until I do because what if I leave it here? Robert worked so hard for it. He and I wouldn't go on dates because he was saving every penny he could to buy it for me. I can't lose it. I just can't. It's the most precious thing I have of him other than you, sweetheart. And well, I can't really wear you around my finger, can I?"

"Actually, Grandma, you do have me wrapped around your finger."

He got the smile out of her he'd been hoping for, but it

was true. There wasn't much he wouldn't do for Grandma. Including having Mac stay here.

But just for one night so he wouldn't have to lie.

"Of course we'll look for it, Mrs. Nolan." Mac sank to the floor beside Grandma and patted her knee. "Right, Jared?"

"Of course."

Grandma patted Mac's shoulder. "Thank you so much, Mary-Alice. You see why I couldn't have someone else clean my house? I couldn't trust just anyone to look thoroughly enough. Your grandmother raised a wonderful son and four wonderful grandkids, so you're the perfect person to be Jared's second pair of eyes."

She looked at Jared. "I'll go get you some water to wash down those pills. Perhaps Mary-Alice can help you get up."

Thank God Grandma turned her back because he got up all right—and not in the way she meant.

"You might want to think about different uniforms, Mac," he said as he took the pills she offered him.

"Oh?"

Damn, he'd swiped the smile off her face. "I just meant, that, you know, the pants . . ."

"What about them?" She looked down, then twisted so she could see over her shoulder.

"They're, uh . . ." Shit. He'd dug himself in deep with this. He should have just left well enough alone and enjoyed the view. What was it to him if she wanted every male customer to ogle her?

Did she have a lot of male customers? And if so, did she personally do their cleaning?

"What, Jared? Did I tear them or something?"

"Or something." Thankfully, Grandma showed up just then with his water, so he didn't have to answer. With luck, Mac would forget the question.

"So what's wrong with them then?" she asked once he'd downed the pills, no distraction whatsoever. "They're the uniform. My brand. If there's something wrong with them, I'd like to know."

"Yes, Jared, what's wrong with them?" Grandma walked a circle around Mac, studying her. "I helped Cate design them."

Of course she did. Why *shouldn't* the grandmothers be responsible for designing a form of torture just for him? They'd probably concocted this whole housecleaning gig just to put him and Mac in the same vicinity. It'd been no secret that they would've liked to have been related all along; marrying off their grandchildren to each other would solidify the deal.

"I don't see anything wrong with them. Do they feel okay, Mary-Alice?" Grandma asked.

"They feel fine." Mac ran her hands down her hips.

Really? Really? He wasn't in deep enough that she had to caress the curves he was trying hard not to stare at?

"They fit nicely and move well when I'm climbing ladders and stuff. I think they're okay." The two of them turned toward him. "So what's your beef, Jared?"

"I . . . uh . . ." He raked his hand through his hair while the two women stared at him. "I just think they might be too flimsy. Don't you think jeans might be a better fit for the job?"

"I'll take it under advisement." Mac nodded and spun on her heel, dismissing him while giving him a view of exactly *what* his beef with those damn tight pants was. "Mrs. Nolan, I finished one of the rooms upstairs and found a few photos and keepsakes behind some of the furniture that you might want."

"Oh, that's lovely, Mary-Alice. Let's go take a look." Grandma looked at him. "Let's get Jared on the sofa and then we'll go up."

"I got this." He didn't want Mac anywhere near him right now.

Gritting his teeth, he pushed himself upright onto his butt. Tightening his abs to move his legs around was painful, but nowhere near what he'd already had to deal with.

Then Mac bent over to pet the kittens.

"God damn." The words were out of his mouth before he thought better of it.

At least he hadn't whistled.

"Oh, Jared." Grandma came running over. "Honey, did you hurt something?"

"Nah. It's just the ribs. They're still sore." Yeah, blame it on them so she wouldn't suspect that he couldn't breathe because Mac in those pants sucked the air right out of him.

"That's it. I am moving back in. I'll go home and grab some clothes. Dafna and the girls will have to play bridge without me tonight. And bunco tomorrow. It's not important."

Like hell it wasn't. Grandma loved her social life at the new place, and he definitely didn't need her eagle eyes watching him around Mac. "Grandma, I'll be fine. You don't have to babysit me."

"But you shouldn't be alone."

"He won't. I'll be here." Mac sounded as happy as a funeral director.

"Are you certain you're okay with babysitting Jared, Mary-Alice?"

Babysitting! "Hello?" He waved a hand. "I'm right here and I don't need babysitting. Mac volunteered to help take care of the kittens, so I'll be fine. Go back to your friends, Grandma. No need to skip your games for me."

"You're certain, dear?" She looked at Mac.

He didn't need Mac's seal of approval. "Of course I'm sure, Grandma. I'm not an invalid."

"I meant Mary-Alice, Jared. I know how grumpy you can be. I do hope you'll be on your best behavior while she's here."

Jared wisely kept his mouth shut.

Mac glared at him. "It'll be fine, Mrs. Nolan. Jared and I have an understanding."

Grandma patted Jared's shoulder as she stood. "Can I get you anything, dear, before Mary-Alice and I go upstairs to see what she's found?"

For a second, he had an overwhelming urge to ask her for a hug. Something so innocuous at times, something so common . . . He'd never realized how much he took them for granted until there was no one to give him any.

Geez, he was getting maudlin. Must be the pain. "No, I'm good. You two go. Me and the stooges will be fine."

Grandma looked at Mac as they left the room. "Stooges?"

"He named the kittens after The Three Stooges," explained Mac.

"But there are four."

"There were more than three as it turns out."

"Then why call themselves The *Three* Stooges?"

"Beats me. It's a guy thing, I think."

Yeah, women didn't get The Stooges. Just like guys didn't get the knick-knack thing. It was surprising the race had survived for so long.

Then he got a side view of Mac in those figure-hugging pants and fitted golf shirt.

Maybe it wasn't so surprising after all.

MILDRED dialed Cate's number, then picked up the chocolate sampler box on her bedroom dresser once she was back in her new place.

"Well?" Cate didn't even bother to say hello.

"They bought it." Mildred tilted open the box lid and smiled at what was inside. The only thing she loved more than chocolate—besides her family and friends—was this ring that Robert had worked so hard for.

She slid it onto her finger. Even for those few hours, she'd felt naked without it. As if she was being unfaithful to him.

But it'd been for a good cause. These two, Jared and Mac, they were perfect for each other and always had been. The sparks that flew between them . . . Phew. They reminded her of her and Robert.

"They didn't suspect anything, did they?"

"Come now, Cate, you know me better than that. Who convinced you she had the mumps back in the day until you were so upset you thought you had to have them, too, so we'd die together?"

"It's cruel of you to remind me of that, and kids these

days have the internet to check facts. They're not as gullible as we were."

"Well I still haven't lost my acting chops. Even got a few tears to eke out."

"Brilliant."

"I know."

"Modest, too."

"Of course. When have you known me to be any different?"

Cate chuckled on the other end of the line. "True. Mildred, you are one of a kind."

Mildred held out her hand to see her tiny, tiny diamond catch the light and wink at her—just like Robert used to. This ring was more precious to her than any of the ten-carat monstrosities celebrities were wearing these days.

"Actually, Cate, that's not true. The two of us are quite the pair and we're going to come out of this with one heck of a winning hand when we get those two together."

Chapter Thirteen

JARED winced as he set Shemp back in the pen and glanced at the grandfather clock in the corner. Mac was going to be back soon, thank God.

He shook his head. He never thought he'd say that.

He straightened, wincing again. Hmmm, maybe he had done some damage after all.

He crutched over to the mirror in the foyer and pulled his shirt over his head, inspecting his ribs.

The bruising was gone. They were still sore, but not any more than they'd been earlier today. Not any more than they were after a good workout actually. But he had lost muscle—one more thing he'd lost because of Camille.

God, how had he been so stupid? So blind? Talk about pride going before a fall; women had been coming on to him since he could remember. He'd never suspected Camille of having a reason other than being attracted to him. He wasn't like some of the other guys whose sole attraction to the opposite sex was the contract and cachet of being a sports star. He'd grown up with these looks. Knew how they affected the opposite sex. Used it to his advantage more times than he was proud of. He'd never suspected Camille had a boyfriend. Or that she was getting gifts from *him* to funnel back to that boyfriend. It made her a whore, but when he'd called her that, she'd just laughed. Said he'd been the one paying for it and how pathetic was that?

Not pathetic. Gullible. Trusting. Wanting to believe in happily-ever-afters.

Mac showed up in the mirror behind him.

"Don't you knock?"

"Given the fact that we've known each other practically our whole lives and I'm here to do you a favor, *plus* I have a key, I didn't think I had to. But if it makes you happy . . ." She knocked on the door. "Mind if I come in?"

Hell yes. And no. And . . . shit. He was acting like an ass. "Sorry, Mac. I'm beat."

"I get that." She shut the door behind her and handed him a business card. "Here. This was on your door."

He didn't get the scorn in her voice until he read what was on the card.

Call me if you're lonely ~Renee.

Really? People actually paid to have these printed? Made him feel just *so* special that he was one out of a box of five hundred.

"You go on up and I'll bring the kittens. In case you're *lonely.*" She swung her duffel bag around to her back.

"Bring them? Where?"

"To your grandmother's room. Don't worry; we won't infringe upon your visit with *Renee.*"

He chose to ignore the sarcasm. "Why are you taking them there?" His grandmother's room was next to his.

"Because I need to be close to them during the night and I don't feel like navigating the stairs in the dark when I'm tired?"

This was turning out to be a nightmare. He didn't want Mac that close. Bad enough she was sleeping under the same roof. "I thought you'd sleep on the sofa."

"Sofas don't lend themselves to a good night's sleep. If I have to pull two AM duty, I want to sleep well the rest of the night. So you and *Renee* are just going to have to keep it down." She hiked a pillow in her arms. "So hop to it there,

Hopalong, so I can get the babies up to bed before feeding time. And before your visitor gets here."

"There will be no Renee." Why was it that the minute she said *babies* the image shifted in his brain? Why on God's earth would he imagine her with *human* babies in her arms, taking them upstairs to cribs?

Because you're exhausted and frustrated. Get upstairs now before you do something you'll regret.

Or because he *wouldn't* do something and he'd regret that even more.

MAC forced herself to turn away and head into the parlor. She didn't care if there'd be a Renee or not, and she wasn't here to ogle Jared. Heck, she was trying desperately not to *want* to ogle him ever again. That's what the Renees of the world were for.

But, damn, the man was one fine specimen.

The *thump thump* of his crutches on the stairs almost drowned out the kittens' meows, but these little guys—and gal—were hungry. Which meant she had to get them fed, *then* move them upstairs, not the other way around.

Mac sighed. She was tired and wanted to climb into bed, but there'd be none of that until her duty was done.

Why had she agreed to do this?

It was a question she kept asking herself the entire time she prepared the bottles and carried them back to the parlor. She didn't have an answer after she got all four set up with some creative pillow/bottle propping, and she gave up trying to come up with one by the time they'd finished eating.

Face it, Manley, you aren't over the guy. Just embrace the knowledge and chalk it up to life lessons. Then get your mind focused on finishing this job so you can get back to real life. That's the plan; stick to it.

She felt better after her conscience's pick-me-up. There was nothing wrong with being attracted to Jared—he was a good-looking guy as the Renees of the world were so blatantly telling her. So she still had a crush . . . Didn't mean she had to act on it.

Now if only he wouldn't kiss her again, she'd be fine.

She herded the kittens into a laundry basket, filled a take-out container with kitty litter, and carried them up the stairs *just* in time to run into Jared leaving the bathroom. Shirtless.

"Uh, bathroom's all yours," he said, scrubbing his damp hair that was dripping water onto his shoulders and tracking in tiny rivulets down his chest.

The one she wasn't supposed to be ogling.

"Thanks." Spending the night here was a really bad idea.

"You know, you didn't have to come back. Grandma wouldn't have known."

"*I* would have known. My word means something to me, Jared."

"Mine means something, too."

"Then why are we having this discussion? Your grandmother asked me to stay; here I am."

He looked at her for a few seconds and swiped a hand over his mouth. "Then let's be clear about this. She didn't ask you to stay indefinitely. So one and done and we're good, right?"

Gee, the guy couldn't make it any more obvious that he didn't want her around. "Loud and clear."

"Good."

"Fine. Anything else?"

He looked at her for a few more seconds, then shook his head. "After you." He held out his hand and she walked past him, hanging a right at her door.

"Good night," he called after her.

"Good night," she said before she leaned against the back of the door to close it. Wow, look at her. Able to manage a complete sentence—okay that didn't *technically* constitute her English teacher's version of a complete sentence, but it was a pretty good result in the state she was in.

With him in the state *he* was in.

IT was a long night. These old houses . . . He could hear every scamper of a mouse, every creak, every gust of wind.

Too bad there wasn't any wind. And he knew for a fact

that his grandmother had had a pest control service out last week, so that killed the mouse theory.

He couldn't even lie to himself. He'd been listening for Mac. And he'd heard her. And it'd been killing him for the last—he picked up his phone and squinted as the screen light came on—four hours.

The kittens shouldn't be awake this long. When he'd fed them last night, they'd eaten, answered Nature's call, then gone back to sleep—half hour tops. Twice.

Something crashed in Mac's room. Jared was on his feet before she'd finished some very inventive cursing and half-way to the door before he realized he didn't have his crutches.

He hobbled back to the bed, yanked the damn things from against the nightstand, and got to her room as fast as he could.

"Are you okay?" He hit the light switch by the door.

"Ack!" Mac shielded her eyes with her forearm—

She slept in very short shorts and a T-shirt. With ruffles around the edges.

Ruffles shouldn't be sexy. But with the amount of abdomen showing . . . Then there was all that leg. Mac might not be tall, but she had legs that went up to her eyeballs. Toned, shapely, smooth . . . They'd wrap around a man's waist just fine.

"I heard a crash." He shut off the light, needing to hide the evidence of what she did to him, but the image of her in those pajamas was seared into his brain. What the hell had happened to the sweatpants she'd shown up in?

She scratched her head, and her hair—no longer in that ponytail—fluffed around her face as moonlight sifted through the lace curtains. "One of the kittens jumped off the bed and knocked the remote off the nightstand."

"He jumped? He could've broken a leg." Her four-poster was high off the floor. "Where'd he go? And which one?"

"The calico."

Larry seemed to be the problem child of the bunch. "Did you see where he went?"

"If I did, do you think I'd be standing here wondering where to look first? It was dark before you turned on the sun, and now I have spots in my eyes from the light."

"Hey, I just wanted to make sure you hadn't impaled yourself on anything."

"Well I didn't, but I'm not so sure about the kitten. Go ahead and turn on the light since I'm prepared now."

Jared had to check to make sure *he* was prepared.

Finding everything in, um, order, he switched on the light.

Her nipples were hard.

It was the first thing he noticed. Dammit.

Then she got down on all fours to look under the bed, and her ass—

He swung around. He didn't need to see how her ass curved beneath shorts that hiked up enough to give him a glimpse—

His crutch knocked into the dresser beside the door and he almost took a header.

"Jared? You okay?"

She looked back over her shoulder at him, and shoot-him-now, the image of that—

"Yeah. Fine."

Not.

He crutched past her, keeping his eyes glued to the floor, ostensibly searching for the kitten.

"There you are, baby. Come on over here." Mac tapped the hardwood floor with her nails.

The words . . . Jesus, he had a serious problem if he was imaging her saying those words to him. "Is he under there?"

"Yes, but he's curled up in a ball under the middle of the bed. Can you use your crutch to scoot him this way?"

"Sure." Yeah, give him something to do other than stand here and fantasize about Mac calling to him like she'd called the kitten.

He got himself onto the floor and swept the crutch softly behind the little thing.

It scampered down toward the bottom of the bed.

"No, come here!" Mac again tapped the floor. "Use your other crutch, too, Jared."

Because, yes, he *was* a giant scissors.

Feeling like Johnny Depp in a title role, Jared lay on his

right shoulder and hip, and scissored the crutches on either side of the kitten, herding him toward Mac.

"Got him!" She plucked the little guy off the floor, then sprang to her feet.

Jared got to his feet in time to see Mac dump the troublemaker back into the laundry basket, then put a pillow across the top.

"You might want to turn that over so they can't climb out," he said, glad to see the ache in his ribs was gone.

The one in his groin when he caught a glimpse of her taught abdomen with a belly ring sparkling in her navel, however, was a different story. That one was growing.

"Okay, Mac. Glad everyone's back where they should be. See you tomorrow." He couldn't get out of her room fast enough.

Which meant that, of *course* he'd trip.

The crutch skewed to the left, he went right, and he ended up on top of Mac with the mattress beneath her.

For a second, time stood still and he was right back to that moment years ago when she'd fallen out of the tree onto his date, those big green eyes of hers wide and staring into his.

Like they were doing now.

Her lips, too, were parted just like they'd been then, only this time . . . Only this time he knew what they tasted like. What they felt like beneath his.

And now he knew what *she* felt like beneath him. Every soft, curvy part of her, and the way her chest fluttered as she sucked air into her lungs—

He groaned and it didn't have anything to do with the pain. Well, not the pain from the accident, but one very tight, very aching pain down low, and it was all because of this woman. This gorgeous sexy woman who'd gripped the waistband of his shorts, her fingers lighting fires under his skin.

"Mac—"

"Jared—"

Someone kissed someone. He wasn't sure who it was, but there was no hesitation on either one's part, and the kiss became full-on carnal in about three seconds.

God, the way her fingertips shot sparks under his skin,

the way the slide of her tongue against his urged him deeper inside, the way her hips cradling his erection made him thrust against her—

The way four sharp claws dug into his ribs—

"Holy mother of—"

Jared reared back, breaking the kiss, and leaving one suddenly very pissed-off woman staring up at him.

"Hey, I didn't invite you to kiss me. If it's so abhorrent, I'd think you wouldn't have done it a second time." Mac wiggled under him and if she only knew that that was *not* the deterrent she was trying to make it be. "Get off me you big, conceited oaf."

"Give me a minute, Mac." He needed to be able to breathe, and between the kittens and Mac, he wasn't sure he'd come out of this alive.

"Jared, get off." She shoved him and there went a whole new round of pain in his ribs.

He rolled off her and onto the mattress, the ribs taking another jarring, but at least the pain made his dick quiet the fuck down.

Mac's effect was a whole other story.

"Do you mind telling me what that was? A woman in your house is an open invitation for a mauling? What gives you the right to just up and kiss me whenever you feel like humiliating me? How dare you—"

"Humiliate you?" Jared rolled onto his side and worked his elbow under him to sit up. "*Humiliate* you? Is that what you think I was doing?"

Mac's shoulders got squarer and she crossed her arms. "I am *not* the same kid who thought you were the cat's meow all those years ago." She glanced at the kittens in the basket. Whichever one had jumped on him wasn't copping to it. Jared had a feeling it'd been Larry. "My apologies, guys. You all are worth way more than this slug."

"Slug?" Jared got to his feet, holding on to the newel post. "*Slug*? You were just as involved in that kiss as I was, Mac, so what does that say about you for kissing a slug?"

"I was not—"

"Don't try to deny it. I was there if you recall. *Right* there. And that was your tongue sliding into my mouth. I wasn't coercing you. I wasn't forcing you. You grabbed hold of me and pulled me against you."

"I—" She crossed her arms tighter and huffed.

"What's the matter? *Cat* got your tongue?" Jared pushed off the post and stood in front of her. "You wanted to kiss me, Mac. Admit it."

She looked up at him, those big green eyes staring a hole right through him. Searing through him. Straight to the middle of his chest, and suddenly *he* was the one who was trying to suck air into his lungs.

"Why did you kiss me, Jared? Why are you playing games with me? Do you think it's funny to play on those feelings I had for you all those years ago? We have to be in this house together for a couple of weeks. Have to work together for Mildred's sake. I can't keep doing this. I can't keep wondering if you're going to try to humiliate me every time I'm here."

Jesus, he never knew words could hurt so much. "I wasn't trying to humiliate you, Mac. I . . . you . . . we were there and it wasn't something I planned. It just . . . happened."

She shoved herself off the bed and scooted toward the footboard. "Then make sure it doesn't happen again, please. I'd hate to disappoint our grandmothers, but I'm not going to stay here and be something to relieve your boredom and give you a laugh or two." She grabbed the bedspread and shook it. "Now if you wouldn't mind, I'd like to settle the kittens down and get some sleep before I have to get up for work in the morning."

He looked at her standing there so rigid. Replayed her words in his head. He hadn't been trying to humiliate her; he'd wanted to kiss her. She'd wanted to kiss him, too.

"I'll get out of here, but only because after that kiss, your bedroom is not the safest place for me to be. For either of our sakes." He yanked the crutches off the floor and shoved them under his arms. "Hide behind your denial, Mac, but you wanted to kiss me every bit as much as I wanted to kiss you. This isn't over."

Chapter Fourteen

JARED scrubbed his head one more time with the towel, which he then tossed onto the washer in the laundry room, shivering as the cold water dripped onto his shoulders. He'd needed a cold shower to wake himself up this morning, since sleeping after that kiss had been as elusive as the no-hitter he'd been hoping to have before his career was over. God willing, he'd still have a chance at that.

A chance with Mac, however . . .

Chemical combustion aside, seeing her soft spot for the kittens and his grandmother, and, hell, even him . . . Mac had a good soul and if someone had told him that when they were kids, he would have told that someone to go dunk their head in the creek because Mac Manley had been a terror.

Funny how time and distance could change a guy's perspective. And, unfortunately, hers.

"Jared!"

"In the kitchen."

She blew back into the kitchen in all her tornado style, but even though he was used to it, he wasn't prepared to see her as she was now.

Mac in a skirt and heels was deadly.

Toss in the ruffles on the edges of her blouse when she removed her suit jacket and she upgraded to catastrophic.

Seriously, ruffles were not supposed to be sexy, but on her . . . Jesus. Even if they didn't remind him about last night, all that leg . . . And those heels.

Black heels.

With a ruffle at the back.

And then there was her hair: loose and flowing around her shoulders as she spun around, waving a pair of keys above her head.

"I got it!"

"Congratulations." And when she smiled like that it lit up her face and stole the breath right out of his lungs. Mac was simply . . . gorgeous.

". . . the financing went through, I could finally let out that breath. But Liam kept me from dancing out of my chair until all the paperwork was signed, and now I am the proud owner of a work van. I just need to get it wrapped with my company logo and contact info and then we'll be ready for business. In the meantime, though, I've got the car magnets, which look great with the green against the white backdrop. Just how I envisioned it."

Mac was nothing like he'd envisioned. All those years when he'd thought about her—*if* he'd thought about her—he'd seen the child she'd been.

She's not a child anymore.

Yeah. He got that.

He cleared his throat. "This calls for a celebration." He limped over to the cabinet and pulled out a pair of wine glasses. "I don't think Grandma has champagne around here, but we could celebrate with a glass of orange juice before you show me the van."

She flopped onto one of the kitchen chairs and stretched her legs out in front of her. "I'd love to, but Liam needed it. He loaned his truck to Cassidy Davenport."

"Cassidy Davenport? What does she need with a pickup

truck? Doesn't her father own a fleet of sports cars? That's more her ticket."

Mac shrugged and the ruffles swished some hair forward, leading right down to the cleavage he was trying desperately not to notice. He headed to the fridge. Maybe a blast of cold air would get his libido under control.

After the cold shower didn't? Good luck with that.

"Apparently those aren't family cars. All I know is she's car-less and Liam has to get to work, and since he fits as well as you did in my truck, I had to give him the van." She chuckled. "It stinks that I can't use it, but I've gone this long without one, I can use the truck a little longer."

As long as he didn't get in it with her. It'd been a tight squeeze, and after last night, he didn't need to be in such close proximity again. He opened the fridge, but the cold air did nothing to stop the heat coursing through him at the memory.

He poured their juice, handed her a glass, and raised his. "Here's to your very own Manley Maids fleet."

"So how are the kittens?" she asked after they'd *chinked* their flutes of juice. "They ought to be sleeping 'til noon after last night."

There was silence for a beat or two. She hadn't forgotten about last night any more than he had.

"Actually, they were pretty active up until about twenty minutes ago. I figure we have a good three hours before they're jumping all over each other again. Time for another chance for you to beat me at rummy."

"Not today." She sat up and pulled her legs under her as she turned to rest her elbows on the table. "No time for fun and games. The attic, remember?" She downed the rest of the OJ and stood up, brushing past him on her way to the sink.

She smelled good. Too good. "We're doing the attic now?" he asked as he headed out of the kitchen after rinsing their glasses.

She'd already made it to the second floor and leaned over the banister, her fingers on the buttons between her breasts. "No time like the present. Your grandmother was upset. We shouldn't keep her waiting. We need to go through the stuff in there anyway to decide what to keep and what to give away." She headed into her room and closed the door.

Give away? He'd played in that attic for hours on rainy days when he'd been younger. Had made forts and foxholes among the trunks and knickknacks Grandma had stored up there.

A hollow feeling settled around his heart and he stopped on the second step from the landing. Giving it away would be like another piece of his life being taken from him. And he'd lost too much already.

He needed some air.

Hopping down the stairs on his good leg, Jared gritted his teeth against the pain in his chest cavity, be it his ribs or his heart. He didn't want to examine it too closely.

At the bottom, he again hopped across the floor and yanked the door open—

There was a woman standing there. With more baked goods.

He so didn't need this right now.

"Hi," she said with that hopeful look in her eye. "I'm Renee. I left a note on your door last night."

"Ah, yes. I got that."

She licked her bottom lip, then pulled it between her teeth, her head tilted and looking up at him from under her lashes.

He'd seen the same move a thousand times before. And this woman—Renee—didn't need the affectation because she was pretty in her own right. But he wasn't interested and, nibbled lip or not, he wasn't going to be.

"I brought you some brownies." She held up the plate.

He wasn't in the mood. Not for the food nor what they represented. "Thanks, Renee, but while I appreciate them, I can't eat them. Gotta keep the weight off, you know?"

Big mistake. Renee took her sweet time checking him out. "You don't seem to have a problem."

Oh yes he did. Two. The life that was spinning out of his control and the five-foot-two sexy, caring dynamo who was, right this minute, probably taking off the rest of her clothes in the room above his head.

He knew which one was the bigger problem.

MAC leaned closer to the window. "*You don't seem to have a problem,*" she repeated in a nasally whisper. "Please. Can't the woman come up with something original? Jared probably hears that a dozen times a day."

The knife that had shown up when the *first* Mrs.-Nolan-Wannabe had come calling the other day twisted half a turn in her gut with this one.

"I'm a physical therapist, actually. I can give you a hand with your rehab."

Geez, the woman didn't give up.

Mac looked down at the blouse she had clutched between her breasts. And the lacy bra she was wearing beneath it.

It would be wrong to lean over the banister like this, right?

She let the smile curve onto her lips. Mildred *had* asked her to help Jared out . . .

She opened the bedroom door and walked to the banister, leaning over enough to see the latest hopeful. "Jared, I'll be out of these clothes in a few minutes if you want to meet me upstairs."

Renee's gaze shot right up the stairs.

Mac waved, trying really really hard not to laugh.

There was silence for a couple of seconds until Jared coughed.

Mac could swear she heard a chuckle in it.

"Uh, yeah. Okay. Be up in a minute."

It took her half that time to hightail it back to her room and grab a T-shirt and shorts. That little show out there had been solely for Renee's benefit. After last night, she wasn't trying to tempt Jared in any way whatsoever. He could call Renee for that. But they had a job to do and the quicker they finished, the quicker she could remove herself from any temptation.

Because she was tempted.

By the time he was *schlumping* up the stairs, she was dressed, had her hair in a ponytail, and was waiting for him in the hallway, ready for business.

"That was bad." Jared's smile didn't back up his statement.

"It got her to leave, didn't it?" She executed a military turn toward the attic stairs, her ponytail swishing over her shoulder.

"Yeah, but it gave her the wrong impression."

"Did you want her to have the right one?" She looked over her shoulder at him. "From what I heard, it sounded like you were trying to get rid of her. I just helped that along."

"And now everyone's going to know that there's a half-naked woman in my house."

She tugged on the old wooden door, but it didn't move. Must've swelled into its frame. "That's what they'll surmise. They won't know. But maybe that will prevent any more snacks from showing up on your doorway with cards and phone numbers."

Jared reached over her shoulder and leaned on the door frame. "Maybe I *want* cards and phone numbers."

She swatted his hand and yanked on the handle again. The thing wouldn't budge. "Then put a basket on the front lawn with a big sign. Guaranteed it'll be filled in under twenty-four hours and I won't have to play butler."

He put his hand atop hers on the handle. "Mac, if I didn't know any better, I'd say you were jealous."

"Of course you would." She slid her hand out. "Because no woman could possibly be in the same room with you and not want you."

"Actually, Mac." He ground out her name as he tugged the door open. "I think Camille proved that that *is* possible. A hard lesson, but one I've learned well." He swept his hand toward the steps. "After you, *Princess*."

There it was, that flash of vulnerability she might have imagined if not for the sarcasm. Jared lashed out when something was bothering him; she'd seen it more than a few times through the years, and her heart, no surprise, had always gone out to him.

As it did now. Camille had hurt him.

Mac felt the reverberation of every step as she climbed into the attic all the way up her spine and circling her heart. A woman had gotten to Jared enough to hurt him.

It hurt that that woman hadn't been her.

And it hurt to admit that she felt that way.

God, why couldn't she be over him? Maybe if he weren't hurt, hadn't lost someone he cared about, wasn't worried about his career, she'd be able to get over him. Hell, with what he'd said to Dave, she *ought* to be able to . . . But she heard his voice, knew how much he loved being a professional athlete, and not only understood his pain, but *saw* it. Recognized his sarcasm as a cover. No surprise in that; she did it herself, and had after that night on Grandma's walk when Nan had let the whole world know he'd shot her down. She'd used it as a shield against the pitying looks and comments.

And maybe he'd done the same thing in that conversation with Dave.

Something to consider . . .

"Wow. Grandma wasn't kidding." Jared used the banister to haul himself up the last couple of stairs. "This place is a disaster. I've never known her to be this messy."

Mac got her brain out of Possibility and planted it firmly in Reality, righting a quilt stand that was leaning against the wooden hobby horse she'd ridden more than a few times when Gran had brought them to visit. "She must have been really upset at losing that ring."

"Yeah. Some story, huh?"

She patted the horse. "I think it's sweet." Mac loved hearing stories of Mildred's husband, Peter. To hear Mildred tell it, Jared's grandfather had been an honest-to-God Prince Charming. It hadn't been tough to make that leap to Jared when she'd been younger and foolish.

"That's what I mean." Jared leaned over to pick up a picture frame off the top of a pile of embroidered pillows. He brushed the glass against his shirt and set it on the old plant stand beside the banister. "I can't imagine doing all my grandfather did to save up for that ring."

She turned away and headed toward an old doll house. "How else was he going to afford it? It's not like your grandfather got a million-dollar contract."

"Neither did I."

She spun around about to call his bluff when she saw a twinkle in his eye.

"It was more than a mil."

She tossed the closest thing to her at him, an ugly old sock monkey that had been all the rage when she'd been a kid. She'd hated those things. Thought they were scary ugly and creepy, and time hadn't changed her opinion. "Is that supposed to impress me?"

He caught the monkey—of course. She'd expect nothing less from a pro ball player. "You *aren't* impressed, are you?"

"I'm happy for you, Jared. You worked hard to get where you are, so I think that's great. But the dollar amount? No, it doesn't impress me. Because it doesn't affect me. You're getting paid to do what you love for a living. If I could make a living doing what I love, I wouldn't care what that number was because getting paid to do it is its own reward."

"You don't love what you do?"

She shrugged. "I don't hate it. I'm good at it, but it's not my passion. Not like baseball is to you."

"So what do you want to do? What *is* your passion?"

"It's nothing." She didn't want to get this personal with him.

He set the monkey down and limped across the worn plank floor until he was within touching distance.

Which he did, raising her chin with a finger. "Doesn't sound like nothing."

She jerked her head away. In this mood, Jared was even more dangerous to her equilibrium than when he'd kissed her. A caring, gentle Jared let her imagine *what if.* "No, really. It is. Nothing, I mean."

He brushed his finger along her cheek. "Anything that

gets your voice husky like that and makes you blink fast *is* something. It's what you want to do. What you believe in. So tell me, Mac, what's your passion?"

His face was too close and his voice too sexy to make her think about anything other than wanting to plaster herself up against that hard body of his and take her time kissing him—

"Kids."

Jared backed away. "Kids?"

Well, gee, if she'd known kids were such a turn-off to him, she would've mentioned them years ago. No kids was a deal breaker, and if he felt so unenthused about them, she could've saved herself years of heartache.

No time like the present to start.

She picked up a box and set it on top of a dresser. Might as well get to work. They had a lot of boxes to go through. "Yes. Kids. You know, young adults? Little people?"

"I know what kids are, but . . . what? You want to have a bunch of babies?"

She shouldn't be picturing his babies. His and hers. With their green eyes and Jared's blond hair.

Okay, her black hair was probably genetically dominant, but it was her fantasy, so she could have them look like him if she wanted.

She wanted.

Dammit.

She tore open the box a little more forcefully than was probably necessary. "Um, no. Not yet. I mean, eventually. When I find the right person." Who she'd wanted to be the guy standing in front of her but he was too stupid to know it, so she had to find the *next* right person. "But I mean kids in general. Working with them. I put programs together for the community center's Kareers for Kids day and teach classes. It's an outreach program for not only the community but kids in foster care, too."

The foster care kids were the ones closest to her heart. If not for Gran, that would've been the only option for her and her brothers.

"Sounds like a worthy cause."

"I've had kids tell me they wanted to become chefs after my cooking classes, which is so gratifying. Many of them lose hope. I've seen it over the years. Not being adopted, bounced from home to home . . . At least I can give them a vision for their future, something to strive for. Some way of knowing they won't always be at others' mercy. That they will be able to provide for themselves in life."

"Hey, take a breath, Mac." Jared put his hand on her shoulder. "You don't have to convince me. Helping kids is a worthy cause."

"You really think so?"

"Well, yeah. Sure. Obviously."

Obviously? There was nothing obvious about it after his recoil. But now she had a chance to test the waters . . . "Worthy enough to consider doing something for them?"

He'd walked into that one. Should have seen it coming, but he'd been socked in the gut at the idea of Mac and babies, and his guard had been down.

For that reason alone, he almost said no, but something stopped him. "What'd you have in mind?"

"Really?"

"You were expecting me to say no? Then why'd you ask?"

"Because if you don't ask, you don't get. And, look, you said yes, so I got what I wanted."

When hadn't she? "I haven't said yes. I just asked what you have in mind."

She tapped her lips and it took all he had not to remember what those lips felt like. The woman was lethal in a whole other way she hadn't been as a kid.

"There's a community center event coming up and you ought to, I don't know, do something with baseball."

"You mean like getting in a dunking booth and seeing who can knock me in?"

Her smile was blinding. "Now there's an idea."

"I am not sitting in a dunking booth."

"Pie-in-the-face booth?"

"No."

"Kissing booth?"

Now *she'd* walked into that one. "You volunteering?"

Damn she was pretty when she blushed.

"Hardly." She cleared her throat. "How about a pickup game or a pitching clinic or something like that?"

He missed baseball. Playing it with Chase the other day—teaching him—had been fun. Different than playing with his teammates, but definitely gratifying. This could actually be fun. "When is it?"

"This weekend."

"As in two days?"

She nodded. "I saw you throwing a ball with that boy. You could do the same thing on Saturday, right?"

"Yeah." He stood on his left leg and used his right toes to keep his balance. "Okay, then I'll start on this side, you start over there, and we'll work our way to the middle and hopefully find Grandma's ring quickly so I can pull something together for Saturday."

"Sounds like a plan." Mac skirted a mishmash of furniture, picture frames, an old sewing machine, and boxes of lord-knew-what to plunk herself as far from him as possible—which he *ought* to be grateful for.

The front doorbell rang.

First time he was grateful for *that*.

Mac looked at him. "Juliette, Maeve, Renee, or someone else?"

"I don't know. It's anybody's guess, but you're going to have to answer it because by the time I get down there, they'll be gone."

"And that's a problem, why? I say we let her leave whatever little goodie she thinks will get from your stomach to your heart, then grab it when we take a break."

"Are you horning in on my bribes?"

She smiled. "Yup."

He smiled back. "Sounds like a plan."

The bell rang a couple more times. Mac peered out the octagonal window, but said she couldn't see anything because of the porch roof. "I'm betting it's Renee. She sounded like she wasn't going to go away earlier. She probably restocked her arsenal and came back with guns blazing. What do you think? Double chocolate devil's food cake or macadamia nut/super chunk chocolate chips?"

"Where do you come up with this?" Jared had to laugh, though any of those were fine with him.

"The stakes seem to be getting bigger. I wouldn't be surprised if you graduated to Baked Alaska or cherries jubilee."

"Why not a nice juicy steak? Seems to me chocolate's more of a chick thing, and a thick slab of beef is more of a guy thing."

"Want me to hand out flyers? Go door-to-door with menus?"

"Cheeky."

"I call it smart. Like I said, if you don't ask, you don't get. Worked for me, didn't it?"

She had him there. "Okay, Princess, I'll take your bet and put my money on chocolate chip cookies."

"How much are we betting?"

He knew what he'd *like* to bet . . . "Not money. How about dinner?"

She tapped her lips. Which only made him look at them.

Dammit.

"Okay. You're on. I say brownies. Out of a box, they're the easiest thing to make if someone can't cook."

"Deal." He opened the next box, which turned out to be full of vinyl records. "Oh, man, remember these?"

And so it went for the rest of the afternoon, one that passed surprisingly quickly. He couldn't believe all the things Grandma had saved. The things he remembered. The things *Mac* remembered. She'd been a bigger part of his childhood than he'd realized. Almost as if they were siblings.

But not.

A fact that was reiterated over and over when he'd catch a glimpse of her bent over to search the bottom of a particularly big box, or when she'd reached up to untangle an electrical cord from Grandma's Tiffany lamp and her shirt hiked halfway up her abdomen. His mouth had gone dry at the sight of all that toned skin—and that freaking sexy bellybutton piercing winking ruby red at him from across the room.

His mind went into overdrive at that. Taking that little dangly thing between his teeth, running his tongue in the dip in her stomach, feeling her muscles flutter with arousal . . .

One of his in particular was doing that right now.

"Oh. My. God."

That's what he said . . . "What?"

Mac's mouth had dropped open and she held up something round and silver. "Home movies."

"Wow. I haven't seen those in I don't know how long. We ought to watch them."

Mac held them as if they were covered in garlic or something. "I think you should have them transferred to DVDs for your grandmother. That'd be a great Christmas present. Just think how much she'd love to see your grandfather in these."

He was thinking that. He'd never known his grandfather. *He'd* like to see his grandfather in them.

"I wonder if there's a projector up here." He scanned the space. "Do you see anything that might be one?"

"No." She set the metal canister down and brushed her hands. "But Gran might have one. I'll check when I go home tonight."

"You're going home?"

"I thought that was the plan? Do you really need me to stay? After sifting through all this stuff, I don't think the kittens will be much of a challenge."

That wasn't why he wanted her to stay.

Which was precisely the reason she ought to go.

Chapter Fifteen

MAC picked up the latest round of neighborly treats—complete with offers of another type of treat—from the table she'd placed beside the front door after she'd tripped on her way out last night over the bottle of wine she and Jared hadn't guessed.

For a moment, she'd been bummed. No dinner bet payoff. Then again, that was a good thing. She shouldn't have made the bet in the first place because dinner out with Jared like that would be weird.

This morning's offering was homemade apple pie. With a little toothpick flag right in the middle with *Sherisse's* name and phone number.

And of course, like every single other woman (or was that every other single woman?), she'd put the thing in an expensive serving container, which meant it had to be returned, ensuring at least one conversation with Jared.

Mac shrugged and unlocked the door. She didn't get these dating tactics, but, hey, she wasn't going to turn down a piece of apple pie. Especially since dinner was out.

She set the extension mop against the grandfather clock,

then checked on the kittens in the pen in the parlor before heading into the kitchen.

It was a mess. There were towels hanging off the back of every chair, one hanging off the wall phone, a couple draped over the cabinet doorknobs, and two hung with thumbtacks from the doorframe to the mudroom door.

Then there were the paper towels crinkled up all over the floor, looking like someone had used them for shoes, the trash can was overflowing, and there was a pile of kitten food on the drain board beside the sink. Probably explained the rug missing from the parlor.

No wonder the kittens were asleep. From the looks of this, Jared should be as well.

But then she heard thumping from upstairs, so she did a quick cleanup, tossing everything into a trash bag or laundry basket, started a load, then took the trash out before heading up to help him out. She really hoped they'd find Mildred's ring today because yesterday's trip down memory lane hadn't been her idea of fun.

Oh sure, she'd smiled at all the right places, poured fake enthusiasm into every find, but the reality was, every time she saw something from her childhood, she remembered the moment attached to it. And invariably, those moments—if they weren't about her parents—had something to do with Jared. Not banner times in her life.

Then the home movies she'd found . . . She'd nudged Mildred's projector under a table and rearranged a drop cloth over it. She didn't want to sit in a darkened room with Jared while watching movies of him at the age she'd first fallen for him.

And then the wine had shown up . . .

That wouldn't have been good.

Really.

Rolling her eyes, she grabbed a dishtowel off the wooden calendar on the wall and tossed it into the washing machine, then headed up the stairs—where she heard Jared talking to someone.

"Hey, yeah, thanks for last night. I really appreciate it."

Please tell her Sherisse didn't stay for breakfast . . .

"Next time, wine's on you."

Next time. There was going to be a next time with Sherisse or Renee or whoever he was talking to.

"Yeah, gotta go. Catch you later."

Ah, his cell phone. At least she wasn't going to have to face whoever drank her portion of the wine.

"So I see the kittens went surfing in the kitchen." She climbed the steps, being sure he knew she was there.

He groaned. "What the hell is in their food? I thought they had a natural instinct to use a litter box?"

"You have to show them. When you see them scratching at a spot, you have to plunk them in the litter so they start to make the correlation."

"I've been doing that."

"Not all yesterday afternoon you didn't. We were up here until dinner."

"And they saved it until sometime in the middle of the night. Made quite the wake-up aroma this morning. Not to mention the amount of cleaning I had to do. The kitchen looks good compared to what that play yard thing looked like."

"I was wondering why you moved it."

"If you'd seen the rug, you'd know. Be thankful I spared you. I'm going to have to buy it from my grandmother because it's not worth saving." He wiped his forehead with the back of his hand. "I got a day's workout in before seven. And now Dave's going to show up wanting more."

She knew the feeling . . .

She straightened her shoulders. And her metaphorical backbone. "I'm only here for the morning. One of my clients put her house up for sale and the realtor decided at the last minute to have an open house all day tomorrow. I have to get over there and clean it today since we have the Kareers for Kids event tomorrow. You're going to be on attic duty yourself today."

He shrugged. "That's fine. There's a lot to get through. I'm still hoping I find a projector. Did your grandmother have one?"

Mac crossed her fingers behind her back. "If she does, I didn't find it." Technically, that wasn't a lie—she hadn't looked for it.

"I wonder if I can rent one." He picked up the box with the reels in them and picked two of them up. "I kept thinking about them last night. I wonder how far back they go. Who's on them." He turned them over. "No dates or anything."

"So it'll be a surprise. Like opening a present."

"Yeah, and check these out." He set the movies down and picked up another box. "A bunch of family photos of people I don't know." He held up one in sepia with a large group of kids. "I'd forgotten that my grandfather had nine brothers and sisters. My dad grew up with a slew of cousins. Wish I'd known them."

"What about family reunions and holiday dinners?"

Jared shook his head. "Are you kidding? My mother eat on paper plates in someone's living room at a card table? Hell no. We always went to the Bijou or Landers' for our holiday dinners, just the three of us. Big elaborate spread, staff dressed to the nines, tons of cocktails, desserts made with gold leaf."

"Wow. That sounds . . ." Mac had to think how to phrase this. "Lonely."

Jared sighed and set down the picture. "Got it in one."

"You should've come to our house." Where her young heart would've gone all aflutter . . . "Gran didn't have a big extended family, but she had a lot of widowed friends. We always had people over. Sometimes people we didn't even know. If there was someone who didn't have anywhere to go, everyone knew to send them to Gran's."

"I know."

"You do?"

"Sure. When we were finished at the restaurant, we came home. With your house being right across the field, I could see the lights and the cars, and if it was nice out, the party would spill out into the yard. I always asked to go over, but my mom didn't understand that I had a standing invitation to your house. She expected one in writing addressed to her and my father. Not that she would've come. Do you know, she's never driven in your neighborhood? It was always 'around the corner.'"

"Is that like the wrong side of the tracks?"

"All that was missing were the railroad ties."

Mrs. Nolan had always seemed so imposing to her. Now she knew why: The Manleys weren't good enough. "Wow. That's . . . um . . ."

"Pretentious." Jared put the photo back into the box. "Welcome to my world."

It was a world she'd wanted to be part of back then. Jared had lived in a big custom-built home with nice furnishings and all the latest technology, with a manicured lawn and a pool. Not to mention that batting cage. His parents had driven expensive cars, and he'd always worn designer clothes, even his sports gear. She'd let the Cinderella fantasy run the full gamut back then, imagining him as her real-life Prince Charming, whisking her away to his wonderful palace, away from the chores of life in Gran's small house.

Never judge a book by its cover.

"But enough about that. I'll take these photos to Grandma next time I visit and see if she wants any for her new place. I guess we'll pitch the rest. I mean, who wants pictures of people you don't know cluttering up the place?" He shrugged and smiled, but the smile didn't reach his eyes.

"Good point."

She studied him while he put the box against the banister. Not having a relationship with his extended family bothered him.

Jared was lonely.

The thought hit her out of the blue. It was a realization so personal, so intimate, that Mac didn't know what to do with it. He certainly wouldn't want to discuss it—would probably deny it—but it made sense in looking back over the years.

Gran must have seen it. She was too sharp not to. And why wouldn't she take him in? She took in anyone who didn't have someone. Just because Jared had all the money and *stuff* and advantages he'd had didn't mean he was any happier than she and her brothers. Matter of fact, Mac would bet that she and her brothers had been happier their entire childhood.

And now.

The thought rocked her. Who *did* he have? He'd said his parents hadn't shown up at the hospital, his teammates were off somewhere doing their job, his ex-girlfriend had pulled a really crappy move on him, right down to kicking him out of his own home, and here he was in his grandmother's attic, alone except for the memories.

And her.

Which, with the sympathy she was feeling, was probably not the safest place for her to be.

"I'm, uh, just going to clean the dining room and then head out. Will you be okay up here?"

He'd say yes. Of course he would.

"Yeah."

But Mac knew better.

Now what she was going to do with that knowledge was something she'd have to think about.

HE almost asked her to stay. To forget about the dining room and keep him company.

But that was dangerous. Mac represented everything he wanted: unconditional love—which he'd stupidly destroyed with his careless and purposely arrogant attitude around her all those years ago—a caring, close family, traditions and holidays that dated back generations and were still going strong today, compassion, love, caring. Then there were the facts that her brothers were his best friends, she'd turned into a woman he hadn't expected, and kissing her was the next best thing to heaven. And he knew if they took it any further, it *would* be heaven.

But . . . did he want Mac for herself or for what she represented?

Chapter Sixteen

"DO you know who's here?" asked a woman walking past Mac's booth the next day at the community center.

"I saw him in the parking lot," said another, fanning herself—and it wasn't that hot out. "I swear, if my husband had been a few more steps ahead of me, I would've gone over."

A third one fluffed her hair. "Well point me in his direction and I *will* go over because mine's out of town. What he doesn't know won't keep me from hitting on the hottest thing in a uniform to come along since a shirtless Bryan Manley in ripped fatigues."

Ewwww ewww ewww. Mac wanted to scrub her brain. She knew which scene from Bryan's movie the woman was talking about and, while she got that her brother was hot, it was just so squidgy to hear these women foaming at the mouth about him. And it didn't help that they were doing it about Jared, too. Hell, he could practically be her brother.

But he's not . . .

True. But still. To hear women talking about him as if he were a piece of meat . . . It just felt wrong.

Or you're jealous.

Whatever. Mac wasn't going there. Today was all about the kids, and those women could take their supercharged hormones someplace else. She now had enough supercharged hormones of her own, thankyouverymuch.

"Hey, Mac!"

She looked up to see Jared limping across the field, his crutches more for balance than transportation.

All three women swung around to look at her.

Mac bit her lip to keep a satisfied smile from it. They could be potential clients and if their interest in Jared got them interested enough in her, maybe she could sign 'em up.

Or . . . judging from the murderous look in their eyes, maybe not.

Okay, so she let some of her satisfaction smile through and waved back to him. "Hey, Jared!"

He came over. "How's it going?"

Much better now that you're here.

"Good. Lots of kids around. I didn't tell anyone you were coming, otherwise you'd be mobbed, but I have a feeling word's going to spread pretty quickly." She looked behind him. Yup, the women were snapping pictures and Mac would bet those would be online in ten seconds.

"I blocked off a spot for you over there." She pointed to the orange cones she'd laid out with CAUTION tape linking them. "You might want to get set up so you're ready when the hordes hit."

"Thanks." He nodded to the backpack he was carrying. "Can you give me a hand with this?"

Which hand and where do you want it to go?

Mac bit her tongue, half afraid she was going to voice those questions, told the kids she was helping with the cookie dough to hang on, and hurried over to him as he slid the backpack off.

She grabbed it but it hit the ground with a thud. "Geez, what's in this thing?"

"Bats, balls, bags, gloves. Couple bottles of water. Sunscreen. Usual pickup game stuff."

"You just had all of this hanging around?"

"No, Liam brought it over the other night. We killed that bottle of wine, by the way. I was going to give it to you, but he and I got to talking and I didn't have any beer left, so it was the wine. I owe you."

Liam. The conversation she'd overheard now made sense in a perfectly no-need-to-be-jealous way.

She couldn't keep the smile off her face. Which irked her to no end. One minute she didn't want him and the next . . .

The next she wanted him as much as she ever had. Which had been a lot. But that'd been puppy love. Now . . .

She wasn't going to examine now.

"Hey, Jared." A blonde in a minidress waved at him as she tossed her hair over her bare shoulder.

"Hey." He gave the quintessential guy head-toss move.

"Friend of yours?" Mac couldn't help asking.

"No clue."

"Really? Sounded pretty chummy to me."

He shrugged and hefted the backpack as if it weighed nothing. "Gotta keep the fans happy. They pay good money to watch me do what I love. I should pay them."

"I wouldn't say that too loudly if I were you or you'll have some takers." Except the women wouldn't want him to pay for *baseball*.

"Hey, did you know there's a petting zoo by the parking lot?" Jared bent over to separate the things he brought into piles.

Mac made sure to look somewhere else. Anywhere else. "The zoo brings the animals here to sell memberships. Plus, a zookeeper is a valid career path and the animals help break the ice with the kids. That and the water ice booth. The owner talks to the kids about owning their own business between giving out samples."

"Let's hope good ol' American baseball can get them interested, too."

It did. And not just the kids.

Or the dads.

The moms came out in full force.

"Choke up on the bat, Kev," Jared said to the kid he was pitching to. "That's it. Now hold it steady so you can connect with the ball."

Jared pitched and the kid swung . . . and missed.

The crowd commiserated, but Jared held out his hands to quiet them down. "You took your eye off the ball. You were looking at me, not the pitch. Let's try that again."

And so it went for the next three hours. Mac caught a glimpse when she could, but preventing the kids with her from eating the cookie batter became a full-time job.

Finally, she slid the last of the cookie trays onto the refrigerated baking rack. "Okay, gang, let's get this round inside to the ovens and then we can clean up while they bake."

"Aw, I don't want to clean up. I'm a chef. Chefs cook things. They don't clean up."

Mac tweaked Calvin's nose. "They do when they're first starting out and so will we. Who else do you think is going to do it?"

"The ants!" said Janey Weston.

Mac chucked Janey under the chin. "Nice try, kiddo. But we're not inviting the ants to our cookie bake, so you'll all have to grab a rag and get busy."

JARED had a blast. God, he loved the game. Coaching kids wasn't like playing in the majors, but as something to get him over the hump 'til he went back, it'd been fun. And it was great to see familiar faces from school and catch up, but after three hours of pitching, his legs and his ribs were protesting.

And as for the kids . . . They were receptive to his advice, excited to learn, and some a little star struck. It was good for his ego, but even more importantly, it was good for his soul. It was nice to be appreciated for something he'd worked so hard to be good at.

He pulled another two-hour stint signing everything from T-shirts to baby strollers and business cards, enjoying himself, smiling until his cheeks hurt, but he could really use a break. With all the physical activity of cleaning up after the kittens, surveying the attic, playing ball with Chase, and working out with Dave, plus this afternoon on top of it all, he was wiped out, and the line wasn't getting any shorter.

"Okay, gang, listen up." Mac showed up with a plate of chocolate chip cookies. He could have kissed her for that.

Well, among other reasons.

"For those of you who already have Jared's autograph, there are more cookies at the baking booth back there. If you head over, the other people in line can have their chance to meet him and we'll be able to finish up. The cleaning crew wants to go home, too." She said that last bit with a big smile, taking the command out of her words.

Too bad the next woman in line didn't listen. God knew, she had more than enough of his stuff to ensure she'd *never* have to wait in line.

"What do you want, Camille?"

She whipped out a piece of paper from the hideous fur purse she'd insisted on buying with his money for her own birthday. Only Camille carried fur year-round. "Your autograph, of course."

Every adult within hearing distance was watching them. Jared hated it. And he hated her for doing it.

He grabbed the paper, ready to sign it just to get her out of here, when he looked at what it was.

"You want me to sign over my *house*? Are you out of your mind? And that's *not* a rhetorical question."

"If you want me to go quietly, you'll sign it." The bitch smiled at him as if she were just another fan.

He was D.O.N.E. with her manipulative bullshit. "Go ahead, Camille. Make a scene. I don't care. You're not getting my house, and as soon as the eviction happens, I'll be the one smiling. So how about you step aside for someone who actually likes me?" He was working very hard to hold on to his temper. There were kids around. They shouldn't see their idol lose it on someone. Even if she did deserve it.

"I've got all night, Jared." Camille crossed her arms and

her smirk got bigger. The red fox bag swung against her hip. "My only plans are to spend the night at home. *My* home."

Jared crinkled the paper into a ball, never taking his eyes from her. "Over my dead body."

"But then you'd have to have put me in your will and I have a feeling you haven't done that." Camille drummed her fingertips on her arm so nonchalantly that he wanted to shake her.

Jesus, he'd never been one for physical violence. He raked a hand through his hair. He wasn't going to start now. Camille wasn't worth it.

"Get out of here, Camille. I don't know what your game is, but I'm not playing it. This piece of paper is worthless." He tossed it onto the table, daring her to take it.

"I have copies, Jared. Did you really think that would make it all go away?"

He wanted *her* to go away. But it wasn't easy to argue with someone who refused to argue, so Jared just crossed his arms to wait her out.

Thankfully, Mac showed up to rescue him once more. She walked up to the table, a smile on her face as if she didn't know who was standing there.

"Excuse me? Is there a problem here?"

She knew. He recognized that tone—the one she reserved for the Renees and Maeves of the world and had used so effectively on his front porch.

Jared sat back. He was going to enjoy this.

"No. There's no problem." Camille didn't even look at Mac when she said it.

Big mistake. Mac didn't like to be ignored.

For the first time, Jared was glad about that.

"Oh, that's good, then. So if you could please step aside? We're trying to move the line along so everyone can get home for dinner. You understand. If you have some personal business with Jared, I'm sure he wouldn't mind waiting until he's met with his *other* fans."

Man, the woman was good. That slight emphasis on

other was a dig so subtle that if it were anyone other than the lying, conniving bitch, they wouldn't see it.

Camille, however, did.

She glared at him. "Oh no. I have no *personal* business with Jared. It's all business. You'll be hearing from my attorney."

She could threaten a lawsuit all she wanted, but he had the deeper pockets and he wasn't afraid to use them to get her out of his life. "Bring it on."

Mac smiled the entire time she thanked Camille then went to the next person in line, bringing him up to Jared.

But Jared could see something simmering below the surface . . . and he wasn't sure he wanted to know what it was. The last person he wanted to discuss Camille with was Mac.

Unfortunately, Mac wasn't on board with that plan. "You lived with that . . . that walking PETA nightmare?" she hissed when the last person left his table and she grabbed the bowl of raffle tickets she'd devised for three lucky winners to win a signed autograph ball.

Besides being a good bouncer, Mac was good for PR, too.

"If it makes you feel better, she's allergic to it. That's as far as her fur fetish can go. She has to put the thing in a plastic bag at home. Ticks her off immensely." Which made him happy as hell. "But, yeah, living with her wasn't one of my more brilliant moves."

Mac set the bowl down, the look of disbelief growing. "Did you just admit that you're not perfect?"

"Of course I'm not perfect, Mac. What gave you the idea that I thought I was?"

"You're arro—um, confidence." Mac slid the bowl to the end of the table and made a big production of gathering up the markers he'd used to sign things—without once looking at him.

"My"—If he weren't already sitting, he would have at that. "You think I'm arrogant?"

"No. Of course not. I mean, you have to be extremely self-confident to do what you do for a living, always being in the public eye, with fans' expectations on your shoulders, always having to step up to the plate—I mean . . . Well, you know. You could crumble under all that pressure if you weren't sure enough of yourself to handle it. Some people could call that arrogance."

She was babbling and it was kind of cute. Mac was embarrassed. He'd never seen her like this. Not even when he'd crushed her young heart with that unforgettably scathing kiss-off he'd delivered all those years ago. Back then, she'd just shut up and backed away.

Jesus, he *was* arrogant. He'd done a number on her that night.

Man, if only he could go back and make it right . . .

Maybe he could.

He stood up, his legs needing a change of position from sitting so long.

"So did you have fun?" Mac made a big production of putting the markers in a cigar box.

"I did. Thanks for suggesting this." He handed her a marker that had rolled away.

"It was nothing."

"It was something, Mac."

She looked up at him then, and Jared didn't even think about what he did next.

He cupped her cheek.

For a few seconds, they stared at each other and Jared could've sworn the rest of the world stopped along with them.

But then Mac took a step back and he reacted just a second too late to keep her from doing so.

"Jared, maybe we should . . ." She tucked the hair that'd fallen from her ponytail back behind her ear. "It's late. We've both had a busy day. We ought to just go home and get some rest."

"I agree, Mac. We should go home."

She swallowed and reached for the cigar box.

He put his hand on hers. "Together, Mac."

Her gaze flew to his. "To . . . Together?"

Oh hell, that hadn't come out right. He wasn't propositioning her for God's sake. "I mean, you should come over and watch the movies with me."

"Oh." She blew out a breath. "Oh. Um . . . that's probably not a good idea."

"Why? Got a hot date?" He hadn't really been teasing the other day when he'd asked her, and he sure as hell wasn't teasing now. He wanted her with him tonight.

She smiled, but it didn't reach her eyes. "Thanks, Jared, but I sweated all day, have goops of melted chocolate chips in my hair, and have licked enough batter off my fingers to make me want an antacid and a pillow. I need to go home."

"So that's a no then?"

Her smile was a little more real at his joke.

But Jared wasn't joking. He had to move slow here. He knew that. Of course she was skittish. He wasn't exactly sure what he was doing either, but what he did know was that he wanted Mac with him on the sofa tonight, even if it was just to watch the movies. Especially when she saw who was in them.

"What if I offered you wine and a pillow to go with the movies? It's not hot and it's not a date, but I found my grandmother's projector and set it up this morning. It still works and I think you'd like to see who's on the film."

"If they're my baby pictures, I'm out." She stacked the raffle bowl on top of the cigar box and tucked them under her arm. "I don't want to sit there while you make comments about me in a diaper."

He laughed. "If there are any of those, I haven't found them." He put a hand on her arm and finally got her to look at him. "But your parents are."

"My . . . parents?"

He nodded. "They're young. Probably not married yet. I haven't watched much, sort of felt like you ought to see them before I do, you know?"

She swallowed a couple of times. Blinked really fast. But it took her a minute or two before she answered him. "Give me a half hour to shower, then I'll be over. Should I bring anything? Cheese? Crackers?"

He didn't let go because he could feel her trembling. "I got it covered, Mac. Just bring yourself. And your pillow if you must."

"It's already there. I left it in Mildred's room."

He didn't know why, but that got to him. Her pillow was in his house. Such an innocuous thing but somehow . . . it wasn't.

You're in a shitload of trouble here, Nolan. You should not *be serving wine on a Saturday night and sitting on the sofa next to a woman who is undoubtedly going to be overly emotional while watching the movies. A woman who'd loved you once.*

Yeah, this was a dangerous move, but one he had to take. Seeing Camille had made him realize that he might have thrown away the best thing that could've ever happened to him and he wasn't going to blow this chance. "Take longer if you like. They're not going anywhere."

"That's because they already did," she whispered. Then, being the Mac he remembered, she straightened her shoulders and put some determination in her smile. "I'll be there in thirty."

Chapter Seventeen

"YOU look like her."

Mac walked into Mildred's parlor, unable to take her eyes from the screen. Jared had stopped the film on her mother's face. She *did* look like her. So much that it was painful.

"Mac? You okay?"

No. God, she missed her parents.

She walked to the nearest piece of furniture—the arm of the sofa. It was as far as her legs would take her.

"Here. Sit down." Jared shifted to the right, giving her room to slide onto the cushion.

"They look so happy." Her parents were cuddled on a wicker chair on the grass just off Mildred's back porch, glasses of what looked like iced tea in their hands, clinking them together, her mother's tiny diamond ring sparkling in the sun.

"They do. From what my grandmother says, they seemed to have been very happy together."

"They were." She cleared her voice. "I don't remember a lot about them because I was so young, but I remember the laughter. My dad would swoop her up in his arms when he came home from work every day. I remember because Mom had just read me a whole bunch of fairy tales and I thought that was how the prince would act. I thought my mom was the luckiest woman in the world." And she'd wanted to be just like her.

Damn, the tears eked out. She quickly dashed them away. Crying solved nothing. They were still gone. And she was no Cinderella.

"It's okay to cry, Mac." Jared reached for her hand.

She let him have it. The emotions were threatening to overwhelm her and she needed something to hold on to.

"Do you want me to turn it off?"

Yes. "No." She shook her head to clear that traitorous *yes* out of it. "No. I've never seen these before."

Gran walked out next, looking so young Mac's mouth dropped. "She looks so pretty."

"Good genes run in your family." He squeezed her hand, making her smile.

Gran waved to the camera, then turned around and circled her arm to someone inside.

Mac's grandfather walked out, his walker leading the way.

Mac's breath caught. "Wow, I didn't realize how bad he was. This might be right at the end." Which just broke her heart all the more. Everyone was so happy, the drinks raised, hugs all around, a neighborly celebration, and it would all be so different all too soon. "God, life can change in an instant, you know? Look at them. They have no idea what's going to happen—"

Her voice disappeared. She couldn't watch any more knowing that they'd be gone in a few short years, yet not wanting to miss a moment of this precious precious gift.

She let go of Jared's hand and reached for the glass of wine he had waiting for her, wanting the relaxation it offered. "Thank you for insisting I see these."

"I didn't insist. I offered."

She raised her eyebrows. "Potato, pot*ah*to."

He picked up his glass of wine. "At least it got you here."

She didn't want to contemplate why he thought that was a good thing; for years, he'd been trying to get rid of her.

"Oh, look. There's your dad." Mac pointed to the screen, glad to have someone else to focus on besides her parents.

A woman walked into the frame and slipped her hand into Mr. Nolan's.

"And that's *not* my mom."

"Who is she?"

Jared took a gulp of his wine. "Not sure. But Dad certainly knows who she is."

Mr. Nolan kissed the woman then, and when they pulled apart, they were laughing as the woman held up her left hand.

"Holy shit. They're engaged, too." Jared leaned forward. "What year is this?"

Mac did some quick calculations.

"That's not possible."

She ran the numbers. "No, actually, it is. If my grandfather was still alive at this point, which we clearly see that he is, that's when my parents got engaged because they got married when he went into the hospital. They had the ceremony in the hospital chapel so he could walk her down the aisle. I'm sure of it. Gran's told me a thousand times about it. He died less than a week later."

"But that would be about seven months before I was born."

They looked at the screen again.

"Um . . ."

"Yeah." Jared fell back against the sofa. "No wonder my mom pulls him around by the nose hairs. He got her pregnant and then asked someone else to marry him."

"But he obviously married your mom."

"But at what cost?" Jared exhaled. "So many things are making sense now. He felt guilty and she never let him forget it. Jesus." He ran his hand through his hair again. "No wonder they've been miserable all these years."

On screen, Mildred walked out of the house carrying another round of drinks, and she had something draped over her arm. She set the drinks down then handed the thing to her son, Jared's father.

He held it up in front of him, a big smile on his face.

"Holy shit! Are you kidding me?" Jared almost jumped out of his seat.

Mr. Nolan was holding a baseball jersey. With NOLAN across the back.

"They didn't make vanity jerseys back then, did they?" Mac asked.

"Hell no." Jared's eyes were glued to the screen and the very visible team logo. "That's real. And it's his."

"So your dad played professional baseball?"

Jared looked at her then, his expression . . . bleak? Confused? Something.

"I have no idea. He never told me. All those years when he was showing me how to hold the bat, how to swing, how to catch . . . He never said a thing."

"Why?"

"That's the question, isn't it?"

"You need to talk to your parents."

"For what? I don't know what I'd say to them. Hell, I don't even *know* them. The pregnancy thing and then him not telling me he played ball . . . How would I even begin that conversation?" He reached for the iPad on the table beside the sofa and brought up the search engine, then typed in his dad's name.

Nothing came up no matter how many different search words they tried.

"You're going to have to ask them."

"What am I supposed to say: Why'd you lie to me my whole life?"

"They didn't lie; they just left a few things out."

"A few *big* things. Are you defending them?"

"Well, no, but you don't know the circumstances. You can't get mad until you know. And to do that you're going to have to ask them. Or you could always ask your grandmother."

"Grandma." Jared shook his head. "She's known all along. She never said anything." Jared sat forward again, resting one hand on his knee, the other scrubbing his chin. "Why didn't anyone say anything? What's the big secret?"

She rubbed his shoulder. The guy was hurting, and even though she ought to stay away from him in the emotional state they were both in, she had to give him some comfort. He looked so lost. "I think *you* were the secret. Remember, out of wedlock pregnancies still weren't acceptable when we were born."

He turned to face her. "Are you kidding me? It was the age of sex and drugs and rock-n-roll. Free love and weed. No one looked twice at out-of-wedlock pregnancies."

"Obviously some people did or we wouldn't be having this discussion. Didn't you ever do that math with your birthday and your parents' wedding day?"

"I never thought about it."

"Because your parents would never do that, right?"

"Uh . . . yeah. I guess. I mean, it's not something that crosses a teenage boy's mind when he's trying to score both on the field and off."

Mac winced. "Yet you turned me down flat out."

His hand dropped to his lap.

Crap. She hadn't meant to say that out loud.

"I'm sorry, Mac."

"For what? Not using me? That's not something you should be sorry for."

"No." He put his hand on her knee. "I'm sorry for how little I regarded your feelings. I was selfish and I hurt you. I'm sorry."

She shrugged, wanting to make it not seem like a big deal, but that seventeen-year-old inside of her wanted to shout for joy. He finally saw her. Finally recognized her feelings. That's all she'd wanted back then, to know that he knew she cared. Well, no, actually she would've liked if *he'd* cared back, but the mocking and teasing that'd come along with him knowing about her crush and not realizing its significance to her . . . While it'd been a lot to ask of him, this was, finally, the validation she'd wanted.

"It's okay, Jared. It's in the past." She patted his hand and for the few seconds that he looked at her, she had to wonder if it *was* in the past.

Thankfully, Jared cleared his throat and removed his hand from beneath hers. "Well, like I said, I'm sorry."

"Apology accepted." Mac leaned back into the cushion and focused on the rest of the film. There was a lot of hugging, a lot of kissing, smiles all around. Everyone had seemed so happy. If they'd only known . . .

Thank God they'd been happy. Her memories of her childhood with her parents were vague, but she remembered laughter. Remembered hugs. Remembered smiles. Remembered snippets of getting tossed in the air by their dad, of loving hugs from her mom—who always smelled like chocolate chip cookies. No surprise that those were her favorites and why she liked to share them with the kids. That part of her childhood had been happy and those memories would be with her forever. Her parents' love would be with her forever.

Jared, on the other hand . . .

What a shock. First, to see his father obviously in love with someone else, then to find out about his parentage . . .

For all the money the Nolans had, she and her brothers had been far richer.

She looked at Jared with new eyes. Saw him not as some god she could never hope to be worthy of, but as a man. With wants and needs and failings and triumphs like the rest of them.

And in that moment, she took him off the pedestal and put him squarely on the sofa next to her.

As a mere mortal, he wasn't half bad. Question was, how did he see her?

Chapter Eighteen

MAC was itching to get back to Jared's house Monday morning.

She caught a glimpse of herself in the rearview mirror as she pulled into his driveway, Bryan's Maserati eating up the road a lot quicker than her old truck. Yes, being excited to be there sounded strange, and with the emotions she'd had tied up in Jared all these years with no reciprocity, it was foolish to want to go back to the scene of the crime, as it were. But after Saturday night's movie fest, she had more insight into him. More insight into herself. She'd made him into Prince Charming and he wasn't. He was a man with the same baggage and needs she had. While it sounded good in theory, no one really wanted to be worshipped as an ideal; they wanted to be loved for who they were.

But that wasn't why she wanted to go back. She wasn't naïve enough to think one night of bonding over home movies would suddenly make him fall in love with her—and she needed to see the real Jared, not her idealized version, to know if she even wanted him to.

But that, too, wasn't why she wanted to get here. She'd been thinking about those movies all weekend, had even mentioned them to Bryan when she'd called him about his impromptu press conference on Saturday, and she remembered that the wicker chair her parents had been sitting in in the film was still on Mildred's back porch. She'd been obsessing ever since. It made no sense, but she wanted that chair.

She let herself in, not sure if Jared was awake or not, and made her way past the kitten enclosure, through the kitchen and mudroom, then out to the porch.

It was there. With the same cushion. The weather had worn a lot of the stitching away and mice had cannibalized the stuffing, but it was still recognizable.

"Mac?" Jared poked his head out the back door, his hair mussed and his T-shirt clinging to some damp skin. "You okay?" He looked behind her. "That's the chair."

She nodded, trying not to notice that he'd been working out. "Can I have it? I'll buy it from your grandmother."

"She's not going to take money from you. Matter of fact, she was pretty adamant that she's going to pay you for cleaning the house anyway, so how about we let the chair be part of your payment?"

"Not part. All. I'm not taking your grandmother's money. This chair is more than enough."

He limped out onto the porch without his crutches. "Good luck getting her to agree to that. And you know, you're never going to get ahead in business if you keep taking garbage for payment."

"One woman's trash is another woman's treasure."

"Good point." Jared walked around her and lifted the chair from the debris that had collected around it. Tarps, old beach towels, a couple of folded lawn chairs. "I think this was my grandmother's to-be-tossed pile. What do you say about us cleaning this corner up for good?"

"Sounds like a plan."

Mac dragged a couple of trash cans around for Jared to dump the debris into, her walking skills at the moment being better than his. "So did you find the ring over the weekend?"

He shook his head. "I've been through two-thirds of that attic and haven't found it. I'm really worried we won't. Grandma will be heartbroken."

"We'll find it. It's not like it grew legs and walked out on its own."

They both stopped what they were doing and looked at each other.

"You don't think—"

"She wouldn't really—"

"No. Of course not. What would be the point?"

"Right. She wouldn't be that devious. Not about something so important to her."

Mac wasn't so sure about that. *Jared* was that important to her and Mildred was friends with Gran. She wouldn't put it past the two of them to have concocted this scenario just to force her and Jared together.

And she wasn't sure how she felt about that.

"Want some help refinishing the chair?" Jared lifted the cushion. "I don't think you're going to be able to save this, but the rattan looks salvageable. A couple weaves in spots and some paint will make it look as good as new."

"You know how to refinish a chair?"

"Hey, just because I throw knuckleballs doesn't mean I'm a knucklehead. I've done some home repair in my time. I know my way around a hammer."

"I'm impressed."

"Hammer usage impresses you, but million-dollar contracts don't?"

She shrugged and took the cushion from him to toss into the can. "One directly affects my life, the other doesn't. So wield your hammer this way, Mr. Nolan, and let's get the nails out of this railing. They may have held up strands of lights for years, but now they're just tetanus fodder."

They made it through all the stuff on the porch and into the mudroom, a well-oiled machine of tossing, organizing, and cleaning, with Jared getting the high parts and Mac tackling the stuff low to the floor, crossing off another item from the To-Do list and bringing their daily interaction closer to an end.

Mac wasn't as gung ho for it to end as she'd been when she'd started.

"You still owe me another game of gin rummy," Jared said, rubbing the towel in his hair from the shower he'd taken while she'd made lunch.

She set the sandwich plates on the table. "Isn't Dave coming today?"

"Are you chicken?" He grabbed two glasses from the cabinet and headed to the fridge for some juice.

"Chicken? Me? I'm the one who took on three Manley men and beat them at their own game. I'm not afraid of anything."

He opened the fridge door. "You're going to have to show me how you did that, Mac. It couldn't have been luck."

"What about skill? Why can't I play poker as well as they do?"

He grabbed the bottle of grapefruit juice. "You can; I just don't think you did."

"Are you calling me a cheater?"

"No." He poured their drinks. "You're too honorable for that. I'm calling you an opportunist. I think you found an advantage and used it."

"You're giving me a lot of credit, Jared."

He handed her a glass, tipping it—if she wasn't mistaken—in salute. "Actually, Mac, I don't think I've ever given you enough."

"GIN." Mac laid down her hand. "That's two for me and how many for you?"

"None." Jared gathered their discarded hands and tapped them on the table. "You are one lucky woman."

"I prefer to think of it as talented." She handed him the rest of the deck, then picked up their plates. "After all, it's not as if I—"

A face appeared at the window above the kitchen sink.

A female face.

Who perked up the minute Jared looked over.

Then the woman waved.

Mac arched an eyebrow at Jared. "Friend of yours?"

He kept his smile on, but said out of the corner of his mouth, "I was hoping she was one of yours."

"Nope. My friends don't go skulking around people's homes in the middle of the day. My friends actually use the front door. Good thing you took a shower before lunch. From the looks of that perfect hair and all that makeup, this one probably wouldn't appreciate you all grungy."

Mac, however, did. Jared looked good all hot and sweaty. Too good. It'd sent her right back down the *what-if* road and if Miss Perfect At The Window hadn't shown up, she might have travelled down it again. Nothing like a dose of reality to put her *what-if*s in perspective. She was letting Saturday night's movies take on too much significance.

As evidenced by the fact that Jared got to his feet to go speak with the woman. "Guess I should see what she wants."

As if they all didn't know . . .

Jared headed out back and Mac made quick work of their dishes. So much for the whole "future" speculation. Her future consisted of finishing this job, getting out of here, and moving on with her life. If Jared had even been the remotest bit interested he wouldn't have jumped up to check out their latest visitor.

The front door rang. Geez, it was Grand Central around here. How was she supposed to get anything accomplished if she had to keep playing butler?

She yanked open the front door all set to give a piece of her mind to—"Dave. Hi."

Dave cocked his head. "You were expecting someone else?"

Mac pointed to the table by the door. A few more offerings at the altar this morning, and she'd left them right where they were. Maybe if women saw that Jared wasn't taking them—and how many others were offering—it might deter them. "You might say that."

"Ah. Anyone camped out yet?"

"No tents yet, but he's out back talking to one who bypassed the front door. I don't get it. How women can be so brazen. It's not as if they even know him. Just because he's an athlete."

"You don't see him that way, do you?"

"Jared? I've known him my whole life. He and my brothers are friends. I know every one of his bad habits, so no, to me he's just Jared. Annoying boy from the block." She was crossing her fingers behind her back.

"That's good to know." Dave put his hand on her arm. "Because I was wondering if you'd like to have dinner with me."

Her first thought was *No.* So was her second. Her third was *What would Jared think?*

Which made her answer be, "That would be nice. Thank you."

YOU trying to kill me, Dave?" Jared asked with a grin as he put down the exercise band and mopped the sweat off his face with a hand towel. Dave knew how to push him and Jared needed the push. Playing ball with the kids the other day only reinforced his need to get back to the game, and the quicker he rehabbed himself, the sooner that'd be. He'd let himself get sidetracked by Mac and the ring and the kittens. But he was back to fighting form and he wanted to put his entire workout regimen back together to get him where he needed to be.

"Wimp."

"Sadist."

Dave tossed a ball at his face.

Jared caught it before it could do some damage.

"Good. Your reflexes are fine. Good eye-hand coordination and motor skills. You keep this up, you'll be back before the season ends."

Jared tossed the ball and the band into the laundry basket with the other instruments of torture. "I plan on it."

Mac appeared in the doorway then. "I'm leaving for the day. See you tomorrow."

"Okay. Do you want me to put the chair in the car?"

"Bryan's Maserati? I doubt it's going to fit and if I scuff up his interior, he'll have my head. No, I'll just leave it here until I can get the van from Liam."

She looked at Dave and smiled.

Jared wanted to punch him. That smile was *his*—

Whoa. What the hell was that? Dave was his friend.

"What time tomorrow, Dave? I can be ready by six."

"Six it is. I'll pick you up then."

Pick her up? What?

Then Mac gave Dave her address.

Oh.

Oh hell.

Oh shit.

Oh *no*.

Dave apparently *wasn't* his friend.

Jared waited until the front door closed behind Mac and she'd walked off the porch before he let the smile slide off his face. "What the fuck, Dave? You're taking Mac on a date?"

"Whoa, Jare." Dave held up his hands. "Chill out. I thought you said you weren't interested?"

"I'm not."

Much.

Liar.

"So then what's the big deal? I think she's pretty, she has a great personality, and she's single. Why can't I go out with her?"

"Because . . ." Jared's reason sputtered out. Yeah, why couldn't Dave take her out? It wasn't as if Jared had any proprietary hold on her. Just because he'd suddenly opened his eyes to Mac the woman didn't mean she'd necessarily wanted him to. Not after how he'd treated her all those years. And then kissing her like that . . .

God, he never should have done that. They'd made baby steps with the movies and with the attic, but she no longer showed any signs of the puppy love she'd once had. Maybe it was over. Maybe they'd moved beyond her crush and could just be friends.

He didn't want to be just friends.

"Jare? You okay?" Dave stood and grabbed his gym bag. "If you really don't want me to go out with her, I can cancel I guess."

He really *didn't* want Dave to go out with her. But it wasn't his call to make. Until he actually made a move—and Mac accepted it—he had no claim on her whatsoever.

And maybe Mac was into Dave. She had, after all, said yes.

"No." He shook his head more to clear the . . . sadness that'd invaded it. "No. Go ahead. Have a nice time."

"You're sure?"

"You don't need my permission. If Mac said yes, then she's interested, so go. Have a good time. Just not too good."

"Not too good? What are you, her father? What's next? Going to ask me my intentions?"

Jared wasn't feeling like her father. And he wasn't feeling like her friend. Or Dave's either for that matter, regardless of the guy's intentions.

He was feeling like a caveman. Wanted to toss her over his shoulder, parade her around the town so everyone would know she was his, then bring her back here, carry her up those stairs, and toss her onto the middle of his bed where they'd spend the next week ordering Chinese takeout.

"Just treat her nice. Bring her roses. Take her someplace elegant, like Sanders' maybe. But know that her brothers are my friends, Dave. I've known her my whole life. Hurt her and you have to answer to me."

"I dunno, Jare. For someone who says he's not interested, you seem an awful lot like you are." Dave hiked the gym bag's strap onto his shoulder and headed toward the door. "It's just dinner. I'll let you know how it goes."

Jared stayed put, gripping the wooden knob on the sofa's armrest like a lifeline. Which it was: Dave's, because Jared wouldn't mind ripping the guy's face off right about now. "Good luck."

Dave stopped in the doorway. "You saying that to me . . . or to yourself?"

Chapter Nineteen

JARED heard Mac on the stairs when he got up the next morning, and he quickly threw on a pair of shorts before meeting her in the hall.

"You're here early."

She looked startled. "I'm, uh, sorry. I was trying to get in here quietly. I wanted to get done early so I can, uh . . ."

"Get ready for your date with Dave?" He tried to keep the sarcasm out of his voice.

"Yes."

"You won't need much time. Dave will be thrilled even if you show up looking like you do now." God knew he would be. The soft green shirt brought out the color of her eyes, all framed in sooty lashes that matched her silky hair, those figure-hugging pants perfect for whetting a man's appetite, and yeah, he might just be that man.

Damn it.

"Give me a minute to toss on a shirt and brush my teeth, and I'll be up to join you."

"Okay. No problem."

Mac seemed a little distracted. Jared put it down to the date with Dave. Was she really looking forward to it?

Well, of course she was. That was a stupid question. Mac wasn't the type to go out with a guy simply for a free meal.

Not like Camille.

Jared grabbed a blue T-shirt and pulled it on, then shoved his feet into a pair of rubber-soled slippers. The doc told him he could put weight on his leg now, so these were safe. Using one crutch, he made it up the steps.

Mac was bent over a large box in the corner, pulling out a bunch of blankets.

"Digging for gold?" he asked her.

Mac's head shot up, her ponytail sailing over her crown. "Do you know what's in here?"

"Blankets?"

"Not just any blankets. These are quilts." She held an all-white one up that had a pair of intersecting rings stitched in the middle. "Wedding quilts. And look. They have all of our names on them. This is mine." She showed him the corner with a very fancy MAM in it. "Here's yours."

His, too, was white and matched hers. Which was . . . interesting.

He felt a little better when she said, "And there's one for Sean, Liam, and Bryan, as well." A pale blue, pale green, and pale yellow. "How sweet is it that your grandmother made them for me and my brothers?"

"You know Grandma." And so did he. He knew exactly why his and Mac's matched and he wouldn't be surprised if Mrs. Manley had helped. The grandmothers had obviously been planning to get him and Mac together for a long time. Too bad neither of them had seen a Dave coming along.

Too bad *he* hadn't seen a Dave coming along . . . "I guess we should each take ours. That'll help clean out the attic." Not that he'd be using his anytime soon. After Camille, marriage was the furthest thing from his mind. Maybe he'd use it for the kittens to sleep on.

"We will not." Mac spread one out and started to fold it.

"These are wedding gifts. They need to stay right here until they're needed."

"That'll be kind of tough when we sell the place."

"Oh. Right." She stopped folding and scrunched her lips. "We're going to have to get them to your grandmother without her knowing we've seen them."

"Come on, Mac. Of course she's going to know. She sent us up here to look for her ring." The one he was coming to suspect wouldn't be found. "She told us to go through every box in the place. Do you really think she's not going to know"—or expect—"that we found them?"

If he knew Grandma, he was guessing she'd moved them up here just *so* they'd find them. No one kept heirloom quilts in a cardboard box in an attic. Mice would turn them into balls of fluff in no time.

"I guess you're right. So what should we do with them?"

"I say we take them to her. Who knows, maybe your date with Dave will turn into something more and you can take it home with you." He plastered a smile on his face, but really wasn't feeling it.

Mac got very interested in folding Liam's quilt back into the bottom of the box. "Uh, yeah. Who knows?"

He hadn't expected her to *agree* with him. "I mean, yeah. Dave's a good guy. You could do a lot worse."

Eyebrows arched, she glanced at him. "*That's* your endorsement of your friend? I'd love to hear what you say about Liam."

"What do you want me to say, Mac? That Dave's a great guy and you should jump his bones?"

Dude, never ask a question you don't want to know the answer to.

"If that's how you feel, then yes, you should."

Case in point.

"Fine. Then go ahead. Sleep with him. See if I care."

Seriously? Are you nuts?

"Fine. Maybe I will."

"Fine. Do that."

"Fine."

They stood there glaring at each other, and Jared could feel his conscience strumming its metaphorical fingers along his spine.

What had he just done? Given her carte blanche to sleep with one of his best friends? Apparently he *was* nuts. "I need to go check on the kittens."

"Fine. You do that."

"I will." He spun around—damn, shouldn't have used his bad leg for that—and headed to the stairs before he said something else he'd regret.

Mac watched Jared leave. What just happened? One minute they'd been talking about wedding quilts and the next, Jared was pimping her out to Dave.

Good lord, the man could drive someone insane.

Well it wasn't going to be her. She was having dinner tonight with a nice, normal man who didn't have any reason not to like her. And if she needed any more proof that Jared wasn't the god she'd thought he was, she'd just gotten it. Nope, her future was definitely not going to include Jared Nolan.

JARED was going stir crazy.

After today's nightmare, he'd stayed with the kittens for the better part of an hour, leaving Mac up in the attic to sort through things he ought to be sorting through, then when he'd gone up, she'd come down to do a thorough cleaning of the parlor, which had then segued into another round of kitten bathing, which they'd done very stiltedly and very silently, until it was more than apparent she couldn't wait to get out of there.

He hadn't blamed her.

He'd been an ass. Of course, this great revelation didn't come to him until she'd been gone not three minutes and he realized he ought to apologize, not send her off on a date with a guy who could actually be good for her, leaving him to sit here and stew about whether or not she was going to sleep with that guy.

And how fucked up was it that he'd even say that to her? Mac wasn't that kind of girl. Of course she wouldn't sleep with Dave on the first date.

Except he'd all but dared her to and he knew how Mac took dares.

He shoved himself off the sofa and raked his hands through his hair. He couldn't sit around here and imagine what was happening on their date. Maybe he should call Renee or Sherisse or Juliette . . . Hell, maybe he should call all three. Get his mind off Mac and see if there was someone out there for him.

He picked up the phone and one of the cards in the basket beside it and dialed the first three digits.

What was he doing? This would start a whole other round of problems he didn't want to deal with. He wasn't interested in them and it would be wrong to lead them on. He didn't need the extra baggage in his life and if he could get over himself, he'd see that.

Jesus. He'd sent Dave and Mac to Sanders'. Of all places. He hated that place; it held too many frustrating memories of sitting there, all trussed up in a suit and tie, having to mind his manners and act like the "perfect little man" while everyone else he'd known was home ripping through piles of wrapping paper or eating homemade turkey and stuffing and mashed potatoes in their sweats and playing video games.

He'd suggested it because he wanted Dave to fail.

But the problem was, Sanders' didn't hold the same memories for Dave and Mac that it held for him, so they might actually have a *nice* time. That *he'd* sent them on.

Damn. He didn't want Mac to like Dave. Not like that.

Which was completely selfish of him.

He picked up his phone and scrolled through his contacts. He needed to get out. There were a few guys from the old neighborhood still around. He'd try one of them because he wasn't about to text Liam. He didn't want to be around any of the Manleys tonight—not if he couldn't be around the one he wanted.

YOU look amazing." Dave stood on her front stoop with a sweet smile and a sweet-smelling bouquet of flowers. "Here. These are for you."

"Wow. I didn't know guys still did this."

"I heard you like roses."

"You did? From whom?" Actually, she liked daisies.

"Jared."

Well that was odd. Jared had given her very first flower to her and it'd been a daisy. She'd skinned her knee and was trying not to cry, then Jared had stuck the daisy under her nose and the tears had dried up. She had a feeling that was when her *what-if*s had started.

"Thank you for these. It was really nice of you. Let me put them in water and then we can go."

He followed her back to the kitchen. "Nice place."

She looked over her shoulder. "Please. It's my grandmother's 1950s throwback that needs a lot of work. She moved into the same place where Jared's grandmother lives, so I'm slowly but surely updating it. Going to take a while, though, with my business."

"Yeah, being self-employed means you're working all the time."

"I hear you, but it beats working for someone else."

She cut the stems an inch, stuck the roses in a vase of ice water, added some sugar, then cleaned up the mess, and brushed off her hands. "Okay, I'm ready. Where are we going?"

"I thought Sanders' would be nice."

Sanders' was the place Jared had spent his holidays.

Damn it, she didn't want to think about Jared tonight. Tonight was about Dave and moving forward with her life.

"I've heard it's wonderful." And she'd make sure it was.

"Jared suggested it. Said we'd like it."

So much for that.

Dave held both the front door and the car door for her, his Prince Charming meter going up quite nicely. Flowers, upscale restaurant, gentlemanly manners . . .

The only thing was, he kept talking about Jared. She heard about the first time they'd met, how they started hanging out, some of the stories from games on the road when Dave had been the team PT . . . It was almost as if Dave was afraid to talk about anything else in case they found out they didn't have anything in common. If a relationship between them was going to happen, they couldn't count on Jared to keep them together. Especially when she was desperately trying *not* to think about the guy. She wanted to think about Dave.

"Dave, why are you bringing up Jared so much? Surely we can find something else to talk about besides him."

Dave shrugged. "He's our common denominator, and since we both care about him, I figured there's no need to *not* talk about him. Is there?"

She got stuck on the caring about him part. Was she that obvious?

"Well, no, but I've heard more about him than I have about you. Do you have any siblings, for example? I know Jared's an only child." And the reason that was suddenly came to her. Growing up, she'd wondered if his parents couldn't have more children; now she wondered if they'd never tried.

"I'm one of three. Middle kid. Only boy. Jared's like the brother I never had."

And they were back to Jared. "How old are your sisters?"

She managed to keep him off the Jared track for the next ten minutes or so while she learned about his family, where he grew up, and the camping trips his parents had taken them on in the pop-up trailer every weekend in the summer for about five years—stories that actually got a pang of envy from her. Gran hadn't been able to afford vacations. A trip to the zoo or the free bible camps had been it for her and her brothers. She'd never been to the beach until one of her friends had invited her for a week in high school with her family.

"We loved going to the chalk mines down South. They had these huge mounds of chalk—well, gypsum—that we loved to climb. We'd get brown paper bags from supermarkets and fill them with the stuff and bring it home. My sisters were the hopscotch queens of the neighborhood. The game boards, or whatever you call the chalk drawings, went along the entire block. I can't tell you how many sprained ankles there were when people kept trying to hop the entire thing."

"Too bad you didn't know then what you were going to do with your life. Just think how much fun you could've had wrapping all those girls' ankles."

"Oh I didn't do so bad even without the wrappings."

Yeah, she could see that. He was good-looking, he was smart, he was funny, and he knew how to hold a conversation. And how to treat a woman. He'd surreptitiously signaled the waiter when her water was getting low, he'd held out her chair, deferred to her for ordering first, offered her some of his shrimp cocktail appetizer . . .

It'd been a long time since she'd been out on a date. Hell, it'd been a long time since she'd had a free night to even consider doing something other than paperwork or prospecting for new clients, both of which she should be doing tonight.

But she wasn't. She was here. Trying to make Dave into the guy she couldn't stop thinking about because putting Jared in that role hadn't worked so well. Even after watching movies together Saturday night, he'd spent twenty minutes talking to Ms. Face-In-The-Window yesterday. Mac didn't need to be clubbed over the head to get it.

"So Jared tells me you guys have been friends your whole lives."

"He actually said that?"

"Yeah, why?"

Mac shrugged, trying to go with the not-so-embarrassing version of their history. "He's friends with my older brothers. I was that tagalong little sister everyone had to take care of. He, needless to say, wasn't thrilled having me around."

"Shame on him. I bet you were cute." Dave picked up the wine bottle and offered her more.

She chuckled as she waved the bottle away. Yes, Dave was definitely charming, but wine on a date wasn't always the smartest move. "I'm sure it got old. After all, he didn't have a sister. He never had to deal with having to take care of someone else. My brothers were used to it."

"Maybe he was jealous."

"Jealous?"

"Think about it. He's got all his parents' expectations about sports, they even hired a trainer for him and built an expensive batting cage in his yard, but the few hours of freedom and play time that he had, he had to spend it with his buddies' little sister. To your brothers, it was just another day hanging out, but to him, his opportunity was hijacked. By you."

"But that'd make him angry, not jealous."

"Unless he'd wanted a little sister. Or liked you."

She sputtered on her water. "It's a nice thought, but no, that definitely wasn't the case for Jared and me." Jared had liked her? Hardly.

"Oh, I don't know, Mac. I was with him through the mess with Camille. From the beginning of the relationship to the rotten end. And I have to say, I've never heard as much about Camille's childhood as I have about yours over the past two days."

"Jared was talking about me?" Now she was completely confused.

Dave reached for her hand. "Oh, I might have asked him some questions. Call me curious."

That got a smile out of her. She wasn't feeling the same spark with Dave that she felt with Jared, but maybe that would change when he kissed her.

IT didn't.

Mac stood on her front stoop, very aware that they were standing there, and that Dave's arms were around her and his lips were on hers, with his head tilted to the right so their noses brushed but didn't bash into each other, his breath warm and wine-scented against her cheek, a few inches taller than she was, with broad shoulders and strong hands that knew how to hold her just right and she felt . . .

Nothing.

Oh, it was pleasant, but the fact that she could hear the crickets and regret that her porch light was on, and know exactly how his nose brushed hers, and how she was standing, and how he was standing, and a whole bunch of other details bummed her out to no end.

When Jared had kissed her, she hadn't been aware of what day it was, let alone where they'd been standing and how his head was angled, because she hadn't been *able* to think. She'd been one big mass of feeling and now . . . she just wasn't.

Dave cupped her cheek as he pulled away, his eyes on hers. "Guess that says it all, huh?"

"What?"

He ran his forefinger down her nose with a little tap at the end. "Thanks for spending time with me tonight, Mac. I've really enjoyed it." He stepped back.

"I had a good time, too, Dave."

He smiled. "But you'd have a better time with someone else."

"That's not—"

He put a finger on her lips. "Don't." He took his finger away. "Don't lie to yourself, Mac. And don't lie to Jared. He's a good guy. He deserves a good woman." He ran his hand down her arm and squeezed her hand. "He deserves you. And I hope he's smart enough to realize it."

Chapter Twenty

"HEY, Jared. This was on your front door."

Mac handed him an envelope when she breezed into his kitchen the next morning looking way too happy for Jared's peace of mind. Did that mean her date had gone well? And *how* well?

She set another dropped-off tray of sweets onto the countertop. "Looks like an invitation."

Was it wrong that his first thought was to ask her to go with him?

"Thanks." He took it from her, being careful not to touch her.

He'd tried to ignore the visions of her and Dave all night with the numerous beers he and the old high school crowd had consumed, getting home late enough that he'd had to deal with another round of kitten cleanup, which woke the little buggers up enough to need to be fed, so he'd had about four hours of sleep and his body hurt like hell from moving a ton of boxes around in the attic yesterday. Then, to see her all perky and happy . . .

He picked up the invitation, knowing before he opened it what it was. He'd received a lot of these over the years.

THE HONOR OF YOUR PRESENCE IS REQUESTED
AT THE DEDICATION OF THE COMMUNITY CENTER POOL
AS OUR HONORED GUEST ON THE PODIUM
AND FOR THE RIBBON-CUTTING CEREMONY.

"So I'm guessing from the look on your face an old girlfriend is getting married and invited you to the wedding." Mac had that smirk that used to bug him but now just made her look adorable.

Not helping . . .

"It's an invitation for a ribbon-cutting ceremony at the community center pool this weekend. They want me on the podium, which means I'll have to come up with a speech, and they'll probably give me a key to the place."

"And that's a bad thing?" She cocked her head and her ponytail fell over her shoulder.

For a second he remembered what her hair had looked like out of the ponytail. In the next second, he was wondering if Dave knew what it looked like.

He probably did. Mac wouldn't wear a ponytail on a date.

"You should wear it like that."

"Excuse me?"

Damn. Not what he meant to say. He shouldn't have had those last couple of beers. And he should have gone to bed earlier. "I, uh, mean, you wouldn't understand. I'm not going."

"You have that right, I guess, but after Saturday, why wouldn't you? People know you're out and about, plus you're a hometown hero. Of course they'd want to honor you. How is that a bad thing?"

"Like this?" He shook his crutches. "It's a pity vote. They couldn't get anyone else because we're in season. No one's available. So they ask the injured guy."

"And you say *I* have a chip on my shoulder? Geez, Jared, maybe they're asking you because you're actually in town for once. No one opens a community center pool in the middle of winter when *you're* available, so the fact that you're actually here is a perfectly good reason to ask you to do this. And they're *honoring* you. It shouldn't be a chore. I don't get why you'd turn them down. Seems like a good way to make a bad impression."

Well when she put it like that . . . "Fine. I guess I'll do it."

"Good. I didn't want to have to go to your grandmother."

"You wouldn't."

She raised the invite. "Don't bet on it. I actually know people on the community center's board."

He studied her. He wasn't used to a Mac who didn't hero-worship him, and even though that'd gotten old back in the day, he would've bet that he'd like one who told him off even less.

That was a bet he would've lost.

He liked that she came back at him. Called him on stuff. That she put him in his place and wasn't bowled over by his profession or his celebrity or his bank account.

He wasn't so thrilled that she'd gone to dinner with his friend, however. "But you have to go with me."

"What? Why? No one wants to see me."

He did.

There. No hiding from that. He wanted Mac with him. If he had to face the pity stares, he wanted someone in his corner who definitely didn't pity him.

Or maybe you want her to go with you just because you want her with you.

"Think of the publicity. You can wear your uniform and hang out beside me—"

"As your *date?*"

Hell yes. "You want publicity for the business? What better way to get it? They'll definitely put me on the air."

"I thought you didn't want me to use you for publicity purposes?"

"Let's call it a mutually beneficial usury."

"But what do you get out of having me there?"

"Protection." He pointed to the latest stack of desserts the neighbors had left this morning. "And think of the press coverage."

"When is it?"

"Saturday at two."

"Will you wear a Manley Maids shirt? I might as well get as much publicity as possible."

"Like what you're wearing?"

She nodded.

"Does it come in any color other than pistachio?"

"It's not pistachio. It's green."

"Pistachio *is* green."

"But not this shade."

"Then what would you call it?"

"Mint."

"Like that's so much better. I'll walk around in a *mint* golf shirt. Bad enough this injury shreds my masculinity, now you're throwing a mint-colored maid's uniform in as part of the deal."

She crossed her arms.

He really wished she wouldn't do that.

"Trust me, Jared, your masculinity is perfectly safe."

His brain went right to his . . . well, *other* brain at that comment. She saw him as masculine. That was a start. But where did his masculinity fall in comparison to Dave's masculinity?

And when had he ever questioned *that*?

Jared shook his head. He needed coffee and lots of it. Never should he face Mac hungover. Especially after she'd been out on a date.

"Still . . . you might want to revamp the uniforms, Mac. At least for the guys. I can't see your brothers in that getup."

"Maybe you should stop by one of their job sites because they are perfectly fine wearing these."

"Then at least give them jeans. Maybe blue instead of green for the shirt?"

"You want to tell our grandmothers that you don't like what they came up with? You're a far braver person than I."

Hell. He was going to wear the green shirt.

MAC mentally patted herself on the back as she closed the French doors to the study. She'd made it through their interaction without doing anything stupid, given that

Dave's comment about Jared deserving a good woman like her had been mulling about in her head all night.

It was nice that Dave thought so, but Jared had had his chance and done nothing. Matter of fact, he'd actually encouraged her to go out with his friend. Couldn't say it any louder than that unless he flat out told her to her face that he wasn't interested. Which he kind of had when she overheard him talking to Dave.

So she'd shoved Dave's comment out of her head, focused on what she was here to do, and made it through their morning hellos. Now she was just going to clean the study, then join Jared in the attic to look for the ring. She'd considered letting him go ring hunting solo, but they couldn't put the house up for sale until it was found.

"Mac, have you see Moe?" Jared opened the study door with three of the kittens in his arms.

"I didn't know it was my turn to watch them." Okay, so maybe she had a bit of an attitude with him. Sue her. A woman could only take so much and she'd had more than her fair share with Jared.

Actually, Dave had it wrong. Jared *didn't* deserve a woman like her and thankfully the guy hadn't done something when he could have.

"Damn." He hiked the kittens a bit higher. "Last I looked, they were all in the play yard, but when I went to change the litter just now, she was gone."

That wasn't good. These guys were babies. They still needed someone to take care of them. Couldn't have them wandering off on their own yet as the almost-catastrophe on the basement steps attested to. "Do you think she crawled out?"

"I don't know how she could. The holes aren't that big."

"We have to find her."

"I know. Can you watch these guys while I grab some chicken wire from the shed? I'll put it around the bottom of the play yard so they can't get out before we go looking for her."

She took the three brothers who were missing their sister.

Oh . . . crud.

She took a seat, a lump in her throat. Four siblings who'd lost their mom. A little sister in need of rescuing. The correlation to her family . . . Maybe that was why she'd been so adamant about Jared keeping them.

Well, hell, they had to find Moe.

Within ten minutes, Mac had cans of tuna spread out around the downstairs and Jared had the play yard lined with chicken wire, as well as a makeshift "lid" to keep the boys where they should be.

Ten minutes after that, Jared did find Moe.

And why wouldn't he? He'd had a lot of practice rescuing damsels in distress.

Mac didn't want to go there. He wasn't Prince Charming and she wasn't Cinderella. Even if she did clean for a living.

She ran down the stairs and reached for Moe. "What were you doing, you little rascal?"

"She went in search of the litter box in the laundry room even though she had a perfectly good one here. Makes no sense."

"Those nasty old boys make a big mess for you?" Mac rubbed Moe's nose with hers. "Were you out exploring all by yourself?"

Wide blue eyes blinked at her.

"I don't think she thought she was lost," Mac stage-whispered out of the corner of her mouth.

"Reminds me of someone else I know." He nudged her with his shoulder. "Like that time we found you in that cave on the trail, remember?"

Mac tucked Moe under her chin, trying to hide a grimace. She hated this story. "I remember."

She hated that she'd had to be found, hated remembering how scared she'd been—she'd just seen the Wizard of Oz for the first time and those "lions, and tigers, and bears, oh my" had been going round and round in her scared little mind. So when she'd seen the overhang of rocks, she'd butted up against the wall, curled her arms around her knees, and tried to bury her head there, figuring if she didn't see the monsters, the monsters wouldn't see her. The logic of a five-year-old.

Jared had been the first to find her—and he'd let her have it verbally until her brothers had shown up.

By then, she'd been so scared and so miserable that she'd gotten yelled at, that she'd yelled back at him, telling him she'd known *exactly* where she was and he was the idiot. When she'd shoved him out of her way, Liam had scooped her into his arms and carried her home.

She'd been scared witless. "You yelled at me."

"I know. I'm sorry. All I could think about was you getting hurt." He leaned against the secretary desk and crossed his arms. "But you scared me, Mac. I'd never lost anyone before. I didn't know what to do. We were frantic, calling you, looking in the creek, looking down the embankments . . . I thought you drowned. Seriously, Mac, I was ten years old and thought you were dead. Then when I found you . . . You have no idea the relief I felt."

"Why?"

"Why?"

"Yes, why? You didn't like me, so why the relief? You made it perfectly clear that you didn't want me around, so it would've been better if I was out of the way."

Jared took Moe from her and set her back in the pen, making sure to latch the lid. Then he walked up to Mac and tilted her chin. "You know how I was with these kittens, all worried about taking care of them?" He waited for her to nod. "I was ten times as bad with you. You were a child. A little girl. Something not of my universe. But I saw how much your brothers cared about you, I saw how much your grandmother cared about you, and I knew we had to protect you. Yet every time I tried to suggest you do it one way, you purposely went and did it the other."

"That's because I didn't like being bossed around."

"What you saw as bossing, I meant as caution." Jared tapped the tip of her nose.

Ohmygod, she felt that all the way down to her—

Wait. That was silly. It was a tap on the nose. The tip of

the nose wasn't an erogenous zone. And, hey, Dave had done the same thing last night and she hadn't gotten that . . . tingle. "And the teasing? The sarcasm?"

Jared winced and leaned back against the desk, taking his tingling fingers with him. "I'm not proud of that, Mac, but I was a teenage boy. You were my best friend's kid sister with a crush. I wasn't sure how to handle it. So I chose the wrong way. It didn't mean that I didn't like you; I just didn't know what to do with you. About you." He touched her arm briefly. "But, hey, remember the zip line? And the hayride? And the time in the cornfield maze when we overheard your brothers who were so scared that we offered to lead them out if they'd buy the ice cream? Remember how hard we tried not to laugh as we stood on the other side of the hedge with the end in sight? Then there was that time at the lake with the inflatable dock thing that we bounced everyone off of. Remember that?"

Jared kept going with the memories and Mac had to take a breath. She *had* forgotten those other times, but they existed.

"Can you forgive me, Mac?"

Could she? Jared had been a kid and it wasn't his fault that she'd looked at him in a whole new light. That she'd gone a few steps further.

She'd been condemning him all those years for something that'd been her doing.

"Of course I can, Jared."

Chapter Twenty-one

YO, Jare, your chariot awaits."

Jared, Liam, and Bryan were at the baseball stadium—he'd gotten last-minute tickets for tonight's game—and Bryan was rattling the wheelchair by the ramp, smiling the shit-eating grin the media called *charismatic* but Jared, Liam, and Sean called *obnoxious*. Worked on women, but it wasn't doing a damn thing for Jared.

"I'm not an invalid, guys."

"Says the guy with a brace on his leg and a set of crutches." Liam handed him the damn things. "Just shut up and get in the wheelchair. You know you want us to cater to your every need."

On a good day, maybe. Now? Not a chance in hell.

But they'd miss the first three innings if he had to gimp his way to their seats, and his leg did hurt like hell. Too much chicken-wire-gathering without his crutches this morning. He'd overdone it. "Fine. Let's go."

He pulled his baseball cap down low on his forehead, wishing Bryan would do the same. Mr. Movie Star, however, enjoyed his publicity, and it would only be a matter of time before someone called him on it.

"Hey, aren't you Bryan Manley?" asked a kid.

Like now.

Damn. They were right by their seats; they'd almost made it.

Liam nudged Bryan. "Looks like you're up, baby bro."

"Don't call me that," Bryan muttered as he handed Lee his food carrier. He turned around to the kid. "Yes, I am. Would you like an autograph?"

"Yeah," said the kid, tugging a teenage girl with him. "On my sister's arm. She says she'll never wash it again if you do and I wanna see that fight with Mom."

Jared had to laugh. He'd never had sibling interaction, but he'd seen the same sort of thing between Lee and his brothers. He'd always wanted a brother, that's why he'd wanted Liam for a friend. The guy came with two more; it was the family he'd never had.

And then there was Mac—

Thankfully, Liam dropped a food carrier onto his lap before he could go too far down that lane. Tonight was about forgetting Mac. It was his time to hang out with the guys and just chill.

"Here, make yourself useful," Liam said. "That bogus injury's not getting you out of doing some work."

"Bogus?" He twisted to look back at Liam while trying not to upend the beer. "If I could get out of this damn contraption, I'd show you bogus. And trust me, I'm working these days. Your sister . . ." He opted for shaking his head. It was one thing to be frustrated by Mac, it was another to bitch about her to her brothers.

"Don't tell me she's put you to work."

In more ways than one.

But he wasn't about to share that with her brothers. They all knew how he felt about her—*had* felt about her. What he was feeling now was his business. "Sorry, Lee, but she's a pain in the ass even if she is your sister."

"Hey, you don't have to tell me."

Good. Because he wasn't about to. The last person he'd want to discuss Mac with was her older brother.

Or Dave.

Dave.

He'd cancelled today's PT session, hadn't wanted to hear how great the date was and when Dave was going to see her again, and if he'd kissed her goodnight—

Actually, he was torn on that subject. He only wanted to hear about it if Dave hadn't enjoyed it.

Of course, Dave would have to be dead for Mac's kiss not to do anything to him. Jared knew that firsthand.

Bryan caught up to them. "Thanks for abandoning me, guys."

"Aw, come on," said Liam, ribbing him yet again. Bryan made it so easy. "You love it. Isn't that why you got into the business? So you could get all the women?"

"That's just wrong. The kid was fifteen."

"Long time to never wash an arm." Guilt spiked through Jared the minute he said it. Here they were, teasing each other about that girl's crush, and she was probably thrilled beyond belief that a movie star had paid attention to her. He'd seen that same hopeful look on Mac's young face that night at her grandmother's.

God, was the guilt ever going to go away?

It was a good thing Mac had tomorrow off. Well, not off from work because she had another client she'd promised Thursday to, but off from coming back to Grandma's. He could use a breather—if only to do some serious thinking about what he wanted out of life and where—and if—Mac fit into that.

And if she'd let herself fit into it.

"I signed her T-shirt," Bryan said. "The one she'd just bought, not the one she was wearing. What kind of pervert do you take me for?"

"Just your average, run-of-the-mill pervert, I guess," Jared said, trying to interject humor he wasn't feeling to get off the subject of a young girl's crush. "What's the difference?"

Bryan slapped the back of his baseball cap so it fell over his face. "Watch it, you. I say your name just a little louder and we'll have a swarm crawling all over you, too."

Jared turned so quickly the cap almost spun off. "Don't you dare, Bry. I don't need that nightmare."

Bryan put up his hands in surrender. "Backing off here. No need to get psycho on me."

Jared straightened his cap, trying to hide his face. People were looking at them. It was no secret he was friends with a movie star, and he didn't need anyone connecting the dots and figuring out who he was, or cameras and cell phones would be going off in seconds. "You're all about publicity these days and I get that, but me? I'm all about recovery since the accident. I don't need cameras and mics in my face asking me how it's going or when I'll be back. If I knew, they'd know, you know? I'm so sick of the intrusion into my privacy. Do they think I *like* having to relearn how to walk? That I *want* to show up in a stadium in a wheelchair? Or hear what my ex-girlfriend who did this to me is doing these days?" Rotting in hell, he hoped. "Why the hell is any of it news? Can't they just leave a guy in peace to do his job?"

Neither of them answered, and a couple people stepped back.

Great. Injured *and* insane. He would make for really good copy right now.

He twisted in his seat and rearranged the food carriers. Just get him to his seat and everything could get back to normal.

There was a poster of a beautiful woman plastered to the wall as they entered their seating area. Cassidy Davenport, local socialite and sole heir to the Davenport hotel and construction empire. She made news just by breathing. Surprisingly, though, even though she was a classic beauty, she couldn't hold a candle to Mac. And that was the God's honest truth.

Jared shook his head. How and when things had shifted was up for debate. But shifted they had.

"Damn, that's a gorgeous woman," he said. Lee would

expect the comment; his playboy reputation wasn't entirely fictionalized. Some of it, yes, because it got him mentioned in the news—professional athletes were no different from other celebrities when it came to that—but if he *were* as romantically active as the tabloids made him out to be, he'd never have time to play ball.

"Steer clear, Jare," Bryan said as he helped him from the wheelchair to a seat. "Woman like that . . . I don't know if you've got enough bank to keep her happy. And if you do, she's only after it. Not the marrying kind."

Jared lifted his leg onto another chair. "Who says I'm in the market to get married? But she might be the *perfect* incentive to get back on my feet." He was saying the words, but he wasn't feeling them. It was as if he was talking about some other Jared Nolan—the one who had let Mac go.

"On your feet isn't where you're planning to be with her." Bryan grabbed one of the plastic cups. "Lee? Here's your beer. You look like you could use it. I bet she's a pain in the ass to work for, right?"

Oh, right. Mac had given Liam Cassidy Davenport as a client. What did Mac have against the poor guy? Lee's last relationship had been with a B-list socialite, whereas Cassidy Davenport was an A-lister all the way. She'd actually been Camille's hero—which should've been his first clue.

Poor Liam.

"I pity the guy who ends up with her." Bry handed Jared a beer next. "We learned to steer clear of daddy's girls. Right, Lee?"

Liam chugged half the beer and Jared didn't blame him. Hell, if he had to work for Cassidy, he'd be drunk *all* the time.

"See what a hardship it is?" Bry cocked his head Liam's way. "He's gotta chug a few after spending the day cleaning her froufrou shit. I bet it's all pink and lacy, am I right?"

Did Mac wear pink and lacy?

Oh hell, he shouldn't be thinking like that. He took another swig of his warm stadium beer. Ah, nothing like it.

Liam wiped his mouth with his arm. "What about the place where you're working, Bry? How's that going?"

Jared noticed Lee hadn't answered the question. Interesting.

"*How*?" Bryan sat down and put his feet up on the railing in front of him. "Well, let's start off with: Beth's a widow. And a mom. Of five."

"*Five*?" Jared practically choked on his beer. He'd always wanted a brother, but five? "Who has five kids anymore? Who'd *want* five kids?"

"You don't like kids?" asked Bryan.

Jared had to think about how to answer that since these guys were two of four, and four wasn't far from five. "I like kids well enough, I guess. But five? That's a little much."

"It's a basketball team."

Jared slathered a hotdog with ketchup. If he had food in his mouth, he couldn't put his foot in it. "It's not enough for a baseball team, so what's the point?"

"Hang on. You want *nine* kids?"

Now he almost choked on his hotdog. He didn't want to discuss kids. Not when that image of Mac holding a baby had popped into his head and he had to see her on a daily basis. "No. I'm just saying, if you're going to go for five, what's another four?"

"Uh, a lot more mouths to feed," said Bryan. "Diapers to buy. College tuitions to pay. Ballgame concession stands to go broke at. I can't imagine having even one."

Oh, Jared could imagine—making them, that was. There was a reason the world was overpopulated.

Still not what he needed to be thinking about, given that Mac was their sister . . . "Yeah, but once you get beyond two, it's just numbers." He finished his hotdog, then picked up another and, in an effort to steer the conversation off this topic, went for the next obvious one. Bryan was easy to pick on. "But a widow, huh? How long's she been single?"

"Seriously?" Bryan's eyes almost bugged out of his head. "Did you not hear me? I said *five* kids. Need I say more?"

The thing was, Bryan probably would. Which was unlike

him. Bryan was the ultimate in chill when it came to women, so this outburst was out of character. Protesting too much maybe?

Jared looked at Liam to see if he was picking up on this.

Liam took a chug of his beer and Jared thought he saw a hint of a smile behind the cup.

"So what's the prognosis, Jared? When're you gonna be back in the game?" Liam, ever the peace-keeper, changed the subject.

But not for the better.

Jared sucked the inside of his cheek and grimaced. "I have to wear this damn brace awhile longer and do a shit-load of rehab. Doc says nine months total. I'm planning on it being sooner."

"Nine months?" Bryan sat back. "That sucks. But you better listen to the doc. Don't want to get back before the body is ready. I did that after I hurt my knee on the set in Sri Lanka, and damn, big regret. 'Course, it might have had to do with the less than stellar medical care, but still, Doc said to take it easy for a month, but I *had* to get back on set. Was worried I'd lose the part." He shook his head. "Stupid. Took another month for it to give out while I was holding Ava Stone." The Bryan Manley wolfish grin made an appearance—not unexpected when discussing the actress. "Not that having Ava Stone land on me was all that much of a hardship."

"Considering it started your relationship with her," said Liam sarcastically, "I can see why it wouldn't be."

"Not a relationship. A mutually beneficial usury."

Jared did choke on his hotdog at that phrase. Rang a little too close to home. Okay, a *lot* too close to home. "So, guys, you have plans for this weekend? I have a ribbon-cutting at the community center. It'd be nice to have some friendly faces there." And keep him from doing something stupid around their sister.

"Gee, Jare, I don't know . . . Go to a stuffy ribbon-cutting ceremony or hang out at home watching a game. Let's see . . ." Bryan curled his wrist toward his forehead in an attempt to reenact Rodin's The Thinker.

Thank God he didn't take his clothes off to do it or there'd be mass hysteria in their seating section.

"Hey, there's no point in watching if I'm not playing." Jared flicked an unused straw at Bryan, going for humor, but the truth was the thought of not being on the mound ate a hole in his gut. The world hadn't stopped for the rest of the population when he'd stopped playing ball.

Bryan broke character to pick up his beer and salute him. "You know? That's true. Weymouth doesn't have what you have. There's no consistency. No style. It's like he's looking at a batting machine when he pitches."

Weymouth was a good pitcher and Jared appreciated Bry's attempt at saving his ego. "Good. So then you can come. I'll save two front-row seats for you guys. Think Sean can make it?"

"No clue," said Liam. "But you'll have to count me out. I've got inspections coming up on the new place and need to get some work done. With this cleaning gig, I'm behind schedule. Gotta work, buddy. Not all of us can make a million dollars."

He didn't correct Liam on the amount. He was almost embarrassed by it. *Almost*, but he wasn't stupid. They wanted to pay him millions? He was taking it because there would come a time when they wouldn't anymore.

He was afraid that this might just be that time.

Chapter Twenty-two

JARED was surprised that he wasn't afraid to admit that he was looking forward to seeing Mac Saturday morning.

He'd missed her the past two days. She'd been off on another job and after a long, disappointing call with his attorney about filing civil charges against Camille and her boyfriend for the attack and more waiting on the eviction, he'd been stuck here alone with the kittens and the cleaning and the attic. He'd gotten through a lot of boxes, but the days had lasted a lifetime. Even the neighbors hadn't shown up with goodies.

He didn't want the neighbors; he wanted Mac. It was almost funny to be excited about seeing her, but there was nothing funny about what he was coming to feel for her.

Jared pushed off the nightstand to get up and tested his bad leg. It took some of his weight without twinging, so that was good. Dave said it was an excellent sign of his recovery.

Dave.

They'd cleared the air yesterday. Dave, as it turned out, had figured out what Jared was feeling about Mac before he did, and had decided to bring the issue to a head by asking her out himself.

"Don't get me wrong, buddy," he'd said as he'd put Jared through his paces. "If she were interested, we'd be having a different conversation, but she isn't, so we won't. The woman, for whatever reason, has it bad for you. So don't blow it or that's what will make you a loser, not this injury."

The ball was firmly back in his court. He just needed to figure out what to do with it.

He hobbled into the tiny mosaic-tile-covered bathroom and turned on the shower. Then he leaned on the bathroom sink and stared at himself in the mirror.

What do *you want, Nolan?*

He looked at himself. Really looked at himself, almost daring himself to answer.

He'd never been one to back down from a dare.

Jared sucked in a fortifying breath, nodding at his reflection.

He wanted not to be alone.

There. He'd admitted it. He didn't want to be alone. He'd been alone growing up, parents distant from each other and from him. They still were. Camille had used him, all her so-called caring a façade. He had Liam and his other friends, but that wasn't what he was talking about, and his teammates were professional associates, not bosom buddies. Baseball was a job. A career. It wasn't a life.

He wanted someone to come home to. Someone who'd be there in the morning, who'd worry about him, think about him. Care about him. Who'd show up at the damn hospital because she couldn't bear the thought of him not being in her world and needed to assure herself he was coming home. To her.

He wanted a family. A real one. All that talk about kids with Liam and Bryan last night . . . Maybe he wouldn't want five, but, then again, why not? It wasn't as if he couldn't afford them.

Steam fogged the mirror and Jared let it. God, was he pathetic or what? Standing here mooning over what he didn't have when he ought to be grateful for what he did.

But he wanted more—No, not more. Something else. People thought fame and fortune were it, but at the end of the day, you couldn't take those with you. They didn't wrap their arms around you when your world turned upside down and tell you they'd stay with you no matter what. They didn't leave a note on your pillow or write lipstick hearts on the bathroom mirror—not that he could see Mac doing that; she'd only have to clean it.

He smiled as he got in the shower, but it was rueful.

Mac.

He'd known her almost his whole life, yet hadn't really known her. What he was learning about her now, he liked. She wasn't the pest he'd thought, and the tornado that surrounded her was because she was doing a million things: helping people, growing her business, being part of her family. She loved her brothers and her grandmother—loved *his* grandmother—helped small animals, didn't put up with his shit, had a smile that could light up a room, and most of all, she was herself. She was Mac Manley and made no apologies for it.

No, he'd been the one to apologize. As he should have.

He turned the spray to cold and sucked in a breath at the shock of the temperature change. Or maybe it was the shock of having blown his chance with her by not realizing that the last time she'd worn her heart on her sleeve around him was the last chance he'd get.

He'd taken Mac and her feelings for him for granted. That they'd always be there. Just like he'd taken it for granted that he'd always be in control of his career.

Camille had proved him wrong on that end, as well.

He scrubbed the washcloth over his chest. It wasn't over 'til the fat lady sang, and right now, no one was singing, least of all him. He'd get Camille out of his house one way or another, and he'd find out if he had a shot with Mac.

He rinsed off, wrapped a towel around his waist, and started coming up with a game plan.

MAC pasted a smile on her face and waved to people she knew. She hadn't thought through the reality of what coming to this event with Jared would entail, with everyone she knew—and people she didn't—seeing them together.

He was wearing a Manley Maids shirt, so that gave her the promotion excuse, but still, her friends knew about her crush. Half the town had known about it back then, and most of the town was still *in* town. And most of those who'd lived here for years were *here*.

Gossip was starting already.

Then the reporters chimed in.

"Nolan, what's your prognosis? When will you be back?"

"You going to be starting next season?"

"Think the team will make it to the Series without you?"

"Is this your new business partner?"

"Cleaning houses these days, Nolan?"

Mac didn't get a lot of the sarcasm and put-downs. Jared was a hometown hero. Why would they want to kick him when he was down?

Jared kicked back with that killer smile of his, however, tilting his baseball cap back, and tugging Mac forward. "Actually, Mike, no. I'm not cleaning houses; I've hired Manley Maids to do it for me. This is Mary-Alice Manley, the owner. Take her card. Best service in town. Satisfaction guaranteed."

They took her cards, though it had more to do with Jared telling them to, but who knew? Maybe she'd get a mention—though his *satisfaction guaranteed* had raised a few eyebrows and gotten a few snickers. Oh, well. She wouldn't mind if it put Jared's picture in her uniform in the paper and, given the shutter-bugging that was going on, maybe *she'd* make it into the papers as well.

Geez, if she'd known it'd be this easy, she could've gotten some sleep instead of learning how to beat her brothers at poker. All she'd needed was Jared.

Seemed to be the mantra of her life.

The ceremony started, with Ted Bakersfield, the community center director, welcoming the crowd then segueing to Jared's intro, all his career highs from when he played for the high school, all through college and into the majors.

Jared fidgeted next to her, almost as if he was embarrassed . . . or worried that those would be his only stats because of his injury.

And once again, her heart went out to him. She was never going to get over him.

"Please welcome Jared Nolan." Ted led the crowd in applause and Jared sucked up his emotions at hearing what he'd done while wondering if he'd get the chance to do more, then took the podium.

"Thank you all for coming out today. I'm proud to have been asked to participate in today's ceremony. As Ted said, I did get my start in baseball right here in our T-ball league, so I'm thrilled to be able to give back." He went on to praise the fund-raising organizers, the donators, the staff for making the well-being of the community a priority with all the activities and services the community center offered. He was sure to mention Kareers for Kids, and tossed Mac's name in the mix while sweeping his hand toward her, working promotion in for her business as smoothly as he'd worked sponsors' names into any interview he'd done. This was old hat; this was what Jared knew. What he was good at.

God, what if management wouldn't take him back? What if, at thirty-five and with these injuries, they thought he wasn't worth the risk? That he couldn't be what he'd been?

It'd kill him. Baseball was all he had. All of these people, they were here because of who he was. Because of what he did for a living. Once it was over, why would they bother?

Why would you want them to? Do they define you?

Thankfully, he'd finished his speech before that little pearl of wisdom bit him in the brain.

No, they didn't define him. *He* defined him. But he'd defined himself through baseball; he wasn't sure who he'd be if he didn't have the game.

He looked into the audience as they handed him the oversized ceremonial ribbon-cutting scissors. Bryan's seat was empty; he'd called and said something had come up with the kids at the house he was cleaning, but Grandma was there along with Mrs. Manley. And then there was Mac.

The people who cared about him.

He sliced the ribbon, feeling that same slice in his heart that his parents weren't there.

Mac was right; he needed to talk to them. For so long he'd used the game as his family. His teammates, the coaching staff, the fans, even the reporters. He knew the regulars by name, and most by sight. He played to them, knowing he'd get validation even if it was just for their story. Validation he hadn't gotten from his parents.

Jared smiled through the pictures, his arm around the director and his staff, but his mind was elsewhere.

For years he'd wanted his parents' approval. Had thought baseball was the way to get it. But even with his success, they hadn't chosen to be there for him when he'd needed it most. He'd stared at those goddamn white walls of his room at the rehab facility, wondering what the hell he'd have to do to get them to show up.

In the end, if a serious injury wasn't it, he didn't know what would be.

But Grandma had come. Mrs. Manley had, too. Liam and the guys . . . He understood why Mac hadn't, but she had sent cookies with Liam that one time . . .

He glanced at her. She was leaning over her grandmother to speak to his, reaching for Grandma's hand, her smile warm and loving and genuine.

Why hadn't he seen this about Mac before? Why had he been so blinded by resentment that he hadn't been able to see what a genuine person she was? Why had he tossed her feelings back in her face?

Because you were in college. Shit happens. Don't beat yourself up about it, fix it.

He planned to.

He finished up with the photo op, patted the director on the back, shook a few hands, then ate up the distance between him and Mac with a couple of long swings between his crutches. The things were worth something at last.

"Hey, you ready to get going?" he asked when he reached her side. "I'm sure the kittens have left me some gifts."

"Oh, but, Jared," said Grandma. "We wanted to speak to someone about the classes for seniors they offer. We'd like to see if they could do them at our community room.

So many of our residents don't travel, and they're missing out."

He'd like to get out of here and spend some alone time with Mac, but he could wait a little longer for his grandmother. "Let's go talk to the director. If it's an issue with money, tell him I'll cover the cost."

"You will?" Grandma beamed at him.

He had to hug her. So many times she'd hugged him when he'd needed it and his mother hadn't been around . . . If he could do this small thing for her and make her happy, he was more than willing to do it. "Of course. You ladies deserve some fun in your life."

"Oh, that's so sweet of you, Jared. You always were such a thoughtful boy."

Mac coughed beside him.

He shot her a glance. Yeah, he got it. Thoughtful with everyone but her. He was going to make that up to her.

He called out to the director and put him in touch with his grandmother and Mrs. Manley. "Whatever they want, Ted," he said as he turned to face Mac, leaving the grandmothers to work their collective persuasive powers on the director. "Want to get some ice cream?"

She cocked her head and looked at him thoughtfully, as if ice cream were a major life decision.

Or maybe it was just a metaphor for one.

"Okay. You're on."

Uh, yeah, he kinda was . . .

It only took them a half hour to reach the ice cream booth across the football field, which was about two hundred autographs later. "Sorry about that," he said when the last kid finally left.

"Don't apologize. Those are your fans. They loved it. Who am I to disappoint them?"

"The woman who's patiently waiting for the ice cream I promised her."

"That woman can wait. I like watching the kids, especially as you give them your autograph. Their own personal hero come to life."

"Geez, Mac, better watch it or I'll get a big head."

"I said that was the kids' impression. Don't worry, Jared, you've got me to give you a reality check."

He liked that. "Keeping me grounded, huh?"

"Someone has to. Between you and Bryan, the two of you could fill a stadium with your hot air if I wasn't around to keep your egos in check."

He wanted to reach for her hand, but didn't because he'd only have to let it go when they started walking again. Besides, he had the rest of his life to hold her hand—

He stumbled.

"Jared!" Mac's arm went around him, steadying him.

Well, not really. That's what she might have done it for, but the touch of her hands on his skin made him anything but steady.

This was so not the place. Especially when there were three camera lenses aimed at him that he could see, and probably half a dozen more he couldn't.

He dragged his stupid crutch to vertical and propped it under his arm, thereby disengaging himself from Mac's embrace. He didn't want their relationship, for lack of a better word, played out in the media for everyone to see. Not at first anyway, though he'd love to shout from the rooftops that he'd finally come to his senses, but he should probably discuss it with her first.

"What would you like?" he asked when it was their turn to order their ice cream.

"I'll take a chocolate dip top on vanilla."

So not the answer he'd wanted.

Jared chuckled to himself.

Pathetic, man. Get a freaking grip.

He'd like to—on her and then sweep her off her feet.

"And you, sir? What would you like?" asked the teenage server.

He had to force himself not to spout exactly what he *would* like. "Ah—"

"He'll have a double chocolate cone with chocolate sprinkles."

Jared looked at her. It was what he always ordered. "You really were paying attention."

She shrugged then looked away, pink creeping across her cheeks. "Some things stay with you."

He couldn't help himself; he ran a finger down her forearm. "I'm glad you did, Mac."

She glanced at him, those green eyes flashing uncertainly, and Jared wanted to kick himself for all the things he hadn't appreciated about her.

"I'm sorry, Mac."

She shook her head and waved her hand, blinking a little too fast. "Don't. I'm fine."

The teenager handed Mac her ice cream and he couldn't blame her for walking away from the cart.

He fished out a couple of bucks to pay, grabbed his ice cream and—

Shit. Now how the hell was he going to use his crutches and hold the cone?

"Mac?"

She turned around with a look on her face that grabbed him by the heart and twisted, but then she looked at his cone and smiled.

"Hang on, Nolan." She strode back to him, plucked the cone from him, and jerked her head toward a bench. "Seriously, what would you do without me?"

It was a rhetorical question, but he was going to answer it anyway.

He followed her to the bench and sat down, leaning his crutches against it, then took his cone. "I don't want to find out what I'd do without you, Mac."

"Huh?" She stopped eating her cone mid-lick.

He cleared his throat to get that image out of his brain. "I was an idiot all those years and I'm sorry. I'm sorry for hurting you and I'm sorry for not appreciating you."

"Where'd this change of heart come from?"

He winced at her sarcasm, but he knew where it came from. When Mac was hurt, she either yelled and called him an idiot, or she came at him with sarcasm.

He knew because he'd invariably been the one to hurt her, a realization he wasn't proud of.

"Let's just say that I finally grew up."

Her gaze flicked over him. "Or it's because you're injured and bored and lonely and I just happen to be handy—"

"Don't." He put a finger on her lips. "Don't denigrate this, please. This is a big deal for me. *You're* a big deal for me and I'm an ass not to have seen it sooner. This isn't because you're here and I'm lonely. It's because you're here and you're you and I finally see that. Would I be feeling like this if we hadn't seen each other day in, day out for the past two weeks? I don't know. I've been so focused on this injury and what it means for my career that I wasn't looking around. That's why I know this is real; you crept beneath my barriers."

"Oh, hey! Look who's over there! Yoo, hoo! Jared!"

Some woman was waving at him from the other side of the football field, her loud voice guaranteed to catch everyone's attention.

Jared bit back a curse. He loved his fans. Even if it meant interrupting him, but this was one of the most important moments of his life and he could do without the attention.

He squeezed Mac's shoulder. "Can we put this discussion on hold until later? I have a lot I want to say to you, Mac. And I hope like hell you want to hear it."

Mac wasn't sure she wanted to hear it. Was this the same guy who'd told her to sleep with his friend? She didn't get it.

But she had more than enough time to try to as she sat beside him through another autograph session, holding his ice cream cone and then eating it when the fans multiplied.

Luckily, the grandmothers showed up after a bit, and the fans parted like the Red Sea then drifted off when they realized who the women were.

"Hi, Grandma. Mrs. Manley." Jared leaned down to peck them on the cheek, and Mac could hear a collective sigh from his female fans as they left.

She smiled to herself. If those women only knew he'd kissed her, too. And not on the cheek.

Damn, she could feel the blush creep up her cheeks at the memory.

"Mary-Alice?" Gran was looking at her expectantly.

Fudge. She'd missed Gran's question. "Yes, Gran?"

"Oh, good. Then that's settled."

"What's settled?" She looked at Jared for help, but he just arched an eyebrow.

"The beach party of course."

"What beach party?"

Gran patted her arm. "The one we're having in the community room. My friends are going to love to see you again. And Jared, too, of course."

"Of course," said Mildred.

Mac wasn't sure she was up to spending more time with him after that cryptic comment. It'd come out of left field and she could use some time to adjust to his change in attitude before she did something stupid like play her *what-if* games again.

"I'm so glad you'll come, Mary-Alice." Gran gave her a quick squeeze. "I missed you at dinner the other night with the boys."

She'd had to work and Gran had known that, so it wasn't fair to use it as leverage.

But that was how, six hours later, Mac had helped set up for the dinner, limbo'ed herself to a trophy—not that big of a deal, considering she was the youngest one there and one of the few without a walker—danced the hula so much she was surprised the older women with her hadn't thrown out a hip, and had enough virgin mai tais to actually regain her virginity. Well, except for the fact that she'd felt Jared's eyes on her the entire time and there was nothing virginal about the way he was looking at her.

Or the way he was making her feel. Especially on the heels of his earlier apology.

"We should get going, Mac." Jared drained the last of his virgin margarita. "I left some soft food for the kittens but I'm not sure they know how to eat it. I should probably go home and feed them."

Which meant that she had to drive him there.

She wasn't sure that was such a good idea. Because she still hadn't figured out where his change of heart was coming from.

And because she might not want to leave.

"YOU were a dancing fiend tonight," Jared said with that killer smile of his when he got into his truck's cab.

"I prefer dancing queen. Sounds more dignified." She pulled on her seat belt. No temptation to slide across the seat in case he continued saying things like he'd said back on the bench earlier.

"Since when is the limbo dignified?"

Jared had a point there. She'd won the contest because she was the only one without arthritis.

He ran a finger along her shoulder. "I had fun tonight, Mac."

Oh boy. Jared in this mood was tough to resist. "Me, too."

"We should do it again."

"Not sure when or where the next limbo contest is, but I'll keep an eye out." She was trying to keep this light because being alone with him in the car, and the darkness, and the sound of the crickets through the open windows were creating an ambiance she wasn't ready for.

Nor was Jared's invitation when she pulled into his driveway. "Will you come in, Mac?" Jared tucked a piece of hair behind her ear.

The shivers racing through her body urged her to say yes. But her battered heart was throwing CAUTION signs all over the place.

"I don't think I should, Jared."

He pursed his lips and nodded. "I get that."

He stared at her awhile longer, his gaze darting to her lips.

He wanted to kiss her.

She wanted to let him.

Instead, she opened his truck door and slid out. She'd been down that road too many times. She had to know Jared meant it before she let herself go there. And right now, she wasn't sure. "I have to get going. I have a busy day tomorrow."

"I thought you didn't work on Sunday."

"I don't work for other people, but I have paperwork and my own place to do. When you work for yourself, you never get a day off."

"Just remember, all work and no play . . ."

Jared would be the *play* part and it was so hard to walk away from that.

Which was why she did.

Chapter Twenty-three

JARED'S butt was the first thing Mac saw when she walked into the attic Monday morning.

Not a bad way to start the week.

"Moon out early today?" Sean snickered over her shoulder.

Jared had apparently been busy yesterday and gone through the attic like a tornado. Still no ring, but a bunch of the stuff was ready to go and Sean was the only one of her brothers free to lend a hand today.

"Oooph!" Jared bashed his head on the sofa he was crawling under.

"Careful, Jare," said Sean, skirting around Mac and lifting the sofa. "I hear professional athletes lose brain cells faster than the rest of us."

"Only the young and stupid ones. Those of us more mature to the game have a better head on our shoulders." He rubbed the top of his. "A sore one, perhaps, but still, better." He set Moe on the cushion, then held out his hand to shake Sean's. "So you're the moving crew?"

"Ahem." Mac spoke up. She was perfectly capable of moving furniture.

"Mac and I." Sean nudged Jared's bad leg. "Since you're in no shape to do it, figured we'd better before you do something foolish like try to carry it all down on one leg."

"I'm not foolish."

"Stubborn . . . foolish . . . Same thing."

"You're only saying that because you know I can't kick your ass now. Just wait until I'm healed."

"Then you still won't because you'll be worried about breaking something else, old man."

Jared handed Moe to Mac. "Here. She escaped again. I swear, this little lady is going to be the death of me."

Mac bit off her smile and took the kitten back down to its brothers. Jared had come a long way from not knowing how to take care of them.

If he changed in that way, could he change in another?

"Wow, I remember this." Sean was holding up a hideous clown when she returned.

"Damn thing was frustrating as hell," said Jared. "Always came back up."

"Until Bryan sat on it that time."

"And almost popped it. My grandmother was not happy."

"We should've done it anyway. This thing gave me nightmares."

Mac took the final steps onto the landing. "Aw, don't tell me you guys are scared of a little clown."

"Look at that thing." Jared swept his hand toward it. "If that's not straight out of a horror film, you can call me Chucky."

The clown was the first thing down the stairs. The old pictures were next, the settee followed, and more boxes of toys and memorabilia that'd been handed down for so many generations no one was sure who was what relation to whom anymore. Mac earmarked some of it for the local historical society and others for a few homeless shelters, but the rest, by and large, was making its way to the thrift shop or the landfill.

Sean was configuring the first load into the back of his pickup and her old work van while she climbed the steps for another. When she reached the top, she saw Jared paging through a book. She was about to ask him what it was when her phone rang.

Mitchell Davenport's office. Her biggest client, not only money-wise, but pain-in-the-neck-wise since he'd kicked his daughter out of her penthouse, and Liam, bleeding heart that he was, had offered her a place to stay.

As far as Mac knew, Mitchell didn't know where Cassidy was and Mac wanted to keep it that way.

"Mac Manley."

"Hello, Ms. Manley. This is Mr. Davenport's assistant. He'd like to discuss a business proposition with you."

"A business proposition with Manley Maids?" Mac made sure to mention her company because she wasn't sure the woman had called the right number.

"Yes. He asks that you be here in twenty minutes to discuss it. He believes you will find it quite lucrative to do so. Shall I send a car for you?"

"Um, no. I'll get there on my own." She never liked being at anyone's mercy and with Mitchell Davenport calling out of the blue like this, given certain circumstances, she *really* didn't want to be at his mercy because she'd probably have to beg for it if he found out where his daughter was.

"Everything okay?" Jared asked when she ended the call.

She tucked her phone into her back pocket. "Business. I have to go. See you later."

Promise? he almost asked, watching her ponytail bounce down the steps, fighting the urge to call her back. All the memories in this attic—and the scrapbook he'd found—were getting to him. Wanting Mac was just one more thing he didn't need on his plate right now. Not with her brother in the house.

That brother poked his head between the banisters. "Hey, Jare, need help with anything else?"

He opted for "This," instead of *your sister* and handed Sean the book.

"Aw, this is nice. Gran did this for us, too, though Bry's is by far the fattest. I don't think she missed even one mention of him in any tabloid. Gotta admit, though, it's kinda freaky to see your own grandmother cutting out articles about your brother and his harem."

"I don't know how he juggles all those women. One's more than enough for me."

"Yeah, she really did a number on you."

It took Jared a few seconds to realize Sean was talking about Camille. Good. He let him think that because he wasn't sure what Sean's reaction would be if he knew he'd meant Mac.

Sean tucked the scrapbook under his arm. "So is there any chance you're going to kick her out?"

Not a chance in hell—oh, again Camille. "My attorney's working on it, but eviction is a pain in the ass." Which was why he had to come up with some other way.

"So where are you going to go once this place sells?"

Jared shrugged. "I'll find something. Or maybe I'll just move back into my place and piss Camille and Burke off enough that they'll move out."

Yeah, that option was out. Even being around Camille for those few minutes at the community center had been too long.

Or maybe he'd move in with Mac in the house he felt more at home in than the one he'd grown up in.

The thought had a certain appeal for many reasons.

MAC was counting to a hundred for the sixth time as she drove over to Liam's latest house-flipping project, trying to figure out what the hell she was going to do about this latest development. She loved her brother, but she also needed to keep her business's reputation pristine, and with that impromptu meeting where Mitchell Davenport had offered her the contract on all his properties in the tristate area, that reputation was more important than ever.

So was the problem she needed to discuss with Liam.

She opened the door to his new place. "Liam! I've got a problem. I need to talk to you."

That problem was climbing down a ladder in the front room.

Liam nodded his head toward the ladder. "Mac. Meet Cassidy. Davenport. Cassidy, my sister, Mac."

"Oh. Uh, hi." Damn it. She didn't want to have this discussion in front of Cassidy. Not until she figured out what she was going to do about it. But she plastered a smile on and nodded. "So nice to meet you. We've spoken on the phone, I believe."

"Actually, that was Deborah. My father's assistant." Cassidy brushed off her hands and held one out. "Hi. Yes, I'm Cassidy. It's nice to meet you."

Mac worked hard not to stare. Cassidy Davenport in clothes that would make her stylist's head spin painting the woodwork? It didn't add up, but then, nothing about the Davenports was adding up these days. She should never have placed Liam in that penthouse. Gran hadn't known what she was talking about, and now it was just one more headache she had to deal with. Liam helping Cassidy out with a place to live had disaster written all over it—*not* that Davenport had had to say anything. He hadn't needed to; the very act of him telling her to call him by his first name put the message out loud and clear: Play on his team or else. "Liam told me what happened, but I didn't think he'd make you do manual labor to pay him back."

"Oh I'm not—"

"Mac, that's not what this is." Liam put a hand on her back. "Come on. Let's go into the kitchen and you can tell me what you need. Cassidy has to get to work on her own projects, actually. Do you mind, Cass?"

"No. You're right. I do have work to do."

Mac allowed Liam to lead her into the kitchen, wondering what sort of project Cassidy had to get to work on—redesigning her closet to handle this season's collection? Must be nice.

Mac shook her head. Cassidy Davenport's closet was the least of her worries. "I got a call from Davenport, Lee. He wants me to handle all of his buildings in the tristate area."

"Hey, that's great! Congrats!"

"No, Lee, you don't get it. I can't sign the contract knowing you have Cassidy in your home."

"Why the hell not? What does it matter what your brother does with his life when it comes to Davenport hiring you?"

"You're not that naïve, Lee. He's dangling this carrot because he knows where she is." And he knew Mac would want the carrot badly enough to do something about it.

"So? Cassidy's a grown woman; she can live where she wants. It's not like he's going to put something in the contract about his daughter."

Mac exhaled. "On second thought, maybe you *are* that naïve. He won't *have to* put anything about her in the contract; if he wants her back, all he'll have to do is threaten to badmouth my company. The guy's got clout. I don't need my business getting bad PR, and I certainly don't need my clients questioning my ethics. I can't risk everything for this one contract."

"And of course you want it."

"Wouldn't you?"

Liam sighed loudly. "You want me to kick her out."

Yes. "Well, no. Obviously I don't want you to have to do that, but how much longer is she going to be staying with you? I don't want to have to keep pretending I don't know. This is a really big opportunity for me, Lee. It could make my company."

"Did he specifically say you needed to hand over his daughter?"

"Well, no, but—"

"Then it's not an issue."

"But it could be."

"Mac, if he hasn't come after her by now, he's not going to. The guy's had plenty of opportunity."

"I wish I could be sure of that."

"Hey, he's a lousy father. You think he's just going to get a change of heart like that?" Liam snapped his fingers. "I mean, how shitty can he be, tossing his daughter away? What I wouldn't give—"

Liam looked away, his voice thick.

Mac got it. She walked up to her brother and hugged him. "I know. It's sad how people don't realize life is short and that they should enjoy each other while they can."

"I miss them, Mac."

"Me, too."

They held each other for a bit, each taking strength from the other. It was what the four of them did.

"We have to cherish every day we have with Gran," Liam said. "She's getting older."

"I know."

"She wants us married."

"I know." Mac was glad her face was buried in Liam's shirt so he wouldn't see the guilt on her face.

"What are we going to do about that?"

"I think they frown on brothers marrying sisters in this state."

"Ha ha." He squeezed her tighter. "I love you, Mary-Alice."

"Watch it, Lee. We might be feeling mushy, but I'll still deck you for using that name."

He squeezed her even tighter. "And you'd do it, too, *Mac*." He kissed the top of her head. "Let's give this Davenport thing a few more days. It might be moot by then."

"Oh? Cassidy going to hit the lottery and be able to move out?"

Liam took a step back, shrugging. "Something like that."

"Now that sounds intriguing."

"Let's just say that Cassidy Davenport isn't the spoiled little socialite I thought she was. Want to come for dinner and see for yourself?"

"Are you saying she's not like Rachel?" The question shot out before Mac could think about it because she was so surprised at the invitation. Ever since Rachel, she and Sean and Bry made a concerted effort *not* to try to fix him up with anyone or talk about the woman who'd broken his heart.

He shrugged again, this time turning away and heading back to the living room. "Let's just say that you can't judge a book by its cover. You really need to get to know the person before you understand what they're all about, and living with Cassidy has taught me a few things."

Mac could only imagine what those things were because one night under the same roof with Jared had shown her a lot.

Mainly that she wanted another.

Chapter Twenty-four

MARY-ALICE has certainly grown up, hasn't she?"

Jared kissed Grandma's cheek after getting into her car for his doctor's appointment on Wednesday. He'd spent yesterday alone again because Mac had had to go put out the fire that erupted when Bryan managed to get his ass canned from the widow's place. For a single mother of five to kick out the hired help—especially a movie star—something big had to have happened. Jared couldn't wait to hear *that* story; he just hoped for Mac's sake that he didn't learn about it in the news. "We've all grown up, Grandma."

She patted his cheek. "Don't remind me, Jared. A lady doesn't like to know she's getting older."

"But you're still as pretty as you ever were."

"Flatterer. No wonder you have groupies."

"Bryan's the one with groupies. I have fans."

"Female ones. A lot."

There was only one who mattered now. And that was a conversation he didn't want to have with his grandmother. Not until it became one that couldn't be avoided. Like when he and Mac started dating—

Jared sat back with a hiss. He was getting way too ahead of himself. Two weeks ago he was done with women for good, Mac hadn't even been on his horizon, and she didn't even like him that way anymore.

"Are you okay, Jared?" Grandma twisted in her seat, concern etched all over her face.

"Ah, yeah. I'm fine. It was just a . . . twinge." At least that wasn't a lie. The twinge had been in his chest, not his leg, but, again, she didn't need to know.

"You're certain?"

"Yes, Grandma, I'm certain. Besides, we're going to the doctor; he'll fix me right up." In about seven months with dozens of therapy sessions, but, hey, at least it was two months less than it'd been when this started.

"How's the attic clean-out coming along?"

He looked at her. Her tone and the look on her face were just a little too innocent.

"It's coming. A little slower than I'd like. Mac has to handle a couple of other clients for a while, so it's just me." A state of being he was coming to loathe. He'd never realized just how much baseball had filled his life on a personal level as well as a professional one until it wasn't there anymore.

"You know, that girl really cared for you. Cate and I had hoped . . ." Grandma glanced at him. "Well, you know what we'd hoped. But we're just being silly. It's not as if you can fall in love on command. I mean, if something were going to happen between the two of you, it would've already." She stole another glance. "Right?"

"Right. It would have." She was fishing, but he wasn't biting. "There is no ring, is there, Grandma?"

"What?" Her head spun his way—and so did the steering wheel.

Jared wrenched it back so they were heading straight.

"Oh . . . oh dear. Thank you, sweetheart." Grandma patted her hair back in place and gripped the wheel until her knuckles were white.

And she didn't answer his question.

Just as he thought. She'd wanted the two of them in that attic together.

"I found the scrapbook."

She glanced over, but this time, didn't jerk the wheel. "Oh, good. I'd hate to get rid of that. All your hard work."

"You mean, all *your* hard work. What'd you do—subscribe to every newspaper in the country?"

"I didn't make that scrapbook, sweetheart."

"You didn't? Then who did?" Certainly not his mother. While he could hope for it, he knew better.

"Mary-Alice did, of course. She'd show me each new page when she made it."

If Jared had bet someone that he couldn't feel worse about how he'd fluffed off Mac's feelings years ago, he would have just lost that bet. The work that had gone into that book . . . It definitely wasn't fluff. "I found a bunch of home movies, too."

The subject change worked perfectly. "You did? I didn't realize they were still there. I wonder if they're any good. I'll have to find a projector."

"You have one, and the movies are fine. I watched one of them."

"Oh? Which one? Was it the one of you after you were born? Your grandfather spent hours getting the lighting just right, then you slept through the entire thing. I think we have an hour of film of you just sleeping." She squeezed his knee. "You were such an adorable baby. I could watch that film over and over."

"Um, no. That wasn't the one I saw."

"Oh, was it our trip to Niagara Falls? I told Peter that no one was going to want to watch a bunch of water going over a cliff on film in forty years, but he just had to film it."

"Nope, not that one either." He sat up straighter in his seat, ready to lunge for the steering wheel when he asked her about his father's mystery woman. "It was the one where Mac's parents got engaged."

"Oh . . . That one . . ."

He watched realization dawn in her face. "Yes. That one. Who was my father engaged to?"

Grandma, to her credit, managed not to drive into a tree and almost convinced him he hadn't seen the dread in her eyes.

But he had.

"Oh, dear, that was a long time ago. I don't even remember. But then he married your mother and had you and what does it matter who she was? It was all over ages ago."

"I don't think it was, Grandma."

"What?" This time the wheel did go to the right, and Jared was glad to see his reflexes weren't shot to hell. Maybe he should have had this conversation someplace else, but the doctor's waiting room wasn't a better choice.

"Do you mean to say that you think your father is having an affair with Olive?"

"Olive? That's the woman's name?"

Grandma's lips slammed shut and she stared out the front window.

Jared sighed. He recognized that look. She wouldn't talk until she was ready. "No, that's not what I meant. What I meant was, I think Dad still has feelings for her."

A tear slid down his grandmother's cheek.

"Pull over, Grandma." He'd been right; this wasn't a conversation to have while she was driving.

He looked at the clock on the dash. They had a few minutes to spare before his appointment.

He directed her to a side road and Grandma pulled into the first spot available.

He reached over and turned off the engine. "Tell me about them."

Grandma smiled. A genuine smile. One that erased the worried look she'd almost driven off the road with. "Olive Tremayne. He'd loved her from the time he was six. She did, too. They were inseparable."

"Then why didn't they get married? You can't tell me Dad fell head over heels in love with Mom because I've lived with them. There were no sonnets and picnics between them."

"Oh, that's not true, Jared—"

"I did the math, Grandma. I know they got married because of me."

Her hand fell away and so did that happy look. “Oh.”

“I just can’t believe I didn’t figure it out sooner.”

“Yes, well, it wasn’t something we wanted to bring up.”

“So what happened?”

Grandma looked at him, her bottom lip quivering. “I think you need to speak to your father about this. It’s not my story to tell.” She ran her fingertips from his temple to his chin, which she then cupped. “Just remember, if things hadn’t happened how they did, I wouldn’t have you. So whatever’s gone on before, none of it is more important than the fact that I have you in my life, Jared.” She leaned over and kissed his cheek.

“But you’d have another grandchild. Maybe more.”

“Would you want a different grandmother?”

“Well, no, but—”

“Exactly. I can’t change the past or what happened, but I can certainly be thankful for the blessing I received from it. You’re here and I love you, sweetheart. The past is in the past. Let it go.”

She was right; he couldn’t change the past.

But he could learn from it.

JARED walked around the back of his parents’ house. He’d never thought of it as his; it was merely the place he slept until he could move out on his own.

His father was on the patio where the housekeeper had said he’d find him, reading the newspaper.

Alone.

Not that he expected any different. Obviously, their vacation hadn’t brought his parents any closer.

“Hey, Dad.”

“Jared.” His father looked over the top of the paper. “This is a surprise. What can I do for you?”

Jared sat down. “I heard you used to play ball.”

His father set the paper down. “Who’d you hear that from?”

“I saw some old movies. You had a jersey.”

"Old movies . . ." His father's shoulders drooped. "The engagement party."

It wasn't a question. "Yeah."

His father sucked in a giant breath, held it for a few seconds, then exhaled. "You want to know why I never told you."

"Yeah."

"Your mother. She hated to hear me talk about it."

"Yet you hired Bill and built me the batting cage."

"You had the talent and I told her it wasn't fair for her to punish you for my mistakes."

"Olive."

His dad sucked in another breath, pain etched across his face. "Yes. Olive. I couldn't blame your mom, so I did what she asked." He kneaded the back of his neck. "It's not a story I'm proud of."

"I still want to hear it."

Dad folded the newspaper in precise, minute detail. "Olive's father decided my aspirations to play pro ball were irresponsible. Said I'd never amount to anything. Forbade me to see her."

"So you drowned your sorrows one night, ended up in Mom's bed, and here I am."

His father winced. "In a nutshell, yes."

"Didn't you ever hear of a thing called a condom?"

"I was drunk, Jared. Drunk and pissed off, and the chances of me making the team really *were* slim. But I had that dream, you know? And everything was still possible. All of it within my grasp. When he told me to stay away from her, I thought . . . I thought I was going to miss out on the best thing to ever happen to me, and, well, what can I say? I was young, drunk, and stupid. And here you are."

"Wow. With that kind of story, it's a wonder you guys decided to keep me at all."

"Come on, Jared. That's not fair. Of course I wanted you. But I didn't know about you in that film you saw. I'd had that night with your mom, then two days later I found out the team wanted me. I high-tailed it to Olive's house, showed her father the offer, and asked for her hand right there. I wasn't going to make a lot, but it was a job. A real job. Suddenly, that made me good enough for his daughter. So I borrowed the money from my parents to get her that ring and I was set. I was the happiest guy in the world."

"And then you found out you were going to become a father."

"Yeah. I had it all. I was on top of the world—"

"And then I came along." So much made sense now. He'd been paying for the sins of his father—from his father. And his mother, come to think of it.

"Does Mom know about Olive?"

"Of course. Everyone knew about Olive. We'd announced our engagement in the paper. Three weeks later, your grandfather showed up at the front door and the rest is history."

"So why didn't you still play ball?"

"The PR. Team didn't want to deal with it. If I hadn't announced the engagement to Olive so publicly, I might have gotten away with it. I could have married your mom and still been able to play. But with it being in the papers and your grandfather not wanting you to be born out of wedlock, there was no choice. The scandal would be worse for the team than losing me. So I lost."

"So you two got married, had me, and lived not-so-happily-ever-after."

"We tried. I did want you, Jared. That was never in question."

"But to have me you had to give up everything you wanted. The game, Olive, the life you'd planned."

"But I worked my ass off to give it all to *you*."

"Then why haven't you been there to enjoy it?"

His father sighed and this time he got out of his chair to walk to the stone wall at the edge of the patio. "I thought I could live vicariously through you. That it wouldn't matter that it wasn't me on the field. That I could be proud of having a professional ball player for a son. And don't get me wrong, I am proud of you. But every time I set foot in that stadium, I realize it could have been me. Should have been me. I made a dumb-ass mistake that cost me everything I'd wanted and it's like a knife every time. And not only did I lose the woman I loved and the career that I'd wanted, but I've lost my ability to enjoy the game."

"You need to see someone, Dad. This isn't healthy. It's been thirty-five years."

"Thirty-six and three months."

Which alone showed he needed to see someone. "Whatever. It's been a long time. You've done well for yourself. You have a career and a home you can be proud of. If you can't come to my games, well, I guess I can understand. But you have to stop beating yourself up over it. You only get one life; you might as well enjoy what's left."

"That's easy for you to say, Jared. You have everything you want."

"Maybe not. They might not take me back with this injury."

"And you're okay with that?"

Jared shrugged. "I have to be. I mean, at some point, we all know we're not going to be the starters anymore. Getting older only brings that day closer. Throw in this sort of injury, and the writing's on the wall. But I have other options. Other things I want to pursue. Other things in my life."

His father looked at him. Really looked at him. In a way he hadn't in a long, long time. Maybe ever. "You're the man I wanted to be."

"You still can, Dad. Your life's not over. You can still make it count. You can still . . ." Jared looked at the sliding glass door where his mother stood watching them. "Fix things."

Dad looked at the door, too.

Mom quickly turned and walked away.

"I think that ship has sailed, Jared."

"I don't think so, Dad. You know Mom. She's not the kind of person to sleep with some random guy."

"True."

"Yet she did with you. Maybe it wasn't just a one-nighter for her. Maybe she wanted you. Because it wasn't for your money back then, right? You didn't have a job and you didn't have a contract. Maybe she just wanted you."

His father's eyes widened and he sat back down in the chair. "No. That's not—" He shook his head. "No. It was just a night out with her girlfriends. A few drinks and—"

"She was with her girlfriends? Dad, have you ever been around a pack of women? There's no way one of them is going home with a guy unless she wants to because women talk each other out of doing shit like that. No, she wanted you, Dad." Jared was crossing his fingers here, though he'd recognized the look on his mother's face.

He should; it'd been the same one Mac had worn around him.

Mom loved Dad. And she'd been waiting all these years for him to love her back. All she'd need would be to hear the words . . .

He stood up and grabbed his crutch. "I have to go, Dad. Think about what I said. You may not have the life you'd envisioned, but the one you have isn't all that bad. Be thankful you have a family at all. So many people don't. Too many lose them too soon."

And some people never realize what having one was all about.

That was *not* going to be him.

JARED zipped into the parking spot in front of Liam's latest project and headed to the door on his crutches before he second-guessed himself out of what could be one of the most important decisions of his life.

The door swung inward. "Jared? What's up?"

"Hey, Lee. I want to go out with your sister."

Chapter Twenty-five

IT took Liam less time to recover from that statement than it took Jared.

"Does she know this?" Liam was, surprisingly, calm.

That made one of them. "No."

"Are you planning to tell her?"

"Obviously."

"But I thought you didn't like my sister." Liam jerked his head as an invitation to enter.

Jared winced as he crossed the threshold. "I lied."

"You lied."

"Yeah."

"Because?"

Jared exhaled. "It's complicated."

"And you think you wanting my sister isn't?" Liam uncapped two beers and held one out. "Start talking, Jare."

Jared took it and headed toward the overturned crate beside the fireplace. He set his bad leg on a bucket of joint compound in front of it and set the beer on the floor beside him. Much as he wouldn't mind easing this conversation with alcohol, he needed a clear head more. "Mac . . . She's . . ." He scratched his jaw. "Geez, Lee. It's complicated."

"Yeah, I get that. She drove you bat shit crazy when we were kids, which is why I don't get you wanting to go out with her out of the blue." Liam took a long swig of his beer, then walked around the sawhorse table. "God, just saying that makes me want to hurl. I mean, you. You're Jared. My best friend. We talked about girls. Shared what we did with them. How the hell am I supposed to look at you if you're with my sister?" He flipped over another empty compound bucket and sat on it, rubbing his temples.

"You don't seem surprised."

Liam looked at him. "I'm not. You two were always like a match to flame. I figure it's inevitable that some of those sparks still remain. But, still . . . my sister?"

"I know, right? I mean, I never made a move on her back then. She's your sister; I get that. But now . . ." Jared's fingers twitched. He wanted that beer. "She's also a woman."

"Don't say any more." Liam rubbed an eye with the ball of his hand. "You. Mac. God." He shook his head. "I need to scrub my brain. It's too bizarre."

"Hey, it's not that weird. I mean, she's gorgeous, and we've known each other practically our whole lives. We played together as kids—"

"No, you teased the crap out of her and made her life hell."

"You're exaggerating, Lee."

Liam leaned forward. "Really? Did *you* find the scraps of paper that said *Mrs. Mary-Alice Nolan* trailing down the hallway? Did *you* have to see the tears when you said something that hurt her? Did *you* have to watch her face fall every time you showed up with a new girlfriend? Mac had the biggest crush on you and you squashed it. I'm shocked she's even talking to you after Camille."

"Drive the knife in a little deeper, why don't you?" Jared pinched the bridge of his nose. "Look, I know I was obnoxious to her. And it would've been weird to date your sister when we were teenagers. We were horny bastards and if I'd tried anything with Mac, you would've had the right to cut off my nuts. But we're adults now and, well, she's . . . she's . . . Mac."

Liam rested his knees on his elbows. "Say that again."

"What? That you can cut off my nuts? No thanks."

"No, the other thing."

Jared scratched his head. "What? That she's Mac?"

Liam smiled and took a sip of his beer. "You like her. You really like her."

"Hey, Sally Field, that's what I've been trying to tell you."

"No, I mean you *like* her. You might even love her."

"Whoa, let's not go that far. I'm just getting used to the idea of wanting her." Love? That was just . . . Just . . .

No. He wasn't in love with Mac. Hell, he was just warming up to the idea of being in *like* with her. Of wanting her. Love? No. Definitely not.

Sure about that?

Liam had his fingers in his ears. "TMI, bro. She is, after all, my sister."

Jared got that. It wasn't exactly sunshine and roses for him, either. Though Mac preferred daisies. How he knew that, he had no clue, but something in the back of his brain was reminding him about that. "Uh, yeah, this has to be weird for you."

"Especially since I can see it for myself. You're different about her."

Jared couldn't even deny it because he was. "Here's hoping I didn't screw up too much in the past and crush all her adolescent dreams out of existence." Though it'd serve him right.

Liam waggled his eyebrows. "Just think how much fun it'll be to fulfill them now."

He had. In minute, Technicolor detail.

Which he wasn't about to share with her brother. "I, uh, think we're heading into weird territory again, Lee."

"Yeah, you're right." Liam laughed and swirled his beer bottle. "I just don't . . . I don't know. I guess it's better than her being with some guy I don't know. What if he was a dweeb or something?"

Jared had already lived that nightmare—and Dave wasn't a dweeb. "So, do I have your permission to pursue this?"

"My permission?" The beer bottle stopped halfway to Liam's mouth. "Jared, you're a grown man. Since when do you need permission?"

Jared picked up the beer. "Since it's my best friend's sister we're talking about and I don't want to screw up our friendship."

"True. Bros before hos." Liam took a swig.

Now it was Jared's turn to stop the bottle before it reached his lips. "Did you just call your sister a ho?"

"What's it to you?" Liam arched an eyebrow in that I'm-smarter-than-you routine he'd used so effectively on his brothers but which didn't work on him for shit.

Jared saluted him with the bottle. "If I were fully recovered, I'd deck you for that."

"You and what army?"

They stared at each other for a heartbeat, then burst out laughing.

"This is weird shit." Jared held out his beer and Liam clinked his against it. He wasn't just talking about this conversation.

"Yeah. It is. But then, given what I'm feeling for Cassidy Davenport, I guess I'm not one to throw stones."

Jared coughed on the swig he'd just taken. "Cassidy Davenport? Are you saying—"

"I don't want to talk about it." Liam finished off the rest of his beer.

Jared had to as well. Loving Mac . . . Cassidy Davenport . . . This little conversation had turned out to be a real eye-opener.

Jared steered the conversation back into safer waters. "What if your sister finds out about Cassidy? Isn't the dad one of her biggest clients?"

"Yeah. And about to get bigger because the guy wants Mac to handle all his properties in the tristate area. You see my dilemma."

"But . . . Cassidy Davenport? Isn't she like a bigger deal than your last girlfriend? Like a socialite on steroids?"

"Again, you see the dilemma. But we're not talking about me. We're talking about you. And my sister." Liam raked a hand through his hair. "Holy fuck."

"Not going there with you, Lee. This is one instance where I do *not* kiss and tell."

"Appreciate that. I don't know that I could stomach it. Just the thought of it . . ."

"Don't think about it. It'll make your head explode."

"You know, if this were anyone but my sister that we were discussing, I'd say something crude." Liam set his bottle down and linked his hands behind his head. "So what are you going to do about Camille?"

"Camille has nothing to do with what I feel for Mac."

"I get that, but still. She's living in your house. At some point you're going to have to cut the strings. I can guarantee my sister isn't going to want your live-in ex around."

A very good point. He wanted Mac to be able to trust him; having Camille in the picture wasn't conducive to that. "I can't legally change the locks if she's living there, and the eviction process is tedious. And no one but me is in any great hurry."

"Come on, Jare, you're a smart guy. I'm sure you can come up with some way to do it. Preferably before things get too serious with my sister. Matter of fact . . ." Liam's eyes narrowed and Jared knew what was coming. "I *bet* you can."

"I'm not taking that bet."

"Chicken."

"Dick."

"Pansy."

Jared ran the rest of the litany in his head: *ass, dork, jerk, minion* . . . They'd had the same running comments for years. And in the end, the bet always won out. "I don't think it's a good idea to bet when Mac's involved."

"If you want to get a chance with her, then you better make sure Camille is gone." Liam held the bottle to his lips. "I'm not budging on this."

Jared looked at him. They might be friends, but Mac was Lee's sister. The guy was dead serious.

Shit. This was a no-win situation unless he came up with something.

"Do we have a deal?"

"Do I have a choice?"

"I love my sister, Jare."

Yeah, Jared got that. "Well Mac has to forgive me first. She sorta has to be in on this for it to work."

"Oh it'll work. You leave that to me. But remember, friend or not, you hurt my sister, I'm going to have to hurt you. And in your condition," Liam nudged his injured leg with his foot, "that's not going to be hard to do."

Lee had that right. Mac not wanting to give this a shot would do a more effective job than her brother ever could.

Chapter Twenty-six

"SORRY, Mac," said Liam when he opened his front door for their dinner, "but Cassidy's not here. She had to work."

"Work? She has a job?" Mac held out the plate of brownies she'd confiscated from Jared's stash. She could bake brownies as well as any of the Maeves or Renees or Juliettes of the world, but why bother when Jared had more than he could eat?

"Yeah, she, um, does some commission work."

"Commission? For what? Personal shopping?"

"Hey, cut her some slack, okay? She's not like that."

Mac followed Liam toward his kitchen, wondering who he was talking about. The Cassidy Davenport she was familiar with had been known to keep local designers in business on one shipping trip alone. Other than that, the woman wasn't qualified to do much of anything other than look good in front of the cameras and spend her father's money. Money Mac wanted a piece of now that she'd offered to return Bryan's client's money and Tina had called out sick for the next few days. Mac couldn't afford to pay someone else to pick up the job, so she was going to have to do it.

Mildred's project just got put on the back burner, but at least Jared was there to keep it moving forward.

"So what are we having?" Mac hiked herself onto one of Liam's barstools and told her stupid hormones to quit crying that they wouldn't see Jared for a while. That was a *good* thing.

"Your choice of Gran's beef stew, Gran's lasagna, or Gran's mac-n-cheese."

Mac smiled and linked her fingers on the countertop. "Yes, please."

"Yes? To what?"

"All of them."

"All? Geez, Mac, don't you ever eat?"

"I do, but I finished the food she made me."

"So now you're hitting my stash?"

"You offered."

"Good point."

He walked around his kitchen, getting out the food, warming it up, plating it . . . Gran had taught them to be self-sufficient. Her brothers were going to make some women very happy. And if Gran had anything to say about it, that'd be sooner rather than later.

She picked up her fork when he set the plate in front of her. "So, about Cassidy, Lee—"

"I don't want to talk about Cassidy." He pulled his bar stool around the end of the peninsula and sat.

"But we have to. I have to figure out how to handle this thing with her father."

"You just say, 'yes sir,' and sign on the dotted line. No conflict. If he does ask, you say that she's staying here. End of your involvement." He put a slice of lasagna on his plate.

Mac scooped some of the mac-n-cheese. No one made mac-n-cheese like Gran. "So then why invite me over if you wanted to keep me out of the Davenport loop? Having dinner and getting to know his daughter seems counterproductive."

"I, ah, had an ulterior motive."

Mac set her fork down, the mac-n-cheese going stale in her mouth. "An ulterior motive?"

"Yeah." Liam waved his forkful of lasagna around. "I want to see how you beat us at poker."

"See how—Are you saying I cheated?" The correct terminology was going to be very important for her indignation. She speared some more mac just for appearance's sake.

"No, you wouldn't cheat. But I'm having a hard time believing that you could come in cold and beat the three of us. You had to have a system."

"Newsflash, big brother: It's all in the draw of the cards." Which, really, it had been. "Unless you're going to accuse me of some fancy prestidigitation?" Which she hadn't done.

"No, it's just . . ."

"Did Jared put you up to this?" Jeez. Just when she thought he might have changed.

"Jared had nothing to do with this." Liam set his fork down. "Let's play a few hands. I want to see you win."

Mac scratched her nose. She'd say he had something up his sleeve, but he was wearing a basketball jersey that didn't have sleeves. If she refused, he'd have grounds to question her. If she played, she could lose and dispel his suspicions. And she might even lose for real.

This was a no-brainer. "Okay. Fine. Whatever. But when I beat you again, are you going to say I cheated?"

"Not unless you do."

She won the first two hands, then lost in the third. There. Suspicion averted.

Lee tapped the long edge of the deck on the counter. "So, did you let me win that one just to prove your point?"

"Do you really think I'm that devious?" She crossed her fingers beneath the ledge. She actually *hadn't* let him win that last hand; she'd lost fair and square. Just like she'd won the first two. It was difficult to count cards when there weren't many being played.

"No, Mac, but no one can be as lucky as you were to beat the three of us with the stakes that high."

"What'll convince you that I didn't do something? You want to bet something so I won't 'lose on purpose'? Like, say, loser has to clean for a month?"

Liam leaned onto his elbows, studying her. Mac wished she could take the offer back. This was a no-win situation. She had to win because she didn't have time to clean for him for a month, but winning would only prove Liam's case.

Liam sat back and tapped the cards on the counter. "Okay, I'll take the bet, but I want to amend it since I don't need you to clean my place."

"Fine. What do you want to wager?"

"A date."

"Seriously, Lee, that's probably as illegal as us getting married."

"*Not* with me, runt." He flicked a couple cards at her. "I want you to go out with a friend of mine."

For a second, she thought he meant Jared. But of course he didn't; he knew how she felt about Jared. Lee might want to beat her, but he wouldn't humiliate her. "A date. So what are we talking? A long bike ride? A movie? Just dinner . . . what? How long do I have to be in this guy's presence?"

"Dinner's fine."

"Who is he? Do I know him?"

"He's a friend. And he's interested. Let's leave it at that because if I don't win, I don't want to embarrass him."

She looked at Liam. That was nice of him, and if he was okaying this date, the guy had to at least be decent. Liam would never set her up with a troll.

"Just dinner?"

"Just dinner."

She didn't want to take the bet. Blind dates were awkward and uncomfortable and carried a whole extra set of expectations. But if she didn't, Liam wouldn't let up about her poker-playing abilities.

She sighed and said, "Fine," even though she didn't want to have dinner with anyone. Not if it couldn't be Jared.

DINNER'S tomorrow night." Liam dragged the "pot" of toothpicks toward him when he won the hand. "He'll pick you up at six."

"Who's going to pick me up?" She gathered the cards and organized the deck. "I don't get a name?"

Liam shrugged. "Like I said, I don't want to embarrass the guy. He might not show."

Something was up. It wasn't like Liam to be this cagey. She thought about calling him on it, but since he'd stopped insisting she'd had "a system," she didn't want to rock the boat.

She set the deck down in front of him and tapped the top card. "Fine. Dinner tomorrow. That's it then, right? We're even after that?"

Lee picked up the deck and got off his barstool to put the cards in the drawer by the fridge. Mac thought she caught a grin before he turned away.

"Oh I don't know, Mac. You might end up owing me big time."

Chapter Twenty-seven

JARED was standing on her front step with a crutch under one arm and a bouquet of flowers in his other hand.

A bouquet of daisies.

"You?" Mac almost closed the door in his face.

Almost.

Jared held up the flowers. "Hi, Mac."

She took them instinctively because she was trying to wrap her brain around the fact that not only must Jared have told Liam he was interested in her, but Liam had obviously given his blessing.

Or had he? Maybe this was payback for the bet?

"You might want to put them in water. No sense having wilted daisies."

"What?" If it *was* payback, she wasn't going to give either of them the satisfaction of seeing her sweat.

And if it wasn't, well, then she might let *Jared* see her sweat.

Really?

She shook herself mentally. Getting way too ahead of herself. Right now she just wanted to get through dinner. "Oh. Right. Hang on."

She headed toward the kitchen, then realized she'd left him standing on the threshold.

She turned around. "Come in. It's not like you don't know your way around."

Maybe not the most hostess-with-the-mostest graciousness, but then, she wasn't feeling the *mostest* of anything right now. Except maybe confused.

"I can hear you thinking, Mac," Jared said from the living room.

"You can't hear anyone thinking. That's not possible."

"Not true. The silence is so loud it's deafening."

She poked her head out from the kitchen. "You can hear silence? We're going to want to get you to the CIA because I'm sure they'll find your superhero power quite handy."

He smiled that damn sexy smile. "So you think I'm Superman?"

She rolled her eyes. She might have been infatuated with him, but she'd never been blind to his ego.

She put the daisies in a vase and smiled. Jared had brought her daisies.

Does that mean he gets a kiss at the end of the night like Dave? And since he brought your favorite flowers, maybe more?

Geez, her conscience needed to give it a rest. Let her enjoy the evening.

As long as you don't enjoy it too much. Do we need another broken heart here?

Valid point.

And, besides, she needed to find out what was up with this date. Jared couldn't suddenly be interested just because he was bored and alone, and think she was going to go along with the program. And *she* needed to be sure she wasn't superimposing her teenage wants and dreams on her grown-up ones.

Well, she already knew she wanted him; that was just plain chemistry. She'd never doubted that for a second. But the rest? That was still to be decided. She had to keep everything in perspective.

But Jared made it difficult. He opened the car door for her, held out her chair, deferred to her for her meal selection . . . And after they'd ordered, he stood when the music came and held out his hand, the one crutch he'd brought with him leaning against his chair. "May I?"

"You want to dance?"

"Absolutely."

It was a slow number. Mac wasn't sure how she felt about that.

But she did know she wasn't going to pass up this opportunity.

He slid his hand around her waist. "Any chance I can get to hold you, Mac."

The words made her melt, as if her teenaged dream had waltzed out of her brain and into her body. But what she was feeling was definitely not teenaged. And definitely not a dream.

His fingers moved against her back. Slightly, but they lit a fire under her skin that she couldn't ignore. His breath was warm against her temple and his chest brushed hers just enough to tease. She should have worn a loose-fitting top because, another couple of dance moves, and it was going to be very obvious that there was some serious chemistry between them.

The twirl, pull-in, and dip were those moves.

When he dipped her, Mac couldn't look away. His green eyes were staring into hers so intently it was as if he could read her thoughts.

"God, you're beautiful, Mac."

She'd say the same thing about him—if she could speak.

He set her upright and put his lips against her ear. "I want to kiss you, you know."

She knew she wanted him to—which was exactly the reason he couldn't.

"No." She took a step back.

He let her. But he didn't let go.

And she didn't make him.

Jared squeezed her fingertips. "If I promise not to, will you finish this song with me?"

If he promised not to, she might cry, but since she was the one who'd put the brakes on, she'd just have to deal.

"Mac?"

She nodded and took that step back into his arms.

"Too fast?"

She nodded.

"I don't think I've ever heard you this quiet."

She smiled against his chest. "I thought you were the one who could hear silence?"

"I'd much rather hear what's going on in that brain of yours."

No he wouldn't. It was a jumbled mess of the past and the present colliding, and even *she* didn't want to hear it.

"Mac?" He pressed her a little closer. "Say something. I'm feeling a little out of my league."

She didn't have a clue what to say. Hell, she didn't have a clue what to *think*. Right now, she just wanted to feel and enjoy and let everything take care of itself.

"Mac?"

She wracked her brain to come up with something coherent. "Our dinners are here," was the best she could do.

Jared pulled back and scanned her face, then he smiled that grin that was hot enough to melt silk.

Which she was wearing.

Under her dress.

"We're not finished with this conversation." Jared led her back to their table, her fingers firmly entwined with his, his limp more pronounced the closer they got to their table.

She scooched her chair in so he wouldn't have to help her and risk setting her skin on fire any more than it already was. "We shouldn't have done that."

"You didn't like it?" He slid into the seat beside her, then flicked his napkin into his lap. "I thought it was nice. A lot more than nice, actually."

"I just meant . . . your leg. Should you be taxing it like that?"

His smile got brittle. Just for an instant, and if she didn't know his every expression, she might have missed it. But she knew Jared like the back of her hand. Always had.

"I'm okay, Mac. The doc says I can put weight on it. We weren't jitterbugging, so it should be fine."

If it were fine, he wouldn't be limping, but she wasn't going to argue with him and ruin tonight. If she never had another night like this, if this *was* all about the poker bet, she was still going to enjoy it. Tonight, she was going to be Cinderella at the ball. Or maybe she'd be Scarlett and think about it all tomorrow.

She sliced into her Chicken Divan. "So how are the kittens?"

"They're good. We've come to an understanding: I don't give them any formula and they don't ruin any rugs." Jared put a slice of his steak in his mouth.

"No formula? But what are they eating?"

"I soak the kitten food in water. Makes it soft, though still firm enough that their, uh, output is firm, too. A little bit more work on the front end, but a whole lot less on the back end. If you catch my drift."

She chuckled. "Got it."

He sliced off another piece of steak, his head bent so he wasn't looking at her. "They miss you, though."

"They're kittens. They don't miss me." It was a nice thought, but still . . .

"Sure they do. They've gotten used to having you around. They perk up when you're there. When you're not, they get lonely." He slid more steak into his mouth.

He wasn't talking about the kittens. She knew that as sure as she knew she wasn't going to make it out of this date with her heart intact. "So now you're adding cat whisperer to your list of superhero powers?"

He put on his charming sideways smile and waggled his eyebrows. "You should see me when I'm about to leap over living room furniture in a single bound. These guys are fascinated with something in the basement. That should be next on the to-be-cleared-out list."

"Then the attic's done?"

"All but the ring. And I'm not so sure it was ever there. When I told Grandma I hadn't found it, she wasn't as heartbroken as I'd expect her to be if it was really missing. I mean, my grandfather worked ten hours a day, six days a week to buy that for her, and she let him, foregoing dates so he could." He squeezed her fingers when he said it. "I used to think he was crazy. That no one was worth that kind of sacrifice. Grandma would've waited, or done without."

Scarlett came out to remind her that the *used to think* part of his statement and its implications were better considered tomorrow. It'd be too easy to go down that path with the soft lights and music, the wine, and Jared sitting beside her looking so incredibly gorgeous in his navy blue button-down. "But that ring was a sign of his commitment. I think it's romantic."

"Romance is highly overrated. Well, given my past experience, that is."

Camille.

Right. How could she have forgotten Camille? The woman Jared had asked to live with him. The woman he might have married if she hadn't hurt him. It'd be one thing if Jared had ended their relationship, but Camille had. He could still have feelings for her.

Pain twisted in Mac's belly. So many times she'd imagined him marrying the woman he'd been with at whatever moment in time she'd looked him up. Yet, in all that time, he never had, and she'd hoped that maybe . . . that he might have been . . . well, waiting for her.

Nice dream, but he'd had his chance and hadn't taken it.

But maybe that was what tonight was about.

God, she hoped so.

Because she was still in love with him.

Mac exhaled and shook her head, then grabbed her glass of water and took a healthy swig.

"Mac? Are you okay? Something wrong?"

That'd depend on how he defined *wrong*. "No. I'm fine." In a please-God-don't-let-me-get-hurt-again sort of way. "So explain to me why we're here, Jared." Might as well get the answer to the question she really wanted to ask. Rip off the bandage, as it were.

He looked at her, his eyebrows in a V. "To have dinner?"

"No, I mean, us. Why are *we* here? How did this come to be? Us."

He took a sip of his wine. "Because Liam said he'd mentioned that I wanted to take you out and you said you'd go? Then he called me and told me to pick you up at six tonight."

"That's it? He didn't tell you how he 'mentioned' it?"

"I'm assuming he said something along the lines of, 'Mac, Jared told me he wanted to take you out,' and you said, 'Okay.'"

"He didn't mention the poker game?"

"What does that game have to do with anything? You cleaning my grandmother's house didn't have anything to do with that bet—Wait." He set down his utensils. "You and Liam played another game. With this dinner as the prize."

He wasn't asking a question.

So she didn't have to answer.

"Oh, hell." He tapped his thumb on the rim of his plate and stared at her. "Lee bet you to go out with me if he won, didn't he? I wasn't the prize. I was the bet you lost."

Sometimes it really sucked that he knew her family as well as he did.

She took another swig of her water.

"Never mind. You don't have to answer that." He swiped a hand over his jaw and sat back in his chair with a muttered, "son of a bitch" beneath his breath.

She ought to be enjoying this. And maybe if she didn't care about him, she would. But she'd loved Jared from the first moment she'd seen him—well, after she'd finished yelling at him about the dirt bike mounds—and nothing had changed since.

He shook his head with a disbelieving look on his face. "Serves me right, huh? I'm sorry for that night, Mac, when you came to me with your heart on your sleeve and I was such a jerk."

"And I'm sorry it looks like you were the bet I lost. You're not."

"No?" He leaned forward. "Then what am I?"

HE'D never wanted an answer more in his life. He'd been thrilled when Liam had said she'd accepted, and he'd attributed her silences tonight to the awkwardness of their past meeting their present. And whatever the future would hold.

But to know that she was only here because she'd lost a bet . . . What game was Lee playing?

"I haven't figured that out. I'm still trying to grasp the concept that you told Liam you wanted to take me to dinner. And that he agreed."

"That's because I told him the truth, Mac. That I was a blind idiot back then and I've opened my eyes now."

"And he believed you."

"Why wouldn't he? It's the truth."

She looked at him then, into his eyes, and, man, the hope he saw in hers . . .

Jesus. How could he make up for breaking her heart?

Give her yours.

Jared swallowed. Oh, sure. Just blurt out that, after years of pushing her away, he'd suddenly fallen in love with her.

Wait. *Had* he fallen in love with her?

Jared sat back. Was it possible?

He looked at her, the candlelight and pale green of her dress making her eyes seem brighter, and the look of hope in them making a beeline right to his chest.

He'd been the boy of her dreams, but in his stupidity of not appreciating that, he'd almost missed out on the woman of his.

He leaned forward again and reached for her hand. "Mary-Alice Catherine Manley, you are an incredible woman and I'm the luckiest guy on the planet to be out to dinner with you. I'm sorry for the hurt I caused you in the past, but if you'll let me, I'll make it up to you."

He waited, not breathing, when she nibbled her bottom lip. Then when her tongue swiped over it. Then again when she opened her mouth to say something, only to think better of it and close it. He'd never begged in his life, but for Mac, he was willing to take that first step. "Please?"

Indecision crossed her face. Hesitation. He got all of that. But that little bit of hope was what he was betting would make her say yes.

"I want to make up for that pain, Mac. I want us to get to know each other as we are now. Explore this side of our relationship without the past tarnishing it. I'd like to start new. Will you give me—us—that chance?"

"Why, Jared? Why now?" Her voice was soft and he hoped to hell it wasn't because there were tears behind it. He'd made her cry too much already.

"Because when you're stuck with only yourself for company, you do some hard thinking. A lot of introspection. I've looked at my life and seen the mistakes I've made as well as the successes. Baseball has been a success, but you . . ."

"I'm a failure? Gee, this conversation's going well." She tugged her hand away and grabbed her glass again.

He stopped her before she could hide behind it. "Not you, Mac. Me. I failed you."

"You didn't owe me anything."

"But I did. I do." He set her glass down and reached for her hand again. "Your feelings for me were a gift that I didn't appreciate. I claim lack of maturity and the self-centeredness of teenagers, but I could have handled it better. I'm not making excuses; I'm asking you to forgive me. Because now I see the gift of what you offered and I . . . I'd like to see if those feelings still exist."

"Why?"

"Because I . . ." How the hell was he going to say this so she'd believe him? "Because I don't want to miss out on the best thing to happen to me."

He held his breath as she looked at him, praying that what she'd once felt for him was still there and it'd be enough to let her risk her heart once more.

"I . . ." She cleared her throat and sat up a little straighter in her chair. "Okay, Jared. I'll give this a try."

He couldn't contain his smile. He did, however, refrain from hauling her into his arms and kissing her senseless. He was going to woo Mac. Make her believe.

And he was going to find some way to get Camille out of his house so Mac would never question his feelings again.

He raised his wine glass. "Then here's to tonight. This dinner. May it be the first of many." He nodded his head and took a sip.

The atmosphere changed then. When Mac wasn't self-conscious about being with him, she was a hell of a lot of fun. Smart, funny, compassionate . . . all things he'd always known about her but was just now starting to appreciate.

They talked about growing up a field away from each other and school. They were far enough apart in age that they hadn't been in the same building, but they'd had friends in the same families. And there were always the community events they'd been at.

"Do you remember that Halloween when Kelly Martinez wore that hideous mask and no one reacted?" Mac asked during dessert. "The look on his face when we just said, 'Hi, Kelly,' like it was no big deal."

"That's because Liam and I told everyone who he was," said Jared. "He'd been planning to scare all of your girlfriends into the arms of the football team and, well, let's just say the football team as a social body wasn't exactly the nicest crew. Crowd-think at its poorest. Pissed Lee and me off. We never had to resort to those tactics." Girls had been coming on to them since they'd been born, so it'd never been an issue. And in his arrogance, he'd lumped Mac in with all the others.

He was learning the error of his ways.

They danced to a few more songs and each time it was getting harder to let her go.

Leaving her at her doorstep was even harder.

He cupped her cheek, brushing his thumb along the soft curve of her jaw, tilting her head back. The moonlight caught the sparkle in her eye just before he lowered his head.

He stopped a breath away from her lips. "Is it okay to kiss you goodnight, Mac?"

She smiled that genuine, light-up-the-room smile she'd always had for him.

Thank God.

"Yes, Jared. You can kiss me."

Then she reached up and twined her fingers in his hair, tugging him down to her, and Jared wrapped his arms around her, hugging her against him, lifting her off her feet.

He often forgot how small Mac was because her presence made her seem bigger than she was. But, right now, in his arms, she was a perfect fit.

The kiss rocked him and it was a good thing he was standing next to the porch roof support. He leaned against it, lifting her a bit higher, kissing her deeply. Mac tasted even better than she had when he'd kissed her before.

She shivered against him and he smiled. It wasn't cold out tonight and even if it was, he was big enough to keep the air off her.

He kissed his way along her jaw. "You get to me, too, Mac." As if she couldn't tell.

She smiled against his cheek. "I should go in, Jared."

Not the words he wanted to hear, but the ones she needed to say. He understood.

One last kiss to that sweet soft spot below her ear and he let her slide down until her feet hit the porch.

"Ooph." She stumbled against him.

"What's wrong?"

She chuckled. "My shoe fell off."

He looked at it, then at her. It was as if the universe was giving him the perfect opportunity. "Allow me, Princess."

It was a totally cheezeball moment, and a totally hot one at the same time as he knelt on his good leg and slid her high heel onto her foot, his fingers caressing her calf a little longer than Prince Charming ought to. Then again, he was no prince. "It fits."

"Oh puhleaze." She swatted his shoulder. "Get up before you hurt yourself, Jared."

Getting up wasn't his problem—oh, she meant *stand up.* Totally different story.

He leveraged himself on the brick base of the roof support and his shoulder brushed her hip when he stood.

Not helping the situation . . .

He stepped down off the porch—making him now eye level with her.

He wasn't looking at her eyes.

Her lips were still puffy from his kiss.

He took another step down. And another. Away from temptation.

"Good night, Mac. Sweet dreams."

His sure would be.

Chapter Twenty-eight

MAC sat in Bryan's Maserati in Mildred's driveway the following morning, staring at the front door. Jared was in there. She should go in.

But what if everything had changed?

Last night had been one of the most magical nights of her life, right down to the real-life Cinderella moment.

Thought you weren't a big believer in Cinderella?

There was only one way to find out. She got out of the car and headed toward the flagstone walkway to the front porch.

Chase, the boy Jared had thrown the baseball with on the front lawn, ran up to her.

With a daisy.

"Here, Miss Manley. Jared said I should give this to you."

"He did, did he?"

"Yes, ma'am. He did. Have a nice day." The boy tugged down his baseball cap—the one with Jared's signature on the brim—and ran down the driveway with a wave.

Mac watched him round the evergreen at the end, her smile making her cheeks hurt. Maybe there was something to this whole fairy-tale business after all.

"Um, miss?" Another boy stepped out from behind the rhododendron next to the porch.

He also held a daisy.

"Hi. Aren't you one of the Bradfords?"

"Yes. I'm Michael. And this is for you. Jared said you like them."

"I do." She took the flower. "Thank you, Michael. Say hi to your parents for me."

"I will and you're welcome. Have a nice day." And he, too, ran down the driveway.

Boys popped out from behind that rhododendron bush like prairie dogs out of their holes. Each one with a daisy.

It took a dozen flowers before she made it to the first porch step.

"Are there many more?" she asked the twelfth kid.

"A few." He scrunched his mouth and cocked his head. "Is this really fun? Jared said you'd think so, but I don't get it. It's just a bunch of flowers."

"It is, but more than the flowers, it's the thought that counts. So thank you for helping Jared let me know he's thinking of me."

The kid shrugged. "Whatever. Seems like a waste of an afternoon when we could be playing ball." He turned to leave, then remembered to wish her a good day.

"You, too," she said as he walked away shaking his head.

Mac still couldn't help smiling. She'd bet he'd do this same thing someday when he understood the significance behind it.

Numbers fourteen through nineteen were repeats, the first boy—Chase—winking at her when it was his turn again. "This sure is mushy. But my mom said she'd love it if my dad did this. And since he's in a chair, I think I'm gonna do it for him. My mom could use a smile like yours."

Mac put her palms to her cheeks, careful not to lose a single daisy. She could feel the blush, but she didn't mind. "You do that, Chase. I guarantee your parents will love it."

"I guess. Well, I hope you like it, 'cause there aren't too many flowers left."

That's what she was counting on.

Jared was flower number twenty. He limped around the rhododendron with a crutch under one arm and a bunch of daisies in his other hand.

"I wanted to give you twenty-nine individually, but we ran out of kids, and preteen boys are only willing to go along with so much mushiness before they lose interest. I'm shocked I got them to make it through nineteen." He stopped in front of her. "Here. They're your favorite, right?"

She could hardly speak.

"You . . ." She sucked in a big breath. "You remembered."

"I might not figure things out right away, Mac, but it does stay in the vault." He tapped his temple. "To be taken out when most needed." He ran a hand down her arm. "I missed you."

She felt like she was seventeen again and this time Jared was saying all the right things.

"Don't look at me like that, Mac, or we might not get to the plans I have for today."

"Plans? I thought we were cleaning."

"You can clean if you want, but I have better things in mind."

"Such as . . . ?"

"Well first we're going to get these in some water." He took the daisies from her. "Don't want all my hard work and coercion tactics with the boys to go to waste. I'm into them for at least two pickup games."

"They're going to love that."

"So will I." He swept his hand toward the steps. "I was thinking that if the team doesn't renew my contract, I might get involved in a youth sports program around here. I'm sure Ted would give me a shot."

"I think Ted will shoot you if you don't." She nudged him with her shoulder as she passed. "It's not every day an MVP offers to coach."

"I don't know about coaching. I was thinking more along the lines of, you know, putting a few games together."

"And then just sitting on the sidelines? Like the parents are going to let you." She looked at the front door. The table was missing. The one for the neighbors to put their goodies on. "Where's the table?"

He opened the screen door. "I moved it."

"Why?"

He reached for her hand and kissed the back of it. "Because I don't want any more baskets with phone numbers."

She could feel herself blush at that.

"Damn, Mac, that makes you even prettier than you already are." His lips hovered over her hand and they stared at each other for a heartbeat or two.

He wanted to kiss her.

She wanted him to.

The kittens, however, had other ideas.

Three of them tumbled over the top of the play yard and came scampering toward the front door.

The open front door.

"Larry, no!" Jared let go of her hand and managed to catch the calico before the door slammed closed on him.

"Shemp, come here!" The gray dodged Mac's legs and was heading toward the wood panel at the bottom of the door when Jared managed to scoop him up as well.

"Grab Curly!" he said as the last one tried launching himself onto the bench beside the door, then wiggled his butt to leap at the screen.

Mac caught him mid-flight. "Gotcha, you little monster." She held out her hand. "Here. Let me have the others. I think we're going to need that chicken wire lid as a permanent structure.

Jared handed the two squirmy things over. "Look. Moe's still in there. Wonder why she didn't tag along."

Mac raised her eyebrows. "Is that supposed to mean something?"

"Huh?" He looked at her, then at Moe. "Oh. Wow. I didn't mean anything by it. I was just saying that if three cats are headed somewhere, I'd expect the fourth to go along, too. It had nothing to do with you and your brothers."

He studied her for a few seconds, then brushed his fingertips down her cheek and she wanted to turn into that caress and make it something more.

"Ow." Thankfully, Larry clawed her arm, demanding her attention before she could. For all the shoe-falling-off action last night, Jared's soft touch didn't mean she was Cinderella, and he was not going to fall in love with her overnight.

"Way to ruin a moment, Larry." Jared picked up the mini Freddy Krueger and tapped him on the nose. "Seriously, cat. I gotta teach you a few things about women."

"Oh and you know so much about them?"

Jared shook his head. "No way am I answering that question. I just got you to like me again."

No he hadn't; she'd never stopped.

"Come on, Mac. Let's get those daisies in water and these guys locked up nice and safe in that pen so we can enjoy our day together. I promise you, you'll have fun."

AND she did. From the limo that pulled up outside Mildred's home five minutes after they'd finished with the kittens, with a bottle of sparkling grape juice on ice inside, to the pair of shorts, T-shirt, and sneakers from a snazzy shop downtown, to the arm he kept around her the entire ride, Mac was putting this day on par with last night's dinner.

"Where are we going?" She looked up at him and wanted to pinch herself to make sure she wasn't dreaming.

Nope. She wasn't.

He smiled that sexy sideways smile. "I'm not telling."

"Is it the zoo?"

"Not telling."

"Applewood Gardens?"

"Not telling."

"La Maison?" The most expensive restaurant in the area.

He arched an eyebrow. "Dream big or go home; good for you. But no. Now sit back and enjoy the ride. I promise you're going to like it."

He had that right; she'd love it because he'd planned it and he was with her.

She never saw the hot air balloon ride coming. "We're going in that?"

"Don't tell me you're scared, Mac. You were the one blasting me over a motocross track."

"I'm not scared. I just hadn't expected this. It's so . . ."

"Scary? Weird? Crazy?"

"Romantic."

"Good. Exactly what I was going for."

She honestly didn't know how to reply to that.

Thankfully, the limo stopped and one of the balloon crew opened the door before she had to.

"Welcome to In-Flight Extravaganza where we hope you'll have the flight of your lives."

She'd been on that ride since opening her door at six o'clock last night.

THE sights were amazing, the feeling of floating in the basket was how she felt when she dreamed she was flying, and having Jared beside her made the ride an unforgettable experience.

"Look. There's your house." Jared wrapped his arm around her shoulder and pointed to the tiny house where she'd grown up. She used to imagine leaving it to live in a bigger place, but now with Gran gone and being on her own, she thought better of it. The house was full of memories. She was never going to sell it and looked forward to raising her family there.

She looked up at Jared who was squinting into the sun. With him perhaps?

She wanted it to be him. Nothing had changed. Jared had stolen her heart years ago and it was still his.

The champagne when they touched down in a farmer's field was the perfect end to a perfect morning.

But Jared still had other tricks up his sleeve.

A tour of a local vineyard, with drinks on the terrace afterward. Then another limo ride to an outdoor restaurant that overlooked the town center lake with its water fountains, and finally, back to Mildred's house.

"Have fun?" Jared asked as the limo drove away.

"You know I did." She leaned against his shoulder. He'd barely taken his arm from around her all day and she hadn't complained. She liked Jared touching her. God knew, she liked touching him.

"Want to have more?"

She could think of so many ways . . . But she wasn't sure they should take it to the next step. After all, while she'd been in love with him forever, he was only just starting to feel something for her. He wasn't quite where she was in the *what-if* arena. "What did you have in mind?"

"Home movies."

It was the perfect end to a perfect day. Watching how it all began, knowing that they'd end up here.

IT was hard for Jared to concentrate on the images on the screen. He remembered those days as if they were yesterday, but he had a whole new perspective on them now that he had Mac on the sofa beside him.

He was in love with her. It shouldn't be a surprise, and wasn't. Not really. The surprise was that he hadn't realized it sooner. He considered himself a smart guy, but he'd been so blinded by his resentment of her that he hadn't seen *her*. Who she was.

He'd been an idiot. Mac knew the value of family. There was a reason he was friends with her brothers, so there should be no surprise that she had those same qualities.

And the fact that he could barely keep his hands off her today . . . He'd intertwined their fingers every chance he got so he wouldn't kiss her until they couldn't see straight. He'd love nothing more than to spend the next week or so locked in his bedroom with her, but Mac had to be able to trust him and what he was feeling for her. He was wracking his brain trying to figure out how to get rid of Camille.

"Hey, I remember that day. We had so much fun." Mac took a handful of the microwave popcorn she'd made before they'd settled down with the bucket and four kittens. "You won that stuffed frog for me."

Jared focused on the screen where he was handing over a giant green amphibian that was almost as big as she was. "I forgot about that. What'd you do with it?"

"Kept it of course."

The unspoken *because you gave it to me* lingered in the air.

"What'd you name it?"

Mac exhaled and looked away, but he saw a smile on her lips. "Jared."

"Ah. I guess I *was* a frog, huh?"

"No, you were supposed to be the prince the frog turned into."

"But that'd mean you would've had to kiss it."

"How do you think I practiced?"

He groaned. "God, I really was stupid, wasn't I? All the kissing practice I could've wanted, and I handed you my replacement." He moved the bucket of popcorn to the table and slid his left arm along the back of the sofa behind her. "Any chance I can get a rain check?"

"It's not raining."

"Then a sun check?"

"It's night time."

"How about a goodnight kiss?"

She slicked a piece of hair back behind her ear with a smirk. "Oh well that's okay, I guess."

It sure as hell was. Better than okay. It was a kiss and so much more.

Mac had seeped through his veins when he hadn't even been looking. She'd been there all along and it was only now, when his life had twisted sideways, that he could finally see clearly.

"I want you, Mac."

She stiffened.

Damn damn damn. So much for his vow to take this slow. *And* his promise—bet—with Liam.

That last one was the least of his worries. "Wait. I—"

She put a finger on his lips. "Sssh. Don't talk, Jared. Just kiss me."

He was more than happy to oblige.

He shifted closer, dislodging the kittens and for once Larry didn't cause a problem, settling down on the pillow at the far end with his siblings.

Jared scooped Mac onto his lap, never breaking the kiss,

the feel of her arms going around him one of the best feelings in the world.

She threaded her fingers through his hair, pulling him closer, and Jared went willingly.

But it wasn't enough. And seated where she was, she had to know it. Had to know how she affected him. How he wanted her.

He shifted her to ease the ache, but it didn't do any good. He could move Mac to the other side of the room and he'd still want her as badly.

"Mac, this isn't going to work."

She scrambled off him so fast he didn't have a chance to explain until she *was* on the other side of the room. "Okay. Fine. Whatever. Where are my keys?"

"Wait. Hang on." His leg made it difficult to get off this sofa. "You misunderstood."

"Don't get up, Jared. I know my way out."

"Damn it, Mac. Hang on a second, will you?' He shoved off the sofa but his damn knee gave out, so he fell back onto it. "I didn't mean this—us—isn't going to work. I meant kissing you on the sofa wasn't going to work."

"Oh."

He held out his hand. "Please, Mac. Come back here."

She didn't move. But she didn't leave, either.

Go slow, Nolan.

"I . . . I care about you, sweetheart. I don't want to hurt you. Never again."

He held his breath as she looked at him. He wished he really could hear her thinking because he wanted to know what was going through her mind.

She took a step toward him.

Then another.

But then she picked up her keys on the projector table. "I want to believe you, Jared. You can't really know how much I want to. But I should go home. We should both sleep on it. See how we feel tomorrow."

"I know how I'm going to feel tomorrow, Mac."

"That makes one of us." She clenched the keys in her fist. "I'll see you tomorrow, Jared. We'll talk then."

Chapter Twenty-nine

THE smell of bacon greeted her when she opened Jared's front door the next morning.

The tang of freshly squeezed orange juice got her taste buds going, and the sweet scent of melted butter had her mouth watering.

As did Jared in only a pair of basketball shorts, a jersey, and flip-flops as he carried a breakfast tray into the foyer, complete with another daisy in a vase on it.

"What's this?"

He lifted the tray. "Breakfast. I thought we'd have it out front."

"Since when do you cook?"

"Since I want to prove that I'm not a self-centered jerk who doesn't think of others' feelings."

"That's not what I said."

"But it's what you thought. I know, Mac, and I get it. I didn't consider your feelings back then, so you have no way of trusting that I do now. I'm going to change that."

She was happy to let him try.

She'd spent a very lonely and very frustrated night in the

room she'd grown up in, looking around, remembering all her hopes and dreams concerning Jared, and she'd kicked herself six ways to Sunday for walking out of here last night.

But yesterday had been almost too good to believe. And then when he'd said it wouldn't work . . . All her old insecurities had choked her and she'd needed some distance.

But she came back because sometime in the early dawn hours she'd realized that she had to take this chance. Because if Jared *did* mean it, if he wanted this—wanted her—then she'd be tossing it away by being afraid.

"Can you get the door?" He nodded toward the screen.

"Sure." She walked out first and held it open. "Are we sitting on the steps?"

"Over there."

She followed his nod and saw the table that used to be by the door under the cherry tree with two chairs beside it.

One was the wicker one from the back porch.

"Here, let me carry that." She took the tray from him.

"Thanks. Didn't want to have to do the butt thing again," he said as he limped down the steps in front of her. "You're looking at my butt, aren't you?"

Yes. "No."

"Liar. Remember, I can hear you thinking."

Jared *had* always been able to make her smile.

She set the tray on the table. He'd put a cushion from the living room in the wicker chair. "You sure this isn't going to cave under me when I sit on it?"

He arched an eyebrow. "Didn't I just say this whole breakfast thing is a trust issue? How trustworthy would I be if I didn't make sure your chair was safe? Sit, Mac. Eat your eggs before they get cold. I've been slaving for hours over a hot stove."

The sweat glistening on his skin attested to that.

It also sparked an appetite that had nothing to do with eggs.

Yes, she was definitely going to give this—them—a shot, and if it blew up in her face, well at least she'd have the memories. And no more *what-if*s to bother her.

"How are your eggs? Dippy enough for you?"

She took a bite. Over easy, just how she liked them. He'd had breakfast at her house often enough growing up to know that, but she was surprised he remembered. "They're perfect. Almost as good as Gran's."

"Almost?"

She shrugged and shoveled in another forkful. They actually *were* as good as Gran's, but after last night, she was playing her cards close to the vest until she figured out exactly where this was going.

"So, Mac. About yesterday."

"Yes?"

"I had a good time."

"Me, too."

"I'd like to do it again."

"You would."

"Yes."

"When?"

"Today? Now? This week?"

"Why?"

"Why?" He dropped his fork. "Were you *not* an active participant in that make out session on the sofa last night? Or the other times we've kissed? Hell, woman, at the very least we have chemistry. That alone is worth exploring."

"But just because we have chemistry doesn't mean there's an *us*."

His eyes narrowed and Mac recognized that look. That was the look he got right before he—

"Wanna bet?"

Dared someone.

"You're daring me to find out if there's an *us*?"

"Yes."

Here it was, her chance. *Their* chance. Go big or go home. "Okay, Jared. You're on. What do you propose? Gin rummy?"

He leaned in. "I thought poker was your game of choice."

"But I'm good at it. You willing to risk losing?"

"I'm not planning to lose, Mac."

Words designed to melt her bones and they did so very nicely. "All right then, you're on. Five-card stud."

He smiled that utterly sexy smile of his. "Princess, I'll be any kind of stud you want me to be."

She couldn't help the smirk. "Does that line really work for you?"

"You tell me." His leaned over and brushed her cheek with his lips.

Damn he smelled good and not just because of the bacon. No, Jared smelled . . . Like Jared.

"You sure you're up for this game?"

"Mac, we've been playing a game our whole lives," he whispered. "At least now, we know the rules."

"I'm glad you do because I don't have a clue what the rules to this game are."

"Sure you do," he said. "Five cards, best hand."

He had great hands. "Do I get to finish my breakfast first?"

"Do you want to?"

Not with his face close enough to kiss, but she wasn't going to just throw herself at him and hope for the best when it all shook out, like a game of fifty-two pickup. "Yes. I do want to finish. And then we're going to play that game. Best out of seven wins."

"Best out of one."

"Five."

Jared ran his index finger down her nose and her lips, tracing over her chin, barely touching her as his finger followed that line right to the base of her throat where he fluttered his fingers over her collarbone in a tantalizingly sexy barely there touch, bringing goose bumps with it. "One."

"Three. And that's my last offer." She worked to put some strength behind her words. If there was going to be an *us*, it had to be equal, each having as much power in the relationship as the other, or they'd never be partners. She'd already been on the powerless side; it wasn't a fun place to be.

He studied her for a few seconds, then smiled. "Three, then. And what does the winner win?"

"You proposed this game. What'd you have in mind?"

"You."

One word. So many possibilities.

Talk about high stakes. "And if I win?"

"Then you get me."

"Isn't that the same thing?"

"Like you, Mac, I don't go into a game if I don't have a chance of winning."

His green eyes were practically boring a hole through her; it was as if he could see into her soul and find every secret desire she'd ever had. But since they'd all been about him, it wasn't as if they were any surprises.

"Eat, Mac."

"Huh?"

He picked up her fork, shoveled some eggs onto it, and held it to her mouth.

"Eat. The sooner you finish, the sooner we can begin."

She had to lick her lips before she took the bite.

When he stared at her mouth, she did it again just for kicks.

"You're killing me."

"Good." She tapped his hand that was holding the empty fork and pointed to her plate.

"You want me to feed you?"

"Don't start something you can't back up, Nolan."

"Oh I can back it up." He scooped more egg onto the fork and held it up.

She took her time opening her mouth around it and sliding it off the fork, making sure she licked off every last drop.

"Damn, woman. That was good."

"Isn't that supposed to be my line, since you cooked the breakfast?"

"Mac, if you eat eggs like that, I'll cook you breakfast every morning for the rest of our lives."

The thought of waking up to him after a night of sleeping with him—in all its connotations—was enough to make her lose her appetite. Well, for food.

"Are you going to want the English muffin?" Jared held it up.

"Why? Hungry?"

"Yes." The way he was staring at her said it wasn't for food.

So she took a bite of the muffin just because.

Butter ran out of the corner of her mouth and she flicked out her tongue.

Jared beat her to it.

Chills raced over her when he licked it off.

"Want some more?" he asked.

"Yes, please." She wasn't talking about any muffin.

"You *really* want to finish this?" Jared held it to her mouth again.

Not really. "Hey, a deal's a deal."

"Then hurry up, woman, because you're holding up the biggest deal of our lives."

She made it through three more bites of the muffin before she gave in.

Chapter Thirty

THEY brought everything back to the kitchen, cleaned up, checked on the kittens—so there'd be no interruptions—then dealt the cards. The highest stakes poker game of her life had just started.

But Mac was having a hard time concentrating and it was all Jared's fault. He kept touching her. First it was his foot on hers. Then that wayward foot started rubbing her ankle. When he slid it up her calf as he crossed it over his other knee, she realized he had a plan.

"You're trying to break my concentration." She resisted the urge to see her hole card. Five-card stud was all about the luck of the draw; the only way counting cards would help was to give her a vague guess at his hole card. And even then, there wouldn't be anything she could do about it.

"Hardly, Mac. I'm definitely trying to get you to concentrate on something. But it ain't cards, Princess." He stuck a toothpick in his Prince Charming smile and waggled his eyebrows.

Even being silly, he was sexy.

He tapped the table between them. "Ante up."

"I didn't think we were putting money into this equation."

"We're not. But you have other things you can wager with."

She didn't trust the look in his eye. "Oh?"

His gaze slid down her body.

"You don't mean—You're not thinking—"

He was. The sly dog.

Mac had to bite back her smile. Strip poker. The guy had all the moves.

But so did she. Jared shouldn't underestimate her. Especially when he was in only a pair of shorts and a jersey.

She reached up and removed an earring. One of five.

She had to bite her lip *really* hard not to smile when he rolled his eyes.

Then she had to bite it even harder when he removed his jersey. For a completely different reason.

He made a big production of balling his shirt up and putting it on top of her earring—which only highlighted the way his pecs rippled. He'd definitely rehabbed himself back into shape. *All* over.

He really was trying to distract her from the game.

He dealt the next card up. Queen for her, three for him.

He didn't say a word as he reached beneath the table, and Mac resisted the urge to see what he had left to remove. Jared probably went commando, in which case, this game was going to be over *real* quick.

His flip-flop joined the pile.

He dealt the next card. Ace for him, ten for her.

She thought about calling his bluff—his very buff bluff—and take off *her* shirt, but she wasn't quite ready for that yet.

A second earring joined the pile.

Jared arched an eyebrow, but merely dealt the next card. Four for him, two for her.

She added the third earring.

"Up or down?" He held her next card.

"Up. Might as well see what we're dealing with."

She could've sworn he muttered, "I'm trying to," as he

put her ten faceup. She had a pair showing. Looked like Jared would be down another shoe.

Yup, his six made that a reality.

One or two pieces of clothing were all he had left, and she wasn't going to ask him what that exact number was.

"Let's see it, Mac."

It took her a second to realize he was talking about her hole card.

Mac flipped it over. Five. So far, she had the winning hand.

Until he turned over a king. Pair of kings beat out a pair of tens.

"No more earrings, Mac. I won, I get to call."

"Should've made that stipulation before we started." She'd learned a thing or two about getting all the fine print out before any game began.

She took out the hoop from her right earlobe.

Jared sighed and dragged his pile of clothes and her earrings to his side of the table. "You play hardball."

"You've known me for years. Did you really expect anything different?"

"That's the thing, Mac. I didn't really know you. Or I would never have put you through the hell I did. I'm sorry."

He kept apologizing and while she appreciated it, it was no longer warranted. "Jared, no more. I accept your apology. I'm a big girl, I know people say and do things they don't mean. I also know people don't *not* like someone on purpose. You had your reasons and they're in the past. You were right. Let's start from here. Who we are now. How we feel about each other now." She held out her hand for the cards. "But I'm still going to kick your ass."

He set the deck in her palm, then closed his hand over it. "Let's make it interesting."

It was her turn to run her gaze over his body. "I'm kinda thinking it already is."

"Oh, trust me, Princess. It's going to get *real* interesting. And quick." He let go of her hand and sat back in the chair, his fingers interlaced on the table between them, looking as if he were discussing which movie to see. “Clothing only. And shoes don’t count.”

“I don’t have enough on to make it through the game if I lose each hand.”

“Now you see why it’s interesting.” He leaned forward and motioned for her to lean in as well. “And I have even less on than you do.”

She ought to be embarrassed. She ought to be nervous, but she wasn’t. The image that jumped into her head . . . She wanted Jared naked. She wanted *her* naked.

Go big or go home.

“Deal.” She shuffled the cards, never taking her gaze off him.

“Then game on.” He balled his shirt up and dropped it into the center of the table. “Ante up.”

Mac pulled a *Flashdance* move and removed the cami beneath her golf shirt, thoroughly enjoying Jared’s glare.

She dealt the hole card to each of them, then flipped his first faceup card vertical but didn’t reveal it.

“Ready for this?”

“Like you wouldn’t believe.”

She liked the sound of that.

She played the card. Seven.

Hers was a two.

Jared’s smile couldn’t possibly get any bigger. “So what else do you have hidden under there?”

Doing one better than her previous move, she toed off her shoes and shimmied her work pants to her knees, then wiggled her thong to the point where, with some judicious gymnastics, she could manage to get out of it while sitting and not reveal too much.

Of course, when she put the thong on the pile, the expression on Jared’s face said it didn’t matter; his imagination was working triple time.

“Just full of surprises, aren’t you?”

“You have no idea.” Damn, her voice was a little huskier than she wanted.

“I won’t mind finding out, though.”

She put the next card down. King for him. Her only hope was to get a pair of something showing.

Eight.

"Off with it, Mac." Jared flicked the sleeve of her shirt.

"Hang on there, Mr. Impatient." The work pants came next. Thankfully, the golf shirt was long enough to cover anything embarrassing.

"Jesus, Mac, if I'd know you were such a tease, I never would've suggested this."

"But you did. And now you have to honor it." She flipped over his next card. Two.

Unless she got an ace, Jared Nolan was going to be sitting naked across from his childhood nemesis.

She got a four.

He planted his hands on the table. "Wanna help since I'm injured?"

No, she wanted to help because she wanted to get her hands on that body. But he was enjoying his loss way too much. She'd wanted Jared for years; she wasn't going to make it too easy for him. The guy had to pay for the angst he'd put her through.

"You should probably sit down and take them off. We don't want you toppling over. You might damage something."

"Chicken." But he stayed seated and with some interesting jiggling around, his shorts magically appeared on top of the pile.

"Last card. Up or down?"

"Don't you want to see if I have anything left?"

Not particularly. Because *she* didn't have much left—and she wasn't talking about clothing. "Up or down, Jared?"

"Now you know, Mac, that that question could be taken a whole bunch of different ways."

"The card game, Jared. Focus."

"Oh I'm focused all right."

She flicked his card. "Up or down."

He sighed and shook his head. "Up. Let's get it all out in the open."

"Seems like you're already doing that." She put the card down.

Queen.

He had King high showing; she needed a pair to beat him.

"Turn it over, Mac." Jared's voice was husky and he flipped his hole card over before he finished the sentence.

Pair of kings.

It didn't matter what she had.

"I win."

"Yes, you do." Mac tugged her shirt down and walked around the table. "Now what are you going to do about it, Jared?"

He stood up slowly. "What do you want me to do about it, Mac? Because I don't want to do anything that'll make you uncomfortable."

"Standing naked in your grandmother's kitchen is comfortable to you?" She tilted her head with a smirk, trying to keep her eyes on his face.

"I know someplace it'd be a lot more comfortable."

"Oh? And where's that, exactly?"

He pointed up.

"So now you're Spiderman, too?"

He laughed at that. "God, Mac. I love that you don't take things so seriously."

"Now that's where you're wrong, Jared. I definitely take standing naked in Mildred's kitchen seriously."

"You're not naked."

She whipped off her shirt. "I am now."

After that, it didn't matter who said what. Jared hauled her up against him and kissed her.

Mac didn't have a chance to get a breath, not that it would've mattered since he stole it anyway, his tongue doing amazing things to her mouth, his hands roaming her back, and one very insistent part of him poking her in the belly.

Then one hand slid down her backside.

Jared wrenched his mouth away and leaned his forehead against hers.

"Jesus, Mac. You feel so incredibly good." His other hand slid to her other cheek and he shifted, lifting her. "Wrap your legs around me."

"But, Jared, your leg—"

"I got this, Mac." He braced himself with a palm on the kitchen table behind her. "Wrap your legs around me."

She did and his cock was right there. Just a few judicious movements and she'd have him inside her.

"Condom," she managed to get out before he kissed her again.

It was a short-lived kiss. "Damn it," he gritted out. "Upstairs."

"Then let's go."

She unwound her legs and flew out the door.

Jared was as motivated as she was, managing to stay right on her heels all the way to the stairs, then up them and into his bedroom, where he scooped her into his arms and, in half a stride, tossed her onto the middle of his bed. Then he yanked open the drawer on the nightstand and dumped a carton of condoms onto the sheet.

"Take your pick," he said as he slid onto his hip beside her.

"Please tell me these aren't flavored." She'd never understood that concept—either you liked the taste of your partner or you didn't. Wild cherry was not going to make the sex hotter.

"No, they glow in the dark."

"Oh yeah, because that's what I want to see in the middle of the night. Some blue-lit lightsaber coming at me."

"Hey, baby, I'll give you any color lightsaber you want."

She rolled her eyes as he picked up the nearest one. "Purple? Really? That just brings to mind too many old bodice-ripper clichés."

"And how would you know about old bodice-rippers?"

"Hey, a girl's gotta have some fantasy life."

"I want to be the only fantasy you have."

And when he kissed her again, sliding his hand from her collar bone down to her thigh, then spanning her belly from hip to hip and delving lower, he was. Oh he so was and he was taking her straight to heaven.

Chapter Thirty-one

JARED was in heaven, loving the feel of her stomach muscles as he skimmed his palm across her skin. None of the other women he'd dated had felt as good as his very own terror-of-the-tree-fort.

God if he'd only known back then—

He slid his tongue into her mouth. Those earlier kisses were nothing compared to this. Mac rubbed her tongue against his, then sucked it in deeper, and he felt that motion all the way down to his balls. He better get that condom on soon because he wanted nothing more than to be inside her right now.

Then she ran her hand down his chest, swirled it over his nipple, and skimmed it along his obliques.

Okay, maybe there was something he wanted more. He wanted Mac to touch him. He wanted her hands on him. Anywhere. Everywhere.

His ass was a good place to start. She slid her hand down his back and curled one leg over his and he shifted, arching against her, his dick throbbing. Hell, there was a reason for those clichés.

He dragged his mouth from hers. "Where's the condom?"

She swiped her hand over the bed behind her head.

"Didn't you have one, Mac?" he panted, his own hand sweeping the covers as well. Where the hell were the damn condoms?

"I think we're lying on them."

He chuckled and shook his head. *Smooth move, Nolan.* The first woman it really mattered with and he'd trapped the condoms off the playing field.

"Hang on." He didn't mean that literally, but he was glad she took it that way as he did a push-up over her and her leg and hand stayed gripped to his ass. "There. Grab a few."

"Got 'em."

Mac was tearing the foil with her teeth while he resumed his place next to her, then she rolled that condom on like a pro.

He shook his head, not wanting to think about Mac doing this with anyone else. Mac was his. She'd always been his; he'd just been too stupid to realize it. Had always taken it for granted that she'd be there. That she'd wait.

Thank God she had.

"There we go." She gave his dick a nice squeeze, but it wasn't enough.

Not nearly enough.

"No, baby, *here* we go." He rolled her onto her back, moved on top of her, and slid inside.

Yeah, heaven.

"God, Mac, you feel incredible."

She nibbled his ear. "You're right. I do." She clenched her muscles around him and Jared had to suck in a breath so he wouldn't come right then.

"Hey, slow it down, sweetheart. I don't want it over too soon."

"You have more than enough condoms for us to do this again, Jared. Right now, I want you to move. I want to feel you pounding inside of me."

Jesus. In that moment she was no longer Liam's little sister, which took that out of the equation. Right now, from this moment forward, she was Mary-Alice Catherine Manley, the woman he wanted.

The woman he loved.

He surged into her. She felt so damn good. Hot and tight and wet around him and he wanted to just move and feel her go with him.

"Yes, Jared. That's it." She pulled her legs back, pressing on his ass with her heels. "God, yes."

She was moaning beneath him now, matching her movements with his, the perfect yin/yang. He should have done this years ago.

He'd worry about the past later. Right now, there was only the here and now.

He surged back in, loving the way she held on to him, and rode the sensation with him.

"Oh . . . Jared . . ."

"That's it, baby. Let me hear how much you want this."

"God, Jared. Yes. Yes." She arched into him when he ran his tongue around her nipple and grazed it with his teeth.

"More." She grabbed his head and held him there, while she locked her ankles over his waist and tilted her pelvis to take him deeper.

Jared was going to lose control that instant if he didn't do something.

So he did—he rocked into her and met her thrust for thrust. They'd slow it down next time. Right now, he had to have her.

He kissed her again, his tongue mimicking what was happening between them, and she whimpered around it. God, he loved the sounds she made. The way she moved against him, her nipples tight, stroking his chest.

He slid a hand beneath her butt and cradled her closer, grinding against her as his balls tightened.

He was going to come and needed to make sure she did.

He pushed himself back up above her, never pulling out entirely, but just enough to make a long, slow slide back in that made them both moan.

"Jared." She grabbed hold of his hips. "What are you doing?" She clenched them tighter. He could feel her nails making indentations in his skin and he didn't give a damn. "Come back here."

"I will, Mac. I will. I promise." And he did. Inch by inch.

The pace was killing him.

"Please, Jared." She arched up, her breasts slick with sweat and it took every ounce of control he had not to fall onto her and finish the job.

Instead, he slid one finger from the base of her throat, down her chest, over her pounding heart, and down her belly, watching it flutter as he moved lower.

She shifted her hips and Jared made sure to do the same with his, stroking her from the inside.

Her head thrashed. "God, Jared. Please."

"I will, baby. I will. I promise."

He slipped his finger below her belly button and let it trail so slowly down . . .

"God, yes!" She arched when he touched her in that spot, so ready for this. Her legs fell to the side, her inner muscles clenching around him, sweat rolling down between his shoulder blades with the concentration it took not to just pound into her for his own satisfaction.

"Please, Jared . . ." She gripped his wrist and pressed his hand against her.

He gave her what she wanted, playing, rubbing, taking her all the way to the peak, then backing off, until Mac couldn't even say his name amid the throaty pleas for release.

He gave it to her, surging back in, matching her rhythm, taking them both to that peak. And just before he allowed them to hurtle over it, he had one last coherent thought.

Nothing was ever going to be the same again.

A little while later, Mac felt the ends of her hair tickling her cheek.

"You know, Mac, you really were overly focused on the card game. Almost gave me a complex."

Mac wisely kept her eyes and her mouth shut. He was fishing for compliments, but crying out his name a dozen times was all the ego boost she was going to give him. She still couldn't believe that she'd done that. That they'd done that. This. Now. Here.

"I know you're awake. I can hear you thinking."

That got a smile out of her.

Jared feathered her hair along her nose. "Cat got your tongue, Princess?"

Her eyes flew open. "The kittens! What time is it? How long were they—?"

"Relax. I took care of them while you were sleeping."

"I fell asleep?"

The Cheshire cat couldn't out-grin him. "Why yes you did. Quite soundly, too. Even snored a little."

"I don't snore."

"Hate to tell you, Princess, but, you do. It's cute, though."

"That's not very gentlemanly of you to point out." She crossed her arms—which pushed her boobs up.

Jared's gaze left her face. "I'm not feeling very gentlemanly at the moment."

"What are you feeling, Jared?" She licked her lips for good measure.

"You."

That answer was worthy of another ego boost.

Or three . . .

But Mac made sure not to fall asleep this time. She didn't want to miss a single moment of spooning with Jared after making love again.

And, yes, she'd been making *love* to him.

He hadn't said the words—she hadn't either, thank God. But she'd felt them.

"You're thinking again." Jared brushed a strand of her hair off her cheek and even that could elicit tingles.

"How are your ribs?" She rolled in his arms, then propped her head up on her palm and tucked the other under her breasts, knowing full well that'd catch his attention. Now that they were on even footing here, she liked to have the upper hand. So to speak.

"My what?" Jared looked up from where he'd been looking.

"Your ribs. You know these?" She stroked them, stopping when he sucked in a harsh breath.

"Do that again, Mac."

Ah. A harsh breath of arousal.

She did as he asked, then slid her hand over his hip and rubbed her palm along that line by his waist. There was something about this part of a man's body that did it for her.

"You better get another condom handy, woman, because I think you've found an erogenous zone I didn't know I had."

It did something for him, too, apparently.

She rubbed him there again.

"That's it. Consider yourself warned."

"Forewarned is forearmed." She held up another condom that'd been under her waist. "Bring it on, Nolan."

And oh how he did.

Chapter Thirty-two

MAC was sore in places she didn't know she had come Monday morning.

And very satisfied in others she knew she did.

She and Jared had spent the entire weekend together and most of it in bed. But not all. They'd found time to take a drive in Bryan's Maserati now that Jared didn't need the brace, and they'd done some window shopping in the village antique shops for nothing in particular, ending Saturday at a local pub with a band. Sunday had been a picnic in the park by the river with Chinese takeout. They'd laughed, they'd held hands, they'd kissed . . . and they'd made love.

Mac was falling deeper in love with Jared and she'd decided to just go with it. If it ended badly, at least she'd have these moments. And if it *didn't* end, well, then she'd have Jared.

"It's really loud in here." Jared walked back into the bedroom with a towel wrapped around his waist and water droplets all over his chest.

She wanted to lick them off. "What are you talking about? It's deathly quiet in here."

"Nuh uh. You're thinking again."

She sat up. "No I wasn't."

"Yes you were. And it was something heavy. You always get a little V right here," he pointed to the spot between his eyebrows, "when you're thinking big thoughts."

"Oh really? Now you're hearing the difference between big thoughts and little thoughts, Superman? What *is* a little thought anyway?"

"Little thoughts are what you're going to wear for the day, which shoe to put on first, when should you go to the bank. Big thoughts are life questions, like will he want to make love this morning or this evening? That sort of thing." He whipped off the towel. "The answer, by the way, is *both*."

"I can see that." She tossed a pillow at his groin. "You're incorrigible, Nolan."

"But you love me anyway."

Now it *was* deadly quiet.

Mac plopped back against the headboard.

"Uh, I mean . . . That's just a figure of speech, Mac. "

She stood and tugged the sheet off the bed, holding it in front of her, his joke making her feel too exposed. She pasted the perfect smile on her face and pretended he hadn't touched a nerve. "Oh I know, Jared. I get it." She wrapped the towel around her back. "My turn in the shower. I hope you left me some hot water. Be back in a few."

Jared could only watch her go, his idiocy robbing him of speech.

Oh, man. She loved him. Of course she did. She had for so long he'd be an idiot not to recognize the signs—and he was through being an idiot. Well, after this latest faux pas.

He had to tell her he loved her, but not like this. Not to cover up some flippant comment he shouldn't have made, in his grandmother's home with both of them in a towel or a sheet. When he told Mac that he loved her, it had to be a moment. Mac deserved nothing less after putting up with so much over the years.

He'd been thinking of a way to do it all weekend. Well, when he'd been able to think. Which hadn't been often. The few times they hadn't been in bed being incoherent together, they'd been doing other things: talking, sightseeing, enjoying each other's company, eating. The timing and the moment hadn't been right.

And now, today, they were spending it with Liam and Sean and a few other people at the estate Sean was cleaning, helping the owner do something . . . He couldn't remember what they were going to be doing, but it was one more reason he couldn't tell her. You didn't just tell a woman you loved her on the fly, then hang out with other people for eight hours.

He sighed and picked up the pillow. He'd come up with something; Mac was too important not to.

And because she meant so much to him, he'd figured out the perfect way to get Camille and her boy toy out of his place, and there was no time like the present to put his plan into action. He didn't want Lee finding out that he hadn't exactly followed the rules where Mac was concerned.

He glanced at the clock, then threw on a pair of shorts. He was about to open the bathroom door to tell Mac he was going out when he thought better of it. If he went in there, they'd end up being late and he'd have to scrap the plan for another day. And he didn't really think she'd appreciate hearing about Camille after last night.

Instead, he scrawled a note on the back of his *Sports Illustrated*. "Had to run out. Will meet you at the estate. –Jared"

He'd almost written "love," but words that important ought to be said in person.

JARED glanced down the street in front of his condo building before he got out of his truck, feeling like a thief. Which was ridiculous. Camille was the one who'd been stealing from him. His trust, his heart, his career, now his goddamned house. A guy had his limits.

He shoved the crutch under his left arm and hiked the box under his right.

"Meow." Larry nudged his nose through the opening where the cardboard flaps crisscrossed.

Jared poked him back in. "Today's the day you learn to meow? You couldn't wait twenty-four hours? I don't want her to hear you before you do what you need to do."

"Hey, Preston." He nodded at the doorman. Preston had been here forever. Knew all the tenants. And all the tenants' secrets. "When Camille goes berserk, can you round these little guys up for me? There are four of them. Oh, and give this guy a call." He slipped Preston the locksmith's card and a grand in hundreds. Cheaper than paying his lawyer and more effective.

Preston peeked in the box. "This ought to be interesting."

"Too bad I won't be here to witness it."

"I'll throw in some pictures free of charge."

"You're a prince, Preston."

"And you, Mr. Nolan, are the devil. She calls you that often enough."

Camille would be calling him a hell of a lot worse once he let these guys loose in the condo. Her allergies were bad enough that one cat ought to do her in; four would make the place uninhabitable. He wasn't able to bring a litter box, but Lee was right; new carpets would be worth the cost of getting her out.

Jared smiled and headed toward the elevator, very glad Mac had insisted he keep the kittens. "See ya, Preston. Gotta go live up to my reputation."

SO where'd you go?" Mac asked him when he arrived at the estate just as she was getting out of her truck.

"Had to run an errand."

"Did it involve the kittens? Are they okay? They weren't in the play yard."

"They're fine. Since we weren't going to be home, I thought they might enjoy a change of scenery." It was risky turning them loose, but Preston would be on it. Camille wouldn't be home until after dinner—her Monday nights out with her girlfriends had shown up on his credit cards regularly back when she'd had access to them—so there'd be complete pandemonium when she walked in to face enough cat fur that she'd barely be able to pack a bag, let alone look for the kittens.

But he and Mac also walked into pandemonium.

Bryan had brought some of the widow's kids with him to the estate. What he was doing back at the widow's house was something Jared wanted to find out, but not now. The boys were running around with lightsabers, barely avoiding the priceless antiques in this place, and there was a pack of dogs chasing them. The little girl—Maggie—was dragging her baby doll behind her and sucking her thumb, trailing after Bryan as if he were the Pied Piper.

"Hey, guys, come on in," said Sean, slapping him on the shoulder. "We can use all the help we can get."

"I should have brought my leg brace," Jared muttered when he saw the ladders propped against the foyer walls. Someone better move them quickly or the boys were going to knock them over like very large, very destructive dominoes.

"Come on, Jared," Mac said, tweaking his ass as she passed him. "Either you're going to help out or not, but you don't get to claim invalid status when it suits you."

She winked at him when she glanced back.

If she didn't want her family to know they were on intimate terms, she better stop doing that.

Though that'd be a damn shame. Jared was enjoying this playful side to their relationship.

Until he caught Lee looking at him.

Oh hell.

"So? How'd things go?" Lee walked over.

"Dinner was good. We had a nice time."

"And?"

"And what? Are you asking me if anything happened with your *sister*, Lee? I thought we were trying to steer away from the weird waters."

"Only weird if something happened."

It definitely hadn't been *weird*. "I put the wheels in motion to get rid of Camille."

Liam arched an eyebrow. "And?"

"I'm expecting a call after dinner that it's been handled."

Liam stared at him long enough that Jared had to pull on every bluffing skill he possessed. He'd played enough poker with Lee to perfect it, but he was still thankful for the dog that ran between them carrying someone's doll.

"Shit." Lee took off after the thing, ending that awkward moment, thank God.

"What'd Liam want?" Mac walked back with something in her hands.

"What's that?"

"A riddle Livvy's grandmother left. We're supposed to be looking for something to do with generations of Martinsons. It could be anywhere in this place." She dropped her hands. "And don't think you're getting out of answering that question. I presume it had to do with me."

"It did."

"So what'd you tell him?"

"What did you want me to tell him?"

"I don't know. What'd he want to know?"

"He wanted to know how our dinner went."

"Oh. Well that's a safe enough topic. So what'd you say?"

"That we'd had a nice time."

"Oh, okay. So no biggie."

"Yeah, imagine if I'd told him what *really* happened?"

He got the blush he'd been going for. And that smile she had just for him.

"Stop it, Nolan. We're in a family zone today. No innuendo."

"Aw, come on, Mac. You're no fun."

"I'll remind you of that later. Trust me, I can do *no fun* better than anyone."

"Big words, Princess. One kiss from me and you'll do fun. I'll make *sure* you do *fun*."

He kept the smile off his face as he walked away because Sean was watching. But he was smiling on the inside because he'd seen the flash of desire in her eyes.

Oh yeah, later was going to be a lot of fun.

The next eight hours, however . . . Not so much. Preston

hadn't called and Sean took the last oil painting in the hallway off the wall. Jared groaned. "More?"

"Come on, wimp." Sean handed him the painting. "We're almost halfway done."

"Halfway?" Mac groaned this time. "You mean there are more? How many generations are we talking?"

Sean pointed down another hallway. "The Martinsons loved to show off every member of their family."

Jared would love to throw in the towel, but he sucked it up and got to work. The quicker they got through this, the quicker he and Mac could go home. And the quicker he could tell her what he'd almost blurted out too many times today.

Seeing Camille's things in his home earlier had gotten to him. To hell with making a moment; the moment would be when he told Mac. He wasn't going to waste one more day without her knowing what she meant to him so they could start their life together.

And he wanted a life with her.

He checked his phone again. Nothing from Preston. He tapped Mac on the arm. "Buck up, buttercup. It'll be over soon." So many things, and he smiled just thinking about the moment he would tell her. Not only did he like the fact that he was in love with her, but he liked that he could make her dreams come true.

"I prefer daisies, and I'd just rather go period," she muttered, hauling herself off the eighteenth-century bench some ancestor had parked in the middle of the long hallway and ran her hands over the back of the portrait looking for God-knew-what. This would be so much easier if they at least had a *clue* what the clue looked like.

"Now where's the fun in that? Where's your sense of adventure?"

"I left it with the 1542 Martinsons." She tapped the top of the frame to give the all-clear. "Those people could suck the life out of any party."

"Just the sixteenth-century ones? Sweetheart, have you been in any other hallway in this place?"

She groaned. "More than I wanted to."

Jared set the frame against the wall and tugged Mac around the corner. He wrapped his arms around her and picked her up, pressing her against the wall to plant a quick kiss on her startled mouth. "I've been wanting to do that all day."

"But you did it so many times this morning."

"Last night, too, but it doesn't seem to be enough."

Mac's grin took him right back to last night and this morning—until it froze on her face when she looked over his shoulder.

The hairs on the back of Jared's neck prickled and he let her slide to the floor before he turned around.

"Hello, darling."

"What the fuck do you think you're doing here, Camille? How did you know where I was?"

She crossed her arms and cocked her hip. "You're not the only one who has someone on the payroll." The bitch smiled that smile he used to think was sexy but now saw for calculating. "Come on, sweetheart. You don't have to pretend in front of everyone. I got the gifts you left for me in the condo today."

He felt Mac stiffen beside him.

"They were so thoughtful." She sauntered up to him and placed a clawed hand on his shoulder with the scantest of glances toward Mac. "Your apology's accepted."

"I'm not apologizing for anything."

"But you're not denying the gifts."

Mac sidestepped away from him.

"Mac, don't listen to her."

That was like telling a bull not to charge a red flag. Unfortunately, Mac chose to storm off without a word, and he couldn't even run after her, thanks to the bitch in front of him.

"My, my, did we break another heart, Jared?" Camille stroked a fingernail down his cheek.

Jared thrust her hand away from him. "Get out, Camille. You've caused enough damage."

"You haven't even begun to see the damage I can cause,

Jared. That little stunt? My lawyer is already drawing up charges."

"Did you go to his office to talk to him about it?"

"Absolutely."

"Did you pack a bag?"

That took her off her high horse. She looked at him suspiciously. "Of course. I'm not about to let my things get polluted by that mess."

"Perfect. Good luck getting back inside the condo."

"You can't toss me out. There are eviction laws against it."

"Considering you left voluntarily—bags packed—we can safely say you left of your own accord." The smirk slid off her face—and onto his. "And there are *trespassing* laws as well, so I suggest you stay off the premises. The locks are being changed as we speak."

"Why—You—" She stomped her foot. He'd paid for those very expensive heels and wouldn't mind if they chose now to fall apart.

Camille spun around and stormed off the way Mac had gone, only to spin around again and head back his way, finger pointing at him like a lance.

"Listen, you hack. Don't you think you can do this to me. I'll destroy you. I'll drag your name through the mud so many times no one will remember what it is. I'll—"

"'Scuse me." Little Maggie ran in from the other hallway. "Are you guys fighting?"

"No."

"Yes." Camille glared at him.

The little girl stuck her thumb in her mouth and looked at the two of them.

Jared glared back, then dropped to Maggie's level. "I'm sorry, Maggie. No, sweetie, we're not fighting. We're having a disagreement."

"Oh. I have disabeements with my brothers. But then they get out the lightsabers and try to chop my head off. You're not gonna do that are you?"

Much as he'd like to, he shook his head. "No, sweetheart. I'm not going to chop off her head with a lightsaber."

Camille crossed her arms and tapped the toe of one of those shoes. "You might as well, Jared. Where do you think we—I mean, where am I supposed to go now?"

"Ask your lawyer if he's so full of answers." He planted a hand on the wall to stand up, then held it out for Maggie. "Now, if you don't mind, Camille, I have other things to deal with. I presume I'll be seeing you in court. Or maybe, since you'll actually havc to start paying rent somewhere, you'll want to save the attorney's fees and just give it up. You've taken enough from me. Call it a day, will you? Don't you get tired of fighting? You had your time in the limelight, now go enjoy obscurity."

"Big words coming from you, Jared, especially since you might never play again."

"Sure he can," said Maggie, the biggest smile on her face. "He can play with me."

Maggie's innocent remark settled around his heart as if it belonged there. "Don't worry about me, Camille. I'll be just fine. Come on, Maggie. Let's go find Mac."

Maggie looked up at him with her big eyes. "Why? Did she get lost?"

"Not if I can help it."

Chapter Thirty-three

MAC swiped the tears off her face.

Dammit. She'd fallen for him again and he'd used her. How could she have forgotten about Camille? The woman he'd fallen in love with. The woman he'd lived with.

The woman he'd gone to *this morning* after spending last night with her.

She had no clue why he'd leave *their* bed and go back to Camille on the same freaking morning! Within the space of half an hour!

She'd misjudged him. All these years, she'd held out the fantasy of him as Prince Charming, and when she'd finally taken him off that pedestal to see him as a man, she still hadn't seen the truth.

The Maeves and Renees and Juliettes of the world should have told her, but she'd been too blind to see it.

Well she was seeing it now. Well, sort of. It was hard to see through tears.

Women were available to Jared whenever he wanted and she'd just become one in a long line.

And she'd let herself fall in love with him. Again. God, she was pathetic.

She slowed to a stop at the next traffic light. Turning right would send her to Mildred's.

She didn't want to go back there.

When the light turned green, she went straight. Straight home. Straight to where she could lick her wounds and soothe her battered heart in the place that had always given her solace.

She pulled up to her street and turned right, then curved around to the left.

She pulled into the driveway of her childhood home. All the memories she'd had here, all the hopes and dreams. And that damn walkway where Jared had broken her heart. She should have remembered that night.

Crud, and she should have remembered her key. Damn, she'd left it at Mildred's.

Mac plunked her butt down on the front porch stoop. She was going to have to go back there. Or she could drive back to the estate and grab a spare from one of her brothers, but that would involve questions about why she'd just up and left without a good-bye to anyone.

Questions she didn't want to answer.

Chapter Thirty-four

JARED found her just where he knew she'd be.

"Hey," he said when he got out of his car in her driveway and saw her sitting on the front step of her grandmother's house. "Forget your key?"

She looked up and, God, the pain he saw there. "It's back at Mildred's and I . . . I didn't feel like going there."

Because he'd be there. Because she thought he'd hurt her again.

He walked up that path that held one of the saddest memories of his life. "I'm sorry, Mac."

"For what exactly, Jared?" She tucked some hair behind her ear.

He sat next to her on the stoop. "I'm sorry I didn't tell you about going to the condo today."

The raw pain he saw in her eyes sliced across his heart.

"Why did you?"

He took her hand in his. "I wanted to get her out."

"But why *today*? After . . . well, after last night?"

He covered her hand with his other one. "Something Liam said."

"Liam? What does he have to do with this? Is he trying to pay me back for winning that damn game?"

"I hope you don't consider me payback, Mac. I was hoping to be the jackpot."

She bit her lip.

It was too soon for jokes.

He slid closer and nudged her with his shoulder. "I went to the condo with the kittens."

"You gave her our kittens?"

He loved the way she called them theirs. "Let's just say I loaned them to her. For a little housekeeping."

"I'm not following."

"She's allergic to fur, remember? The place will now have to be fumigated for her to live there. So she left, and because she packed a bag, she can't say I evicted her. So I had the right to change the locks. Which I did."

"But why today?"

His heart broke at the pain in her voice. "I wanted her out of my life before I started anything with you, but, well, we got that a little out of order. This morning was the first chance I had."

"But why didn't you tell me?"

"Lee pointed out that you wouldn't appreciate Camille being in the picture, so I didn't want to mention her at all. I never expected her to pull the stunt she did."

"*What* did you and Lee talk about?"

"You, Mac. We talked about you. About how I was an idiot and how much you loved me."

She looked away, a blush creeping up her throat.

He put a finger under her chin and turned her to face him. "Don't look away, Mac. Those are the sweetest words I've ever heard."

"I've never said them."

"You don't have to. I saw how you looked at me while I was making love to you—and I *was* making love to you, sweetheart."

She blinked and her eyes filled with tears.

He brushed the corner of her eye with his thumb. "Don't

cry, Mac. No more sad tears. It's okay. Because I love you back."

Her eyes got big and she blinked faster. "You . . . you do?"

"I do. I should have told you the minute I realized it, but I wanted to make it this grand gesture. Something big and memorable so you'd never forget it."

"That is not going to happen, Jared."

Her answer sucked the wind out of him.

Jesus, he'd blown it. After all of this, after everything they'd been through, after finally realizing what he should have known all along, he'd ruined it.

"Are you sure, Mac? You can't find it in your heart to forgive me? To let me make it right, let me show you how much I love you? I will, Mac. I do. I promise. I should have told you about going to Camille's. Hell, I should have told you everything I was thinking and feeling, but—"

She put a finger on his lips.

He kissed it. He had to. He had to convince her that what he felt for her was real. That she could believe in it.

"No, Jared. That's not what I meant. I've loved you forever; that hasn't changed. No, what I meant is, you've given me that moment." She leaned in and kissed him on the cheek—a soft, sweet, forever kind of kiss. "And I never *will* forget it."

Three months later.

He gave her an even more memorable moment. One they could tell their grandkids about.

Because there *would* be grandkids.

"You ready, guys?" he whispered to the troops lined up behind his grandmother's house. He'd bought it for the two of them, and for the family they'd raise here, but hadn't told Mac yet. He knew she wanted to live in her grandmother's house, but it would be too small once they started having a family, because he wanted a lot of kids with her.

She was in the front yard, thinking the yellow mums she was planting were for putting the house on the market.

He couldn't wait to tell her they were to commemorate this moment. He would've preferred daisies, but they needed to be planted in the spring and he wasn't waiting until then.

He wasn't waiting one more moment.

"Do we really have to do this *again*?" Kevin groaned. "Wasn't once enough?"

Nicky tapped the baseball cap down so Kevin couldn't see. "Shut up, dork. The guy's gonna propose. Let him do it the way he wants to."

"Jerk."

"Loser."

"Guys? Can it wait? 'Cause I can't." Jared had been dying to do this for the past three months. He'd known he wanted to marry her the moment he'd fallen in love with her. He *should* marry her; it was as right as breathing. And *he'd* been the dork who had been too stupid to notice. "Ready?"

Kevin sighed. "I guess."

Chase nudged him behind the knees, almost taking him down. "Then man up, Kev. Most important moment of a guy's life according to my dad. We gotta make it count."

"Whatever. Let's just get it over with so we can go play ball."

Jared wanted to get it over with so he could start planning his future with Mac.

He nudged Nicky out first.

The look of surprise and happiness on Mac's face was everything he'd hoped it'd be.

The boys continued giving her the daisies, each one coming back for more. That'd been the stipulation he'd made to take on the coaching job; that they'd each give her half a dozen flowers. One for every year he wanted with her. Sixty ought to cover it. And if not, well, there were the three dozen more in his hands.

She was laughing by the time they were at thirty, and had tears in her eyes at fifty.

When he walked out with the rest, those tears slipped down her cheeks.

"I love you, Mary-Alice Catherine Manley," he said.

She tried to say something, but had to sniff back the tears. "I'm not even going to get mad that you used my whole name."

"Good. Because I have to use it again." He handed her the flowers—well, he fit them in among the rest. Crud, he hadn't really thought these logistics through because she needed both hands to hold all the flowers and he needed one for the ring.

"You do?"

He nodded then took some of the flowers from her, kneeling to put them on the ground around her.

He didn't get up.

Instead, he pulled Grandma's ring from his pocket. She'd been thrilled to give it to him.

Mac's tears started flowing faster. They were happy tears; he could tell by her smile. Happy tears were okay.

"Jared Nolan, what are you doing?"

"You'll see." He took her hand. "Will you, Mary-Alice Catherine Manley, marry me and be my wife? To have and to hold in million-dollar contracts or community center coaching salaries, with broken legs and cracked ribs, leaping furniture in a single bound, and taking in stray kittens wherever we find them until one of us kicks the bucket—and that'll be the *only* way we're ever separated—amen?"

She was crying *and* laughing by the time he finished, so much that he couldn't get an answer out of her.

So he kissed her.

Hell, he knew her answer. She'd marry him.

Epilogue

Six months after that on the far side of the dance floor . . .

"I'M telling you, Lois, it can work."

"Eh?" Lois Gayle put a hand to her ear to listen to what Cate Manley was trying to tell her. These dang parties were always so noisy that it made it tough to hear.

Though that's not what her granddaughter would say. Jennifer was a sweet girl, smart as a whip that one, but her fancy vet degree didn't teach her a thing about humans getting older. Hearing aids were for deaf people, not those who didn't want to listen to the noise. Lois liked her peace and quiet, thank you very much.

"You just need to come up with a plan. Mildred and I married off all of our grandkids. Two of them to each other."

"To each other? Isn't that illegal? I'd watch out for the babies on that one, I would." Lois's third-cousin-once-removed had married her first cousin, and Lois would swear that's why their son Bill ended up in prison. Just wasn't right mixing the genes that way.

"No, not to each other. My granddaughter, Mary-Alice Catherine, married Mildred's grandson, Jared. That's who got married today."

Lois looked at the two of them, smiling so happily. Mildred and Cate had been talking about their plan for so long it was a wonder their grandkids hadn't heard anything about it. Why, Lois had heard and she'd been trying *not* to listen.

Still, the plan had obviously worked, since Cate was spouting off about three more weddings.

Hmmm. Maybe she *should* have a chat with these two. After all, Jennifer wasn't getting any younger and Lois would like to have some great-grandchildren of her own.

She patted the chairs beside her. "Have a seat, ladies, and tell me what I should do."

TURN THE PAGE FOR A PREVIEW OF
THE FIRST MANLEY MAIDS NOVEL

What a Woman Wants

*AVAILABLE NOW FROM
BERKLEY SENSATION!*

Guys' Night . . . Plus One

SEAN Patrick Manley stared at the straight flush, nine high, in his hand. He really hated that he was going to win this game. Oh, he didn't mind taking his brothers to the cleaners, but taking his hardworking sister's money wasn't anything to gloat about. Still . . . she *had* asked . . .

"All in." He kept his poker face steady and slid the balance of his chips to the center of the table.

Bryan and Liam raised their eyebrows, but Sean didn't say a word. Mary-Alice Catherine had wanted to play "like one of the boys" and this was how they played: cutthroat. No slack because she was a poker novice—or their younger sister.

Bryan glanced at his cards, flicking the edges as usual. Distracting habit, which was obviously why Bryan had affected it. "I'm in." He stacked his remaining chips alongside Sean's pile.

Sean hid his smile. He didn't mind taking Bryan's money.

Liam leaned back in his chair and tapped the back of his cards with his index finger, unreadable as ever. "Mary-Alice, are you sure—"

"Don't, Liam," Mac said, bristling as usual at the use of her given name. "Play the hand as you normally would."

Liam tapped his cards. "Fine." His stack joined the pile.

Sean eyed it, then his brother. He could never tell with Liam.

Mac chewed on her bottom lip and fidgeted in her chair. Sean almost felt bad for her. Almost. But she'd bugged them enough to get in on their game. They'd tried to tell her that she couldn't afford the stakes, but she wouldn't listen. So, to shut her up once and for all, they'd let her in, figuring that once she lost the figurative shirt off her back, she'd stop bothering them. There were some things sisters just weren't supposed to be a part of.

"Okay, so how do I raise you guys if I don't have enough chips?"

"Mac, just put the rest of yours in. Don't go upping the ante. You can't afford to lose any more." Sean smiled at her.

He was surprised when she tossed him a look of pure anger. Who knew she had it in her? She'd always cajoled them into doing her will as a child. The fact that she'd been treated like a princess all her life by them, her knights chivalric, probably had something to do with it, so this behavior was out of character for her.

"Just answer the question. What rules do you guys have for that?"

Bryan ruffled his cards again. "We throw something big in. Like Sean's place for a week or my Maserati or Liam's island getaway. Since you don't have anything comparable, just call."

Mac looked at her hand again, now nibbling on the opposite corner of her mouth. She swept a strand of hair behind her ear. "I'm raising all of you."

Sean started to protest, but Bryan raised his hand. "What's the wager, Mac?"

Mac placed her cards facedown on the green felt in front of her. "If I lose, winner gets four weeks of housekeeping for free."

"And if you win?" Liam asked.

Mac folded her hands over her cards. "If I win, you each owe me four weeks' work, free of charge, for Manley Maids."

"What? Are you crazy? I'm not going to be someone's maid for four *hours*, let alone four weeks." Bryan rammed back in his chair as if someone had electrified the poker table.

"Oh, well, if you don't think you can beat me . . ." She looked at Liam.

Liam studied her through narrowed eyes. "Four weeks, huh?" He tapped his cards. "I'll call. With the Kiawah place for the same time period."

Sean studied Liam. A bluff? Nah. The rent for the vacation home wouldn't break his brother, but Liam wouldn't risk servitude. He had to have a winning hand. If it was better than his straight flush, Sean would only be out the cash and the hotel stay, not be in danger of putting on an apron. "Me, too. A week at the resort when it's up and running." *If* it got up and running, but he wasn't planning on losing. Not with this hand. And not the resort, either.

Bryan looked at the three of them as if they'd lost their minds. "So, one of us is going to end up with two vacations, maid service, and the use of a Maserati for four weeks?"

"Unless I win," Mac said, drumming her nails on the felt. Typical newbie response. She was too anxious.

"You calling?" Sean nudged Bryan with his elbow.

"Hell yeah." Bryan threw a full house onto the table. "Come to Papa." He reached for the pile of chips.

"Hold on, Bry." Liam flicked his hand to the table. Four threes stared back at them. "Sorry about that, Mac." Liam stood.

Sean wasn't surprised about not getting an apology from Liam. The brothers each had had their turns winning. The money was immaterial; they enjoyed outplaying each other and getting together once a month. But Mac . . .

Still, he had to set Liam straight. "Good hand, Lee, but not good enough." Sean flourished the straight flush.

"Shit." Liam sat back down.

"Son of a bitch." Bryan always insisted on having the last word.

Only Mac didn't react. But at least there'd be no question of her joining them again.

Sean started stacking the chips, planning when he could take off long enough for the vacation he'd just won from his brother. Sooner rather than later, since there wasn't much he could do on the Martinson project until the whole inheritance mess was finalized.

Silence descended on the table as he stacked the chips. Over three grand. Not bad.

His brothers were trying not to look at Mac. Sean, too, but he did catch the flicker of her lips. Probably trying not to cry. Yeah, a grand was a big deal to Mac, especially when she was pouring everything she had into her cleaning business. Maybe he'd slip it to her when Liam and Bry weren't looking.

"Sorry, Mac, but that's how the game's played."

"Yeah, Mac. We warned you," Bryan added.

"I know." She cleared her throat. "It's just . . ."

"What, Mac?" Liam leaned an elbow on the table.

"It's just that . . . doesn't a jack beat a nine?"

"Jack?" Liam's face turned green.

Sean's stomach turned to ice. "Jack?"

Bryan's mouth opened, but, for once, he was speechless.

"Yes. Jack." Mac fanned her cards onto the table. Five hearts, in ascending order.

Jack high.

"I believe, dear brothers, you all need to be fitted for Manley Maids uniforms."

Chapter One

THE doors to Hell—aka her familial estate—were wide and welcoming.

Well, there was a first time for everything.

Livvy Carolla jerked her duffel out of the back of the Baja and slung it over her shoulder, flouncing the bottom of her peasant skirt around her, which sent the peacock that was meandering around the well-manicured lawn of her grandmother's estate scurrying to safety.

Who had peacocks roaming their lawn in suburban Philadelphia as if they were maharajahs or something?

Her paternal blueblood relatives, that's who.

Home sweet freakin' home. Wouldn't *Daddy dear* pitch a hissy if he knew she was here?

There was some satisfaction in entering the old man's lair. Especially now that it was hers.

Who would've believed it? That her reputation-protecting, society-conscious, paternal grandmother would outlive her reprobate of a son and leave it all—*all*—to the granddaughter she'd barely acknowledged.

Mr. Scanlon, the estate's attorney, had assured her that all she had to do was fulfill the stipulations in the will over the next two weeks, and the house and the accompanying funds would be hers to command.

Ah, the irony. Her grandmother, from what her mother had told her in a rare lucid—make that *sober*—moment before Livvy had been taken away, had threatened to disown her own twenty-year-old son who'd dared impregnate a barely-high-school-graduate from the wrong side of town with zero money to her name and less than zero prospects other than trapping the local rich boy in the oldest way possible.

So Merriweather Martinson had swooped in and finagled a way (translation: bought Mom off) into gaining custody of Livvy, who, at the tender age of five, had wanted nothing more than a loving family with food on the table, since Mom wasn't capable of the latter and Dad had been . . . well, *absent* was a kind description. Then there was the car accident that had taken him from her life for good.

So Livvy had found herself shipped off to boarding schools without so much as an acknowledgment of their blood ties or a kind word from her new guardian. Hell, the woman had never even cracked a smile, and Livvy's letters begging for some kind of a connection, a visit, a trip home, *something*, went unanswered.

Except for that one time when she was seven. That was it. The old lady had allowed her one visit, and then Livvy had never wanted to return.

Yet here she was. All by virtue of that very same grandmother who'd wanted nothing to do with her. Too bad Mom wasn't alive to see it, but then, the twenty-four-year-old single parent hadn't done much in the way of keeping in touch after selling her child, er, signing over custody, so perhaps *Mom* wouldn't really care that Livvy was back at the scene of the crime.

Ah, but it was water under the proverbial bridge. She'd survived, managed to keep herself employed, and lived her life on her terms. If not for a stipulation in Merriweather's will, she wouldn't even be here.

But here she was, so best to get on with it.

Taking one last bite of her apple, she gazed up at the monstrosity. That was how she'd always thought of this place. The Martinsons, her father's family, were ancient English nobles who'd immigrated back in the eighteen hundreds, apparently bringing half their English manor with them, complete with mullioned Tudor windows and carved oak doors the size of elephants. Stone lions guarded the drive, and the gargoyles on the roofline blended into the backdrop of gathering clouds. Ominous. Foreboding. She'd been overwhelmed on so many levels during that one visit, and her feelings hadn't changed. The place was ostentatious. Overdone. Obscene.

And now it was hers.

Livvy tossed the apple core into the flower bed—good compost—and grabbed Orwell's travel cage from the back seat, being careful the cover didn't allow any glimpse of the scenery. The African Grey went nuts when he was caged outside, so what the loudmouth didn't know wouldn't hurt her ears.

She hiked up the white marble steps to the front door, her boots leaving scuffmarks. Oh well. Something for the butler to do.

"Hello?" She pushed open the door to an empty hallway. Strange, twenty years ago the butler—Rupert? Jeeves?—had guarded the door like a mother bear. Clearly, things had slipped since her grandmother's death.

Grandmother. The word felt odd. Livvy closed the doors, realizing she'd never really thought of the old woman as her grandmother. But, technically, as the bearer of the worm who'd knocked up her mother then took off at the first sign of pregnancy, that was who Merriweather Knightsbridge Martinson was.

"Anyone home?" Livvy peered around the massive foyer, vividly remembering the burgundy and cream striped walls crammed with gilt-framed, musty paintings of portly ancestors trussed up like Easter eggs. It'd probably been centuries since anything had changed here. These people were so hung up on their heritage that she could feel the heavy mantle of Martinson ancestry forming a chokehold around her throat.

Not that she'd have anything to do with it. They hadn't wanted her as a child; she sure as hell didn't want them as an adult.

"Hello? Rupert? Jeeves?" *What was his name?* She stepped farther into the silent entranceway.

"No Rupert or Jeeves here."

She jumped as a guy walked out of the doorway on the left. Tall, dark, and yummy, with the body of an Olympic athlete and the face of one of their gods, he had wavy black hair that swept the top of his collar and set off a pair of eyes so blue they might have been fake—except there was nothing fake about this guy. From the set of shoulders that appeared to have been created solely for the purpose of wrapping strong arms around a woman, to washboard abs that had her mouth watering, to legs with muscles that strained the seams of his pants, this guy was all man.

"What can I do for you?"

There was probably a lot he could do for her. And to her, and with her . . .

"Who are you?" She tugged the front of her blouse closed over her camisole, but it was kind of hard to do one-handed.

"Who are *you*?" he shot back, hefting a . . . *vacuum*? in his hands.

"I asked you first." What was he doing with a vacuum?

"You . . . *what*?"

"Uh, I mean . . ." She tossed her curls and raised her chin, trying to make herself appear taller. Not that she was ashamed of her height—or lack thereof—but it helped when she was feeling out of her element. And she definitely was, because being in this place, with a hot guy holding a vacuum cleaner, was so foreign she wouldn't be surprised if she had fallen down Alice's rabbit hole. "I, um, asked you a question."

"And?" He set the canister down, then leaned on the wand attachment.

"And I'd like an answer."

"And I'd like to be hanging out on a tropical beach, but we don't always get what we want now, do we?"

"You know, you're pretty cheeky for the pool boy."

"In case it's escaped your notice, *this*," he rattled the wand, "is not a skimming net. It's a vacuum cleaner."

"So that makes you, what? The maid?"

He glanced away. Score one for her.

"Look, who are you and what do you want? I don't have time to stand here all day." His jaw was doing some furious ticking.

"Why? Got some shelves to dust?"

Red crept up his neck from where his mint green polo shirt opened in a V, revealing some nice curly black chest hair just to the left of the insignia . . .

Manley Maids.

Oh, man. He *was* the maid. This was just perfect!

"Look, miss. Is there something you need?"

Uh . . . yeah. She bit her lip trying to swallow a smile. Her grandmother obviously had had one hell of a sense of humor. Maybe it wasn't such a good thing she'd never gotten to know the old battle-axe. "Okay. Sorry. It's just that I'm Livvy Carolla and I was looking for the guy who runs this mausoleum."

"*You're* Livvy Carolla? *Olivia* Carolla?"

She hated that name. Olive, Oliver Twist, Olivia Fig Newton-John . . . The nicknames hadn't been fun. Boarding school "chums" were simply better-dressed playground bullies.

"I prefer Livvy. And, yes, that's me. Why?"

Pool Boy—*Maid Man*—groaned.

"Hey, really, it's not cause for a meltdown. The name's Livvy and I need to see Jeeves. Rupert. Whatever."

"It figures," muttered Pool Boy, er, Maid Man.

She wished he *was* the pool boy—much better uniform. "I'd like to get settled, so if you could point me in his direction, I'd much appreciate it."

She set Orwell's cage on the floor to readjust the strap of her duffel. A few feathers and seed husks puffed out from beneath the cover to scatter on the floor.

"Hey, I just cleaned that," Pool Boy said.

"You're kidding."

"No, I'm not." An eyebrow went north. "And it was a pain to do, so if you wouldn't mind cleaning that up, I'd appreciate that."

He looked so indignant. "Okay, *Mr. Belvedere*, I'll make you a deal. I'll clean up the mess if you tell Rupert I'm here."

"Sorry, lady, right now it's just me, and, well, me."

"You."

"Me."

She raised her eyebrows. She'd been working on raising just one, but so far that trick had eluded her. "So, you're running the place then?"

"Princess, running this place is nothing compared to what I do in real life."

"Oh? So this is some fantasy you're acting out? Not quite the maid's outfit that typically goes along with that sort of thing, but whatever floats your boat. Just don't call me *Princess*."

"Sorry." Pool Boy scratched his chin. "Okay, so here's the deal. The will pensioned off every single employee. Right down to the ten-year-old newspaper delivery boy. No one's here but me. And now you. And as I understand it, you're now in possession of this, what'd you call it? Mausoleum?"

She nodded, her amusement tempered. Everyone was gone? Was this some challenge the old battle-axe was issuing from the grave? Something to make Livvy prove she was worthy of the Martinson name?

Or to prove she *wasn't*?

Well, she wasn't about to jump to that woman's tune, especially not in death. In fact, Livvy was glad everyone was gone. That way she wouldn't have to fire them when she sold the place, which she would do as soon as she found out what stupid stipulations her grandmother had come up with to force her to live here for two weeks.

Okay, so maybe she was still jumping a little bit to the woman's tune. But not for much longer. Soon she'd be home free with millions to do with as she wanted. And she wanted to do so much good with them. Unlike her *illustrious* so-called family.

"So." Livvy hiked the duffel onto her shoulder and knelt to scoop the feathers into her hand. "This changes things. I was hoping the butler could show me the ropes, but I guess that's not happening." She repositioned the duffel as she stood.

"The only ropes I've seen are tying back some curtains in the living room, though I think there's a real bellpull in the chapel tower," said Hot Guy With A Vacuum.

"Yeah. It rings obnoxiously early, too." Oh how she remembered waking to it one Sunday morning. She still couldn't believe there was an actual chapel on the other side of the property. That seemed more than a little overboard even for *her* family.

Pool Boy smiled. "Actually, it's been quiet since I got here. No one to ring it."

She shared the smile. "A plus to the situation. Very good. Well, in that case, why don't I get my stuff upstairs"—she hefted the duffel and cage—"then I'll come back down and we can chat."

"Sure. Fine. I'll be in the . . ." He flicked his hand toward the far corner. "Whatever that room is, finishing up."

"Okay. See you then."

"Fine." He turned around.

"Uh, hey?"

"Yeah?" He looked back over his shoulder. Man, the way those pants hugged his butt . . .

"Your name? I didn't catch it."

"That's 'cause I didn't toss it."

"Funny. So what is it?"

"Um . . . Sean."

"Well, Um Sean, I'll see you in a bit."

SEAN felt her eyes on him all the way through the door. Her gorgeous amber eyes. On a five-foot-nothing body of screaming sex appeal with more curves than a racetrack, lips ripe for kissing, a face that'd put Helen of Troy to shame, and all the attitude to back it up.

How was he supposed to kick her out of this place when his first instinct was to drag her over to the closest piece of furniture, rip those gypsy clothes off that delectable body, and devour her for hours on end? Grab those auburn curls that tumbled down her back like an invitation and wrap them around his fist, arching her neck so he could—

Sonofabitch. The private eye he'd hired to investigate the will's stipulations hadn't mentioned that the granddaughter was a babe.

He also hadn't mentioned that she'd be moving in, or that they'd be the sole inhabitants of Casa Martinson. He'd thought living in was a good idea when Mac had gone over the job's specs, but now . . .

Sean set the vacuum down and headed to the curio cabinet. With the way he reacted to her, he'd better find out what those stipulations were and soon. Failure was not an option. This property was going to make his name in the resort industry and validate everything he'd been working for. He was banking on it, to the tune of millions of dollars in revenue.

His Heritage Corporation bought historic buildings, most in disrepair, and brought them back to their former standard and beauty as bed & breakfasts. So far, it'd been a win-win situation. Localities loved saving their old buildings, and he loved the bottom line.

But his dream had always been to be bigger. He wanted luxury resorts. He wanted to be *the* destination in this part of the state, with an eye toward growing into other areas. To be as successful in his career as his siblings were in theirs.

The Martinson property was his chance to start expanding the company. The next tier of his dream. And as long as there was a chance to make it happen, he wasn't about to call it quits.

So when Merriweather had thrown the wrench in, jeopardizing his name, his bank account, and his brothers' money, his back was to the wall. He *had* to buy this place at the below-market-value price she'd promised or he'd lose everything. He really didn't need her change of heart or his sense of misplaced lust screwing this up.

Screwing was a bad word choice.

Sean replaced the porcelain statues in the glass-fronted case, careful not to ding them against each other. There were some prize pieces here. What in God's name had possessed the woman to leave this place to a granddaughter she'd never acknowledged? According to the detective, Mrs. Martinson hadn't sent even a birthday card to her only living descendant. No contact even when her son, Olivia's father, had died. Talk about cold. He hadn't had a doubt that his plan would pan out as she'd promised.

Yet there was obviously no figuring what was in someone's mind at the end of her life. And the old woman was thorough, dammit. His lawyer had tried to find some way to break the bequest, but no dice. It was airtight. Olivia Bombshell Carolla held all the cards.

The poker reference was ironically appropriate.

He'd thought Mac's win was a homerun when he'd seen the Martinson name on her client list. He'd jumped at it; if Lady Luck had given him the means to secure the place for himself, he wasn't one to question her.

Until now.

Because with millions at stake, a babe for a boss, and just under three weeks to kick her out of her home, instead of being lord of the manor, he was the freaking *maid*.